I0460394

~ Beyond The Black Earth ~

John Williamson was born in London rather a long time ago, but apart from a brief spell in South Africa, has spent most of his life living in the gentle countryside of Cambridgeshire.

Beyond the Black Earth is a novel in two parts, comprising *The Chronicles of Talakhonsu*. Book II, *Beyond the Pyrene,* will be published in November of 2016.

Visit www.johnwilliamsonbooks.com for further insights into the author, his works and influences.

Also by John Williamson

The poetry of John Williamson
features in the following
collections of verse

Reverence of Rune
(ID: 214845 – www.lulu.com)

Threads
(ISBN 978-0-557-07491-4)

~ Beyond The Black Earth ~

The Chronicles of Talakhonsu
Book I

John Williamson

STOUT
HOUSE

Published by Stout House Publishing
For further information on
other Stout House titles,
visit:

www.johnwilliamsonbooks.com
www.clandestine-books.co.uk

Cover art by Trif TwinArtDesign,
via www.99designs.com

Maps by John Williamson

Beyond The Black Earth
John Williamson

For Natasha

Great Middle Sea

Naukratis

PERSIA

LOWER

KEMET

Menefer

Asyut

Dendera

Waset
(Thebes)

Khnum

Edfu

Kom Ombo

The Syene

UPPER

NARROW SEA

Temple of
Rameses
The Great

KEMET

Buhen
Fortress

Soleb

Napata

KUSH

Atbara River

Meroe

Map of Kush (Land of the Bow)
and Kemet (Land of the Black Earth)

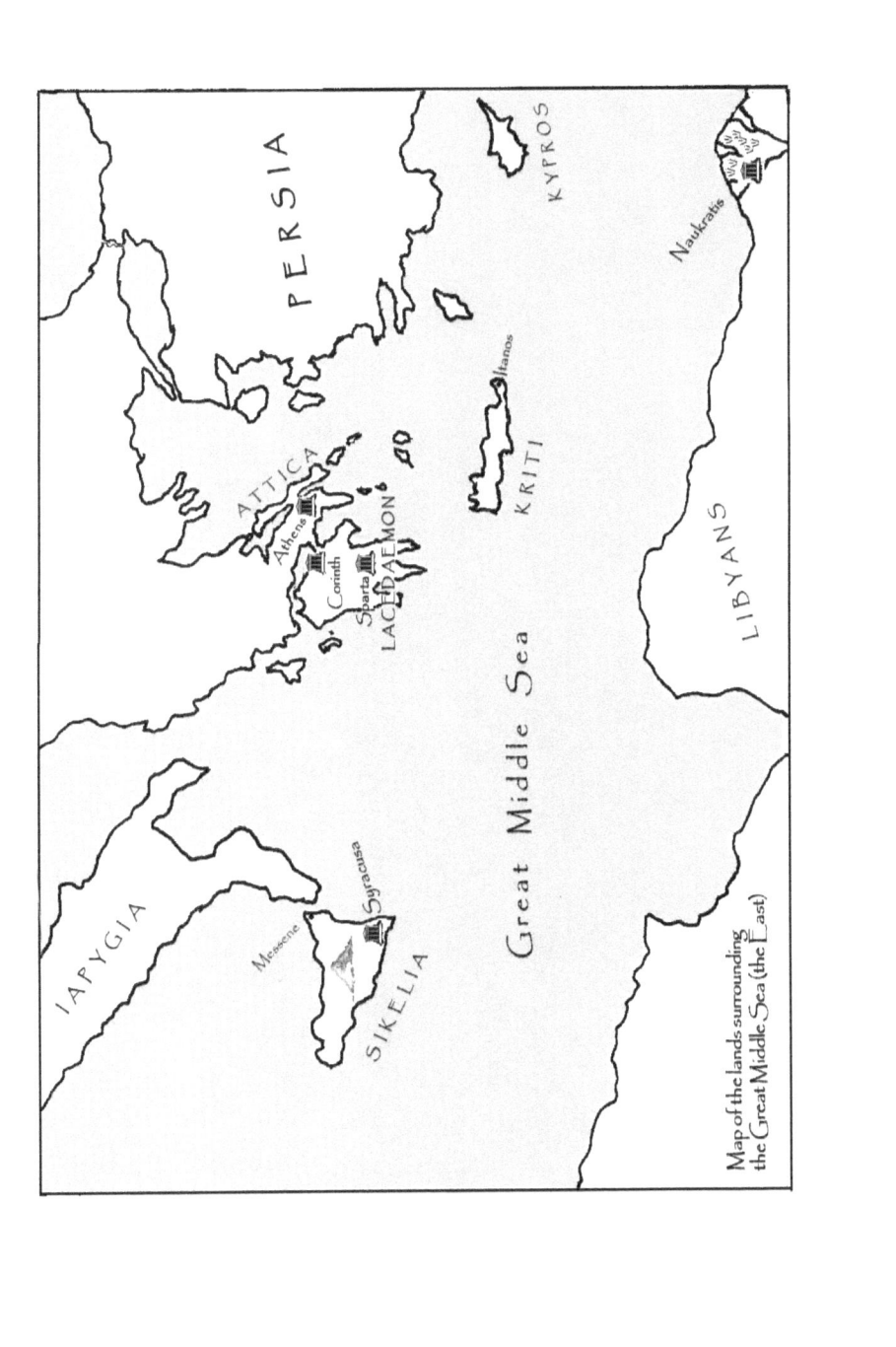

Map of the lands surrounding
the Great Middle Sea (the East)

Chapter 1

Llan Huell

Pelia smiled as she hummed to herself, remembering fondly her mother singing her softly to sleep as a child. The fire was low in the darkened hut and it was starting to get cold again, so she carefully settled a small birch log down in amongst the embers and gently blew the fire back into life.

With the evening still some while off it was better to save the ash and the oak for the bitter cold of the night to come. For in the harsh midwinter, every effort was precious and so every log had to be valued. She watched the swirling smoke and the first licks of flame as they sprang from the new wood, holding her hands close to the welcome heat while Sealgair the hound slumbered on. Her hut was small, its thatched roof timbers reaching down to the low stone wall that encircled a round patch of stamped earth, with dry rushes laid down a safe distance from the reach of the fire. The hut was big enough for perhaps four or so to sleep there with space enough about them. For Pelia and her hound it was more than enough, and that is all anyone can ask for.

She waited thoughtfully, her mind wandering to the start of the day when her old childhood friend Olwen had mentioned a visiting cousin of hers, and asked if she might send her to stay and learn from Pelia. There were some mischievous spirits in her, Olwen had said, and perhaps there were at that.

Pelia had seen this girl Cerian before, a one of perhaps sixteen summers now, on the cusp of her full womanhood and yet with no marriage in sight. An age of unquiet minds, of arguments and strong will, at least if Pelia's own first years after the coming of her blood were anything to go by.

Now somebody's footfall approached, lightly stepping across the crisp, frosty leaves towards Pelia's hut.

'Aunt Pelia,' a girl's voice called. The bright and clear voice of youth.

One of the hound Sealgair's ears lifted a little, but he did not stir from his sleep, hearing no threat in the girl's gentle voice.

'Come in Cerian,' Pelia called, but the girl was hesitant and so Pelia crouched forward to lift aside the weighted leather flap that hung from the doorframe.

'Quickly now,' she called as the girl ducked under the low opening and sat opposite her. 'And don't call me aunt!' she smiled. 'It's not so many summers since I was your age.'

Pelia noted the girl's fine, pale skin that seemed almost to shine like the moon as she crouched in the firelight. Cerian, 'the beautiful one'. Rarely had a name fitted a girl so easily.

'Come, sit beside me,' she beckoned. 'Better that we both share the fire's warmest side. The frost will be all the harder when night falls.'

Cerian nodded, but her glance at Sealgair's dark form beside Pelia gave away her nervousness of the hunting hound.

'Don't fear Sealgair,' Pelia calmed her. 'He is a gentle beast despite his name, unless someone was to raise their voice to me. And then... not so gentle!' she laughed.

Cerian smiled back as she skirted the fire and sat to warm her hands.

'Sit closer. There is no need to be afraid of me,' Pelia beckoned again, and this time the younger one did so, lifting her tawny woollen dress as she shuffled around the hearth.

'Thank you, but I am not afraid of you,' Cerian said quietly, staring into to the glowing fire. 'It is only your skin that is dark, Olwen says.'

'Then that is good,' Pelia smiled, looking at Cerian, though the girl would not hold her gaze. She was well made Pelia noted, with the curves that men lust for, swelling under her long plaits of dark hair. Her eyes seemed dark too at first, but when the firelight flickered, they shone hazel-green, like those of a vixen fox.

'You are happy then Cerian, to see your Olwen and to be

here?' Pelia asked, seeking some common ground with her guest.

'I suppose I am, yes,' Cerian said without much feeling in her voice. 'Olwen is a good woman, a good wife... that is why I am here I guess.'

'To learn to be like her?'

'That and to catch the eye of a man,' Cerian answered, a sullenness in her voice. 'Is that why Olwen brought me to you?'

'Perhaps that is her reason. She did not say,' Pelia hid the truth of the matter. 'Olwen wants only what she thinks is best for you.'

'So my path is to be here in this place, guided by you and your folk instead of my own?' Cerian said bluntly as she turned her eyes on Pelia. 'I think I know my own mind well enough without need of that.'

'You do? Then truly you are as wise as any of us,' Pelia raised an eyebrow.

The warm blood of anger came to Cerian's fine cheeks then. 'Don't mock me,' she said coolly. 'What do you know of...'

'Of love? Of life? Of dreams and wishes? Of curses and hate?' Pelia interrupted her. 'I know something of all of these things, but I also know each of us has our own path to follow, woman and man. I cannot help you if you don't want my help, and I would not change you either, not for Olwen's sake or anyone else's. You are what your nature tells you to be.

'As the years pass you will learn that sometimes life will bring you good things, and sometimes not. Only you know what will make you happy. If you don't know it then nobody else will.'

Cerian pulled her knees up to her chin with a deep sigh and stared into the fire again.

Pelia left her to her silence, whilst she sought out a small, lidded pot from a number of vessels that stood neatly around the low hut wall. Untying the cord that held tight its hide cover, she used a small wand to draw out some honey from within and let it drizzle into a pot of water that was heating through at the edge of the hearth. The younger girl watched from the corner of her eye, then looked away again as Pelia dipped a small cup into the pot and offered it to her guest.

'Thank you,' Cerian relented, her hand on her heart. 'A rare gift so late in the year,' she said, sipping the sweet liquid.

'You are welcome,' Pelia said warmly. 'Many who come to my hut are old or sick, or with child and it is of these matters that they wish to talk to me, so it is good to speak about other things.'

This caught Cerian's shyness again and the girl turned away to look into the fire once more. Pelia left her to her thoughts and poured a draft of the honeyed water into a cup for herself.

'The honey...' Cerian began. 'You are a great healer, or that is what I have heard anyway.'

'Doubtless you've heard other things about me too,' Pelia said wryly. 'But yes, the gift of healing was passed to me by my mother, may her spirit always find peace. Her own gift was greater than mine, and she knew so much about the healing ways... Ah, but I am not her. Even so the people hereabouts still look to me for help in their time of need.'

'Where does it come from, the gift?' Cerian asked with some doubt in her voice. 'The spirit men have the magic. Is yours the same?'

'No, mine is not from the same root as theirs,' Pelia laughed. 'Do you think they would let me, a mere woman, live untroubled in their midst if they thought I intruded on their power?'

She could see Cerian was a sensitive one, so she spoke her next words more gently.

'There are many things that we women can learn and share between us, Cerian. The gods and spirits leave their small magic for us in the trees, and in the flowers, and in the plants and their roots. When you come to know these things as I do, then you can add them together to make a more powerful magic still.'

'Like a potion?' Cerian said her face coming alive with a keen interest.

'Yes a potion, either to drink or to breathe in its vapours, and so take the magic into your body,' Pelia continued. 'But whether these things work depends also on the nature of the heart. If the heart is strong, then the body will be too you see?'

'Yes,' Cerian nodded, though she still looked a little doubtful.

'Sometimes,' Pelia explained, 'people just don't have the strength of will to get better, and this also is where the healer may try to help, by lifting up their spirit. But come, let us talk of other things. Girls of your age grow bored easily I know, and no doubt your mind is already wandering among the young men you've seen here.'

'It is not!' Cerian cried indignantly before calming herself. 'I'd like to hear more of your healing, for there is no talk in my village except for the boasts of the men, and the gossip of the old women. Few are as lucky as you are, to be a slave to no man.'

'We all have our bonds Cerian, even me,' Pelia sighed. 'All here look to the chieftain's protection if raiders come. In return he has our oaths, including mine.'

Cerian thought on that whilst the two sipped their drinks and the fire glow started to fade.

'Is it true what they say of your mother?' she said suddenly, as Pelia settled another log onto the hearth.

The hut grew cold as the hungry spirit of the fire goddess Brid strove to lick fresh flames from the wood. Pelia shivered and gathered her great grey wolf pelt cloak about her.

'I know what some of the men say,' she said looking into the embers. 'That the man my mother got me by was a spirit come across from the shadow world.'

Cerian hung her head, afraid to speak.

'But of course he was a man, just as any other,' Pelia continued. 'People always fear what they don't understand.'

'Your skin though…'

'Is darker than yours, yes,' Pelia smiled patiently. She had known looks and comments like these all her life.

'Yes, and your eyes…'

'My eyes?' Pelia laughed.

5

'I only meant they are very beautiful.'

'Thank you. But don't concern yourself Cerian, these things that make me different, I like them all. Even when my own people sometimes forget that I am just the same as they are inside.'

'Does that not annoy you?'

'No!' Pelia laughed, as the fire finally kindled itself back to life. 'A handsome warrior once told me my skin was the colour of the sweetest honey, and that my eyes were like a golden sky at sunset.'

'That is beautiful,' Cerian smiled. 'The words are very true.'

'Thank you,' Pelia said. 'I lay with him for those words, and others that he spoke to me, though not many know that part.'

Cerian blushed a little at that.

'Did he die?' she asked quietly.

'No. He still lives as far as I know, but I did not want a husband then, just as I don't want one now.'

'Oh.'

'It is nothing,' Pelia waved the talk away.

'And your hair...' Cerian said, changing the subject. 'Can I touch it?'

'Yes, of course you can. This I have been asked many times by men and women alike.'

Cerian lifted the mass of spiral curls that hung a little past Pelia's shoulders, unwinding them a little, only for them to jump back up into their former shape as she let go. A look of wonder crossed her face. 'Could you make my hair like yours?' she asked eagerly.

'I don't think so,' Pelia smiled. 'My mother always told me it was a gift from my father, from his seed. My hair is always the same and I like it, but sometimes I wish it could be like yours is, long and straight.'

Cerian grinned at that. 'It seems to me that we always long for those things that others have.'

'That is true enough,' Pelia nodded, as she offered her guest some more of the honeyed water which was by now steaming in its pot.

'What of your father then?' Cerian asked. 'He was a warrior too I have heard?'

'I do not remember him,' said Pelia quietly. 'I know of him only through my mother's words, as he left her before I was born.'

'That is sad...' Cerian reached out and touched her arm. 'Did he not love her? Why did he leave?'

'It is a long story,' Pelia patted the younger girl's hand. 'Far too long to trouble you with.'

'I would like to hear it still, if you would like to tell me. That is if...' Cerian stopped herself. 'I'm sorry. It hurts you to remember these things.'

'No, no,' Pelia shook her head. 'There is no shame for me in the tale of my mother and father, but all the same I doubt you would want to hear it all. Much of it would have little meaning for you.'

'But why not?' Cerian frowned.

'Because it isn't just a story of this land or your people.'

'But you are one of us too, are you not?'

'I am that, but my father was an outlander you see, from a place far beyond your knowing, or mine come to that, though I have kept in my mind the many strange things he told my mother of. No-one here, other than high chieftain Heilyn has much interest in my story, for they have tales of their own forbears and their deeds. These and the legends of the old people who moved the great stones are what they like to hear about.'

'And the high chieftain?' Cerian puzzled. 'Why is your story important to him, but not to others here?'

Pelia bit her lip thoughtfully.

'He has his reasons,' she said. 'In part you see, my story is also his story.'

Cerian frowned again. 'How can that be? Did he know your father?'

'No. Like me, Heilyn was not even born when my father left this place. To understand these things you would need to hear the story from the beginning,' said Pelia. 'And as I have already told you, it is a very long story that would take many moons to tell.'

'I would like to hear all the same,' Cerian said, the firelight catching the eagerness in her young eyes. 'I am in no hurry to be paired off with a man, if that is what Olwen wants for me.'

'Your cousin wants what is best for you, but...' Pelia hesitated before making her mind up. 'I will speak to her and then we will see.'

Cerian's brow wrinkled, but she bit her tongue.

'You are her ward while you are here, after all,' Pelia said thoughtfully. 'But she might be persuaded to pass you into my care if I also teach you something of my ways. There are things I know of healing. And the knack of bringing babies more easily from the womb.'

'Ach,' sighed Cerian.

'Never mind, ach,' Pelia said sternly, her finger raised as her mother had often done to her. 'You may not yet want babies yourself, but with what you learn from me you might one day save two lives by saving one. How many of the young do you know who have had to live without the love of their mother?'

Cerian hung her head shamefully, for she had spoken without thinking.

'I would learn if you would teach me,' she said quietly.

Pelia nodded, satisfied. 'Yes, you will learn I think and quickly. You have a sharp mind and that will grow into wisdom in the years to come. Others will be glad of you, if you learn the things that I know.'

Cerian did not know what to say, the awkwardness of her youth holding her tongue still.

'Go back to Olwen,' Pelia said warmly. 'And sleep well. There will be many jobs for you here in the days to come if we are both not to go hungry.'

'Thank you, I will,' Cerian nodded respectfully, as she got up and crouched toward the doorway.

'And be always kind to Olwen,' Pelia said quietly. 'She is a good woman.'

Cerian nodded again, lifting the leather door flap before

stepping outside into the chill evening.

Pelia sat up by the fire with her thoughts for a while after Cerian had left, until the flames slowly ebbed away. When the fire was down to embers, she rubbed her tired eyes and sighed, as she roused Sealgair from his sleep. She pushed the hound out into the night air so that he could empty himself against the high stockade wall behind her hut while she too made herself comfortable for the night.

Outside all was still and quiet, even the long hall of Heilyn the high chieftain, off a way in the middle of the settlement.

'Heilyn the cautious,' they called him. Not a man like his father. No, Huell the great chief who had fathered him had been a very different man.

Her own father had once counted Huell as a brother until things had soured between them. After all, it was only down to her father's help that Huell had united his people, so that he could raise up this place of Llan Huell that took his name. Pride swelled in Pelia's lonely heart at this thought.

The stars overhead shone brightly in the moonless sky, outlining the shapes of the heroes and the gods, named by the elders in their many stories. Perhaps, she thought, her father looked down upon her from up there, for it was at their side that he surely deserved to be if he was gone from this world. Pelia ushered the hound Sealgair back in to the warmth of her hearth and consoled herself with this thought as she sought the dream world that comes with sleep.

The next day Pelia spoke to Olwen of young Cerian and what would be best for her, so that Olwen soon saw the wisdom in her words.

Cerian came to the hut early the following morning, bringing newly gathered firewood and her things wrapped in her woollen cloak to Pelia's door. This was on Olwen's strict condition that the girl would obey Pelia's will and would be beaten if she was lazy.

After the two of them had shared a thin but warming porridge of barley and oats, Pelia made sure that the younger girl was set to work, checking and setting eel traps in the chill shallows of the river. Cerian's feet throbbed with the cold, yet she did not complain. Luckily for them both there was a fat eel and a thinner one too for their trouble, so they had cause to give thanks to the water spirits for their gifts when they reset the traps. Then there was wood to be chopped with Pelia's small axe, which soon had them warm again as they fetched and carried.

When they had stacked the logs outside Pelia's hut, there was cord to be plaited from the inner bark of the longer green branches they had collected. Then Pelia gave Cerian a hare skin that had soaked in some weak ash water, and set her to scrapping off the hairs so that it could be worked into fine leather. Finally, there was corn to be ground between the quern stones for the next day's bread. Easy enough these things might be in the warmth of summer, but they sapped the strength in the cold, lean months of winter.

At last, when Pelia was satisfied with the flour the younger girl had ground, she handed Cerian the fatter of the still squirming, slimy eels to skin, gut and chop up for their stew with some green winter herbs from the forest. All the while, Cerian listened patiently as Pelia told her a few things of the birthing ways. These were the ways of the midwife, some of them common enough knowledge for a girl of Cerian's years, but others were usually in the keep of only the wisest of women.

When the pungent eel stew was ready, they ate it all hungrily down. Cerian wiped her wooden bowel clean with a last piece of bread crust, while Pelia rebuilt the fire anew to restore flames to the cooking embers and then made herself comfortable. Sealgair, next to her as always, gnawed on an old boar knuckle bone he had dug out from a hiding place somewhere.

'And now Cerian, if you are sure, I will tell you a little of the story of my father and how he came from a far off land to this place,' Pelia said quietly. 'But first I would ask you to promise something.'

'I have eaten your bread and shared your hearth, and so you can ask of me anything I am free to give,' Cerian said, in the formal way of things that pass between a guest and their host.

'It is only this,' Pelia began seriously. 'There are some things you will learn from me, if I decide to tell you of them that is, that must stay between us. If you were to speak of them to others, it would cause me trouble.'

Cerian was puzzled, wondering how she could promise what she did not know and might never be told, but she nodded her agreement all the same.

'I will keep your words to myself if you tell me to do this,' the girl said, her hand on her heart.

Pelia smiled and she nodded to herself. She was a little sad, but also at the same time glad in her heart that she could now bring something of the spirit of her mother back from where she now dwelt in the shadow world. Back into the knowing of another soul, so that for a while longer her mother, and her father too, would live again in Pelia's words and Cerian's imaginings. Perhaps this was part of what her old friend Olwen had intended by sending her the girl.

'We will begin then,' Pelia said, her eyes of gold and green glistening in the firelight. 'Tell me Cerian,' she began, gathering her wolf skin cloak about her. 'Do you know where we are, here in this place?'

'Yes... Of course,' Cerian hesitated, surprised by such a silly question. 'We are in your hut, in my cousin Olwen's place, the place that is called Llan Huell.'

'And beyond Llan Huell?'

'Beyond?' Cerian thought for a moment. 'Well, they say that if you walk towards the setting sun for three days, you will reach the sea,' Cerian said proudly.

'Very good,' Pelia nodded.

'But others say,' Cerian continued, 'that the sea, though a long way off is all around us except perhaps to the north. There they say you can walk forever and still not come to it.'

'What do you think of this?' Pelia asked curiously.

'I cannot say. I have never seen the sea,' Cerian said, a small sadness in her voice.

'Nor I,' replied Pelia. 'I know it only from the stories my

mother told me, but in my mind I can see it in all of its moods just the same. It is the endless realm they say of great Llyr, the god of the sea. He is the one who thunders against the towering cliffs of the land on white horses that he raises up from the water. He is the bringer of the winter storms that shake the trees and his realm is all around us.'

'To the north as well?'

'Yes, to the north and all points of the sun and the stars,' Pelia smiled, now that she had caught Cerian's imagination.

'Éiru, land of the setting sun, lies beyond the western seas, while to the south the Sound of Dyfneint divides us from a vast land much bigger than our own.'

Cerian listened keenly, for these were the things told by the men in their halls when they feasted and drank mead, things that rarely came to the ears of a young girl.

'Though shallow near the shore, the seas are soon deeper than any lake,' Pelia continued, 'and their waters are full of salt, so that you cannot drink them without being sick. The mood of the sea follows the mood of the sky, so some of the wiser elders say. It can be iron-grey like the snowy skies at the time of the Imbolc feast when the land lies frozen. Or it can be a warm blue, like the sky on a clear summer's day.'

'Or the colour of your eyes?'

'Perhaps,' Pelia laughed a little as she ran her fingers through Sealgair's dark fur. 'These things are important to my story, for there is much crossing and re-crossing of the seas in what I will tell you. The sea surrounds all lands you see, not just our own.'

Pelia paused awhile, as she could see that Cerian was deep in thought about all the things she had been told.

The girl picked up a stick from the edge of the hearth and made a mark in the ashes.

'So we are here...' Cerian frowned. 'With the sea to the west, to the south, to the east and to the north. It is all around us?' she asked as she traced a rough circle in the ashes.

'Aye, well done!'

'We are an island then?' Cerian said excitedly, surprised at herself. 'Like those in the rivers where the swans build their nests?'

'Exactly like those, but bigger than you or I can dream of. There are legends of what lies in the far north, stories of giants and dragons. And far beyond that, at the edge of the world there is a land bound in ice forever, where the sun will never rise.'

Pelia shivered at her own words, making the finger sign against evil with one hand, whilst she stroked the bear claw charms on her necklace with the other.

Cerian too grew anxious and held her hands clasped against her chest in fear. It was that same great fear of the unknown that brings nightmares, and Pelia could see that it was too soon to speak of such nameless things to her guest.

'I am sorry,' she said, putting her hand on Cerian's shoulder to reassure her. 'Perhaps you should not hear my story. It is bloodthirsty at times and after all there is much bitterness in it.'

'But also,' Cerian said, 'there will be much pride for you in the telling. My father says that when we honour the dead, their spirits hear us in the shadow world. As you said, perhaps your mother and father will hear you when you speak of them?'

Those words brightened both of their moods, and Pelia sat up proudly, as if her father's eyes might be upon her.

'You are a wise one Cerian, as is your father,' she smiled. 'Thank you for your words. Ah, but where to begin?' Pelia laughed to herself. 'Where to start?'

'What was your father's name?' Cerian asked brightly.

'The name my mother told me was Talakh,' Pelia said with a smile. 'Not easy to say.'

'Ta-laa-tch.'

'Not quite, but a good try,' Pelia laughed again. 'Talakh was his friend-name, for those who knew him well and those who loved him, but his given name in full was Talakhonsu. He came from far away where peoples' words are as different from ours as the colour of my skin is from yours. I will tell you his story if you will listen,' Pelia smiled.

And so she began.

13

Chapter 2

The Night River and the Moon

On the night that Talakhonsu was born, the bright, full disc of the moon god Khonsu had risen over the great stone temple of Amun of the four winds. Amun was the greatest of the gods of those far off desert lands of Napata and father of the moon god Khonsu too, so for this reason the priests declared that the newborn should be named Talakhonsu.

The holy men watched over the boy as he grew and then when he was five years old his mother sent him to live with them in the great temple, so that he could be taught the god Amun's ways and start on his path to become one of their order. Talakhonsu's mother was proud of him and glad that the fates had smiled on her son, for she could see that with luck he would grow to have power and influence amongst his people. This was something that would have otherwise been impossible, despite her own noble birth, since he had no father to stand behind him. Of course at first Talakhonsu had been sad to leave his mother, but the servants of Amun treated him well and taught him much, so that slowly his happiness returned.

One priest in particular, a blind elder named Prainke, became almost as an oldfather to him as the years passed and Talakh grew. From Prainke he learned that he must look for omens, both in the sky and on the Great River that brought life to the parched lands around Napata.

But though his eyes did not see, still old Prainke saw much that others did not. He always thought foolish those who said that one day the young king Siaspiqa would take back their ancestral territories in the land of Kemet far to the north, where once his ancestors had ruled. The people of Kemet were the ancient enemy of Napata and none more so than the false priests of Amun in Kemet, who claimed the great god of the four winds and the sky for their own. They would be made to eat their words in the years to come and the temples of their great city of Waset would be burned to the ground, so Siaspiqa and his advisors boasted.

This then was the dream of Siaspiqa, king of Napata of Kush, but it was not the dream of Prainke. He was wise enough to see not just that Siaspiqa would grow to be a weak ruler, but also that the nobles of Kemet still had their teeth, together with a deep hatred for their old Kushite enemy.

Sure enough, after many years of uneasy peace between the two lands, a large war band of skulking Kemet warriors came unseen to Napata one fateful night. They soon began their work, killing all who crossed their path in a blood thirst that would not be slaked until the sun returned to the sky.

As the slaughter began, the boy Talakhonsu was roused from his bed by Prainke, whose keen ears had heard the first strangled cries echoing in the night. The old priest, heedless for his own safety, ordered Talakhonsu to run and hide in the marshes, where no doubt the women would take the children if they could. Yet as the old man pushed him outside, their way was blocked by a desperate fight between the Kemet raiders and the few warriors of Napata who had found their feet and their bows. Talakhonsu ran past them and he did not stop until he came down to the Great River, breathless with fear and longing for the safety of his mother's arms as the screams and cries rose higher behind him. There at the river were the places he would play in the cool of the evening with his friends in the times before he had been sent to the temple. There at the river he would hide, and in turn seek, with the other children amongst the reeds that grew thick along its shallow banks.

'Beware the khamsa,' his mother had often warned. 'The servants of the Lord Sobek have sharp teeth beyond number in their long jaws and they like nothing more than to drag young boys down into the underworld so that he can feed on them in his dark halls.'

Talakhonsu had not heeded her then, but now there was a worse danger for him still. His throat swelled with fear as he stumbled and sobbed along the river bank through the dark, smoke filled night. Suddenly an old man loomed out of the blackness and grasped his arms.

'Where are you going boy?' he rasped with the voice of a crow, a jagged wound across his bleeding face. 'Amun has deserted us! Run if you will, but you will die just the same. We will all die tonight, all of us, do you hear me?'

Talakhonsu twisted away from the man's wiry grip and fell back into the dust, before scrabbling away as fast as he could, sobbing even harder now.

'All dead, boy!' the old man called out after him. 'All dead, all of us...'

Talakhonsu ran on, unheeding and breathless until finally he came to a place where he could hide. The Great River was far from its lowest mark and there were strong currents too, yet he had no choice but to wade into her cool waters to lose himself amongst the reed beds.

Now all grew quiet, all peaceful except for the boy's heaving sobs and the night wind whispering through the reeds. Talakhonsu tried to be brave and waded up to his shoulders in the dark waters, pushing against the flow as he sought out a mud bank that he knew must be there, though it was now almost covered by the river. Only a tiny island fringed with reeds remained and there he dragged himself ashore, exhausted and terrified. A desolate tiredness closed his eyes and though the night was clear and cold, still he fell into a troubled sleep, his young ears mercifully spared the worst of the distant screams that rang out as the Napatans were slaughtered.

When at last the morning came, the great sun brought the warriors of Kemet to the river, a few at first but then many more. They seized the larger boats and set to work loading them with treasures of gold and other precious things they had plundered from the temples and the houses of the rich. There had always been a few Kemet slaves in Napata, taken no doubt from the disputed border lands to the north. These warriors shared the same dark skin, yet not so dark as the peoples of Nubia to whom Talakhonsu and the Napatans belonged.

All of these things Talakhonsu saw through fresh tears as he lay numb with the cold, a shadow amongst the reeds, while yet more warriors arrived with their spoils. Some of the boats started to raise sail and it was then that Talakhonsu heard a great crying and sorrowing coming down toward the river. A long line of his own people came into sight, tied together in bonds as they were goaded and beaten before the hated men of Kemet. For this was a great raid, a taking and a burning. A dishonouring of all that was Napata. The warriors of Kemet now formed into a long line along the bank of the Great River, so close to the boy's hiding place that he could almost smell the sweat and bitter blood on their bodies.

They were light of limb these men, their heads shaved for the most part, except for a short band above their necks, just as Prainke had taught him about them. They wore kilts too, but where once their cloth might have been white, now it was soiled with dust and dark spats of blood. Napatan blood. Talakhonsu looked on them in fear and horror, in disgust too for they were as wolves among sheep, knowing only how to kill and savage.

The Kemet warriors were shouting now, some wielding long wooden clubs above their heads in triumph, while others jabbed their spears at their prisoners' feet, taunting them mercilessly. Anger grew heavy in young Talakhonsu's throat as his heart pounded in his chest. He gritted his teeth and clenched his small bony fists in his impotent rage.

Just then a man's voice called loud from amongst the warriors, a voice of authority. Of course Talakhonsu could not understand the tongue of the strangers, but the voice was level, cold and hard, the voice of a leader. The line of warriors in front of him parted to reveal a tall noble, his kilt pure white against those of his blood stained soldiers. He had broad, well muscled shoulders, with a gold circlet around his neck and a cruel smile on his face.

To his horror, Talakhonsu saw then that amongst the prisoners at the noble's feet was old Prainke. The blind priest's face was a bloody mess, the bone of his cheek showing a shocking white through his old leathery skin. Talakhonsu's heart fell at the sight of it.

The noble barked another order and suddenly Kemet hands were laid on the old priest, cutting carelessly at the thong that tethered him about his neck to the others. Blood oozed from Prainke's neck as he was thrown, moaning to the ground. The old man curled up in a ball, knowing what must surely come next.

But Talakhonsu, boy priest of the temple of Amun of Napata did not know, did not guess, could not imagine until the first club was raised high over the head of a Kemet warrior. For a moment the heavy black war club paused in midair, before two clenched fists brought it down with all of the warrior's strength on the bare back of Prainke, splintering his ribs with a sound that was both a loud crack and a hollow thud all at the same time. In an instant other clubs fell on the old man's collapsed body which was already in the last throes of death.

Before he knew it, before he even had time to think, the boy Talakhonsu was already in the water, wading at first and then running, splashing through the shallows and onto the shore. A small part of his mind cried to him in fear, but the rest of his body was filled with such a rage that it blanked out almost everything else. He was running, but not running away from the evil ones. No, he ran toward them, falling on one of the warriors from behind, his small fists flailing uselessly at the man's bare back. The boy suddenly felt his legs become light and the world began to spin as another man picked him up bodily and threw him to the ground next to Prainke. A shadow fell across him, blocking the light of the sun, the shadow of death with its war club raised high again. Talakhonsu closed his eyes and braced himself for the pain of what was to come, but just then the cold voice of the Kemet noble shouted another order. The shadow of death moved aside to be replaced by that of the noble himself.

The Kemet noble's dark, soulless eyes pierced Talakhonsu through and he was suddenly afraid as the last of his anger vanished like the morning mists under the heat of the sun. The man muttered something to himself as he dragged Talakhonsu to his feet by the hair. The last that the boy priest remembered was a rush of air as the noble's hand struck him hard on the temple, and then the world tumbled into a black void that flared with bright stars and pain.

It was dark when Talakhonsu awoke with a start and tried to sit up, though his throbbing head told him straight away that this was not wise. He lay back down on the hard rock, pins and needles casting a cold spider's web over his numb back and arms, before he slipped back into unconsciousness once more.

As the boy's spirit crossed back into the land of dreams, he saw a great bird high above him in a darkened sky. It was the lammergeyer, the sharp beaked swallower of bones, its mighty wings beating silently as they pushed the air down so hard that he felt a cold wind on his face. The great bird, as big as any eagle, swooped down onto a hill made of the bones of men, its mighty wing beats dislodging the skulls of the dead so that they tumbled to the ground, where they smashed into pieces like eggshells. The lammergeyer seized a thigh bone in its claw and reared up, soaring high into the black sky, its feathers burnished a dark bronze by the dead sun.

Talakhonsu's spirit-self shuddered as the great bird dropped the bone, watching it fall end over end until it shattered on the rocks below. He knew what would come next and sure enough the great devourer swept down again to feast on the broken shards, swallowing them whole down into its craw. Some said that the lammergeyer was a god, smashing the bones of the dead to release evil spirits from them so that they could return to their own dark lands, but Talakhonsu saw only horror in the grisly nightmare.

Thankfully, the dream faded as quickly as it had come. The world of the living called his wandering spirit back into his body again and he woke with a start, his eyes already wet with fresh tears.

'There, boy,' a voice whispered to him from the darkness.

19

'Don't let those Kemet curs hear you cry. We must all be strong if we are to survive.'

Talakhonsu said nothing. Confused and in pain, he stifled his tears as best as he could, knowing not what had become of him nor what would happen next. He tried to sit up again, this time more slowly, and opened his mouth as if to speak, but no sound came from his parched throat. For an awful moment he thought perhaps the soldiers had cut out his tongue. Something was tied around his neck, and his wrists too were tightly bound together.

'Here,' the voice came again, and this time he could make out the eyes of a man, then the lighter palms of his outstretched hands holding out a small water skin in the darkness.

'It is the water of the Great River. It is not so sweet here, but none of us has been sick from it yet.'

Talakhonsu took the skin from the stranger, his bound hands so weak that he could barely support it, and let some of the water fall into his mouth. It was warm and a little sour, but it salved his dry throat nonetheless. His mother had warned him not to drink water straight from the Great River, and this he usually obeyed, for the water from the cool mountain wells always tasted better. Yet as he swallowed, he felt his painful tongue come unstuck from the sides of his throat. For that at least he offered his thanks to the stranger.

'It is nothing,' the man said quietly. 'How do you feel?'

'I don't know... I feel dizzy, like I am still half asleep,' Talakhonsu croaked.

'You have a small fever,' the man replied in a kindly voice. 'But we can hope that the bad spirits have left you now.'

'Where am I?' Talakhonsu croaked again. 'What has happened to us?'

'We are in one of the cave tombs of the old people,' the man answered, 'held prisoner here by the Kemet war band. They are feasting, up there on the bank above us.'

Talakhonsu could smell the roasting meat now as his senses slowly came back to him. With them came a sudden hunger, worse than any he had ever known.

'What do they want with us?' he asked fearfully. 'Will they kill us?'

'No, they mean to take us back to Kemet as slaves, those of us who survive the journey. They stole our boats and sailed through last night to take their spoils as far from Napata as they could. Now they feel safe.'

'My mother...' the boy started to say.

'There is no easy way to tell you this, lad. She has gone over into the land of shadows. Your mother is in the care of the gods of the dead now.'

Talakhonsu could do nothing but sob as the burning tears came like fire to his eyes. Dark sorrow hung heavy in his young heart and he felt then that he too should have died with his mother and Prainke. He tried to imagine her whole again and smiling, as she was led by the jackal-headed one through the gentle light of the shadow world to where perhaps his lost father waited in a beautiful garden. There they would all live one day. This was the way of death that the other priests had taught him, but still his heart was so heavy that it brought him little comfort.

'Try to sleep boy,' the man consoled him with a hand on his shoulder. 'I am called Korkamani. I will watch over you.'

Talakhonsu took another draught of the water and handed the skin back to the man, before slumping back down onto the bare rock of the cave floor, sobbing still. He started to shiver, and the man laid a tattered cloak over his bare chest.

'Thank you,' Talakhonsu said as bravely as he could.

'It is nothing,' Korkamani said gently. 'Now sleep.'

There was something familiar about the man, Talakhonsu thought. He was tall and well made from what he could make out in the darkness, a grown man but still with the strength of his youth.

'How do you know of my mother?' he asked.

'There will be time for talk tomorrow,' Korkamani said with sadness in his voice as he turned away.

Talakhonsu could do nothing but close his eyes tight against the bitter world that had taken all that was precious from him. First, his father had died when he was just a baby,

21

so that Talakhonsu had no memory of him. Now his mother and Prainke were gone too. The tears came again and though he tried to fight them back as best as he could, still they ran down his cheeks, warm over his skin. As he lay there in the dark, the boy plaintively asked the great god Amun of the skies and the winds to watch over his mother and the old priest as they made their journey to the world of shadows.

When Talakhonsu next awoke it was to the harsh shouts of the warriors of Kemet, as they pulled the captured Napatans from the cave by the tethers that were looped around their necks.

'Come,' the man Korkamani said, taking Talakhonsu's thin arm and pulling him upright. 'Better that we walk proudly than be dragged like dogs.'

The boy did as he was asked and gathered to his chest the old cloak Korkamani had given him. When they left the twilight of the cave and emerged blinking into the early morning light, he noticed that there was only one large boat to be seen. There were fewer Napatans too, perhaps only a dozen and a half, and so fewer warriors to guard them. 'Where are the others? The women...?' he whispered. 'Are they all killed?'

'One thing you will learn quickly Talakh, is that the army of Kemet values gold first, then women, and then us,' Korkamani said, spitting on the floor with disgust at this evil. 'The women and girls have been taken ahead with the gold and jewels. Their leader will not rest until the things of most value are safely back in Kemet lands, and so the faster boats were rowed on ahead through the night.'

'You called me Talakh. How do you know of me? How do you know of my mother?' the boy asked again.

'I know of you through your mother, who I knew from the hall of our king,' Korkamani replied, the sadness returning to his stern face. 'You do not mind me calling you by your friend-name?'

'No, I like it better. Do you have one?'

'No, there is only Korkamani. Korkamani and nothing

else,' he said with a quick flash of a smile that let his white teeth shine in the bright sun. 'But come, we must give them no reason to beat us. Be brave now Talakh.'

At spear point, the Kemet guards dragged and goaded their Napatan prisoners down a plank that led over the low side of a large vessel. Once aboard they were made to sit in a huddle, their backs facing outwards while a rope was passed through their bound hands, so that they could not easily gaze upon their oppressors.

'What will happen now?' Talakh whispered.

'You will grow hungrier still, for they will not feed us,' Korkamani replied quietly. 'The journey will be hard and some will doubtless die, but our captors will show no pity. When great Amun holds back the wind from their sail, we will be made to shoulder the oars. And whether there is a fair wind or not, the sun will bake our skins just the same. Our tongues will cry out for water, but the Kemet curs will not care.'

Talakh swallowed hard as his young mind struggled to come to terms with the woes that Korkamani had laid out.

'But,' Korkamani whispered, leaning close to him, 'you and I will survive, have no doubt of it. Despite everything that has happened, our gods will not abandon us.'

'But how can you be sure of these things after all that has passed?'

Korkamani breathed deeply, sitting up to his full height, and stared deep into Talakh's eyes, as if he were looking for something. Talakh thought then that with his thin, long face he looked a proud man. A leader of men, despite his bonds.

'I saw your anger when the old priest was murdered by those cowards,' Korkamani's eyes flashed towards the guards with their blood stained kilts. 'It was a brave thing you did, to run at them when you could have remained hidden. Foolish, but brave all the same. In that moment I thought you would surely be hacked down, and yet Amun spared you to live another day.'

'I remember a man who hit me,' Talakh said looking at his feet in shame.

'Yes, that one is called Khaemwaset. He is the leader of the Kemet soldiers and from a noble family,' Korkamani whispered, looking up to make sure no-one was listening to them. 'He is an evil man, a cold blooded killer of men and women alike.'

'Then why did he not kill me?'

'That I do not know. Perhaps he found it amusing to see a boy attacking grown men? Whatever the reason, I heard him order that one over there to watch for your safety,' Korkamani pointed with another flick of his eyes.

Talakh followed the glance to his side, where a big man with a fat belly stood, his hands on the waistband of his kilt. He had a broken nose and his cheekbone was sunken beneath one eye.

'Yes, I know. Looks like he's lost a few fights doesn't he?' Korkamani allowed himself a grin. 'But he is still here, so his enemies are probably all dead. He is Khaemwaset's right hand man and a hardened warrior without doubt.'

At this point the man with the broken nose barked an order and the boat cast off from the river bank, the men unfurling the sail which flapped lazily in the small breeze as the slow current took them out onto the Great River. Talakh noticed that the men of Kemet had already daubed on the canvas a crude all seeing eye, the Udjat symbol, to invoke the protection of their gods. The mark was the colour of dried blood.

'Great Amun sends the wind to carry us onward,' Korkamani whispered. 'We are spared the oar for the morning at least.'

In spite of his grief and despair, questions started to come to Talakh's mind now as the Great River carried them slowly northwards through a desolate, abandoned land.

'Korkamani?' he asked. 'How do you know their leader's name?'

Korkamani leant forward, and whispered so quietly that Talakh had to strain to hear him.

'I speak their tongue,' he said. 'We must keep this a secret though, you and I. As long as they think we don't understand, they will be careless with their words.'

'But what are we to do?' Talakh sighed, the hunger that burned in his belly already moving him to thoughts of despair.

'I do not know, Talakh,' Korkamani shook his head. 'I could perhaps try to escape myself, but then what would become of you and the others? It is down to the will of mighty Amun, king of gods, to protect us. We must trust to him and look for whatever chance he may give us.'

Talakh hung his head again, looking at his bare, dirty feet. He did not understand any of this. Perhaps it was an awful dream, like the dream of the lammergeyer, he thought. But in his heart he knew that it was not.

The day that followed seemed to be almost without end, as the boat and its slave cargo sailed slowly down the Great River, on through the barren desert. As far as the eye could see, all around there was nothing but sand and rock beyond the few reeds of the riverbank. Sometimes the land rose up into low hills, sometimes to high crags and cliffs that loomed above the boat. But of life, there was little sign. No cattle, no settlements, no wild beasts to be heard or seen except for the shrieks of vultures high overhead under the burning sun and the cry of the desert fox during the cold, windblown night that followed. Despite the great tract of water that the boat sailed upon, the guards would only let the prisoners of Napata drink sparingly, and of food there was none for them.

The next day as afternoon wore on, Korkamani pointed to a plume of smoke rising over some sand dunes up ahead.

'You have heard of Kawa no doubt from your priest teachers?' he said grimly.

'Yes,' Talakh nodded, glad that he knew one thing at least that might impress his protector. 'It is the place where Taharqa, our greatest king of old built his temple to Amun. This was to thank the great god for our victory over the armies of Kemet.'

'You remember your lessons well,' Korkamani smiled. 'Yes, it was once the second city of our people, though it is not much of a place now. Sadly it seems that what I overheard from the guards is true. Khaemwaset will have burned Kawa before raiding Napata.'

'But why has he put it to fire?' Talakh whispered.

'Perhaps because he knows he cannot hold it for himself,' Korkamani answered. 'Or perhaps just because he took amusement from it. It seems that Khaemwaset hoped to take our king prisoner, but Siaspiqa is away hunting to the south.

'The king is young and weak,' Korkamani sighed, shaking his head. 'Yet the land of Kemet is also weak despite this raid of Khaemwaset. I will tell you more of this later. You will know what I know.'

'But why?' Talakh asked. 'What can I do to change the way things are? I am only a boy.'

'You are not so young,' Korkamani said with a wry grin. 'I have seen the Great River bring its flood to our lands ten times now since your mother brought you into the world. Yet when I was your age I had already killed a deer with my bow. Then, when I was four years older than that, I travelled many days to the south with my father and his warriors to fight the people of the marshes who at that time were raiding our cattle. That was when I first killed another man.'

Talakh felt his heart pound in his chest and his dry throat became drier still.

'But I know only the ways of the temple,' he said quietly. 'I don't know how to fight.'

'Up until now you have led a sheltered life with the priests, it is true. But you will learn Talakh. If Amun wills it, you will learn.'

Talakh nodded silently. He knew that he must be strong if he was to survive. For only if he lived to be a man could he seek revenge on those who had taken his mother.

'Great Amun, king of all the gods, hear my prayer,' the boy whispered to the wind. 'Give me the strength to avenge my mother and I will offer at your shrine and serve you all of my days.'

Korkamani placed his hand on the boy's shoulder again.

'You ask for much, but you offer the great god your

devotions in return,' he said solemnly. 'Let us hope great Amun, who hears all things across the winds, will grant your wish. But know this Talakh, the one above all others responsible for our loss is Khaemwaset. You and I must wait our chance, no matter how long it takes or how much hardship we suffer. Khaemwaset's death must be our aim in all that we do.'

'It will be as you say Korkamani,' Talakh nodded. 'One day if Amun wills it, we will take his life, just as he took the lives of Prainke and my mother. I swear it.'

That night the soldiers went ashore to stretch their legs and eat their supper of stewed brown beans and barley grain. They cooked also a huge fish they had netted from the river as the boat had drifted along. These smells drove the prisoners to despair, the hunger gnawing at their bellies. To add to their misery, the one with the broken nose would not let them ashore and so they lay tethered in the wide bottom of the boat, while a guard goaded them with his spear for amusement until he grew bored with that. Truly it seemed that the gods had abandoned the Napatans as they all sat silent in their misery.

At last the guard swapped with another so that he could eat, and this other warrior was so full of food and barley ale that he started to doze, despite the cold, whistling wind of the desert.

'Korkamani,' Talakh whispered.

'Korkamani,' he whispered again more urgently when there was no answer.

His protector seemed to be dozing too, his head sunk on his shoulders. Yet he was not.

'I know, boy,' he said quietly. 'I have seen him.'

'Should we not try to escape?' Talakh whispered again.

'You cannot see,' Korkamani said without lifting his head, 'but there is another guard on the ridge over there to my right. He will not be resting, for he will be the first to be killed if our kinsmen come after us across the desert.

'Anyway, the others are too worn down Talakh. Look at

27

them, their spirits are broken. They would be sure to panic if I tried to take the guard and we would all end up stuck like pigs on the Kemet spears.'

A small, squat man who lay at Korkamani's feet started at this as if in answer to Korkamani's fears. He was in his middle years, his youth long behind him.

'Besides,' the man said sourly, 'there is nowhere for us to hide but the banks of the river. We would not last more than a day in the desert without skins for water.'

Talakhonsu looked away angrily at that, thinking the man a coward.

'He is right,' Korkamani said quietly. 'We are all weak with hunger and thirst. We would be easy meat for the Kemet spears, and they would take great sport in hunting us down if they had the excuse. We are nothing but animals to them Talakh, remember that.'

'Then we are without hope,' Talakh hung his head despondently.

'Ah, there is always hope,' Korkamani flashed a brave smile. 'Khaemwaset wants us all alive, both for his prestige and to sell us as slaves. So even though he despises us, still we are of no use to him dead.

'As I said before, his men starve us to break our spirit. They ration the water to keep us weak and make us despair when we see the Great River running beside us. But if we do nothing to anger them, then we should survive. We must keep our hope alive Talakh. If we still have that, then we still have a chance.'

Silence descended between them then and Talakh had his thoughts to himself for a while. Korkamani's words had given him a little heart and though he was just a boy, still Amun and Korkamani watched over him, so he took courage from this and turned his thoughts instead to hatred for these murderers from the north.

'Korkamani?' he whispered again in the darkness.

'Yes boy, what is it?'

'What else do you know of this Khaemwaset?'

'Well, they say that although he is high born, he only came

28

to his power through treachery. Many men he has bought off with his gold and many enemies have died at his sword.'

'But if he is rich, then why did he risk leading his men to raid our lands?' Talakh asked with a frown.

Korkamani stared hard at the boy, his eyes screwed up as if he were trying to see something far away.

'You have a wise head, Talakhonsu,' he said quietly. 'It is this way with Khaemwaset. He was born the second son of a rich man, and from the beginning he strove to outdo his older brother who stood to gain all when their father died. Khaemwaset trained to fight with the warriors in his father's guard, trained hard until even when still not yet fully a man he could beat any of them with a bow or a staff in his fury. That is what they say of him.'

Talakh said nothing, but inside he could feel his muscles knotting and his tendons straining, as if he was about to run very fast. He was thinking about what he had seen this evil one do to Prainke and the blood ran cold in his veins at this. Cold with fear, but also with anger and vengeance.

'Khaemwaset's father saw that he was tainted with an evil madness,' Korkamani continued, 'and so he always favoured the older son, though perhaps not just for this reason alone. You see, the dark earth of Kemet and all of the riches that come from it have been ruled for some time by the great king of Persia. Khaemwaset's older brother spoke their tongue well, practised their ways too and so the Persians saw him almost as one of them. In this way he gained still greater influence for his father. Unfortunately for the elder brother, he did not live long enough to come to his just birthright though. One day when the two brothers were practising their arms, he fell from the chariot which was driven by Khaemwaset and his skull was cracked wide open.'

'It was no accident then?'

'You are shrewd for one of your age Talakhonsu,' Korkamani nodded with satisfaction, a wry grin on his face. 'No, it seems the evil one drove the chariot over a rock, a risky thing for him to do. The difference was that Khaemwaset knew when the fall was to come and so he knew how to roll when he hit the ground, so that he could save himself.

'Even so, while his brother's eyes never opened again, the evil one too was injured so that he could do nothing but lie still in his father's house for some days afterwards. Perhaps Khaemwaset thought he would now assume the favoured place in his father's eyes as first son. Well, that was not to be. The old man was heartbroken so they say, and he would not receive Khaemwaset or even acknowledge him as his son in public. Nothing could be proven against the evil one, but all of the great city of Waset suspected his treachery. This is what I have heard of him.'

'What happened then?' Talakh said eagerly.

'Shhh...' Korkamani whispered back, putting his finger to his lips.

The dozing guard had lifted his head, but after sleepily glancing around, his chin sank back down to his chest again.

'Khaemwaset's father was an old man as I have said,' Korkamani continued quietly. 'But he still had good health on his side and strength in his arm too, despite his sadness. Then one day he began to suddenly weaken and quickly fell into a fevered sleep from which he never awoke.

'Of course, Khaemwaset had poisoned him without any doubt, but when suspicion fell on the evil one, he said he had found an empty vessel of poison in a servant's belongings. You can imagine what torture was put to the poor servant because of the word of that treacherous snake, until finally he admitted his guilt,' Korkamani shook his head in disgust.

'You asked why Khaemwaset raided our lands. Well, it seems from the boasting of the guards that the Kemet nobles have finally turned against their Persian rulers and overthrown them. There is a struggle now amongst the nobles of Kemet as to who will rule, and Khaemwaset means to be that man. You can be sure he has riches enough to buy men and he is feared, but he has little favour amongst his people for all that. I am sure this is why he raided our land, for in this way he hopes he will gain support for his claim to be chief among the nobles, what they call Pharaoh.'

'You said before that he is mad though, Korkamani.'

'I did.'

Talakh thought on this a moment.

'And yet also he is very cunning. Can he then be truly mad?'

'There are many forms of madness Talakh,' Korkamani answered. 'His is one of spite and rage and lust for power over all men. That is madness enough. Now you should rest boy. There are hard days ahead of us and we need to save what strength we have left.'

'I am too hungry to sleep I think.'

'Aye, but sleep you must. We will come soon to a place where the Great River is barred by many rocks and islands set close, one upon the other so that they block the path of the waters. We will need all our strength then,' Korkamani said grimly.

'You see, the Great River rushes through these barriers of rock in torrents of white foam that can snap a boat like a twig. For many, many days ahead the river is like this off and on, no sooner calming itself, before more rocks and rapids spring up to bar its path.'

'And yet the evil one sends his own men through these dangers?'

'Aye, and himself too, so I overheard,' Korkamani shook his head, 'even though he risks losing his own life and many of his soldiers amongst the rapids of the Great River. When a man behaves without fear like this, he is like a mad dog that runs onto the point of a spear, when it could easily have run away.'

'Will he become ruler of Kemet then? Will he be the Pharaoh?'

'Only the gods know that Talakh, but if he does rule, it will not be for long. Only a fool chooses to make enemies of the Persians. Their army will return soon enough and when it does, Khaemwaset will be no match for them.'

'But when will they come?' Talakh asked eagerly.

'The empire of the Persians spans the world far across the seas to the north and the east. So vast is it, that like some great beast it is ponderous and takes time to decide upon an action.

31

But when the Persian king Darius marches, they say the earth trembles under the footsteps of his armies. Kemet will fall to them again just as easily as a fish finds itself landed in the heron's beak. Now, enough of my stories, you must try to rest.'

Later as Talakh lay awake parched with thirst, another guard came aboard the boat and threw a water skin in to the crowd of prisoners. How the man laughed as they squabbled over the water in the darkness, until Korkamani took charge to make sure everyone got a share. Then, exhausted from hunger and fatigue they one by one fell asleep, even Korkamani himself.

Young Talakh could not sleep though. His mind, whilst bitter and sad at all that he had seen, was also buzzing with thoughts like a hive full of bees. He looked at the man who had become his protector. Korkamani lay with his shoulder resting against the side of the boat, getting what rest he could despite his bound hands and tethered neck. Asleep, Korkamani had a stern character, his deep-set eyes making him look a little annoyed. He had a straight, thin nose too, whereas Talakh's own was wider and flatter like most of the other Napatans. Korkamani's hair was not the same either, being thicker and more curly than wiry. Then there were his ears. Talakh smiled to himself, for they were much bigger than was usual amongst his people. Yet despite all of these things, Korkamani still had a handsome, proud face.

Just then Talakh felt a nudge in his side, and he squirmed round to face the youth who sat behind him.

'My name is Hynka,' the young man whispered. 'Is he your uncle?' he nodded back with his head to point to Korkamani.

'No, not my uncle, Talakh replied. 'He is... he was my father's friend,' he lied, not wanting to admit that Korkamani knew only his mother.

'You are lucky to have someone to watch over you. My father was away with the king, but he will come to find me and my mother, I am sure of it,' Hynka said quietly, though his voice quivered with doubt.

'If great Amun wills it,' Talakh whispered, the thoughts of his own loss steadied by a slow burning anger that kept the cold of the night wind at bay.

Hynka said nothing more, but Talakh could feel the young man's chest heaving as he sobbed himself silently to sleep.

Soon only the eyes of Talakh remained open to see the moon rise high above all as it filled the low cliffs and the river itself with its cold, silvery light. The guards drank their ale and sang their songs of victory and slaughter, their harsh voices echoing around the banks. Tied and tethered, aching and hungry, Talakhonsu hated them all the more for that.

Chapter 3

The Servants of Sobek

The next day on that boat of suffering passed unbearably slowly, the prisoners now with weals around their wrists and necks where their coarse hide tethers and bindings had dried out and rubbed into their skin. Vivid red sores had started to appear on the elbows, knees and shoulder blades of some of the less fortunate, through lying on the bare wooden bottom of the boat.

With hunger gnawing at them, every prisoner had their share of misery, although this day at least the guards allowed more water to be passed around.

'They do it not out of kindness,' Korkamani had said. 'They just know that if we grow any weaker, too many will die, and they do not wish to tell Khaemwaset they have lost all of his slaves.'

Already, a man in his middle years had tried to jump over the side of the boat, almost dragging two others with him by their tethers, before one of the Kemet warriors clubbed him viciously on the head. They hauled him back aboard then like a dead fish. No-one knew whether he had been trying to escape, or as was perhaps more likely, trying to take his own life. Now he lay face down where they had thrown him, as still as death while a pool of blood slowly seeped from his broken head and the flies gathered.

'Will he die?' Talakh asked as the baking heat of the afternoon wore slowly on.

'He is dead already,' Korkamani answered coldly. 'They leave him there as a warning to the rest of us.'

But while the flies overran the man's corpse and annoyed the prisoners, so they also annoyed the guards with their attentions.

Finally the Kemet leader, who Talakh had now come to

think of as 'Broken Nose', relented and steered the boat over toward the river bank. For they could not throw the body into the sacred river – that was an evil that even these soldiers of Kemet would not commit. The guards cut the man loose from his neck tether, then ordered Korkamani and another prisoner to drag the body ashore, up onto the low cliffs that bordered the river.

Talakh watched the terrible scene with pity in his heart as the weakened pair struggled with their burden, the dead man's head hanging down between his shoulders, his toes dragging over the harsh rocks.

They had just crested the cliff edge when a shout came up from the guards. It sounded like a warning and Talakh's heart lifted, as at once many thoughts flew through his young mind.

Could it be rescue?

Were the warriors of Napata, led by the king himself, marching to revenge themselves on the men of Kemet?

But no, it was not to be for as Korkamani and the other Napatan were pushed back down the riverbank at the point of the Kemet spears, the other guards were already taking the sail down rather than putting it up.

'What is it,' Talakh whispered excitedly to Korkamani as he staggered back down into the bottom of the boat, his raw wrists bound with wet rope once again.

Korkamani's face, drawn and beaded with sweat, looked grim.

'A sandstorm is coming,' he said, his breathing ragged with his efforts under the hot sun. 'The biggest I have ever seen. We must take whatever shelter we can Talakh, for it towers to the roof of the sky!'

Whilst Broken Nose barked his orders, the guards untied the lowered sail from its boom to make a shelter for themselves over a part of the boat. Korkamani gave orders of his own to the prisoners, who at his word wedged themselves on their sides against the side of the boat, covering their faces with their hands as the wind picked up suddenly.

Talakh had seen storms like this before, blowing from nowhere out of the desert to blast the poor goats and cattle outside. They had seemed bad enough then from the shelter of his mother's house with the door barred and the windows shut up. Now he was wedged between Korkamani and another, older man with wiry grey hair, their shoulders rising above his as they lay on their sides. He drew his ragged cloak over his head for shelter as best as he could and peered out from under it, curious to see when the storm would come, in spite of his fear.

At first he thought he must be dreaming, for looming high into the sky almost to touch the blazing sun disk itself, there loomed a solid wall of orange sand like a giant sail pushed along by the breath of mighty Amun, king of gods. The boy swallowed hard, but he could not tear his eyes away from the awful sight as the wall of sand rose higher and higher overhead, as if at any moment it might come crashing down on their heads like a great wave.

And then the wind and sand broke upon them with a roar and a hot blast that beat and scoured the exposed prisoners like the claws of a wild beast, sweeping away their cries as soon as they were uttered. Talakh covered his face with the cloak and screwed his eyes shut, but even so the dust was so thick he could feel it probing for a way in to choke the life from him. On the tormenting storm continued, on and on, sometimes riven by a higher shriek than even the wind itself, as some poor Napatan soul gave up his senses to the merciless storm.

Talakhonsu prayed again and again to Lord Amun, caster of the desert winds, bringer of storms, for the god's anger to subside. He promised always to offer to the god of gods when he had food to give or scented woods to burn, but in his mind he did not know who it was that Amun sought to punish? He thought of poor Prainke and his teachings. Already these things seemed so long ago, as if he had now grown as ancient and white haired as the old priest himself.

Despite the storm, Amun sent a blessing to Talakh then, letting the boy's thoughts pass away from his ordeal to happier times in the house of the priests. His dream took him on to sit at his mother's knee once more as she ruffled his hair and spoke soothing words that he did not understand, but which comforted him nonetheless as he slept. Talakh was still a dreamer and it was this as much as the shelter of the men either side of him and the cloak over his head that spared the boy the worst of the trials of the storm.

When evening came, the storm at last abated almost as suddenly as it had come and to his shock, Talakh realised that the man he was tethered to, the man who had been his shield against the driving sand, was not moving.

'Do not look Talakh,' Korkamani comforted the boy. 'There is nothing we can do to help him now.'

Who could say whether the man died of thirst, hunger or despair? Whatever the cause, his body was taken to join the other dead prisoner at the top of the cliffs.

The boat was now awash with sand, as were the guard's supplies, but thirsty though they were there was little relief for guard or prisoner from the river either. Its waters ran thick with sand and dirt for some while and were terrible to drink before slowly they started to clear.

When dusk came, the guards took most of the prisoners ashore, leaving Korkamani and one other poor unfortunate to clean out the bottom of the boat, sand, foulness and all. For Broken Nose knew that disease and death often followed such ill smelling things.

That night, while the Napatans sat miserably nearby, the men of Kemet lit a small fire by the dying light of the sun and some of the younger guards were set to work making a stew, muttering as they sifted the sand from their dried fish and beans. Once that was cooking, they then made flat breads which were baked on a rock in the fire's ashes. The smells of stew and new bread on the chill night air drove the starving prisoners almost to the point of madness, but they could do nothing but turn to sit facing away, as the guards hungrily ate their shares. All except Korkamani, who sat muttering curses under his breath, while the young Kemet warrior who stood watch over them shifted uneasily.

Broken Nose grunted an order and at his command one of the guards threw two small loaves to the prisoners. There was a wild scramble as the strongest of the prisoners pushed and strained against their cords to reach the bread. Fortunately for Talakh, Korkamani was one of these and he grabbed a piece for the boy and himself in the darkness. But for some, like Hynka the young man who had spoken with Talakh the previous night, there was nothing but further despair. Talakh ate quickly, stuffing the dry, gritty bread into his mouth, though his throat was so dry he could hardly swallow.

'Why did they give us the bread Korkamani?' he whispered later. 'Two are dead already. Do they think we will all die here?'

'We won't die boy,' Korkamani looked him in the eye. 'Perhaps they fear they have offended the gods. Or more likely, they fear what Khaemwaset will do to them if any more of us perish. Be sure of one thing though, these men of Kemet have no pity for us.'

'But why do they hate us so much?'

'Because we are the underdog Talakh. To them we are weak, there to be raided whenever their leaders seek an easy victory. In this way men like Khaemwaset increase their popularity with their own people. From now on, at least until the Persians return, they will raid us like this, take slaves and steal what we have.'

'We should fight them then.'

'Once, a long time ago, we did Talakh. Our ancestors rose up and defeated the Kemet armies. Then our king took *their* lands and *their* grain, and even became their Pharaoh King, ruling far to the north even to the Middle Seas. For that disgrace, Kemet will never forgive us.'

Talakh nodded thoughtfully. The world was harsh, and violent, and unfair, this much he knew now. Good men like Prainke died at the hands of those with evil in their hearts. And where were the gods in all of this? Exhausted by the hardships of the day, the boy lay down on his side in the still warm sand and fell into a deep, dreamless sleep.

'Sleep well,' Korkamani said under his breath, pressing Talakh's shoulder. 'We will all need our strength when tomorrow comes.'

The next day dawned with a cool wind and the sun glinting low on the Great River, which had by now cleansed itself of the choking dirt of the sandstorm. The guards let the prisoners drink their fill, and the river water, though far from sweet, tasted like honey to the thirsty Napatans and their guards alike. For all had felt the harshness of the desert sands.

Though his hunger was terrible, Talakh felt a little stronger now and his mind turned again to thoughts of vengeance as he imagined holding a knife to the throat of the evil Khaemwaset.

'Well you might look grim, boy,' Korkamani said, reading Talakh's mood.

He said no more, but Talakh knew from Korkamani's own face that they would soon come to the new danger he had spoken of, where the Great River would rage amongst the rocks.

The boat pushed off from the river bank and into a troublesome breeze that slowed their pace, for here the river had widened, slowing her flow northward. For the first time the oars were unshipped and the prisoners forced to row at the crack of a hide whip, until they began to slump exhausted over the oars in spite of the pain. Then the guards would kick them to the back of the boat and take another group to the two oar benches. Only Talakh was spared, though he wished he could have shared the suffering of the others to prove himself a man.

The boat rowed on like this all the morning long through the deserted lands, passing only one small settlement. This too had been sacked and burnt out by Khaemwaset's men, if the laughter and cheers of the guards was anything to go by. Now only a few dogs were left alive, barking their warnings in vain, for their dead masters could hear them no longer.

Just after noon, when the sun had risen to its highest place in the roof of the sky and the prisoners at the oars had been flogged almost to a standstill, the wind finally started to swing round to their backs. Now the guards cheerfully raised the flapping sail. The oars were shipped again and the prisoners kicked and shoved back to join their kinsmen on the floor as the boat surged forward at the hand of Amun, great god of the high places and the winds. But still for the prisoners who nursed their wounds and their aching bellies, the wind gave little relief from the merciless sun. So things continued until late afternoon, when the broken nosed one strode forward to the front of the boat.

'What is he doing?' Talakh wondered aloud, as the commander silenced his men with a wave of his scarred arm.

'He listens,' Korkamani said quietly.

'Is it another sandstorm?'

'No, it is something still more dangerous than that, boy.'

Broken Nose barked an order at his men, and six of the strongest took their spears and clubs forwards to the boat's prow, piling them at the feet of their commander. Two then went to the small platform at the rear of the boat and manned the heavy steering oar that dipped into the water. The other men lifted the main oars and rested these on the boat's sides. Some of the guards looked worried, whilst others who took down the sail seemed to be boasting to each other, as if before battle. Poor Talakhonsu was confused by all of these strange things, but in the heat of the sun he was no longer very sure of his own senses.

'Why do the guards take to the oars Korkamani?' he asked.

'Listen!' Korkamani said, his eyes narrowed with concentration. 'Do you hear that?'

'It sounds like thunder, but there are no clouds in the sky.'

'It is no thunder Talakh. Up ahead the Great River is starting to roar!' Korkamani said, as the other prisoners one by one started from their daze.

Fear gripped the boat now, as prisoner and guard alike peered forward to where the river was quickly becoming a maze of channels that rushed between boulders and small islands.

'The sea peoples in the north have a name for these places,' Korkamani said, iron in his voice. 'They call them cataracts, where the rocky teeth of the land seek to block the Great River's flow.'

Talakh nodded, his eyes wide with excitement, as he

looked from the river, to Korkamani, and back again.

'There are many of these cataracts ahead of us in the days to come, and this one is not the worst of them,' Korkamani muttered as the noise of the waters rose still higher. 'Let us hope that the river goddess shows us mercy.'

Broken Nose began shouting orders at his men, his deep voice rising a little as the current picked up and the boat slewed across it, threatening to hit the rocks and capsize. The men at the stern strained against the steering oar, trying to keep her straight as she picked up speed rapidly now, heading straight for two jagged rocks that channelled a part of the river between them in a violent, foaming torrent. Then through the glistening spray Talakh saw it, a fall where the river seemed about to flow of the edge of the world itself.

'Brace yourselves!' he heard Korkamani yell through the deafening roar as the boat sped still faster and the terrible rocks drew close.

Talakhonsu clung to Korkamani's arm as best as he could with his bound hands, while above him the Kemet soldiers readied their oars to fend the boat away from the danger.

Now Broken Nose shouted again at the top of his voice, above even the roar of the river, and the boat slewed again, surely aiming straight for a great boulder that loomed large in front of them.

Korkamani's lips were moving, but the only word Talakh could make out above the deafening roar of the torrent was the name of the great god Amun himself. He was truly afraid now, fear rising from the small of his back up to the nape of his neck, like the cold hand of the dead on his skin. For a moment the boat seemed to grow wings as it surged upwards on a rolling wave of water, like a great wooden swan trying to fly from the river's danger. Then just as suddenly she plunged downwards as if the hands of the dark gods themselves had reached up from the underworld to pull her beneath the water and into the realm of the damned.

There were wild cries now, as the water boiled all around them, drenching guard and prisoner alike in a rush of spray that threatened to inundate them.

41

And then as quickly as her battle with the raging river had begun, the torrent spat the boat out like a piece of chaff into a wide pool where she quickly steadied herself once more.

Talakhonsu glanced up at Korkamani who looked somehow untroubled, neither scared nor relieved.

'Their commander knows the river well,' he said. 'But our trials are not at an end, Talakh. This one was just a ripple compared to those that lie ahead.'

'Have you come this way before then Korkamani?' Talakh asked a question that had been at the back of his mind for some while.

Korkamani looked at the guards, who were boasting to each other and not paying the terrified prisoners much attention.

'Yes boy, I have passed this way before,' he said quietly. 'Though not by boat. Ask me no more questions on this Talakh. It is dangerous for me to talk of such things when others can hear.'

And so the boat glided on, its sail raised again as it found a meandering path through the last of the channels and islands. Still here, though the river was once again calm, the prisoners were not. For amongst the shallows and shoals were huge scaly lizard beasts, their great, green eyes glistening in the sun as they waited in ambush for an easy meal. These then were the terrible, many-toothed monsters of the river, earthly servants of the underworld god Sobek with whom they shared kinship, or so some believed. Talakhonsu had seen small ones before in Napata, but never full grown monsters like these that were as long as three men or more. The awful creatures held their long jaws wide open and then snapped their jagged teeth shut again, thrashing their crested tails as they fought each other viciously in the shallows.

'Do not trouble yourselves,' Korkamani told the frightened prisoners. 'They cannot harm us. The boat is too big for them to tip it over.'

Despite his calming words though, the Napatans still shook with fear, already defeated by pain and hunger. The men of Kemet on the other hand were in good heart, as the threat of pursuit receded further behind them and they drew ever closer to the safety of their own lands. That evening they threw a few more scraps of bread to their prisoners when camp was made ashore, though this did little to lift the spirits of their beaten down captives.

The next day quickly bought the slave boat to another cataract, bigger by far than the one they had already passed through. This time, there was not one, but many rock shelves and torrents to be descended, each threatening to smash the boat into pieces, as it crashed against shoals and submerged boulders. Those guards not at the oars now cowered like the prisoners in the bottom of the boat, all except Broken Nose who steadfastly held his place in the prow, barking his orders.

It was at the moment of greatest danger that Korkamani showed his strength and bravery, for the two guards manning the steering oar were suddenly thrown into the water as the boat was baulked sideways by a rock. Despite the bellowing of Broken Nose at his men, it seemed that none of the warriors of Kemet could summon the courage to climb the steering platform and take the oar.

But then, as the boat lurched over and all aboard thought they must surely die, Korkamani stretched his wet bonds just enough to free himself and raced to the back of the boat. All eyes were on him now as he leapt up to the thrashing oar and grabbed it from behind, clamping it under his arm and pulling with all his might so that the oar took strain against the current. Slowly the boat straightened herself while Korkamani stood like a hero, his black skin glistening with the spray as he stared ahead, wrestling the current.

Almost at once the boat plunged down another torrent, and a wave broke over her from one end almost to the other as the raging waters sought again to destroy her. Yet still the boat rose up again from the heaving waters and as men shouted and others wailed in their fear, it seemed that this time perhaps the worst was behind them. The channel widened and the Great River's roar receded behind them now, its tormented waters at last smoothed out into a calmer flow.

Talakhonsu took all of this in, pride swelling in his chest as he looked from Korkamani at the back of the boat, to Broken Nose at the front. Of all of the men aboard, only these two now had their feet and they stared hard at each other for a moment, before the Kemet commander's temper broke. In a blast of fury he jumped down amongst his own men, kicking at those who still cowered until in his rage he hauled one of them up by the throat. This one he punched full in the face so hard that as he fell to the floor senseless, a spray of blood showering them both. Now there were two broken noses on the boat, Talakh thought to himself with a grin, for he was glad to see the soldiers of Kemet fight amongst themselves like this. The guards remembered themselves then and raised their spears at Korkamani.

For a moment Talakh feared his protector would be put to death, and once again he felt his body jump into action without him even thinking. Just as when Prainke had been killed, suddenly his stiff legs had a life of their own, raising him upright and pushing him toward the guards as if forced by an unseen hand. This then was the moment when the warrior's heart, even in a boy, can push fear away and he moves as if in a dream. Luckily for Talakhonsu, the tethers by which he was bound to the other prisoners held him fast so that he could take no more than a step or two forward, though he strained with all his might.

'Stay!' Broken Nose bellowed, snapping the boy to his senses.

The word was one of those common to both the tongue of Kemet and Napata, and the harsh call sapped the strength from Talakh, his legs buckling beneath him as he sank back down.

The warriors of Kemet now lowered their spears a little, and gestured to Korkamani to come down from the platform, fear still on their faces, for they had seen two of their number taken into the world of shadows by the mighty river.

Of course Korkamani had seen Talakhonsu's bravery too, but also he saw the anger of Broken Nose at the cowardice of his own men, and so he came back down meekly, to be bound once again by the guards. This was no time to challenge the Kemet leader's authority, nor that of his men. As the boat coasted away from the danger of the rocks, they saw the body of one of the drowned men float by. The soldiers reached out to it with the oars, but the current carried the dead man off away into the shallows, where more of the giant lizard beasts lay in wait.

All on board now watched in silence, unable to look away as the creatures ran into the water on their short legs, their long, scaly tails thrashing. Soon the river ran red with the dead man's blood as many jagged teeth ripped at his flesh until between them they had torn the body to pieces. Even then they squabbled and fought each other over the scraps in their blood frenzy. Broken Nose himself threw a spear at one in his rage, but though it found its target, the beast's scaly skin was too thick for the iron point to penetrate and it glanced off harmlessly. The big man beat the side of the boat with his fists in his anger, but there was nothing that he could do but turn his head away.

Yet still the Great River had not finished with them. A little further downstream another body, stripped almost naked by the jagged rocks, lay bloody and broken at the water's edge. Broken Nose ordered his men to beach the boat on a nearby muddy shoal and then they quickly picked up the dead man and passed him back over the side as the lizard beasts swam toward them, eager for another meal.

One of the war band, perhaps a friend or kinsman, knelt weeping over his drowned comrade and closed his still, bloodshot eyes. Even though this dead man was his enemy, Talakh could not help but pity him as he watched the terrible scene, unable to turn away. Others among the warriors laid his knife and his few other possessions on his chest, and then they wrapped his lifeless body in his cloak, so that his face was covered.

'You should not look on these things,' Korkamani shook his head.

'I have seen the rites of the dead before many times, when

45

the priests prepare the body for the afterlife,' Talakh answered. 'For me to become a priest, these are ways which already I have had to learn.'

Korkamani was again taken aback by the boy's boldness, but he knew already that Talakh had a way of speaking the truth and that he meant no disrespect by it.

With all aboard silent again in fear and grief, the boat drifted along for a while as the current slackened off, only then to come to more of the terrifying rapids. It seemed a long time until she had safely negotiated the last rocky outposts of that terrible cataract, and although no more were lost to the thundering waters, still when the battered boat emerged into calmer waters and came to a dejected halt, soldiers and prisoners alike were exhausted. As the sun set and the light started to fade, the men of Kemet buried their comrade under the emerging stars, praying that he would be guided to their afterlife. Their sombre chants carried on far into the night as they drank what little of the Napatan beer they had left.

The prisoners too had another of their number to bury under the shifting sands, for the sun, thirst and fright had been too much for him. Talakhonsu, mindful of his oaths and teachings as a boy priest, asked Korkamani to bind his unruly hair into a side lock with a piece of reed, and then did what he could to speak the spells of the dead for the poor man. He hoped that the ritual, simple though it was, would be enough for the gods to offer the poor man's spirit some protection from evil on his journey into the afterlife. How many more times would he have to speak those same spells before this tortured journey came to an end? The young Napatan shivered at the thought.

The next morning, Talakhonsu awoke early just as the reborn sun had started to crest the horizon to bring the gift of the new day. In the temples of Napata, this time was always one of celebration, when the priests would give thanks to their gods with the burning of scented woods, offerings of food and the chimes of their cymbals. But for Talakhonsu, gnawed by hunger and bruised and battered as he was, the new day brought him no joy. Despair was his constant shadow, no matter that he tried to be strong, and it seemed that only death could free him now. Yet his desire for revenge was strong. As long as he drew breath there was a chance, however slight, that he might one day escape and live to see Khaemwaset dead. It was this and this alone that kept him going.

'What are you thinking boy?' Korkamani asked, his voice cracked with thirst.

'I was thinking of the great god,' Talakh answered. 'We have travelled so far north now from Napata and the throne of Amun... will he still see us out here in the desert?'

Korkamani thought on that for a moment, rubbing the stubble on his chin.

'Well, what you say is true Talakh, we are a long way from our own lands. But do not forget that the priests of Kemet have also raised their own temples to Amun. The great god is everywhere on this earth, all the way to the city of Waset and beyond that to where the Great River meets the sea.'

'Prainke taught me that Amun favours us above all others, because only we people of Napata worship him at his mountain throne,' Talakh said. 'But then still I wonder why it is that he has let our enemies take us as slaves?'

'The gods have no enemies,' Korkamani said firmly. 'They have no need to serve mortal men, be they of Kemet or Nubia, so our squabbles are not their concern. We can ask for their guidance and protection in return for our offerings, but it is for the gods to decide who they will favour.'

'So Prainke was wrong?'

'No Talakh, he was not wrong,' Korkamani said more gently. 'His was the view of a priest and their words help us to travel our path wisely through this life and into the next one.

'But still my father taught me a valuable lesson and it was this: we do well if we seek the protection of the gods, pay honour to them and do nothing to bring their anger upon us. The gods bring the sun in the morning and the flood to the river to break the drought. They send plagues when they are angry, and good harvests if they are content. But battles and wars, Talakh… Those we have to fight those by the strength of our arms and the wit of our brains.'

As the two of them grew silent again, the boat sailed on under the brilliant blue sky. On and on down the Great River she drifted, through a barren world that seemed to have no end, while Broken Nose stood grimly in the prow, the fates of all aboard in his hands and his alone.

Pelia paused in the telling of her story, for it was late now and the fire was now just dull embers amidst grey ash. In the darkness of the hut Cerian breathed slow and steady, fast asleep where she lay wrapped in her cloak next to the great hound Sealgair. Perhaps it was no surprise, for the girl was young and only now on the edge of her full womanhood. The story of Talakhonsu would have to wait until tomorrow and there would be many more nights yet before it was told in full.

Pelia rubbed her own eyes, which were dry with weariness, and went outside as all must if they want to avoid the cold walk in the dead of the night. As chill as it had grown in the hut, the night air was bitterly cold and a white frost already gripped the ground. The sows that had survived the Samhain feast would be lying close to each other for warmth on nights like these and Pelia could hear their ill tempered grunts coming from the pound as they tried to sleep. Even their boar was not much solace to them now, penned as he was close to the chieftain's long hall. Despite all of his scheming and plans, chief Heilyn was still a superstitious young man and so he thought of that old boar as a talisman that he should keep close, to ward off any ill luck.

Once, when Pelia was called to calm a fever that had struck Heilyn down, he told her a rambling story, while she mopped his brow. It seemed that when a young boy, he had gone into the great forest one spring to look for birds eggs and had crossed the path of a great boar. The wild beast had charged him, but at the last minute, just as he fell back on his haunches against a tree, so it had stopped in its tracks scattering leaves and twigs over him. In the morning chill, he had seen the boar's sharp, yellow tusks looming over him from within great gouts of steaming breath that blasted from its nostrils. Heilyn's eyes had met those of the beast then and strangely his fear left him, or so he said, for the boar turned aside and vanished back into the forest. Heilyn thought that it could only have been the spirit of an ancestor whispering in the ear of the boar which made it spare his life.

Perhaps he was right in this, or perhaps it was just that the boar thought him not worth the trouble. Whatever the truth of it, from that time on he had taken the wild boars of the forest as his spirit animal, refusing to hunt them even when others went to the chase. Of course telling Pelia these things was against Heilyn's nature, as he never liked to lower his guard. Always afterwards he was ill at ease with her, though she had done him no wrong and had only helped him to get better.

Pelia put these memories to the back of her mind and raised her eyes to the stars which burned bright and still in the darkness above, her thoughts turning to her father as they often did when the day was done and all was quiet. She shivered suddenly as she thought of the time when she too would pass from the world of the living and a tear came to her green-gold eyes. Though she had friends there in Llan Huell, and now Cerian to keep her company, still in the deep of the night there was no family gathered about her to keep at bay the loneliness. At times like these she missed her mother all the more.

Early the next morning, Pelia tied up the old hide flap that served to cover the low doorway into her darkened hut and brought in a bundle of dry sticks and twigs, waking Cerian as the light of the day flooded in.

'Here!' Pelia scolded the girl gently, 'Make use of yourself and bring the fire back to life.'

Cerian rubbed her eyes and flushed for a moment before she realised her teacher was smiling. She returned the smile, happy enough as she was with her new lot, and sat up to gently part the ashes with a stick until a few bright red embers of charcoal were revealed. The hut of Pelia was a cheerful place where Cerian felt a young woman now, rather than a girl, and she respected Pelia for that. Of course there was hard work to be done finding enough food and gathering firewood. Nothing came easily in the deep of the winter. Yet also there were the teachings of the wise woman, and these things fed Cerian's restless young mind.

'Pelia?' she asked, when the other returned with a jug of water from the stream. 'Did you ever doubt any of your mother's stories?'

For a moment Pelia was hurt by this, though just as quickly she realised that this was just the honesty of the young, whose minds have not yet learned to hide such things. 'No, I never doubted it. I know it is all true in my heart,' she said calmly.

'I meant no harm,' Cerian said, casting her gaze down at the small kindling as it finally crackled into life on the fire. 'It's just that the desert and the temples, the boat, the lizard beasts with their scaly skin and long jaws... I barely can imagine such things.'

'Then I have not made a good job of telling the story,' Pelia smiled wryly. 'Are you sure you can't see in your mind the great storm of sand I told you of? Or the Great River with its thundering waters? Or the scaly servants of the Lord Sobek, with their thrashing tails? Close your eyes and think of what I told you.'

Cerian did as she was asked, pressing her eyelids tight. But then just as quickly her expression changed to a troubled frown, for Pelia's words had conjured an image of the giant lizard beast into her mind.

'There, you see?' Pelia said as she poured some water into a drinking cup. 'Sometimes when we dream it seems so real that we believe in what we have seen, even after we awake. Our minds are powerful things and if we let them wander, then we can see in them the mighty river and the sun scorched lands of Napata.'

'That is true,' Cerian nodded thoughtfully.

'Ah, but what it would be to feel the hot sun again though!' she said, a wistfulness in her voice. 'It seems already so long since the summer ended, and still so long till the next.'

Pelia nodded and carefully placed some small twigs onto the newly awoken hearth, welcoming back the magic of the fire, without which all the races of men would surely be lost.

'Aye,' the wise woman said. 'But the sun can be a curse as well as a blessing, as you have heard. In the lands of Napata and Kemet the sun god is far stronger than here, and he pours his heat onto the parched earth without mercy all the year long. There, they have no rain to speak of and rare are the days when the clouds hide the sun's face.'

'The Great River then?' Cerian asked. 'Where does it come from if the sun is so hot and there is so little rain?'

'Ah, the river,' Pelia smiled to herself again at the sharpness of the girl's mind. 'Yes, it somehow manages to flood over the land every year to water it and make the crops grow, yet as I have said there is almost no rain in the lands it passes through.

'They say that the flood is the gift of the gods and goddesses of that land, who cause it to appear when they are pleased with the people, or to fail when they are angry so that the crops wither and die and the people starve. That is the way of things when the land is all sun and no rain. So you see, cold as our winter is, perhaps we should be grateful for the rain that comes with it. As long as there is not too much!'

Cerian laughed at that as she carefully stirred a pot of oatmeal at the hearth's edge, so that it would not catch. The fire was warm now and Pelia saw that before the work of the day started again there was perhaps time to tell a little more of her story.

Chapter 4

The Soleb Priesthood

The boat continued on down the Great River, carrying the ever weakening Napatan slaves toward their fate as the sun beat down fiercely upon them. Even though they navigated the next cataract they came to without further loss or injury, the mood of the warriors of Kemet was dark too and they sat in silence for the most part as they sharpened their knives and their spear points. At least for now, their defeat of the Napatans had been forgotten.

The prisoners were silent in their own thoughts too, the spirits of most now broken beyond the hope of any rescue.

Then, as noon approached and the sun scorched them at its hottest, the Kemet warrior Broken Nose roared out an order that shook them all from their torpor.

'What does he say?' Talakh nudged Korkamani, as the fat man got to his feet and started barking orders to his soldiers.

'He puts us to the oars,' Korkamani said quietly. 'You see that small mountain over there above the left bank?'

'Yes?'

'The people here call it the mountain of the sun god, and close to the river below it there lies the old fortress of Sesibi.'

The two watched quietly as others were taken from their number and put to the oars.

'But why do they make us row when there is a good wind?' Talakh wondered aloud.

'The fat one wants to make a good show for the people here,' Korkamani answered quietly. 'Perhaps he also wants to rouse the spirits of his men by humiliating us. Then they will forget the loss of their brothers for a while.'

A short time later the boat rowed into sight of Sesibi itself, set back a little from the Great River and sheltered in the lea of a craggy hill. Talakhonsu's eyes were caught by a tumble of high, broken walls of mud brick, with tall palm trees and houses rising amongst them. It did not look much like a fortress, but still it looked far from friendly either. There were a few ships and smaller boats moored near the walls, and to his dismay Talakh could make out armed men standing around here and there.

'More Kemet soldiers,' Korkamani muttered, echoing the boy's thoughts.

Every thought of escape left the Napatan prisoners now, for truly they were deep in the lands of their enemies.

'Be strong,' Korkamani hissed under his breath to the others as a soldier flogged at the rowers with a length of wet rope, making them cry out in their pain. 'They want to humiliate us, but we are worth more to them alive than dead, remember that.'

By now the people of this place called Sesibi were starting to come down to the river. Some, darker skinned like the Napatans themselves, turned their heads away and Talakh sensed that perhaps these were their own long lost kinsmen. Others amongst the growing crowd raised their arms and cheered as they saw the beaten prisoners.

'They see the old days returning for them,' Korkamani said quietly, as he looked on at the cheering men and women. 'The days when their Pharaohs ruled all.'

'But the Persians?' Talakh asked.

'Yes, the Persians...,' Korkamani said distantly. 'They won't forget the Kemet rebellion and neither will we Napatans'

In a few moments more, the prow of the boat nudged the bank and two of the Kemet soldiers leapt ashore to tether it to mooring stakes. At the word of Broken Nose, the boarding plank was put across and the prisoners were marched off at spear point in a tethered line. As his stiff limbs struggled to hold him upright on the bouncing plank, Talakh thought of all the hazards his kinsmen and their captors had shared, and for a moment he longed to be back on the boat, if only for its awful certainty. For who knew what their fate might now be amongst these people?

The prisoners were taken through a broken gateway in the outer wall of the fortress, the crowd parting warily before them only to quickly close in behind, while some of the children spitefully threw handfuls of dirt in their faces. Talakh blinked through the dust as they stepped from sunlight into the shadow of a second, more massive wall. Ahead of them lay a huge ruined gateway that rose above them to the height of the palm trees.

'This is where our trials truly begin,' Korkamani's voice whispered uneasily from behind Talakh. 'There will be no rescue for us now boy. All that we can do is wait and hope for a chance to escape. You must learn the ways of these people as best you can and make yourself useful to them until our time comes.'

Talakhonsu tried to speak, but his throat was dry and he could not loosen his tongue. Fear and thirst had swallowed his voice down into the pit of his empty stomach, but yet for all that, his eyes were now wide at what he saw around him.

Truly this place of Sesibi was unlike anything he had seen before, a strange mix of ruin and order with houses of all shapes and sizes. Some were tall and some were squat, but all were placed in straight lines along wide tracks that crossed each other every so often. The poorer dwellings were bare mud brick and had only the leafy broad boughs of the palm tree for a roof, but the better houses had been plastered smooth and painted the colour of red earth, or a dull white. These ones had flat roofs of sun baked clay, just like those of his far off home. For in this parched land, just as in his own, it hardly rained at all.

Though Sesibi was not a big place, still a lot of people seemed to be crammed within the shelter of its walls. Talakh wondered where they kept their cattle and how they fed themselves, for apart from the date fruits that hung high in the tall palms, there seemed little good land to farm along this parched and rocky stretch of the Great River.

They came at last to a small, walled enclosure that reeked of dung and piss, and the soldiers herded the Napatans into it like goats, barring the gate behind them. In the corner there was a low trough of dirty water set out for the beasts that would normally be penned there, but after they were shut in the Napatans drank it anyway, even though it was warm and rank.

'Don't get your bonds wet,' Korkamani reminded the others. 'If the hide gets damp, it will tighten further still when it dries out.'

'What does it matter?' a young man called Arkenesi sighed. 'We will die soon anyway.'

Talakh looked at him with pity, but also some hardness in his heart. Arkenesi's spirit was broken, that was plain enough and his head slumped forward in defeat on shoulders that were red from the lashing he'd received at the oar. Korkamani shuffled over to the young man, wincing at the pain from the sores on his own tethered ankles.

'Sit up,' he said firmly. 'Sit up if you want to live.'

Arkenesi would not meet his eye. 'There is no living to be done for us now,' he said as he started to cry piteously. 'They will kill us all!'

'Listen to me!' Korkamani's voice rose angrily. 'All of you listen to me! The strong among us will survive because the strong will be useful to the Kemet slave traders. The strong will work and the strong will be fed and watered. Some of you will work the land. Some of you may be traded to faraway places and if you are lucky your work there may be easier still.'

'You talk of this as if to be cast into slavery is a good thing,' said an older man, whose ragged sores shone bright red against his dark skin. 'I may have my best years behind me, but I still have my pride. We are better off dead than to live like this, at the mercy of our enemies. Those same enemies who took our wives and our children!'

'That is why you must live,' Korkamani said firmly. 'One day the Persians will come to take back Kemet, and then will come the chance for all slaves in these lands to rise up and escape in the confusion. Will you leave your wives and children to their chances? If Amun wills it, perhaps some of you may still have a chance to find your loved ones again if they still live. Do not give up hope!'

Korkamani looked around then, staring at each of them until he had caught the eye of all of the Napatan survivors, so that they took heart from his strength of will against the hardships to come.

'We are the sons of our fathers and we will not dishonour them by giving up,' he said firmly as he struggled to his feet, raised himself up to his full height and beat his bound fists loudly on his chest, so that the sound echoed from the high walls. 'I will never give up my hope to these Kemet curs. Never!'

The others nodded, and some of the other men said, 'Aye!' and beat their own chests too.

'Soon we will be split up into smaller groups and you may end up on your own,' Korkamani continued, his voice low again as he looked around the men and youths until finally his eye settled on Talakh himself. 'Remember my words and keep hope in your hearts, no matter how bad things may seem.'

Talakh felt fear again in the pit of his stomach at these words, as the thought came to him that after all their hardships together he and Korkamani might now be separated by their captors. The face of evil Khaemwaset flashed into his mind. Khaemwaset, the leader of the raid on Napata and the man responsible for the death of his mother and old Prainke. Talakh beat his own small fist against his ribs then in his anger, though for him there was not much of a noise from it.

'Korkamani is right,' he said, his voice trembling with both fear and anger. 'We must bide our time, and hope for our revenge on those who beat us. I give my oath that I will not give up.'

Arkenesi, the young man whose despair had moved Korkamani to speak, now joined his oath to that of Talakh's.

'If a boy can find the courage to go on, then we must all follow his example,' he said, though his voice still quaked. 'Let them do what they will to us, and we will bide our time.'

Korkamani and the others nodded and the older man who

had spoken earlier of his pride, touched Arkenesi gently on the shoulder with his bound hands.

'Then let us all rest as best we can in the shade of the wall,' Korkamani said. 'Get what sleep you can.'

For the rest of the day, the prisoners were left to suffer by the Kemet soldiers, who were no doubt entertaining themselves with beer and fresh food at the expense of the people of Sesibi. The prisoners grew drowsy and some found comfort in sleep as they slumped in the shade against the rough, mud brick wall. Talakh too slept, for he was still young and with the hardships and fever he had borne, he was too tired and too hungry for words.

In the early evening when the heat had finally gone from the setting sun, the soldiers of Kemet returned with Broken Nose at their head. Dozing though he was Talakh awoke in an instant at the noise of the approaching men.

'Get up!' Korkamani said quickly to the others. 'Let them see we still have our pride.'

At his words the prisoners shuffled painfully to their feet, stifling their groans as best they could. As the warriors lined up opposite them, their spears at the ready, Talakh felt the fear like a lump in the back of his throat.

Broken Nose lifted a thumb and jabbed it in the direction it seemed of Talakh and Korkamani, muttering an order to one of his men. The soldier now approached them with a knife that caught the cool evening light in its shining blade.

'He is cutting us loose from the others,' whispered Korkamani to try to reassure the boy, though he sounded ill at ease himself. 'Do as they say unless I tell you otherwise.'

The soldier cut the neck tether tying Talakh and Korkamani to the other prisoners and jabbed the point of his spear into the small of Korkamani's back as he marched them away to the far side of the yard. There he forced them to squat on the ground while he stood guard.

As they watched, Broken Nose spoke to two men in rich robes, who had come into the yard and were now looking over the other captives.

It was clear enough that these ones were traders in slaves and their voices quickly rose into a fierce exchange with much waving of hands and pointing at the Napatans. For his part, Broken Nose threatened them both, while they in turn pointed their fingers at him, until Talakh thought that surely it would end in violence.

Finally, Broken Nose spat on his hand and, with a curse, offered it to one of the men to agree a deal. The man said something and then laughed as he pointed towards Talakhonsu and Korkamani. Talakh could see that the man stared at him now and him alone. Scared as he was already, a new fear took root in the boy at the slaver's leering.

There was silence then, a dangerous silence as Broken Nose started to shake with rage. In the blink of an eye he drew a long dagger and thrust its wicked point in front of the slaver's eye, bellowing and spitting as he pulled off the terrified man's fine braided hairpiece and trampled it in the dirt, while the other slaver backed away in fear. The man protested, but this only made Broken Nose angrier and he punched the newly bald man in the face and threw him to the ground to join his false hair amongst the dirt and dung. Still Broken Nose was not finished with him and he kicked the slaver's backside out of the yard as he crawled along in the dirt, sobbing in terror for his life. When he had done with this one, the Kemet war chief turned to the other slaver, spitting on his palm again before offering it. The man mumbled something, his voice shaking with fear, and clapped the warrior's hand with his own.

'A deal has been struck,' Korkamani said quietly, ignoring the guard who glared at him as he spoke. 'The others have been bought by that man, who will sell them on to others.'

'But what did the other one want with us?' Talakh asked fearfully.

'What he wanted was with you alone,' Korkamani said through gritted teeth. 'Some men favour only boys, but it seems that Broken Nose cannot abide such things, even when it comes to a Napatan. Besides, he has other plans for us, which is why we were not offered to the slavers in the first place.'

Before Talakh could ask another question, the guard waved his spear point in Korkamani's face and kicked him in the side. The message was clear and for the moment Korkamani had to bite his tongue.

Now they could only watch as their fellow Napatans were led out under guard through the gateway. As they went, the young Arkenesi shot an accusing glance at Korkamani, for he was the kind who could not see his fate was in the hands of the gods as much as in the hands of men.

After they had gone it was the turn of Korkamani and Talakh to be led out of the yard and back through the streets of the fortress town. Talakh stared down at his feet, so grey with dust and grit that they looked like someone else's, and tried to ignore the fresh jeers of the people of Sesibi, until at last they were pushed into a small storeroom in the lee of the fortress walls. Broken Nose, whose anger had now subsided, made sure they were given some stale flat bread, a bowl of cold stewed beans and a jug of water. This was some comfort at least to them.

As he looked around their new prison, Talakh saw that the store was disused and had no roof, but the rough, crumbling walls were far too high to climb even if they had managed to undo the knotted leather cords that still bound their swollen wrists tight.

Korkamani divided up the bread as best he could and let Talakh eat half of the beans, before taking his share, even though as a man he needed far more. When they had wolfed down the last of the bread like starving dogs, Talakh could finally talk with Korkamani again.

'Korkamani?' he asked. 'What will become of the others?'

Korkamani shook his head sadly. 'They are slaves now,' he said quietly. 'As I told them earlier, if they prove their worth and earn their keep, they will not starve. They will be put to the fields. They will unload the ships. They will quarry stone for the Kemet temples, just as slaves must do in our own lands.'

'Will they ever be free again?'

'If they have their strength, some might escape. But those trying to get away will be sorely punished by their masters if they get caught,' he said bitterly, spitting on the ground against the evil in those words.

'Besides, you have seen how barren the banks of the Great River are in the lands we've passed through. Should a man follow the river toward our own lands, he would soon be hunted down if he didn't starve first. And then if he struck out across the desert with no water, the vultures would feast on his bones in no more than a day or so.'

Talakh's head sunk down in sorrow and with a heavy heart he recited one of the prayers to great Amun which he had been taught, afterwards asking that the god would watch over their former companions.

Korkamani listened to this in respectful silence, before also asking Amun for his protection, pouring a little of the precious water on the dirt floor in meagre offering to their god.

When a moment of silence had passed in respect of the god, Talakh asked a further question that hung over his mind.

'Korkamani?' he asked. 'Why were we not traded to the slavers with the others?'

'All that I know is that the evil one Khaemwaset wanted you brought to him in the place they call Waset, from the moment you were captured. I do not know why. Perhaps as a serving boy? As for me, I am not sure.'

'You are wise and you will find out soon, O Korkamani. Broken Nose is bound to speak of it to his men sooner or later and then you will know.'

'Perhaps not boy,' Korkamani shook his head. 'The fat one is cleverer than he looks; he knows I understand him and so he guards his words more carefully now. We can only wait and see what comes.'

Talakh could not think of an answer as he looked at his protector, once again taking in his curious features. The more he thought about it, Korkamani did not really look like a Napatan at all, but neither did he look like the men of Kemet. He had Talakh's dark skin, but his neck was long, his nose long too and thin. With his tall, lean build perhaps, thought Talakh, Korkamani was descended from the mysterious people of the high mountains, far away to the south of Napata. There were those big ears of his too, the boy grinned to himself. So funny to look at, when his own ones felt so small!

'Why do you smile?' Korkamani said suddenly. 'What do you think of that makes you happy in this grim place?'

'I meant no offence,' Talakh's guilt made him blurt out. 'It just came to me that perhaps your father, or your mother...?' his voice tailed off.

'You wonder if I am a true blood like you?' said Korkamani with a gentler voice. 'Well, my mother was Napatan that much I am certain of. But my father, he was a traveller so she told me, one of those who trade across the deserts to the great Middle Seas and beyond. His fathers, going back through the ages, came from the four corners of the world and so in his blood was the seed of many lands and many peoples. Perhaps there is a far off place where everyone has a long nose like mine,' he said with a flashing smile.

Talakh smiled too, glad that although the fates had been cruel to him, still he had Korkamani as a companion and protector. As the evening light faded into darkness and the stars appeared overhead, Korkamani taught Talakh a little of the tongue of the Kemet people, starting with the most basic words that speak of food and water, of greetings, of commands and so on. In fact to the boy's surprise he already knew some of the words from listening to the guards, and his mind was hungry to learn more, so that in this way he too could hear what Korkamani heard. In the way that all of us like the things that we are good at, and in the same way are good at the things we like, the boy priest found a strange excitement in learning the tongue of his enemies.

As the night deepened, the thick mud walls around them gave out the stored warmth from the hot sun, keeping the cold desert air from the two prisoners, while they talked until the fortress town around them grew quiet with sleep.

'You should get some rest now boy,' Korkamani said. 'We

cannot know what hardships tomorrow will bring, so offer your thanks to Amun a final time and let us trust in him that he watches over us still.'

Talakh made his last offering of the day to the god as he had often seen old Prainke do and then curled up in the dust close by the warmth of the wall. But although he was tired, still his mind was too excited to sleep just yet. 'Korkamani,' he whispered.

The tall man looked fast asleep, his bare chest slowly rising and falling in the darkness.

'Korkamani,' the boy whispered again.

'What is it boy?' came back a half sighed answer.

'Please do not be offended, but... I was wondering how you come to know the ways of these people so well?'

Korkamani stifled a laugh at that.

'Perhaps I am a spy,' his teeth flashed white again in the gloom. 'Now go to sleep young priest.'

Talakh grew only more curious now, for in his heart he suspected that there lay some grain of truth in Korkamani's joke. His restless young mind toiled late into the night, looking for answers that would not come, while Korkamani slept and the moon after which he was named slowly ascended amongst the stars. Always his thoughts at these times returned to the bitter sadness of his mother's death. For although he was brave and his heart was strong, he was still only a boy.

Pelia paused in her story again, her mind's eye leaving her father and his protector Korkamani far off in the land of Kemet, as she found herself once more staring at the crackling fire in the darkness of the hut.

Cerian looked up from ruffling Sealgair's wiry fur. She had taken the great hound to her heart and he lay contented alongside her, gnawing an old bone.

'Is something the matter Pelia?' she broke the silence.

'No, I'm fine,' Pelia replied with a gentle smile. 'My mother was a woman who could weave her words finer than the finest cloth. Sometimes her story takes me so close to my father, I feel I could almost reach out and touch his face,' she said, her eyes still far away. 'Ah, but the porridge will be thick as clay now! Let us eat, you must be as hungry as Sealgair by now.'

Cerian put her hand to Pelia's as she lifted the spoon. 'Poor Talakhonsu...' she said gently. 'To be made a slave after all that had happened to him.'

'Yes, he was still a boy then,' Pelia smiled sadly. 'But even so his gods had already woven the fates for him. In time, as you will see, they took him still further from Napata, beyond the land of Kemet and on to our own shores.'

'I cannot wait to hear of how he escapes!' Cerian said excitedly.

'Then you must be patient,' Pelia said, her eyes brightening in the gloom of the fireside. 'There are many things which must unfold before I can tell you of that. Now let us eat and then, after the jobs for the day are done, I will carry on his story.'

Cerian had been Pelia's guest for some weeks now and the two had fallen into a pattern of life together, sharing the work, good and bad, between them. In the deep of winter, to be outside was rarely a pleasure, but the wicker traps had still to be checked. For an eel, or a fish, or a crayfish was too rare a treat to be passed up, even on the grimmest of days. Then there was water to be brought from the spring that bubbled up clear and pure at the edge of the village. Always there was kindling to be gathered, and always corn and barley to be ground into flour too.

Sometimes the two of them would tend to the sick, and Cerian would watch then, to learn Pelia's ways.

Still other times, for the gift of some small meat or offal, they would scrape the animal skins of Aneurin the hunter. He traded in things such as these when he could. This one Aneurin felt a strong duty to live up to his name as 'the honourable one' and this meant that to Pelia he owed his eternal thanks, for she had time and again nursed his sister back from the brink of death, until finally the marsh fever had carried her off to the world of shadows.

Cerian sometimes caught a longing in Aneurin's eye when he looked at Pelia, but despite the love he no doubt bore for her, he was ever shy and anyway Pelia herself said often enough that she had no need of a man.

Still, there was much time when the hunters were away and there was nothing to be done upon the cold, sodden land. Much time when the warriors were listless, and the children too, as they kept their strength for the days that would be colder still. At these times, when drips of rain fell through the smoke hole in the roof and hissed on the fire, Pelia returned to the story of the faraway land of Kemet.

For two days, Korkamani and Talakhonsu were kept in the roofless storeroom, baked by the merciless midday sun that soared high overhead to banish all shade. As bad as that could be, Broken Nose made sure that they were at least fed and watered, even if this was done in the manner of cattle. It was little joy for them to brush the grit and dirt off the stale bread which was thrown on the ground by the soldiers, still less to wash it down with the muddy water that was left for them to drink. Even so, their hunger abated a little and as Korkamani said, each day they survived with their spirits intact was a small victory over their oppressors.

Early in the morning of the third day, before the sun god had yet brought any light to the darkened sky, the two were woken with a start by the men of Broken Nose unbarring the door.

'Get to your feet!' one of the soldiers shouted at Korkamani, prodding his chest with the butt of his spear. 'Come on Napatan scum, I know you understand my words!'

For a moment, Korkamani looked as if he might spring at the man, woken violently as he was from sleep, but then he glanced at Talakh and carefully, slowly, he got to his feet. The soldiers led them away through the deserted town, to where Broken Nose and the rest of his war band warmed themselves by a fire against the cold of the desert night.

'Where do they take us?' Talakh whispered, rubbing the sleep from his eyes with his bound hands.

'North to Waset, I think. They could sail again, but something tells me they will go on foot, following the Great River through the desert,' Korkamani replied quietly. 'That is why we are starting so early, to move fast before the heat of the sun becomes too hard to bear. You must forge your will from iron Talakh. The way will be hard and long for many days to come now.'

And so it proved to be. Through the half light before the dawn, the soldiers set off. Broken Nose was at their head and the fat man set a harsh pace in spite of his bulk, until all of them, prisoner and soldier alike, glistened with sweat. The soldiers travelled light, carrying only their weapons, their light shields of wood and hide, and small sacks of flour and dried beans. Korkamani, his hands now untied, was made to carry two large skins of water slung over his shoulders. Talakh in turn was given a smaller wineskin, but in his weakened state this was a heavy burden indeed. He prayed to Amun that Broken Nose and his men would drink the wine dry that night, to spare him the load in the coming days.

In the hottest part of the day, the party rested, finding shelter where they could among the rocks on the river bank. In spite of their fear of the sharp fanged lizard beasts, which had consumed their brother soldiers a few days before, the heat was such that some of the men lolled in the river shallows to cool themselves, whilst others vainly sought out fish with their spears.

Still, in the cool of the evening, while a few of the soldiers hunted a small reed bed for fowl and others baked their flat breads on a rock over a small fire, there was time for Korkamani to teach Talakh a little more of the Kemet tongue.

Later when darkness fell, they talked of other matters whilst they waited for sleep to come to them.

'Why did Broken Nose not take the boat instead of walking?' Talakh asked again. 'Do you think he is scared of the river now?'

'No, I think not,' said Korkamani quietly. 'I have heard that the river is far easier to sail from now on anyway. Perhaps he wants to drill his men? Or it may be that with only you and I as prisoners now, he would have had to put his own men to the oar if there were a headwind. All in all, as we can cut across the bends in the river it will be quicker to march than to sail.'

But of what was to become of them when they reached the great temples of Waset, Korkamani would not guess and Talakh did not press him on this, for he knew it could not be good.

The next few days passed for the two Napatans in the harsh extremes of the desert, from the baking heat of the day, to the cold winds of the night that carried the blood curdling howls of the jackal and the hyena, the fox and the wolf of those forbidding lands. Broken Nose drank little from the wineskin, so that Talakh's burden seemed to grow no lighter as they trudged wearily on across the hot sands and bare rocks.

Here and there when they marched along the river bank, the war band would come across small settlements. At these places, if there were more than five young men of fighting age, the strongest of these would be seized by Broken Nose, despite the cries of their mothers and fathers. The Kemet soldiers would take fresh food and beer too at the end of their spears, for they had nothing they wished to trade with these outlying people but threats and oaths.

So it was that the Kemet war band slowly grew, the soldiers teaching the captive villagers the craft of war in the cool of the evening, though most of it only amounted to bullying of the young men. Still, most of these herders' sons had their own light wooden spears for fishing, their slings and perhaps a small knife or axe. One, of them, probably with a better arm for throwing than most, had two stout throwing sticks looped onto his hide belt, at which the soldiers laughed heartily, saying they were nothing but children's toys. Korkamani inclined his head toward this tall one, who had been taken that day from the first village they had passed.

'His name is Meketra,' he said quietly. 'Wait and see what he can do with those throwing sticks if he gets the chance.'

This one Meketra had the darker skin of Talakh's own people and he was taller by far than the rest. He looked strong, his long limbs wrapped tightly with muscle and sinew that twanged like bowstrings when he moved. He for one did not seem to mind that he was now to be a soldier, perhaps because he was young and looked for adventure. Unlike the others, he stood proud and aloof, as if he was already an equal with the men of Broken Nose, whatever they might think.

Later that evening as the sun was setting, the long limbed Meketra went down quietly to the river bank with one of Broken Nose's best hunters, Seneb. Whilst the warrior wielded a spear and a small, weighted fowling net, Meketra carried his two throwing sticks, one in each hand. They were carved from a dark wood and took a curving shape like the stiff bodies of dead snakes, but with a broad, flat head at each end. It was clear from their exchanges that these two were setting out to prove who was the better hunter.

'See,' Korkamani said, his keen eyes following the line of his long thin nose toward the men. 'The ends of those throwing sticks of Meketra are bound in beaten strips of iron. No-one would waste the metal of war on such a thing unless they found their target well. But he will lose them to the fire unless he betters that one Seneb in the hunt. That is their wager.'

Broken Nose and his men looked on as the two hunters divided, Seneb wading upriver, whilst Meketra waded down until they were both out of sight amongst the rocks and the reeds.

'Is Broken Nose not worried that Meketra might escape

67

back to his people?' asked Talakh.

'No, boy. He is a good judge of men. He knows when a man has fight in him and anyone can see that Meketra is not made to till his father's stony fields all of his life. Besides, if he runs those same fields will be burning before tomorrow has passed, and the home of his family too. Broken Nose has his reputation, and where he passes, those beneath him must bend to his will or suffer the consequences.'

Talakh nodded, but he did not really understand what made men like Broken Nose the way they were. For now he shared the world of soldiers with their curses, boasts and oaths of loyalty to their brothers. Oaths of fighting together and of dying together if need be. Tears felt like they would come to him at the ugliness of these things, but they did not and he was glad of that. Glad that he would not shame himself in front of Korkamani. He did not realise it then, but he was already losing a part of himself. The harmless, innocent side of his boyhood was passing from him.

It was some time later as the night gathered in and a few straggling fowl flew over, heading to their roosts, that Seneb the hunter returned, angrily throwing his spear point into the ground as he reported to Broken Nose.

'It seems I was wrong about Meketra,' Korkamani said, listening carefully to the angry words between the two men, as the other soldiers gathered around. 'He has fled and the gods have not favoured Seneb's hunt either. Seneb is in a foul mood now.'

But if Seneb's mood was foul, it was as nothing to the rage of Broken Nose. He beat Seneb about the head with the flats of his hands in his frustration and anger, which was of course as much at himself as it was at Seneb. For Broken Nose had been made a fool of, and his pride would not stand that.

When the worst of his temper had passed, the big man grabbed the still almost full wineskin that had been cooling at the river's edge and set to emptying it in between a raft of curses and oaths of what he would do to Meketra and his kin when the morning came. It would be fruitless to pursue him in the darkness, so the Kemet soldiers sat down in a group muttering to themselves, whilst Broken Nose drank himself toward a headache and Seneb rubbed his battered ears.

When they ate their food, there was little thought among the soldiers for the hunger or thirst of their two prisoners. For Broken Nose had issued no orders and so his men were only too happy to see the Napatans suffer.

Talakh looked on, the cheer he had taken from watching the men of Kemet fight and argue amongst themselves now overtaken by the empty ache of his stomach. To watch them eat was a torture that seemed to last an age, but then when he thought he could bear it no more a voice called out from the gloom of the river bank. Now the soldiers drew knives and readied their spears, as they always did when surprised.

'It is that cursed dog of a farm boy,' Seneb shouted angrily, jumping to his feet to confront the reason for his beating at the hands of Broken Nose.

Meketra strode up from the river, his long limbs quickly covering the ground between them and he seemed to have no fear of what might await him. Seneb held up his spear, its iron point glinting bright with threat in the firelight, but then as it seemed he would surely skewer the villager, Meketra held up his hand and tossed to the soldier's feet a fine pair of fowl, a broad smile on his face.

Still Seneb came forward, his anger if anything even greater now that the sinewy farmer's son had shown himself the better hunter. Meketra only now reacted, drawing his own small dagger. He was no match for an experienced spearman and he quickly backed away before turning and running toward the fire, where the other soldiers sat cheering Seneb on. Seneb was confident now, but as he rushed forward in pursuit, it was Meketra who struck first. Drawing one of the dark wooden throwing sticks from the cord around his waist, in a flash his long arm whipped back over his head for an instant before it snapped forward and down with the speed of the viper's strike. With a crack, the heavy iron bands of the stick found their mark against the spear arm of Seneb, dropping the warrior to the ground with a cry of agony, his arm hanging limp and broken.

Now other soldiers started to rush forward, only to hesitate as Meketra drew his other throwing stick.

'Enough!' Broken Nose suddenly roared, as he roused himself from his sullen mood and got to his feet. 'There will be no more fighting tonight!' he raged, marching past his own men and straight up to Meketra, who bowed his head and held his empty palms up in respect.

'Hmmph!' Broken Nose snorted, before turning on his men. 'This one will not be harmed,' he commanded them. 'He won his wager fair and square. I need fighters like him, so from now on he is your brother, do you hear me? Your brother!'

At that, Seneb who was sweating and moaning with pain, uttered another string of curses.

'Whilst you serve under me, this man is under my protection, Seneb,' the commander said with dark menace in his voice. 'You can kill each other when I no longer have need of you, but until then you are my men and the men of Khaemwaset!

'Now, you,' he turned to Meketra, 'pluck those fowl and do not cause me any more trouble, or I will have your head! You will roast the birds for us, but you will not eat tonight, nor tomorrow.'

Meketra lifted his head a little, but only so that he could lower it again to show his obedience. But though he said nothing, Talakh thought he saw the flicker of a smile on the young man's face.

'Let him drink and then fix his arm!' Broken Nose commanded one of his men, as he dropped the wineskin at Seneb's knees, so that the injured man could numb his pain.

There was much that Talakh did not understand about what had just taken place. Later, Korkamani explained to him that the Kemet commander had to be seen to be fair to the farmers' sons he had pressed into his war band, otherwise he might never have their full loyalty in battle.

Still Korkamani was sure that this Meketra had provoked Seneb deliberately. There was a pride in the young farmer that would not allow him to answer to a lesser man, and he had a deadly aim with those throwing sticks of his. He also had an enemy now, yet he had shown he was a man who could fight. A man to be feared, like Broken Nose himself. If they had any sense, the other soldiers would think hard before they crossed him, young though he still was.

Talakhonsu was too weary to think on such things for long and soon he fell into a deep sleep, even while Seneb's drunken screams rent the night air as his friends set his broken arm straight as best they could with strips of desert bone and leather.

In his dreams, Talakhonsu felt himself slowly drifting away from his cold and listless body lying in the dirt and into a realm of welcome memories. His friends ran with him once more toward the river in the gentle warmth of the twilight, whilst high overhead the gods started to light their countless beacons, bright and still in the darkening sky. Frogs croaked lazily. Dragon flies buzzed around, hunting for insects in the reeds and Talakhonsu smiled at the beauty of it all. But then with a heavy sadness in his heart, the boy priest saw in his dream that the Great River was disappearing, flowing away from him into the distance until it was out of sight, leaving only muddy banks behind. The empty river bed began to dry and crack before his dreaming eyes as the great sun god rose again at the east, too soon back into the sky.

As the boy's limbs began to tremble, the land started to burn under the merciless sun, while frogs and flapping fish shrivelled on the shimmering clay until their eyes were white and their bones shone through. Talakhonsu looked around him, but his friends had gone and he was alone now, alone in a desert dreamland where nothing lived and all was despair. The great god Amun forsook the land, summoning a mighty north wind that blasted the boy with sand. Despite the great heat of the sun, he grew cold, shivering as he crouched down in the dirt, his cries for help unheeded. All he could do then was sob quietly, for in his heart he felt that his time on the earth was coming to an end.

It was late into the cold night when something awoke

Korkamani. Perhaps it was the chill desert wind, or perhaps the nagging ache of hunger. Whatever it was, straight away he knew that something was wrong with Talakhonsu. Reaching out his hand, he felt a raging fever on the boy's soaked brow, and knew that his life was again in danger, for this was a common fever that took many lives among the young and the old alike along the Great River. Korkamani drew the shivering boy close to him, to warm Talakh as best he could, for the boy only had the tattered cloak to cover himself with. Steeling himself, Korkamani called out the true name of the one they had taken to calling Broken Nose. His shout awoke the sentry guard, a mean spirited little man known as Unas.

'Shut your mouth, Napatan,' Unas spat, 'or I'll send you to join your ancestors.'

Korkamani stared hard at the man, who in turn with the bravery of a spear in his hand, would not look away either.

'Wake your commander,' Korkamani said with iron in his voice. 'The boy has the fever. He will die unless you help him.'

'Hah!' the man Unas sneered, spitting in the sand to make his point. 'What is it to me if a Napatan brat dies!'

'It is nothing to you, you think?' a deep voice rumbled out of the gloom. The voice of Broken Nose himself.

'Yet, if the boy dies,' he said, his great hulk looming out of the dark, 'then Khaemwaset will be displeased with me. And then, do you think it will still be nothing to you? Bring the boy to the fire! Give him a cloak and some clean water.'

So it was that having nearly taken the spirit of the boy priest by neglect, the Kemet soldiers now were duty bound to keep him alive. Though his hands were still bound, Korkamani was given a strip of rough cloth and some water, so that he could mop the boy's fevered brow as he struggled to live through the long, sleepless night.

When the great sun god Ra rose above the horizon to once more bring warmth and light to the day, Broken Nose came to check on his two prisoners.

'How is the boy?' he asked in his own tongue, knowing that Korkamani understood.

'His spirit weakens. What has he to live for, now that his mother is dead?' Korkamani said bluntly.

'He has you, Napatan,' Broken Nose said, brushing aside Korkamani's anger. 'It is clear to me that you have some... relation to him. That is the only reason you two are still together. Soon we will come to the temple of Soleb, and there we will see what the holy men can do for him. My men will give you some food and then you will carry the boy,' Broken Nose ordered him.

His words set Korkamani to wonder again at the fat man's cunning. Broken Nose was a watcher of men, as all those who lead must be.

The next morning, the journey to the temple of Soleb proved to be mercifully short, although it seemed longer than Korkamani remembered it, for he had passed this way before, many years ago. His arms soon ached from carrying the thin boy, yet Korkamani cared not for this. All of his thoughts were for Talakh's shortening life, as the boy's breathing became shallower and he slipped deeper into the grip of the fever.

Yet despite his low spirits, Korkamani still felt a surge of unexpected excitement when he first caught sight of another cataract of rocks and shoals across the river. He knew that beyond it stood the great temple itself, its mighty stone gateways rising up high above its enclosing walls. Set in a green swathe of palm trees and fields, the halls of the god here were almost the equal of those in his own lands and yet he knew that far off to the north were temples greater still.

The war band of Broken Nose approached the prosperous settlement before the temple. This was nourished by the Great River, which in its yearly flood washed over a flat, fertile plain defying the barren desert sands surrounding it. Yet still, Korkamani knew that the priests of Soleb were diminished in their power from their former times of great wealth and influence.

Since those far distant days, many armies had passed this

way and the temple had suffered mixed fortunes at their hands. Now, glorious as it still was, some of the mighty stone pillars of its halls had fallen in tumbles of huge blocks. In this border land between the peoples of Kemet and Napata, the temple of Soleb was starting to crumble, slowly but surely losing its power over the hearts and minds of the people.

Broken Nose set his men to rest in the shade of some palms down by the riverbank below the temple, whilst an old man tilling his fields looked on in bemusement at the travel-worn soldiers. A naked child ran off shouting into the village.

'Wait here and don't cause any trouble,' Broken Nose ordered his men as he went to the temple with Seneb. The Kemet soldier, whose broken arm had grown swollen and red, groaned in agony with every step he took.

'Touch nothing. Take nothing,' Broken Nose shouted over his shoulder as he strode off. 'Everything here belongs to the priests of Amun!'

Whilst Broken Nose went to seek an audience with the head priest, Korkamani tended the boy.

'Some water,' Meketra offered in the Nubian tongue, as Korkamani fanned the boy to keep the flies from his face. 'Let me help him. I once helped my mother nurse my sister through the fever.'

Korkamani nodded and watched as the young man dipped a strip of cloth into the pot, and then let the drips run into Talakhonsu's open mouth.

'It is not much, but this is all that we can do for him,' Meketra said grimly. 'He is in the hands of the gods. Perhaps the holy men can help him.'

Korkamani nodded sadly, as he looked down at Talakhonsu's drawn face. The boy had endured much already. His skin was cold and clammy now, and his lungs rustled like a faint breeze through the trees as he struggled for life.

Chapter 5

The Gates of Kemet

On the instruction of Broken Nose, who in turn wielded the influence of the Kemet lord Khaemwaset, the priests made offerings to stone carvings of their god in the great temple. It was their way to wrap those sick with the fever in cloths steeped in hot water and if the great god Amun blew his cool wind from the north, to place them in the shade outside, so that the life giving breath of the great one might restore them. Scented woods were burned and cymbals were chimed to please the gods. Spells were uttered late into the night, and magical charms placed on the heart and brow of Talakhonsu. All of these things and more were done to save the boy, for Broken Nose had been sworn to bring him alive to the land of Kemet and he was not in the habit of breaking his oath.

In the mornings, when Ra returned to spread light into the world once more, so Korkamani prayed for the life of the boy. Broken Nose had him put to work in the fields of the priests, and as he tilled the earth, so he sang prayers to the gods then too. The tall Napatan, now thinner than he had ever been despite the better food that the foreman of the fields gave him, had not seen the boy for three days now and he could not think for worrying at Talakhonsu's fate.

Then one afternoon as he sheltered from the hottest rays of the sun under a palm tree with the other labourers, he saw the grim figure of Broken Nose stamping along the riverbank toward him. The commander's face looked stern, as it always did, the face of a leader who took no slight from any man. Korkamani feared the worst, but as Broken Nose drew nearer and the other men got to their feet out of respect, so he waved the Napatan's concern away.

'The boy will live,' he said bluntly, as was his way. 'His fever has broken.'

'Thank you for your care of him,' Korkamani said honestly. 'He would have died without the help of the priests.'

'Humph,' Broken Nose waved his thanks away. 'You there,' he gestured to the other labourers. 'Stop standing around and get back to your fields.'

The men took up their tools and scattered away, not needing to be told twice by the man with the sword at his belt. When they had gone, Broken Nose spoke again.

'Your people are sworn enemies of mine,' he said firmly. 'Yet there was something that I owed you, Napatan. You saved my vessel and my men when their courage deserted them on the Great River. Consider the favour returned, but you will say nothing of this to anyone else.'

'You have my word,' Korkamani nodded.

'Of course my man Seneb has a broken arm, thanks to his own stupidity, and so I needed to bring him here anyway for the priests to tend him.'

'And what of Khaemwaset?' Korkamani spat in the dust at the evil one's name. 'What does he want with the boy?'

Broken Nose glared at him with eyes of iron.

'My Lord Khaemwaset is no concern of yours!' the fat one shook his fist angrily. 'You are a brave man, Napatan, an honourable man,' he said, leaning forward until his scarred face was inches from that of Korkamani. 'But know this. While Khaemwaset is my lord and you are his enemy, so you are my enemy too, do you understand? If you give me cause I will take your life as easily as I would snuff out the light from a rush.'

'I ask again, what are your lord's plans for the boy?' Korkamani asked unflinchingly.

For a moment Broken Nose looked as if he would lash out, but then he looked away and sighed heavily.

'I see how you care for that boy more than you do for your own skin,' he said, his voice softening a little. 'I have a boy with my woman...'

It was an awkward moment between the two proud men, before the iron returned to the voice of the Kemet commander.

'I can say no more than that the boy's fate still rests in the hands of the gods,' he shook his head. 'Pray to your Amun, Napatan, that he may be spared again as he has been spared from the fever.'

Korkamani looked into the dark eyes of Broken Nose, but found only the harshness of a man whose life was bound by orders and discipline. A man of stone, who others feared.

'When the boy is fully rested and Seneb is ready to travel again, we will continue north,' Broken Nose said flatly. 'Until then we stay here. Now back to your fields,' he barked, as he turned his back and strode off towards the temple.

Korkamani watched him go, and held his silence as he too wandered off to where the other workers were clearing a ditch that carried the Great River's life giving waters into the fields. Despite himself he felt a grudging respect for the Kemet commander who seemed not to know fear. There was a chance they would fight one day if he and Talakh were ever to escape. Despite the blazing heat of the day, the prospect sent a chill down the Napatan's spine.

It was another five days before the boy Talakhonsu was returned to Korkamani and although the priests had fed him well so that he might recover his strength, still he looked drawn and weak. The two hugged each other and there were tears in the eyes of them both at their reunion.

'I am glad to see you boy,' Korkamani smiled, pushing back the side lock of hair from Talakh's temple.

The priests had shaved the boy's scalp as was the practice in those lands with children, leaving only the side lock, which was tied neatly with a strip of binding, like the tail of a pony.

'And I you,' Talakhonsu replied, smiling to himself at the change in Korkamani, whose pinched face was by now disappearing under a beard that rose high up his cheeks. 'The priests say that the fever spirits have left me now. I am to stay with you again.'

Korkamani knew this meant that Broken Nose would have his men bind and tether them again when they resumed their journey north. He had grown used to his freedom in the fields, for the Kemet war chief had known that he would never abandon the boy.

'They will starve us again no doubt, but you will be glad of a rest from the spells of the priests,' Korkamani said wryly.

'They were kind to me though,' Talakh shrugged.

'Yes they were,' Korkamani agreed. 'It is easy to forget that even in this land of our enemies there are still good men to be found.'

Broken Nose kept his war band at the temple of Soleb for another two days, before they set off again early one morning when the first light of the dawn was showing in the sky. Within a few hours it was as if nothing had happened to halt their journey north. The soldiers swore and cursed at their prisoners, goading Korkamani at the point of their spears to sate their boredom. They passed another stone temple, this one a ruin peopled only by two young goatherds and their small flock, as the land quickly grew barren again. The walking was hard for the Napatans, the stony ground leaving them footsore in spite of the makeshift rush sandals Korkamani had made for them. Yes, very quickly it seemed that little had changed.

And yet by the time they camped that afternoon in a small settlement near a large tree-clad island, things were a little better than they had been for the prisoners. Korkamani guessed that Broken Nose was using Seneb's broken arm as an excuse now to slow their pace to a level that would not exhaust the still weakened Talakhonsu. A small cooking fire was lit outside an empty storehouse that the soldiers had commandeered and as dusk drew in, the prisoners were fed on much the same food as the soldiers, even if their rations were meagre.

Every now and again too, Korkamani would catch the eye of Broken Nose, as the fat man glanced at the boy for any signs that his sickness might be returning. But still, Talakh and Korkamani could talk freely and their guard paid them no heed, so Korkamani again began to teach the boy some more words of the Kemet tongue.

'You are a quick learner, Talakh,' the Napatan praised his pupil. 'Soon you will hear what I hear when our enemy speaks. Then you will start to learn about their lands and their ways.'

Talakhonsu nodded. He was tired now, his eyelids suddenly heavy with sleep.

'Lie down boy,' Korkamani said gently, covering him with an old goatskin that Meketra, the hunter of the throwing sticks, had come by. 'You must sleep. There will be time enough yet for your learning.'

Talakhonsu did as he was bid, closing his eyes and letting the tiredness seep from his aching limbs, but he found he could not sleep. Across the still, night air he could hear the voices of many hundreds of people, singing and drumming. There were smells too of roasting meat and fresh bread and the sounds of great joy. Perhaps the joining of a man and his wife, or the birth of a long awaited son. The nearby island held a large settlement so it seemed, and much later when he turned aside to relieve himself, its outline was revealed by a host of twinkling yellow lights from the torches of the dwelling places there. It seemed all too familiar to him and for a moment Talakh imagined himself back in his own lands, looking back at the lights of Napata from the darkness of the riverbank. But there was no comfort in such memories. They brought only pain, for everyone he loved in that place was now dead or stolen away.

He looked down at bearded Korkamani with his long narrow nose and his large ears, lying dead to the world in a deep sleep. His protector looked so thin and drawn now, lying there in the dirt. The tall Napatan had endured much to watch over Talakh when he could easily have escaped on his own, and the boy again swore an oath to himself that despite his own loss, despite his sorrow, he would try not to disappoint his guardian.

The next morning Broken Nose commandeered a boat from the settlement to take them further down the river. Perhaps he had grown tired of walking, but whatever the reason the wind was at their backs now and there was no need for prisoner or soldier to bend to the oar as the days passed. So, despite the discomfort of their tethers, the Napatans used their time for Talakh to learn more of the Kemet tongue. That is when they were not dozing under the hot sun, or watching the land slowly slip past as the boat journeyed on north, down the Great River.

There were often temples dotted along the river banks, though many of them were crumbling into the dust, or swamped by the desert sands. Strikingly green against the barren desert wastes were small groups of tall, waving palm trees, hung heavy with branches of fruit, whilst rarer still were the small fields of wheat that sprang up amongst the rocks and sands, nourished by the cool waters of the Great River. But apart from more sightings of the great lizard beasts from time to time, there was little to stir the soldiers or their prisoners from their torpor. In the evenings the soldiers would sometimes hunt, with tall Meketra's throwing sticks finding their mark amongst the rushes time and again. Despite his youth, he was now among the more favoured men of their commander.

They soon came to Seneb's home settlement. The soldier's arm was healing, but he would never throw a spear again in anger and he now was no use to a war band. Broken Nose paid him off there with some cattle that he had bought from a farmer, though Seneb's mood was sour and it was clear that there was bad blood now between him and his former commander. Meketra for one was glad to see the back of him.

'A man like Seneb will make enemies wherever he goes,' he said to Korkamani, and the young warrior was no doubt right in this.

On and on they travelled across this vast land, where the gods watch over men through their animal messengers of hawk and vulture, jackal and desert dog. The boat came to another fearsome cataract of boulders, shoals and islands where the Great River was hemmed in on one side by a high ridge that forced it to wander across the land in countless, tumbling streams. Broken Nose enlisted some local men to guide them through the maze of waters that shimmered with the sparkling light of the sun, until at last they came safely to a great cliff that towered over them. Here amongst the calmer waters lurked great lumbering water cows with their smooth, dark skin, gaping pink mouths and fearsome tusks. All who knew the Great River had cause to fear these huge beasts, for they would attack for no reason and could overturn all but the largest of boats if they were provoked to anger. In spite of his strength and courage in battle, Broken Nose knew well to avoid these dangerous creatures. The boat left the high cliffs and the water cows safely behind as the waters grew calm again.

When cool evening came at last, the mood of Korkamani grew thoughtful as they passed a massive fortress on a rise of land that loomed over the river.

'The great fortress of Buhen,' Korkamani said solemnly.

Talakhonsu looked up with awe at the towering walls, expecting to see men with spears guarding their heights. But instead there were only a few goats scrambling amongst the crumbling ramparts.

'Our own warriors took this place by force once, a long time ago when we conquered the land of Kemet,' Korkamani said distantly.

Talakhonsu had heard this story before, and to be here in this place where his ancestors had put the Kemet armies to flight made his heart fill with pride.

'They have not taken it back though?' he asked.

'No, boy,' Korkamani answered grimly. 'Only the desert can claim Buhen now. They may have overthrown the Persians and raided our lands, but we can only hope that the Kemet nobles will never be strong enough to hold this place again.

'Make no mistake, though,' he said, gazing up at the stern ramparts. 'The great cataract back there was the last of the barriers that the gods set to divide our lands from theirs. We have passed within the gates of old Kemet now.'

The next evening the words of Korkamani came back to

Talakhonsu. As the boat rounded a bend in the river, the rays of the setting sun coloured the mountains to their right a beautiful rose pink, while long, purple shadows were cast across the river from the high cliffs to their left.

Broken Nose went to the front of the boat then and stood with his palms upwards in the manner of a prayer.

'Great Rameses!' he said in his deep, booming voice. 'Warrior god of Kemet, we thank you for our victory against your enemies!'

Talakhonsu watched as the soldiers cheered their leader's words, unsure what sign had moved Broken Nose to offer thanks to this god.

'Korkamani?' he turned to ask, but the tall Napatan just raised his head, inviting the boy to follow his gaze.

'Others would tell you to look away,' Korkamani said grimly. 'But I say we must look our enemy and their false god in the eye and not bow down before them.'

Talakhonsu followed his protector's gaze ahead of the boat to the mountains beyond and gasped out loud at what he saw. For resting their backs against the mountainside sat four giant kings, made of stone.

'The temple of Rameses,' Korkamani said quietly, 'greatest of all kings of Kemet. Can you see? The ancient ones carved his image from the mountainside not once, but four times.'

Talakh's mouth grew as wide as his eyes.

'Do not fear them Talakh,' Korkamani said. 'Their power is no more. When we grow nearer you will see that the statues are being swallowed by the desert sands, blown along by Amun's breath. This is Amun's sign to us that even the greatest son of Kemet has lost his favour now.'

Talakh nodded, watching in silence as the stone giants grew slowly closer in the fading light until they loomed high overhead.

Long after the boat had put ashore at a small island and darkness had fallen, the boy could still make out the cold, stone eyes peering out into the night across the river, steadily watching him.

-ϕ-

As Pelia stopped talking, so Cerian closed her mouth, which had been wide open with wonder as her mind's eye saw something of what Talakhonsu had seen many years ago in the far off land of Kemet.

'Good, I have told my story well,' Pelia smiled. 'Ah, but I must not overtire you while you are still sick.'

Cerian coughed again, her lungs rattling with the cold that had laid her low the past few weeks.

'The story takes my mind away from things,' Cerian said, when she had recovered her breath. 'Besides, I'm nearly better now.'

Pelia nodded her agreement, but she had seen enough in her time as a healer to know that even the young and strong could be quickly cut down by illness.

'The broth will be ready now,' she said, lifting the clay pot from the fire with an old piece of hide to protect her hands. 'So, we will eat our supper and if you are still awake after that, then maybe I'll continue for a short while.'

For the two young women, as for everyone else in the village, times were hard and food, any food, was something always to be treasured in this, the deepest time of winter. Chief Heilyn's holy man had declared midwinter's eve some weeks before, a time that had seemed too long in coming.

Back then, despite the cold and drizzle on midwinter's dawn, all had left the shelter of their homes to greet the coming sun at the sacred stones. All asked for an early return of spring. The men uttered their oaths to be kinder to their wives in the year to come, whilst the women in their turn offered their promise to keep their families well. The young pledged their whispered love for their sweethearts, while the old wished only to see the coming year out. Offerings were made, chants were sung and an old ram was slaughtered to honour the gods, Chief Heilyn ensuring that all had their share when the tough old beast was taken back to Llan Huell and roasted slowly outside his hall.

Pelia cast her mind back now to that cold, wet midwinter day. Perhaps it had been then that the cold had got inside Cerian, for it had surely carried off widow Maer, a few days later, despite Pelia's remedies and care for the old woman.

'Did you make an oath to yourself, for the year to come, back at the midwinter?' Pelia asked, as she blew clouds of steam from her broth in between sips.

Cerian looked into her bowl, a twinkle in her eye in the firelight. 'Nothing really,' she answered, still looking away.

'A boy?' Pelia teased.

'No.'

'A man then?'

'No!' Cerian said even more firmly. 'No,' she repeated a third time, but the look in her eyes said that perhaps there was someone who had turned her head.

'You'll find a man soon,' Pelia smiled. 'Maybe sooner than you think?'

'I am still young,' Cerian shook her head. 'There will be time enough for me when the right one comes. For now, I want to stay with you and learn your ways of healing.'

'I sometimes wonder if I really have my mother's gift at all, let alone the skill to pass it on to someone else,' Pelia frowned, thinking of those she had been unable to save as the cold had taken its toll of young and old that winter in the lands around Llan Huell. 'Our people choose to put their hopes in me, but sometimes there is nothing that I can do.'

Cerian shook her head. 'No, no, you must not doubt yourself,' she said. 'You cannot save those who are fated to die. But for every one who passes over, there are others you've made well again. People still have faith in you.'

Pelia smiled a little, heartened by the younger woman's wise words.

'Of all the women in this place,' Cerian continued, 'you are the one that the girls want to be like. You are the one the women respect, and the one their men want to lie with!' she laughed, until the cough caught in her throat again.

'Now, will you tell me again of the temple with its giants

of stone? How were they made? Did the giants build them, like the great stones of the plain?'

'No. Korkamani told my father that men carved these ones from the stone of the mountains at the command of their king Rameses many, many lifetimes ago.'

'But can men really do such things?' Cerian said, doubtfully.

'You can be sure that if a leader comes to the people, one who inspires them with bravery and wisdom, then what at first seems impossible can be done.'

'It sounds like your father was such a man.'

'No, though it is true enough that he helped the old chieftain Huell to regain his birthright,' Pelia frowned. 'But we are getting ahead of the story. First I must tell you more of the journey into the heart of Kemet.'

Cerian yawned, a wide, silent yawn that she could not stifle. 'I am sorry!' she said, embarrassed at herself.

'Don't worry, I am tired too,' Pelia smiled at the guileless Cerian. 'You must put this cold behind you, and to do that you need your rest. So sleep now and perhaps you will dream of your love,' she smiled. 'We will continue the story again tomorrow.'

The next day dawned cold enough to freeze the marrow of the living, and Pelia again confined Cerian to the hut while she went out with Sealgair to gather more wood from the forest. There had been a storm a few weeks ago and the trip was worthwhile because of this, for the forest floor was covered in the dead twigs that caught fire so easily in the morning embers of the hearth. By the time Pelia returned to the settlement, her back was bent over with the weight of a huge bundle of faggots, tied together with strips of young bark she had pared from a lime branch.

That evening the wise woman built a rare fire over two large ironstones that she kept for the purpose, a way off from her hut. While Pelia worked to tend the blaze and keep it fed, so the children of the village came to peer in curiosity before they were called in by their mothers. There was little enough to amuse the young in the dark of the year.

'Go on with you!' a tall figure in a long cloak tussled the head of one of the boys as he ran off.

In the fire light Pelia saw the face of one she knew well. 'Aneurin,' she nodded.

'Pelia,' the hunter bowed his head in greeting. 'You are heating the sweating stones I see. Is Cerian no better?'

'With the grace of Keridwen she will be well soon,' Pelia said, holding out her palms to show her honour for the goddess.

'Aye,' Aneurin acknowledged, making his own small gesture. 'You are well yourself?'

'I have no complaint,' she answered with good nature.

The two of them stood awkwardly for a moment. Things had changed since Cerian had pointed out the hunter's eye for Pelia and now she was more guarded in her affection for him. Thus, it was Aneurin who spoke first, in spite of his shyness around her.

'The logs will soon burn low...' he said quietly. 'The hot stones will be heavy. I can help you to carry them in.'

'Thank you,' Pelia said gently. 'But then you must go.'

'Of course, I have no wish to intrude,' the tall hunter shook his head. 'I only want to help where I can.'

Pelia smiled and placed her hand lightly on his arm, looking into his green eyes that shone so brightly in the firelight with their steady gaze. Aneurin was a kind man, those eyes told her, though her heart already knew this to be true from their long friendship.

'Thank you,' she said. 'We will move the stones together then.'

The two warmed themselves by the glowing logs as the flames slowly died down, Pelia agreeing to let Aneurin take the hound Sealgair from her to hunt with him the next morning, as the sweating was no place for a dog.

At last, when the big stones were heated through, Aneurin rolled them out of the embers and levered one of them up, so that Pelia was able to slide two green poles underneath it.

'Quickly now!' she urged.

With an effort they now raised the heavy stone from the ground as the wooden poles hissed with the heat, and then carried it into Pelia's hut, where Cerian sat waiting, gathered up in her cloak by the hearth. The two of them quickly returned with the other stone, and then Aneurin helped Pelia to collect the fire embers from her hearth into an earthenware bowl.

'I will take this and keep your fire burning for you outside my door,' Aneurin said, knowing it would bring bad luck if Pelia let her fire go out. Then, the good spirits that protected her hut might leave the hearth for a better home, never to return.

Now that Aneurin was gone, Pelia covered the smoke hole in the roof with a piece of hide, tucked under the roof timbers and thatch. Next she placed her furs and clothes outside and sealed the door flap, placing some logs against it to keep out the draft. It was very dark in the hut now but for a small rush light, though Pelia could still feel the great heat of the stones on the hearth and next to them she found the water skin that she had earlier filled from the sacred spring. She had performed this magic many times on others and as her mind now relaxed, she splashed a little of the water on the stones. A cloud of hot steam came off them as the spirits of water and stone were released to fill the hut with their wreaths. Then she placed wet mosses and some sacred herbs onto the stones, together with a cup filled with water and feverfew, for Cerian to drink when it had heated through a little.

'Take off your clothes and sit by the stones,' Pelia said, as she did likewise. 'The heat will better enter your body this way.'

Cerian did as Pelia asked, shivering at first, while Pelia stuffed their clothes into some hide bags to keep the damp from them.

'Let your arms relax by your side,' Pelia said quietly, as the heat and steam started to build in the darkened hut. 'Let your breaths come long and slow.'

At first Cerian could do nothing but cough as the fragrance of the potent herbs entered her lungs, but gradually her chest loosened a little. Sweat gathered on their backs and Pelia poured a little more of the sacred spring water onto the stones to bring forward another great rush of steam and heat.

'You must let your mind be content,' she said gently, 'Then the spirit of the goddess in the water may drive out the ill spirits that have keep you unwell.'

Cerian sat in silence for what seemed an age, peaceful and calm, letting her body soak up the heat until she felt she could take no more and her head grew light as if she had drunk too much mead at a feast.

'Drink this and be well,' Pelia blessed her at last, her dark hand touching Cerian's arm to offer the warm draught of feverfew.

When Pelia felt Cerian returning the cup, she refilled it with more water and herbs, waiting for it to warm again on the stones, before offering it back with the same blessing.

After she had done this a third time, for three was always the blessed number, the wise woman bathed Cerian with a ball of cool moss that she had gathered under the full moon from a great stone of the old people that stood alone, deep in the forest. The cool moss soothed Cerian's hot skin and she felt lighter than air now, her chest easier than it had been for many weeks.

When the heat had finally started to go out of the ironstones, Pelia rolled them carefully out of the door, then quickly dressed and went to the hut of Aneurin. True to his word, he had made a small hearth of stones near his door and left a small fire burning steadily there. She collected the embers in her pot, thanking the hunter, who tonight had forgone the company of the long hall of chief Heilyn to do this task for her.

Cerian was sitting up and looking much brighter when Pelia returned.

'I will make the fire anew,' Pelia said, tipping the embers onto a heap of thin twigs on the hearth and breathing new life into them. 'Now you must sleep, for the heat will have drawn out some of your strength, as well as the bad spirits. Lie down and close your eyes,' she said gently. 'While sleep comes to you, I will tell you a little of what my father saw at the temple of King Rameses.'

Chapter 6

Temple of the Fallen God

The soldiers of Kemet, proud in the feats of their forebears, sang their war songs long into the night after their boat had moored up opposite the mighty temple of Rameses.

'What do they sing of now?' Talakhonsu asked Korkamani, though in truth he had already guessed the answer from the way the warriors beat their spears on the tight drums of their hide shields, and chanted at the tops of their voices.

'They boast of their victories over the Persians and the sea peoples,' Korkamani said bitterly as he listened.

'And of their battles with the bearded ones who challenged their great kings long before the Persians came. But most of all they boast of trampling the Kushites underfoot as they raided our lands.'

Talakhonsu cursed under his breath. These curses he had learned from the other prisoners, before they had been sold into slavery by Broken Nose. It was the first time he had used such a curse and the power in the words made him feel a little less helpless, despite his bonds. Korkamani gave him a strange look. Perhaps he now realised that Talakh had already lost the innocence of his boyhood and that it was his fate to become a man before his time.

'They sing of their old victories against us,' the tall Napatan continued. 'It was their great king Rameses whose long arm reached far beyond the land of Kemet in all directions, taking many away into slavery. The stories of those times are carved into the walls of their temples. I have seen them with my own eyes.

'But,' he said wryly, 'they seem to have forgotten their own defeats at the hands of our armies. Long after the sands had already started to swallow up this temple, our warriors marched north past it to defeat the kings of Kemet in their own heartland. Like the sands that are always shifting, the triumphs of men and their kings pass quickly.'

'I see that,' the boy nodded.

'Soon the Persians will return to Kemet with a great army that will stretch from horizon to horizon. They will crush men like Broken Nose and Khaemwaset as if they were ants,' Korkamani said, spitting against the evil one's name as he always did.

The men of Broken Nose did not stir until late the next morning. They had all sung long into the night, drinking their beer and their wine, whilst casting insults as sharp as spears at their two prisoners. Barring the sentry guard who watched sleepily over the Napatans, Talakh was the first in the camp to open his eyes to the day as the early morning sun crested the rocky crags to the east. In the warm, orange glow cast over the great temple, he now saw three of the stone giants in all their glory, the embodiment of great Rameses, a king made god in all his might. The head and shoulders of the fourth giant were broken though and fallen to the ground, while the barren sands had gathered in huge drifts around them all, rising over their unseen feet and up their legs as they sat on their stone thrones. Despite the sly smiles and the coiled snakes frozen in stone waiting to strike from the three remaining heads, he did not fear them. Just as Korkamani had said, the power of Rameses had long been spent. Even so, Talakh could still imagine the whispering spirit of the long dead god king, wandering deep in the permanent darkness of the temple, and a shiver went up his spine all the same.

When Broken Nose ordered the boat to set off again down the river away from the great temple, they passed its neighbour just up the bank, smaller but still mighty with more giants hewn from the rock.

'The goddess Hathor, giver of life in the Kemet lands,' Korkamani pointed at one of them as the boat passed, and he lowered his head out of respect.

Soon they had left the mountains behind them altogether and the land about them on either side of the river grew flat and ever more desolate. These were places where the foot of man rarely trod unless, as with Broken Nose's Kemet war band, they were passing through on the way to somewhere else.

'Why do men fight over places such as these?' Talakh asked Korkamani.

'They say that long ago the land was rich and people farmed here, before the winds drowned their fields in sand,' Korkamani replied thoughtfully as he rubbed his ever more bushy beard against his bound hands.

'You are very wise, O Korkamani,' Talakh said with all respect. 'When you had the chance to escape, you should have left me and returned to our people. They need men like you to guide them.'

'Perhaps I can serve them better here,' Korkamani, said quietly.

'What do you mean?'

'Over the years I have travelled these lands and far beyond in the service of the old king, finding out what I could for him about the land of Kemet and its Persian masters. But you must breathe nothing of this, or I am dead,' he whispered, staring intently into the boy's eyes.

'I will say nothing,' Talakh said solemnly.

'Our young king Siaspiqa has to learn from his mistakes and rebuild his strength,' Korkamani continued. 'Meanwhile the Persians are no doubt readying their armies to take back Kemet. So I think the fates guide me to watch over what happens across the land of the black earth at the heart of Kemet, just as they guide me to watch over you.

'If great Amun wills it that we survive, then perhaps we can escape when the Persians return. Then we will return to Napata and tell our king of all that has happened. Maybe then Khaemwaset can be made to pay, if he still lives.'

Talakhonsu nodded, thinking on what had been said for a moment.

'But how did the evil one surprise us, when our king had you to advise him?' he asked.

'A good question,' Korkamani sighed. 'But unfortunately

kings do not always listen to their advisors, you see? When I brought the news that the lords of Kemet were rebelling against their Persian masters, I warned the king that if they succeeded they would waste no time in sending their soldiers against us. Instead of listening to my advice, he chose to ignore it. Siaspiqa has much to learn if he wants to remain our king.'

'Then he shares the blame for what happened!' Talakh said angrily.

'Yes, boy,' Korkamani nodded, sadness in his deep set eyes. 'The young fool's mind dwells too much on Meroe and our lands to the south. He forgets about the north. Yet only he can unite our people against Kemet. As long as he is king, no-one else can do it. Do you see that Talakh?'

The boy trembled with rage as once more the bitter memories came fresh to his mind. 'I can see only that one day when I grow to be a man I will kill Khaemwaset if I get the chance,' he said through gritted teeth. 'I swear to it.'

'And if the gods will it, I too will be there with you to see him fall in the dust,' Korkamani said quietly, leaning gently against the boy's shoulder to console him.

In the following days after they had left behind the great temple of Rameses, the boat of Broken Nose and his men made slow progress as the river wound through the Nubian deserts deeper into Kemet. Korkamani was put to the oar along with the new men of Broken Nose, including tall Meketra. But though these men were given their rest in between turns, Korkamani was not so lucky and he was forced to row on through the wastes.

Soon, Broken Nose was again reduced to robbing any settlements they came across for food, such was the desolation of the land. Here were no fowl to catch, no date palms to climb, no game to hunt. Even the fish seemed to have left the Great River, for whenever a net was cast it always came back empty. The land was hungry and those few that lived there were gnawed by hunger, their existence a miserable one. All of these things made Talakhonsu ponder ever more why men should fight over such empty places, only to build temples and fortresses that were doomed to stand lonely and abandoned as the sands slowly swallowed them up.

Yet full of hardships as this journey was for the Napatan captives, still an unexpected friendship of sorts grew between sinewy Meketra, the farmer's son turned soldier, and the boy Talakhonsu. It was a strange thing that was never explained, though Korkamani guessed that perhaps the young man had lost a brother of Talakh's own age at some time. Whatever the reason, Meketra taught the boy some of his skill with the throwing sticks, roughly carving a lighter one that Talakhonsu could throw, from a piece of driftwood he had plucked from the river.

In the evening Meketra would free the boy from his bonds and take him a little way from the soldier's camp so that they could throw for practice at stiff reeds that the young Nubian had plucked from the riverbank and planted in the sand. Other times there would be the white skull of a long dead goat to aim for, stuck on the long bones of its own sun bleached carcass. Talakh often missed, but Meketra rarely did, his throwing sticks splitting the dry skulls open in a spray of white shards.

'Do not try to throw too hard,' Meketra advised him in his strange Nubian accent. 'Over a long distance you must flight the stick in a curve, so that it drops from the sky onto your target.'

'But you throw it straight!' Talakh protested.

Meketra laughed heartily at that. 'Yes, but I am a man, while you are only a boy!' he said proudly. 'Your bones are not yet set and you must grow into your full height before you can use all of your strength like me, otherwise you will pull your shoulder. Once that happens, your arm will always be weak. I have seen this happen, so heed my words.'

Little by little the boy's aim improved, Korkamani noted as he watched Talakh learn the skill of the throwing stick. He sometimes caught Broken Nose watching too. The boy no doubt reminded the Kemet commander of his own son, who was growing up out of his sight and care far to the north.

By the time the boat at last made its slow and weary way out of the sands of Nubia, Talakhonsu was mastering the commonplace words of the Kemet tongue and with a good eye for the throwing stick, his health and strength were also now returning. There had been more temples glimpsed along the way, some nothing more than stumps of tumbled columns that endless time had drowned under the wandering sands. Others were more complete and, though long abandoned, in his mind's eye Talakh could still imagine the priests of old holding their processions of music and singing to praise the gods.

Finally they came to the approaches of what Korkamani assured him would be the final cataract on the Great River, the place known as the Syene. There had been few boats on the river as it passed through the desert wastes, yet now suddenly a host of sails were before them, white against the blue-green waters and the brighter blue of the sky above. The rocky hills that encompassed the cataract itself drew in closer, but the wind and current were thankfully in their favour.

Broken Nose had them weave through the mass of boats, most of them traders or fishermen, though a few also carried small parties of soldiers. These ones eyed Broken Nose and his men suspiciously, shouting questions as they drifted by on the breath of Amun.

One such boat full of armed men threw a rope to them and drew alongside. A large, staring eye outlined in blue and black was painted on its prow, the sign of the hawk god, who seeing this mark would give his protection from evil and danger. The man in charge of this boat was young and agile, with the lighter skin of the Kemet people. Without asking first, he leapt aboard and was almost bounced straight back onto his own vessel, as Broken Nose stepped forward to bar the way with his great bulk. The two threw angry words at each other, and for a moment it looked as if blood might be spilt as the men on both sides drew their weapons. Korkamani leant across Talakhonsu to shield the boy with his body.

'What do they say?' Talakh whispered excitedly, for the words were so quick he could not make them out.

95

'The other man demands a tax on behalf of his lord, the high priest of one of the temples here, for entering their waters,' Korkamani answered quietly. 'It is the way in the Syene when strangers arrive, but Broken Nose is too proud to kneel to a lesser man such as this one.'

'What does the man say now?' Talakh whispered.

'He brings news that Darius, the great Persian king is dead, and that his own lord now rules these lands unopposed.'

Korkamani paused and swallowed hard, his tongue dry in his mouth.

'Now he asks for one of us 'slaves' as payment, but Broken Nose says we are the property of his own lord, Khaemwaset. Broken Nose says he will take a tax of this man's head and those of all his men in return if they insist on this. Those are his terms.'

Talakhonsu was struck by the bravery and pride of the fat man, who stood with his hands on his waist, his battle scarred face defying the other to make the first move. The Kemet commander did not blink and there was a terrible look on his face, as hard and unyielding as stone.

The other man, who Talakh had gleaned was called Sehura, switched his eyes quickly around the war band of Broken Nose. There was Meketra, standing tall and proud, his sinews moving like snakes under his skin as he toyed with one of his throwing sticks, throwing it in the air and catching it again, no trace of fear on his face. Then there were the grim faces of the other warriors in their dirty kilts that still bore the stains of the slaughter of Napata, though their weapons were bright enough in the sun. All of them looked strained and thin, but also hungry for a fight, a wild look in their eyes like a pack of desert dogs.

Yes, the men of Broken Nose were all fighters, for he tolerated no others within his war band. By contrast Sehura's own men were clean shaven, their short wigs of black hair all the same as each other and their kilts as white as the pristine sail that fluttered from their mast in the hot breeze.

Broken Nose smiled, though it was a smile as cold as

death. Now he stepped forward so that his sandal rested on top of his new enemy's toes. This was a rare insult and aboard both of the boats, all held their breath.

For what seemed like an age, Sehura did not move, but finally he lost his nerve and with a curse muttered under his breath, he turned on his heel and jumped back to his own boat. As Meketra threw their rope over the side into the water in further insult, all Sehura could do was shout oaths at his men and kick out at them left and right, while the laughter of the men of Broken Nose echoed in his ears. When the wind had put enough distance between them, Broken Nose spoke to his men.

'It will not surprise you that there is no welcome for us here in the Syene,' he bellowed. 'We have made a new enemy in that young pup and his men, but more importantly in the lord he serves. If what he said is true and Darius is dead, then a great many things will now quickly change.'

The men listened intently to their commander, as did Talakh and Korkamani, for what Broken Nose had to say concerned them all.

'With Darius gone, there is nothing to keep the lords of Kemet united against him,' he continued.

'What will the nobles do?' Korkamani asked him in the Kemet tongue.

Broken Nose looked at Korkamani with a look that at once said many things. There was surprise. There was grudging respect. There was also the stern authority that the commander always exuded.

'It is not your place to speak,' he growled. 'But you know the answer to your own question anyway. The lord priests will squabble amongst themselves for land and power. They will divide the strength of Kemet, and what then when the Persians have a new king and a new army?

'There will be no welcome for us here,' he turned to his men. 'We must return to our lord Khaemwaset with all haste. He will have need of our spears.'

As Broken Nose turned his back on his men after ordering them to the oars, Talakh thought he heard the Kemet leader sigh. Though his men talked excitedly about the death of Darius the Great, Broken Nose had the look of a man who was growing weary of the world. His boat was ill provisioned, his men hungry for food, beer and the feel of land under their legs. Yet Broken Nose dared not set foot ashore, and so instead they sailed on amongst the many green islands that marked the great cataract of the Syene. The boat of Sehura dogged them from behind as they went, though it dared not approach them too closely.

'Be thankful they have no bowmen aboard,' Korkamani said, as he and Talakh looked back. 'We will be lucky if we pass through this place alive.'

Yet despite the new danger that now menaced them, there were many fresh wonders to lift the heart of a boy like Talakh. Before his eyes there came the great beauty of a small temple of golden stone, perched amidst deep, shaded trees on the loveliest island the boy had yet seen.

'What gods are worshipped there?' he asked Korkamani, his voice hushed with the same awe he had felt when he had first seen the far distant temple of Rameses.

'I have seen this place many years ago,' Korkamani replied with a sad smile as he remembered happier times when he had been here as a free man. 'The shrine is to the worship of Hathor, the escort of the dead in the lands of the after world. For the mothers of Kemet, she flows through their milk, so they say, bringing life to their newborn babies. Just as we do, they hold the cow sacred to her in this place too.'

Now with the wind and current in her favour the boat sailed past the beauty of Hathor's shrine, quickly on through the maze of huge boulders and wooded islands that channelled the Great River. The boat shot down one last small rapid, but here there was little danger and soon they were back into the more familiar calm of the Great River as it spread its banks far off to each side in a vast lake strewn with many hundreds of small islands. Talakh stared around him at the straggling trees overhanging from the larger islands, and the dark bushes that covered the smaller ones.

'It is all so green,' he found himself saying.

'Aye, it is,' Korkamani allowed himself a thin smile.

Talakhonsu could only watch in wonder, his hunger forgotten for now, as they drifted close by a mass of huge boulders of many colours that rose from the lapping waters. For a brief moment amongst the dappled sunlight and shadows of those islands of the last cataract, the boy priest forgot the bonds of his captivity and all of the hardships he had endured.

'Sehura has given up the chase,' Korkamani said, bringing Talakh's thoughts back to the grim reality of their plight.

'He will have orders to stay in the upper passage to guard the river, for if they once journey down here it is no easy task for a boat to be hauled back up until the river floods full again.'

'Will other men of Sehura's be waiting for us up ahead?' Talakh asked.

'That is a good question,' Korkamani answered. 'Perhaps it would be safer for him to do nothing, rather than admit to others that he let Broken Nose pass.'

'I see that,' Talakh said.

The boy paused, and looked Korkamani in the eye searchingly. 'What would you have done if you had been Sehura, Korkamani?'

'I would have fought,' Korkamani said grimly. 'For when you serve a lord, as Broken Nose does, this is what you are bound to do come what may. There is no other way without losing honour and the respect of your men. The fates are not kind to those who hide from their duty.'

The boat passed on without further challenge, lost amongst the mass of traders and fishermen that passed to and fro across the river. They came then to another great, tree shrouded island, the biggest yet by far.

'They call this the Island of Ivory,' Korkamani said. 'It is named for the huge, curved tusks of the elephant.'

'I have heard of them,' Talakh said, eager to show his learning. 'They are giant beasts as tall as a tree, with long, long noses.'

'So they say,' Korkamani smiled. 'But if they were once

here, they are long gone from this land now. Over there is the city of Syene,' he nodded at the sprawling mass of mud brick houses, grain stores and walls on the bank opposite the great island. 'There will be many traders in that place from far distant lands across the great Middle Sea.

'But the people here, from the farmers even to some of the priests themselves, have a strange view of the Great River,' Korkamani continued thoughtfully. 'You see they insist that the floods of the river rise up from amongst the rocks in this place and then reach far south up the river toward our lands, as well as all the way north down to the sea,' he shook his head.

Talakhonsu tried not to laugh.

'How can they think such things?' he shook his head. 'The flood must surely start beyond our own lands and flow down to here, otherwise the current of the Great River would not have carried us to this place?'

'Sometimes people believe what they are told, even though their own eyes should tell them otherwise,' said Korkamani.

The boat passed by Syene on the following wind, but still there was no sign of pursuit and soon they had left the city behind altogether while the river gathered in on itself again and bore them on past fertile farmlands and settlements rich in cattle. Now where the soil was tilled, Talakh could see clearly why Kemet was named the land of the black earth.

That evening they moored on a small deserted island under cover of the date palm trees, for Broken Nose was still wary of pursuit. The soldiers had caught a few fish that day by towing their net behind the boat, while Meketra and some others hunted down some fowl in the reeds at the islands edge in the last of the light, so finally there was a little more food to sustain them.

As he and Korkamani sat eating their meagre share with their bound hands, Talakh could not keep from his mind the dangers behind them and the dangers still to come.

'Korkamani?' he said. 'How long is it now until we come to the place they call Waset?'

'Well,' Korkamani frowned. 'It could be as little as seven

days walk from here, though it may be even slower by boat if the wind is not in our favour. Still I don't think Broken Nose will risk taking to the land yet. We may not be safe from the reach of Sehura's men until we come to Khaemwaset's own lands.'

Korkamani was again proven right. For the next five days the boat that carried Broken Nose and his war band kept to the midstream and the islands of the Great River as it passed through the fertile land of Kemet, stopping only to trade some food from the small settlements they passed along the way.

For now this was no lordless outland where a strong man could take what he wanted from the weak. Already Broken Nose had made enemies in the Syene and now in the heart of Kemet itself even he would not risk offending the interests of the powerful lords who sought to rule the land of the black earth.

-φ-

Pelia paused in her story, seeing Cerian's eyes grow heavy. The cold of winter had lost its grip on the land for the past few weeks, though it was sure to return soon enough, and in the darkened hut it was for once quite warm by the fireside.

'Why do you stop?' Cerian said, yawning as she sat up.

'You were near asleep!' laughed Pelia. 'Once again I keep you up too long.'

'No, no!' Cerian protested. 'I want to hear what happens next. And when you tell me, then I want to hear what happens after that.'

Pelia smiled. 'It is good that you enjoy the story. Only through the telling can I keep it alive.'

'But how do you remember all of it?' Cerian asked. 'There is so much!'

'There is, but ask yourself this. How do we remember everything that happens through our lives as we have grown from children to where we now sat in this hut talking together?'

Cerian thought for a moment.

'It is those things that have happened to us,' she answered. 'Things of happiness and sadness. Things we will always remember.'

'Exactly,' Pelia smiled. 'My mother told me this story many, many times from when I was just a small girl, and so it is almost as if I was there with my father and Korkamani on the Great River. But even so, there are parts that I remember some times and other times not.

'For example, I forgot to mention that in the lands they were passing through, the people worship as gods the lizard beast. In those lands they call them 'khamsa', while further north they are hated and are called 'crocodile'.'

'Cro-co-dile,' Cerian said, playing with the word on her tongue.

'Yes, and in spite of its great claws and jagged teeth, they take these khamsa, these crocodile, as very holy things in the Syene. If they find a young one apart from its mother, they will take it to their temple and praise it as a god until it dies of old age, by which time it has been fed so full of fish and other offerings that it grows vast and bloated, but tame like Sealgair.'

Cerian frowned at the thought of that strangeness.

'And also they paint the beasts many bright colours and put torques of pure gold around their legs.'

Now Cerian frowned all the more at the thought of the great, scaled beast with its narrow eyes and long fangs, being pampered in such a way.

'Surely you play a joke on me!' she said. 'They aren't afraid it will eat them?'

'Would Sealgair eat us?' Pelia smiled, patting the big hound's shaggy head.

'No, of course not.'

'Yet, is he so different from the wolves that range over the hills?'

'Yes, I see what you mean. The crocodile attacks men because he is hungry, but if he is raised by men and kept well fed by them, then he has no need of his fangs.'

'And then the people are free to worship him, if that is their wish.' Pelia added. 'So perhaps this story is not so hard to believe after all. Anyway, you should listen to your body and sleep now. Put your cares aside and dream of the green islands of the Syene.'

Chapter 7

House of the Evil One

The heat of the day had long since faded into the cool of night when Broken Nose finally led his men and their prisoners past the first outlying farms that lay on the approaches to Waset, eternal city of white and gold. This was the city of the great god Amun, famed throughout Kemet for its vast and rich temples. Yet it was not one city, but two. While Waset lay on the eastern shore of the Great River, a city of the dead lay on the western bank toward the setting sun. This was the last resting place of the god kings of old, those ones who were called Pharaoh.

As the war band edged their way along a track through the moonless night, the sharp bark of a dog heralded their passing, and it was soon joined by another and then more still, until the air was filled with a chorus of howls. An ignoble way for the men of a victorious war band to return to their homes, stealing their way through the dark like thieves.

Prisoner and soldier alike had endured a long and arduous journey and so tired were they that if they had not been so close to Waset, doubtless they would have been happy to fall to their knees and lie down in the dirt until morning came.

At last though, they came to another farm, much larger than the rest. Broken Nose led them through an entrance way into a yard surrounded by a group of low, mud brick buildings where a snarling dog strained against its leash to get at his men.

'Siamun!' Broken Nose shouted above the dog's barking. 'Siamun! Come out, before I kill this dog of yours!'

'Who's there?' a hoarse voice answered.

'Your master, you swine, now open up and feed my men!'

The man Siamun unbarred the door and rushed out naked but for a small waistcloth.

'Master, the gods bless us with your return,' the man Siamun babbled as he fell on his knees at the feet of Broken Nose.

'Never mind that,' Broken Nose said grumpily. 'The men are hungry and weary. Get up off your knees and make sure they are well fed. And give these slaves any scraps you have left,' he nodded to Korkamani and Talakh.

There was little enough food ready to eat, but all were too tired to wait for the woman of Siamun to cook anything. So with only a little stale bread and some cold gruel and dried fish to fill their bellies, the soldiers bedded down where they could in the grain stores and biers of the farm of Siamun. For the Napatan captives there was only the cool dust to lie in, but still they were glad of that just the same, weary as they were.

Broken Nose himself, as was his right, took the bed of Siamun and his wife, who in any case now rushed to and fro, preparing a feast for the next day to honour their returning master. Everyone else slept the sleep of the dead that night, even the guard set to watch over the prisoners.

'Get up you dogs of the desert!' Broken Nose shouted, giving his men good natured pokes with his sandaled feet as they lay in the straw in the coming light of a fine morning.

'Talakh,' Korkamani said, gently shaking the boy awake. 'You must wake up now. Today may decide our fate. We must be ready for whatever comes.'

'What do you mean?' Talakh asked sleepily. 'Where are we?

'We are very close now to Waset. I think today our time with Broken Nose and his men will come to an end.'

Talakh's sleepy mind tried to think this through.

'What will become of us then?'

'I do not know,' Korkamani said honestly. 'All we can do is pray that the gods will intervene for us against Khaemwaset.'

Talakh felt like crying, but he forced the tears back for Korkamani's sake, seeing the worried look on his protector's face. There were grey flecks in Korkamani's beard, he noticed. Thin with hunger, he looked suddenly frail and much older.

'We will go on,' Talakhonsu said bravely, resting his head on Korkamani's dusty shoulder. 'After all that we have suffered, it cannot end for us here. I know it in my heart.'

Tears were almost in Korkamani's eyes too now.

'Your mother would be very proud of you,' he said with a sad smile that creased his drawn face into many wrinkles. 'One day if I live to see you a little older Talakh, I will tell you something of your past. Something that perhaps you will be ready to hear then.'

Though he was a little puzzled, Talakh thought nothing more of those last words of Korkamani then. In the years to come when he grew to be a man, he would hear them again from time to time when he searched his mind's eye for Korkamani's once familiar face.

After rousing his men, Broken Nose stomped off into the half light of dawn with Meketra and another for company, leaving the rest of the war band to guard their prisoners and make mischief with the timid Siamun, who soon disappeared off into the fields rather than face their ridicule.

It was coming almost to noon by the time the war chief returned, his men leading a cart that was laden with heaps of flat breads, baskets of fresh fish, haunches of meat, skins of beer and wine, and other good things. Talakh and Korkamani had to look twice to see that it was indeed Broken Nose, for he was fresh shaven, a pure white kilt about his waist and a belt picked out with gold about that. Strangest of all though, he wore a wig of coiled black hair on his bald head that reached down to cover his ears. Talakh had to try very hard not to laugh, for in truth Broken Nose was a fighter by nature, not a lord and he did not look comfortable in his finery.

While Siamun's woman and his family took the food inside to add to the feast they were preparing, the commander drew up his men in a half circle in front of him. He stood with his hands on his hips, his huge arms jutting out either side of him under the hot sun that already baked the yard. Each man in turn he looked in the eye, but none looked away. They saw in his gaze of iron the respect that the fearless warrior had for them, for they were his men. Men who had fought by his side and survived to see this day of feasting and celebration.

'Men,' he said, his simple words carrying great weight. 'You have always followed me without question despite the hardships and dangers we faced in the lands of our enemies. Always you fought bravely at my right hand, and at my left. You have honoured Kemet and our lord Khaemwaset.'

The men let out a great cheer, whilst Korkamani's eyes narrowed in hate.

'Our great lord does not forget those who fight in his name,' Broken Nose continued, thumping his broad chest loudly with his fist.

'Meketra,' he beckoned the tall young warrior forward and counted pieces of gold and copper into his open hand. Now the farmer's son was a paid warrior.

So it was with the other men of the war band. Broken Nose paid them all with Khaemwaset's stolen gold and copper. When it came to it, these warriors had fought not for land and not just for their master. No, they had fought and killed for just a few small pieces of precious metal and what could be traded for them in Waset. Talakhonsu's blood ran cold at the sight of it. When all were paid off, Broken Nose passed around the jugs of beer that had been brought back from the city.

'Now we drink!' he roared. 'Let us remember the comrades who fell at our sides and drink to them in the afterlife,' he raised a cup of beer to his lips solemnly. 'But also,' he gave half a smile, 'let us remember our sons and our women too!'

The men cheered again and then they all sat down to their great feast, not caring for the hot sun that made it unwise to drink strong beer before the evening. Soon they were roaring their songs of battle and of victory as the beer took hold.

Later that afternoon, when the soldiers had feasted until they could eat no more, the kindly woman of Siamun finally brought the two prisoners some food where they sat under the shade of a tree.

'Thank you,' Korkamani said in the Kemet tongue, as she set the bowls of stewed beans down.

'I can't sit by and see a young boy starve,' she said gently.

'And I can't feed him without feeding you as well.'

Korkamani bowed his head in thanks at this kindness.

'What is your name?' she asked.

'I am called Korkamani, lady.'

'Does he also speak my tongue?' the woman asked, looking to the boy.

'A little,' Korkamani nodded. 'He learns it well.'

The woman smiled at Talakh. In truth she was the first woman that he had spoken with for many weeks. He looked into her eyes and saw a kindness there. Siamun's woman smiled again, showing teeth that were as worn as her sun-creased face.

'What is your name, boy?' she asked.

'I am Talakhonsu, lady,' he answered respectfully.

'You are named for the moon god?' she said, turning to Korkamani with a puzzled look.

'Yes, so the priests said he should be named. He was brought up in the service of Amun,' Korkamani said quietly.

'As we all are,' she held her hands out, palms to the sky in respect for great Amun. Then a sudden look of fear crossed the face of Siamun's woman.

'His name...' she said. 'He was to be a priest then?'

'I cannot say,' Korkamani replied.

'I am called Naphren,' the woman said hurriedly. 'And though I can never be a friend to you, still for the sake of the boy I would not wish to be your enemy.'

Korkamani looked for deceit in her dark eyes, but saw none there. 'I thank you again for your kindness, lady Naphren,' he said bowing his head a little.

'It would be best not to mention the boy's past,' Naphren whispered. 'If you know our tongue and our ways, then perhaps you know that the priests of Waset have no love for your Amun of Napata. They call your people false believers in Amun.'

'I think it may already be too late for that. Your lord Khaemwaset is a wicked man. A murderer,' he spat in the dust, 'but why he chose to have me and the boy brought here, I cannot guess.'

They both looked at Talakh, but he had caught only a little of their quickly whispered words.

Just then Siamun called out to his wife.

'Naphren! You neglect our guests,' his harsh voice croaked.

'I must go,' Naphren whispered, a look of pain on her aged face. 'Do not fear, I will say nothing of this. I will bring you some fresh water when I can.'

Korkamani watched her go, wondering if he should have said anything at all to her. But as he later told Talakh, it was his business as a spy for the Napatan king to know when he could trust someone and when he could not. He and Talakh had not a single friend in this foreign land and he had seen only gentleness in Naphren's eyes. Perhaps Talakh reminded her of a lost son, but whatever the reason, her kindness was as welcome as the food she had brought them.

That evening the men of Broken Nose all slept like hogs, for the food, the beer and the sun had done their work well on the soldiers' worn out bodies. But Broken Nose had held back whilst the others drank and, his wig now abandoned somewhere, he came over to where his Napatan prisoners lay, listless with tiredness under the small tree to which they were tethered like goats. Korkamani saw him approach, his half opened eyes now suddenly alert as Broken Nose drew a small dagger from his belt.

'What do you want?' he said warily.

'The boy is to come with me,' Broken Nose answered gruffly, cutting the bonds that bound Talakh to the tree.

'Then I must come too,' said Korkamani firmly, struggling against his bonds to get to his feet as Talakh woke from his stupor.

'My master has no wish to see you, slave,' growled Broken Nose, his voice as sharp as the blade he now brought close to Korkamani's throat. 'You should be grateful for that.'

'You are a brave man when you have a knife in your hand and your enemy is unarmed and bound to a tree!' Korkamani spat, ignoring the blade at his throat as he looked Broken

Nose squarely in the eye.

The eyes of Broken Nose narrowed with rage as Talakh looked on in horror, and in that moment he knew that Korkamani's life hung in the balance, at the mercy of a merciless man.

'Stop! Don't harm him,' the boy pleaded. 'I will go with you.'

Now the angry gaze of Broken Nose turned on Talakh, fixing him with a look that turned his blood cold, though he did not flinch and instead held the warrior's gaze as Korkamani had done. Broken Nose was taken aback by this, and the fat man shook his head as the malice disappeared from his face like the morning mist on the river.

'You are a brave one, boy,' he said grimly. 'Now listen here,' he turned to Korkamani. 'No doubt my word is worthless to you, but I swear an oath that I will do nothing to harm him.'

'Your word is not worthless to me,' Korkamani said bluntly. 'But what about your master? What does he want with the boy?'

'I cannot answer for him.'

'Then I swear an oath too, that if the boy is harmed I will kill your master and then I will seek my vengeance on you, in the next life if not in this one.'

Broken Nose, unable to contain his temper any longer, dealt Korkamani a heavy blow in the stomach with his fist and the Napatan fell back winded in the dust. No more words came from his mouth as he struggled for air.

'Come boy,' Broken Nose spat in the dust at Korkamani's feet. 'We have kept Lord Khaemwaset waiting long enough!'

When they left the farm of Siamun in the gathering gloom, Broken Nose was wearing his wig again and Talakh consoled himself with the thought that this made him look very silly as it sat lopsided on his great, wide head. Somehow this helped him keep up his spirits in spite of having seen Korkamani so abused by the big man. The Kemet war chief and the Napatan boy said nothing to each other as they passed along by other farms until they came to the edge of the great city itself. Ahead of them a high, white wall ran off into the gloom, its end out of sight in the darkness.

'What is this place?' Talakh found himself mumbling aloud.

'Look in wonder, boy,' Broken Nose said proudly. 'This is the temple of Mut. Mighty Amun himself comes to this place every year in great festival, to hold court and be joined with his wife so the priests say.'

Though he understood the meaning of the warrior's words, Talakh said nothing, for how could Amun be here, when all knew that he watched the affairs of men from atop his mountain throne at Napata? There could not be two separate Amun's, he told himself. Either they were one and the same, or the Amun of Waset must be a false god created by the cunning priests for their own ends. Surely the true god would have his revenge on them in the end for that insult?

The two walked on further into the sacred heart of Waset until the great temple wall turned a corner. Here they left it behind, crossing a long, straight road paved in stones that were worn and uneven with great age. As they walked they passed a dark shape on one side. Lying forlornly on its side in the dust was a great beast, sleeping in stone. Talakh thought this one might be the wolf beast of the desert, the fearsome devourer of men called lion, though its head was broken off so he could not be sure.

'This is the procession way of the priests,' Broken Nose said as they walked down the road. 'There are many great temples here in Waset, and across the river in the city of the dead too. One is named for the son of Amun and Mut, after whom you are called.'

'I would like to see that,' Talakh found the words leaving his mouth.

'Hah! Well you may wish boy.'

Talakh ignored the fat man's harsh words as he looked down the wide procession way stretching off out of sight ahead of them. A thin crescent moon hung low in the sky to the west, and though it cast little enough light, still Talakh

111

could make out the dim shapes of vast buildings all around them. The presence of the gods hung heavy in the night air.

'This way,' Broken Nose said gruffly, pushing the boy from the paved stone of the road.

Now the two walked past a guard at the torch lit gate of a walled enclosure filled with the dark shapes of trees. Here the path was also made of stone slabs, but these were smooth and flat, their edges meeting so neatly there was hardly space for a blade of grass between them. At the end of the path a huge, wide house of a ghostly white loomed out from the darkness.

'The palace of Lord Khaemwaset,' Broken Nose said with a certain pride as a servant came running out of the open hall that marked the entrance. The fat man said something to the servant that Talakh did not catch and then turned back to him again.

'Stay here with this man until you are sent for,' he grunted.

Talakh watched as the big man strode off, straightening his wig as he went, until he disappeared into the hall. He looked up at the servant who had been left to watch him. This one was a man in his middle years, who hid his bad teeth behind his hand when he yawned, which he did often. For a moment, Talakh thought about running away. He was sure he could outpace the old servant. But how to find Korkamani? He was not sure if he could find his way back to Siamun's farm in the darkness and even if he did, how would he free him from the soldiers?

No, Talakh saw straight away that such an attempt would only fail. His fate rested in the hands of great Amun, whose winds carry men they know not where. His thoughts were dark with hate for evil Khaemwaset who had brought him and Korkamani to this place and he spat on the ground at that thought, as Korkamani might have done if he had been there. The servant glared at Talakh, and raised his arm, about to strike the boy for his insolence.

Just then another appeared. By her middle years and her bearing she was the keeper of the household of Khaemwaset. The servant dropped his arm under her glare.

'Come with me,' she ordered the boy sternly.

Talakh obeyed, following her as she walked briskly through the hall and into an open courtyard, lit by torches that flared bright against the white walls. A square pool of water in the centre calmly reflected the flickering lights as the woman led him past small trees and carved stone seats. This was a scene of such impossible beauty that Talakh thought it all the more strange that one so harsh and evil could live there. They came to two great wooden doors, guarded on each side by lean warriors armed with sword and spear, who stood so still they might easily have been carved from wood. As they approached, the doors opened as if by some strange magic, though Talakh saw as he passed through that a serving girl stood behind each of them to draw them open.

In the lamp lit gloom within, Talakh found himself in the gilded lair of Khaemwaset. The evil one sat on a golden throne, raised up on a stepped platform so that, though seated, he would always look down on those of his court, whether they stood or not.

On rugs and cushions to his left and right many beautiful girls lounged, clothed in white and gold. Their light skin was revealed at their waists and shoulders and their eyes, circled with black, all fixed on him like sinuous cats watching a mouse they might eat. Yet, though still a boy, Talakh was struck by their loveliness all the same and he felt as if he was floating in some awful dream. His eyes returned to the figure on the golden throne and he remembered where he was and who had brought him there. Khaemwaset, the man responsible for the sacking of Napata. The man who had caused the murder of both his mother and old Prainke.

The evil one wore a long wig now, crowned with a circlet of gold that shone in the lamplight, and his muscled chest was partly covered with a white robe, but there was no mistaking him. No mistaking the malevolence in those eyes that shone like black jewels in the gloom. Behind and to one side stood the bulky figure of Broken Nose.

'Bring the Kush brat forward,' the evil one said, beckoning with a gesture of a hand that was weighted down with gold rings and bracelets.

The keeper of the household reached for Talakh's hand, but he stepped forward of his own will, rather than be led to Khaemwaset's feet. Perhaps it was bravery, perhaps stubbornness, but Talakh told himself that he would not show fear whatever happened, and he held Khaemwaset's eye as he slowly walked toward the evil one.

'Hah!' Khaemwaset laughed, his deep voice booming around the walls. 'It seems we have a Kush warrior in our midst. See how he stares like a trapped rat? See how he starts to cry? And still he is braver than his miserable kinsmen were!'

Broken Nose shifted uncomfortably on his feet, for to bully children for entertainment was not his way, yet Talakh did not cry. Instead he stared on at Khaemwaset, even though his head told him that this was not wise and that he should look only at his feet.

Khaemwaset eased himself back into his throne, and a benign smile came over his face. A smile that said, I am powerful and you are nothing. I am lord here and all will bow down before me, even as they bow down to the gods. Talakh had seen this smile before. It was the same smile worn by the great stone face of Rameses carved into the rock at his mighty temple in the Nubian sands. The evil one wore it well.

For a few moments more, the two were bound in a battle of wills, the boy refusing to look away, and the noble looking mildly amused by his insolence. Then something suddenly snapped in Khaemwaset and he leapt down from his chair as a hawk swoops on its prey, slapping Talakh so hard about the face that the boy was unconscious before he hit the floor. And that is all that Talakh remembered of his second meeting with Khaemwaset.

When at last he opened his eyes to the morning light, Talakhonsu saw the housekeeper of the evil one kneeling next to him, her brow furrowed. His head was aching, filled with the sound of buzzing bees and when he put his hand to his face, it was bruised and tender.

'Ach!' the cry came from his lips before he could stop it.

'Come, you must eat something,' the woman said to him, a small kindness in her voice. 'The day will be long for you I think.'

The memory came to Talakh now of where he was and the danger he must still be in. He sat up and saw that he had been dressed in a fine kilt of pure white, but his head felt strangely bare. True enough, as well as changing his clothes whilst he slept, someone had also shaved his scalp close again, so that only his side lock of hair remained. That too had been tended to, straightened with hot irons and oil it seemed, and then plaited so that it looked and felt no longer like his own as he held it before his eyes.

'You are to be taken to the great temple this morning, so you must try to eat something,' the woman said, though this meant little to him in his confused state.

With that she left him alone in the small, cool room. Next to the thick mat of rushes on which he had been lying was a flat loaf with some cooked fish on top of it and next to that a cup of water. Hungry as he was it was a slow and painful breakfast for Talakh, for his jaw and cheek bone ached from the heavy blow that Khaemwaset had dealt him.

When the woman returned some time later, the morning sun had already sailed high into the sky. Now he was taken by the servant with the bad teeth and another, out of the house of the evil one and into the city itself, which was alive with a throng of many people. Talakh's head ached dizzily under the hot sun as he walked, but even so he could not help but be astonished at what he saw.

To the right, back along the way was the great temple that Broken Nose had led him past the previous night. A gateway was let into high, steeply sloping walls that were etched with the striding outlines of giant warriors, painted in many colours so that they looked alive. To Talakh's eyes it seemed as though they might spring from the rock at any moment and come running down the way toward him wielding their spears and clubs.

Even more awe inspiring were the two giants in stone, seated on their thrones either side of the gateway. The long, tapering crowns of kingship were carved atop their heads and flanking them were two impossibly tall stones that tapered to fine points like needles. All were carved with a great many strange symbols.

'The halls of the gods,' Talakh whispered to himself, hardly able to believe his aching eyes, but the servants would not let him rest and roughly pushed him onward away from the great temple, along the endless way of the processions.

'I thought I was to be taken to the great temple?' he found himself asking, though in truth he expected no reply.

The servant with the bad teeth giggled behind his hand.

'Fool!' the other servant said harshly. 'Have you no eyes boy? The great temple is over there.'

Talakh looked ahead to where the man's finger pointed. There, far off in the shimmering heat of the day stood a yet more magnificent temple, so large that it stretched from one side of his view almost to the other.

'The hand of Amun...' Talakh whispered, for surely only through the great god could the glory of these twin temples of Waset have been accomplished.

As they walked on it seemed that the far temple grew no nearer at first. Its walls were spread so wide and it was so vast that it was akin to walking toward a distant hill, only to find that it was much farther away than it at first appeared. Talakh peered intently into the haze, forgetting now the pain in his head, forgetting even the danger he was in, as he picked up his pace so that the dawdling servants had to walk faster than they would have liked.

'See how he hurries off to his fate?' the servant with the bad teeth said behind his hand.

But the boy priest hardly heard him. It was as if some great force pulled him toward that temple, the voice of Amun silently calling his servant to come to him.

At that moment, Talakh knew in his heart that the Amun of his people, Amun of Napata, was here in Waset too. Whatever the priests might say, he was suddenly sure that there was only one Amun, though his people were spread far and wide along the Great River, all the way from Napata to

Kemet and perhaps even beyond that.

Korkamani had spent a long and sleepless night, though he was bedded down comfortably enough in some straw by kindly Naphren, the wife of Siamun. Most of the soldiers had gone now, back to their villages to see their wives while they waited on the call of Broken Nose. Only Meketra and a few others remained at the farm, and they paid the Napatan little heed, for they knew well enough that he would not flee without Talakhonsu.

When the sun rose, all the Napatan could do was to sit under the small tree in the yard and wait for news of the boy. So the day wore on, bringing visitors to the farm, each one raising Korkamani's hopes that Talakh might have returned.

Time passed and anger burned in him as he thought about what he might do if the boy was harmed or, Amun forbid it, if he was dead. Korkamani pictured himself escaping and seeking out the house of Khaemwaset, for all in this great city of Waset must surely know of him. He would find the evil one and throttle the life out of him with his bare hands if need be. The treacherous snake deserved nothing less than that for all he had done. Korkamani asked Amun for a blessing that the boy might yet live, making a meagre offering of some spilt water and a crust of bread to the great god, that Talakh would be returned to him unharmed. The day passed ever slowly and even when the sun started to sink back down toward the horizon, still there was no news.

Just as Korkamani thought he could bear the strain no more, he heard the sound of someone approaching and looked up to see Talakh at last, walking at the side of Broken Nose. Korkamani struggled to his feet, but his legs felt weak and for a moment he thought he might be knocked over as the boy ran into his embrace. A wide smile crossed Talakh's face as best as it could, for one of his cheeks was swollen and he had a bruised eye that had almost closed up. Korkamani's joy turned to a blind rage.

'This is your doing, oath breaker!' he spat at Broken Nose.

'No Korkamani!' the boy cried. 'It wasn't him, it was

Khaemwaset who hit me.'

'I would not harm this boy!' Broken Nose said angrily.

'And that stopped you doing your master's bidding when you put Napata to the torch?' Korkamani snarled.

The Kemet war chief shook with rage, but in words alone he had no answer to this truth.

'I am thirsty,' Talakh said, trying to halt the angry exchange between the two men. 'Is there some water, Korkamani?'

Korkamani looked into the eyes of Talakhonsu and the rage in his eyes faded as he drew the boy close and hugged him as best he could with his bound hands.

'Siamun's woman will bring you water,' Broken Nose said sullenly as he stomped off to talk to his remaining men.

Talakhonsu breathed a sigh of relief. He had saved his protector Korkamani from a confrontation with the big man that would have surely cost him a severe beating, perhaps even his life. He sat down with Korkamani in the shade of the small tree as Siamun's wife Naphren brought them a small jug of fresh water, and both of them again offered their thanks to great Amun for not forsaking them. Now Talakh spoke of his audience with the evil one the previous evening and how Khaemwaset had struck him down.

'But this morning, they fed me and took me to the great temple,' the boy continued. 'We entered through a huge gateway, past some temple guards who asked the servants where they were taking me,' Talakh said, his voice full of excitement. 'And then one of them led us to a great courtyard and beyond that a hall filled with many columns of stone, all carved with animals and other strange things.'

'Those symbols are what the Kemet scribes use to record their stories,' Korkamani nodded. 'I have seen the priests in our own lands read such things too, though I think perhaps they guess at the meaning much of the time. What happened then?'

'I saw the evil one again, sitting on a chair in the shade,' Talakh continued. 'He was dressed like a king, with gold bands about his arms and his neck, and his eyes were painted in black circles like the Kemet women. Then a man appeared with his servants, the chief priest of the temple I think. He was dressed even more richly than Khaemwaset.'

'And then?' asked Korkamani, eager to know more of what had passed.

'I could not make out all of their words. At first they both smiled and greeted each other like old friends, but then Khaemwaset pointed to me and after this the priest grew angry and the two started to argue.'

'And then?'

'The priest turned his back on Khaemwaset and walked away. The evil one was furious and he shouted oaths and curses after him. The guard came back then and led us away. I felt sure that I would die, but Broken Nose appeared as we left the temple and after a few words with his master, he told the two servants to take me back to Khaemwaset's house.'

'And then you were brought here?'

'Yes, after the housekeeper of Khaemwaset had given me some more bread, Broken Nose came and brought me back here.'

Korkamani looked very puzzled by all of this.

'That is all?'

'No, not all. When we were walking back here I asked Broken Nose why they had taken me to the temple. He said there were many smaller shrines within the walls of the great temple itself, and it was to one of these that I had been taken, the one after whom I am named.'

'They took you to see the high priest of Khonsu?' Korkamani said a furrow between his eyes.

'Yes, I think so. Broken Nose said that Khaemwaset had offered me to the temple as a token of his allegiance with the high priest.' the boy continued. 'But the priest did not want me. Now we are both to be set to work in the fields, Broken Nose says.'

'That is all he told you? Hmm...'

Korkamani grew quiet now as he thought of what these things might mean, the furrows on his forehead grew deeper until at last he spoke.

'So,' he said, thinking aloud, 'Khaemwaset seeks to strengthen his position in Waset. The priests have power over the people, so Khaemwaset tries to ingratiate himself with them.'

'The Persians!' Talakh said suddenly, as those words leapt into his mind. 'He fears the return of the Persians.'

'Yes boy,' Korkamani beamed, proudly. 'You have a quick mind Talakh. As you saw when we encountered the men of the high priest at Syene, the evil one is not the only lord whose power has increased since the rebellion against the Persian king. They all want power and wealth, but Khaemwaset, he would be like the Pharaohs of old and that will come to nought when the new Persian king sets his eye on reclaiming Kemet. Khaemwaset needs strong allies. He knows that only then will he have any chance.'

'But still the Persian army will defeat the Kemet lords, will it not?' Talakh asked.

'Yes Talakh. When they come, as they surely will, the Persians will cover the sands from horizon to horizon and the soldiers of Kemet will be swept aside like so many flies. If Khaemwaset stands and fights, then his fate will be as good as sealed. We can pray to Amun for that day to come and for it to come soon.'

For nine new moons Korkamani and Talakhonsu were forced to work the lands of Broken Nose under the ever watchful eye of Siamun the overseer, yet at least they were no longer bound. At first the work was hard for the boy, but his strength slowly grew, as in truth none of the workers on Siamun's farm ever went hungry. Talakhonsu had special reason to give thanks to kindly Naphren, who often gave him a piece of fresh bread or a small cake.

As well as the heavy work of tilling the fields, raising water and harvesting the crops, there were also the waterways to be kept clear. These had been dug by men in times past to bring the Great River out into the sun baked fields so that the crops could be easily watered, but often they became choked with weeds.

One morning, Korkamani and Talakh were told to join a party of men from neighbouring farms who had been drawn together to clear a long stretch of one of the main waterways that was overgrown. The men were up to their waists in the cooling water when a sudden cry of terror pierced the air behind them. Talakh looked behind him and saw to his horror that the jagged jaws of a large khamsa had seized the leg of one of the men and were thrashing him through the water, left and right, as the beast sought to tear him limb from limb.

'Out of the water!' Korkamani shouted, pushing Talakh toward the bank. 'Quickly now!'

Talakh had already seen what the lizard beast could do to a man, and he quickly scrambled up the steep bank.

With a glance to make sure the boy was safe, Korkamani raced off to pick up a sharp digging pick which lay on the bank and jumped back into the reddening water. The beast's tail narrowly missed him as it thrashed back and forth, and it was well that it did, for the jagged scales that covered it could cleave a man's flesh to the bone. Korkamani stumbled and for a moment sank up to his chest, but then in a great leap, he rose up out of the water and swung the point of the heavy pick down so that it smashed into the side of the raging khamsa.

Now, the lizard beast is well armoured with bony scales that can deflect the sharpest spear, but Korkamani struck him just behind a leg and there the pick drove in and stuck fast. The monstrous creature opened its great jaws as if it might bellow with pain, but no sound came out except for the screams of the man as he fell bleeding from its long jaws.

'Korkamani!' Talakh cried, as the beast thrashed itself around to try to get at its attacker.

But Korkamani was quick and he was already astride the crocodile's back, working the head of the pick around with all of his strength to open the wound still further. The other men were finally stung into action and dragged the crocodile's victim out of the river, while Talakh stood on the riverbank, throwing stones which bounced harmlessly off the beast's head as it tried to roll itself upside down to throw off its attacker.

Yet Korkamani was not done with the creature yet and with all of his strength, he pulled out the pick in a great gout of blood that turned the churning water redder still. The fight was over now and the khamsa's thrashing grew weaker until finally it slumped down into the water, the last of its life blood draining from its scaly body.

When Korkamani emerged from the river, his dark skin dripped with mud and blood, some of it his own. The lizard beast had dealt him many deep cuts with scale and claw, and it was all he could do to fall exhausted to his knees.

'Is he alive?' he gasped from between breaths.

Talakh looked toward the body lying on the bank surrounded by his grieving kinsmen, and shook his head.

'Thank Amun you are safe,' Korkamani said, catching his breath. 'The Khamsa could have taken any one of us.'

And he was right, for the cunning khamsa could disguise itself as a sunken log and easily take its victims by surprise in that way.

One by one, the grieving kinsmen came to Korkamani as he washed his wounds and gave him their thanks for trying to save their brother. From that point on all of the workers looked on the two Napatans as they would their own. When they had borne away the man's tattered body, singing their songs of grief as they went, Korkamani summoned his strength again as best he could and organised those men who remained to fetch a cart so that the lizard beast's carcass could be carried back to the farm of Siamun. Korkamani said that it should not be left to rot where it was and that its scaly hide was of value, but Talakh could see that the main reason for claiming the beast was to again show Broken Nose who he was. For though Korkamani contented himself to be a slave for the sake of Talakh, he was nonetheless a brave and proud man.

When the men finally dragged the lizard beast from the oxen cart into the slaughter yard where Siamun killed his livestock, the routines of the farm were thrown into uproar as Siamun was called back from the fields by one of his servants.

'What do you mean by bringing such a thing here?' Siamun demanded. 'You will offend the gods.'

'It killed one of your neighbour's men, so I killed it,' Korkamani said bluntly.'

'Well it can't stay there!' Siamun's harsh voice croaked. 'The dogs will come, and the flies. And the vultures.'

'We will skin it and roast its meat,' Korkamani answered coldly. 'And then we can all feast on it in return for the life it took.'

Siamun looked horrified. 'But it ate him.'

'No, the poor man bled to death, just as the khamsa has. In my land this is our way. We take the flesh of the scaly one into ourselves and this serves as a warning to others of its kind.'

Talakh had not heard of this himself, but the other men looked at each other and muttered their agreement to this new way just the same.

'It is not my way here!' Siamun protested again.

It seemed that there would be a stalemate now between the two. For Korkamani would not back down to a lesser man, while Siamun, though no fighter, was compelled by his position as the overseer of the farm not to lose face either.

'Korkamani has done well,' the familiar voice of Meketra called across the yard. 'Our master will be pleased, as you should be Siamun,' he said, fixing his eyes on the overseer. 'The khamsa had a taste for the flesh of men, and the lands of our master are well rid of it.'

For a moment Siamun looked as if he might pick an argument with the tall warrior. But only for a moment, for Meketra was now the right hand man of Broken Nose and every man in the city of Waset knew that his sinewy muscles could speak of great violence if he was crossed.

'As you say, Meketra,' he said sullenly. 'The master will be pleased.'

'When the head is severed, you should take it into the fields Korkamani,' Meketra grinned. 'The ants will soon pick it clean and the sun will bleach the skull white. Then it can be sold along with the hide, if that is our master's wish.'

To kill the lizard beast was no easy task, but to butcher it was almost as hard in the heat of the day, for its hide was like armour and the knife that Naphren had lent them for the purpose was too small and light for the task of separating sinew, bone and hide from such an animal as this. Still when all was at last done, kindly Naphren gave Talakh some clean water and strips of cloth to bind the worst of Korkamani's wounds and so keep at bay the many flies that had gathered. That night the men of Siamun and some of those of the surrounding farms made a great feast of the lizard beast's flesh, roasting the white meat wrapped in wet leaves over the coals of a fire.

When all had eaten their fill, the two Napatans lay quietly by the fire pit, half dozing as they rested their weary bones.

'Korkamani,' Talakh said at length. 'Were you afraid when you fought the khamsa?'

Korkamani laughed, quietly at first, and then a great hearty laugh that showed his white teeth.

'Afraid?' he said. 'Of course I was afraid boy! Did you not see those teeth, set like daggers in its jaws? Did you not see its evil eye and its thrashing tail? Afraid? Yes, I was afraid!' he grinned, his dark eyes twinkling in the firelight.

'You could have been killed,' Talakh said seriously.

'Yes, but we could not have left that man to be eaten alive. Unfortunately there was no saving him, but if I had not tried his face would have haunted my dreams for the rest of my life.'

'I see that,' Talakh nodded thoughtfully. 'But it happened so quickly... how did you know what you had to do?'

'Ah, that is all part of growing up to be a man. When you truly know yourself, then you will learn to trust your heart at times like this. For if you trust your head when there is danger, you will not think straight. Remember that, Talakh. Mark it well.'

Talakh grew quiet again, hoping that one day he could somehow gain the wisdom of Korkamani.

Much later, when the stars had filled the heavens above with the tiny, flickering torches of the distant gods, the boy priest found an old question bothering him again.

'Korkamani,' he said again.

'Yes lad, what is it?' Korkamani said without opening his eyes.

'When will be the time for our escape?' he asked. 'I am older now and...'

'Yes you are older, but the time is not yet right. For now, we have no choice but to serve Siamun.'

'I hate him,' Talakh spat.

'I have no love for him either, but this land is full of enemies for us Talakh. Better for us to keep with those enemies whose ways we know, rather than chance our luck amongst those we do not.'

Over the next few days, Korkamani's wounds healed quickly, helped he said by eating the flesh of the khamsa that had caused them, and it was true to say that his standing amongst the working folk of the farms increased greatly through his victory over the lizard beast. The wife of the man whom the khamsa had claimed came to Korkamani, even though she was mourning her loss, to thank him for saving her husband's body so that she could send him to the afterlife. Broken Nose too was pleased, for Siamun made a gift to him of the monster's scaly hide, which he had made into plates of war armour to cover his chest and back. Indeed, so tough was the armour that only the sharpest blade would ever pierce it.

Time passed on the farm of Siamun. In the evenings when the day's work was done and the heat had left the setting sun, Korkamani and Talakh would take a net they had woven and cast for small fish in the waterways that ran across the fields. Then they would prepare their supper on the hearth of the small makeshift shelter Siamun had allowed them to build at the edge of the farmyard. Yes, in these times food was plentiful and the two Napatans slowly forgot the weeks of hunger they had suffered during the long journey from their homeland.

Whether the work of the fields was light or heavy, on most evenings the beat of drums and the singing of other farmers called to them from across the fields. There were many nights when the Napatans answered those calls and were welcomed into the simple homes of the labourers and their families, as they sang and danced to remember their ancestors, or the heroes of old. Siamun did nothing to prevent this, for he knew well enough that Korkamani was no dog to be whipped back into line. There was an unspoken truce between them, though neither liked the other. The truth was that Siamun knew Korkamani would not risk Talakh's life by attempting an escape, not until the boy was old enough to fight for himself at any rate.

But still these little freedoms and passing diversions could not change the fact that Korkamani and Talakh were slaves, with all the thankless hard labour that this involved. Their fate remained in the hands of their enemies and the days passed slowly for them as they thought of what they had lost.

One evening, Meketra arrived at the farm of Siamun and sought out the Napatans, as he did from time to time. In truth, although he had become the right hand man of Broken Nose, responsible for maintaining his war band, still he had not forgotten the perils they had faced together, nor the bravery Korkamani had always shown in the face of danger.

'Show me your best throw, Talakh,' he grinned at the boy.

This was something he always did when the two met, for he had tried to pass on to Talakh his own skill with the throwing stick.

Talakh gripped the stick that was tucked into the cloth belt around his kilt and looked around the farmyard for a target. Wandering off amongst the reeds on the far side of the yard was one of the tall, curved beaked fowl that were everywhere in these lands. Yet he could not strike it, as these birds were sacred to the people of Kemet, who saw in them the face and the wisdom of one of their gods. Talakh instead fixed his eyes on a pole that was stuck in the ground on the other side of the yard.

'I will hit that pole,' he said as convincingly as he could. 'I will strike it at my head height.'

Meketra grinned at Korkamani, but said nothing as Talakh weighed the curved stick in his hand, fixing his eye on the pole. He had chosen a difficult target, narrow as it was, and when he drew back his arm and threw with all his might, the stick hit the ground well short of the pole.

Talakh cursed his disappointment under his breath, looking from Korkamani to Meketra with shame in his face.

Meketra smiled kindly.

'You try too hard Talakh,' he said. 'Remember what I told you before. Your strength will come in time, but first you must train your eye. Try again, but this time imagine you are just trying to clip the pole, not strike it hard. Your aim must be high, so that the stick falls from the sky onto the pole. Like this,' he said, taking one of his weighted sticks from his belt and throwing it at the pole in one swift movement.

Talakh watched as the stick gracefully sailed high through the air in an arc that brought it down squarely onto the pole with a clatter.

'As light as a feather?' Korkamani said wryly, but in truth he was just as impressed by the swiftness of the shot as Talakh was.

'Hmm... perhaps the boy will do better?' Meketra grinned as Talakh brought back the two sticks.

Talakh's next throw soared too high and so fell short. Then he found the right distance but the stick went wide. Only on his fourth throw did he finally hit the pole, the stick kissing it as gently as a mother kisses her baby.

'Good!' Meketra said. 'Keep practicing in this way and one day you might even be better than me.'

Talakh nodded, smiling, for he valued Meketra's praise second only to that of Korkamani. Although Meketra was now Broken Nose's man, still he came from the far south of Kemet among the lands of Nubia and this made him different to the people of Waset. In fact in his manners and looks, he could almost have passed for Napatan until he spoke.

But now Meketra seemed to remember himself and the lightness of his mood passed into a frown. 'I must talk with you Korkamani,' he said seriously. 'Alone.'

'Whatever you tell me, I will tell the boy anyway,' Korkamani replied. 'What I know, he knows.'

'Then he must keep what I have to say a secret, at least for a few days, or it will cause trouble for me.'

'I will keep my silence,' Talakhonsu gave his oath.

'As will I,' Korkamani said. You are the friend of my enemy, but you are an honourable man and you have shown the boy many small kindnesses.'

'Your people and mine are not so different Korkamani,' Meketra shrugged. 'Listen then and I will tell you what I know. You will have no doubt heard many false rumours of the new Persian king and his army?'

'Who has not?' Korkamani answered. In the many months they had passed in captivity rarely had a week gone by without some new rumour of an invasion.

'Well they are rumours no longer,' Meketra said coolly. 'The lords of Waset have received word that an advance guard of the Persian army has crossed the Narrow Sea and landed far off to the east on the other side of the desert. My master has taken some of his men to scout ahead and gather information.'

'And yet you remain here...' Korkamani pondered aloud.

'Yes, I remain. I have my orders to gather together my war band and go through the farms to recruit others for the cause of Lord Khaemwaset.'

Korkamani spat in the dust at the mention of the evil one's name. 'And why do you tell us this Meketra?'

'We will fight bravely for Kemet,' Meketra said proudly. 'We will wash the sands red with Persian blood and their bones will bleach white under the eye of the sun god.

'But we cannot win against the Persians,' he said lowering his head. 'The Persians will be too many for us, too many by far. Perhaps you will have your chance then to save yourself and the boy.'

'Perhaps,' nodded Korkamani cautiously.

'Well, you must be ready for whatever comes,' Meketra said, his face now deadly serious. 'That is why I give you this warning. Who knows, tomorrow the whole of Waset may hear of it, but for now I ask you to keep your silence.'

'You have my oath on it,' Korkamani said solemnly. 'And

for what good it may do us, I thank you.'

The smile returned to Meketra's long, narrow face.

'Good luck Napatan,' he said, and then strode off.

Talakh watched him go, wondering if they would ever see the tall warrior again.

The next morning as Korkamani and Talakh weeded the crops, sure enough the fields were alive with more rumours. When the men stopped under the noon sun to eat their bread, there was much talk of the Persian army.

'They say the new Persian king is a giant, twice the height of an ordinary man!' one said.

'Yes and I have heard that his archers can shoot arrows as long as a spear, twice as far as our archers can!' said another.

Korkamani said nothing, for he had spent his life sifting the grains of truth from wild stories such as these.

'What do you say Korkamani?' one of the older men asked.

'What would you have me say?' Korkamani replied. The Persians are men no different to you or I. There are just more of them, that is all. Besides, provided that they do us no harm I have no quarrel with them. They are not my enemy.'

'And what of us, Korkamani?' another spoke up. 'What will become of us if the Persians defeat our armies and take our lands again?'

Korkamani stood up now and looked around him.

'Where are your lands?' he said coldly. 'You work these fields, but they are not yours. They belong to your masters, do they not? Ask yourself this. Would you spill your own blood for them? Would you spill the blood of your sons?'

The men muttered amongst themselves resentfully, for the truth hurt what pride they owned.

'Perhaps the Persians would be no better than your masters, but they would struggle to be worse than that piece of dung Khaemwaset,' Korkamani cursed, spitting on the ground.

'You would be wise to curb your tongue where our lord is concerned, O Korkamani,' one of the older men said. 'You have much respect amongst us, but our lord has ears everywhere and he is not a man to suffer those who curse his name.'

'When the Persians come, your lord's head will end up on a spear!' Korkamani laughed harshly. 'I for one will look forward to that day.'

Again the men muttered amongst themselves disapprovingly, but no more was said on the matter.

A week later word came that Broken Nose had returned, though by all accounts he had lost some of his men to the Persians whilst others still were wounded. The people of Waset could see this only as a bad omen, and now they prayed to their gods more earnestly than ever for the Persian threat to be thwarted.

Whilst these events unfolded around them, Korkamani and Talakhonsu bided their time, hiding what fish they could dry up a tall palm tree. Provisions against the hard times that were sure to follow their planned escape.

Chapter 8

The Unstoppable Tide

Early one morning when the eye of the great sun god was still just creeping over the horizon, Korkamani and Talakh were walking out to the fields with the other men when they heard a loud clamour of voices from Siamun's farm.

'Listen,' Korkamani said quietly, holding up his hand as he stopped and turned around.

'What is it?' Talakh asked.

'I don't know, but we will go back a way to see if anyone comes along the road.'

'Siamun will be annoyed if he doesn't find us in the fields when he comes around,' Talakh said mischievously.

'Hah!' said Korkamani, rising to the bait like fish rise for stale bread. 'Siamun can moan as much as he likes, if he dares! Come, we'll go back and see what the noise is.'

And so they walked the short path back in the cool early morning light, Talakh's thoughts dwelling on how beautiful this foreign land was at this time of day, when the air was still and the tall palm trees stood dark against the lightening sky. He had grown used to his life here with Korkamani and though the work was at times hard, still there was food and friendship enough. Even his anger had gradually faded a little these last months as he slowly became a carefree boy again.

When the two of them arrived back at the farm of Siamun, the yard was in a disorganised panic. Siamun stood in the centre of it all pointing this way and that, trying to make himself heard above the crying of his children and the shouting of the servants of his household, not to mention his wife. No-one took much notice of Siamun these days and the man was at the edge of his wits. Korkamani ignored him too and walked straight to Naphren, Siamun's wife.

'Oh, Korkamani,' she said with tears in her eyes, 'what will become of us all?'

'The Persians are coming then at last?' Korkamani guessed.

'Yes, this is what they say. The household of our master fled last night in fear of their wrath and now our master's lady and his son have come to us asking for our protection. They hide in the house but they cannot stay here, for all will know that our master fights for Khaemwaset. What will we do?' she asked, as the tears welled in her kind eyes.

'Korkamani!' Siamun shouted angrily, his short whip in his hand. 'Get back to the fields, this is no business of yours!'

'Try using that whip on me, and I'll wrap it around your scrawny neck, Siamun,' Korkamani said with a sure threat in his calm voice.

'No, please,' Naphren pleaded. 'You must not fight! We are all in danger if the Persians come.'

Siamun took his eyes from Korkamani and stared at the ground, his anger giving way to despair.

'Yes, danger comes with the Persians,' Korkamani said turning to her. 'But you are wrong lady, it is not a danger for all. The lords, the landowners, and the rich, they should fear the most. These Persians ruled the people of Kemet with an easy hand before. They let you keep your gods and your customs, granting you many favours. But their new king will not forget nor forgive those who rose against his father.'

'Then what should we do?' Siamun croaked sullenly.

'Not this,' Korkamani said coldly, looking on as the belongings of Siamun's household were loaded onto a cart. 'How far do you expect to get, Siamun? Where will you run? The Persian armies will reach all the way to the borders of my own lands, perhaps even beyond them.

'No,' Korkamani said, turning to Naphren again. 'You would do better to stay here and dig a cache in a secret place to hide only your most valuable things.'

'My children are what I treasure most,' Naphren said with tears in her eyes. 'If the gods will it that everything else must be taken away, I will be content as long as I still have them and my husband.'

'But the Persians will know that our master fights for Lord

Khaemwaset!' Siamun protested again. 'They will not leave us in peace, they will kill us all!'

'You must forsake Broken Nose then, and swear obedience to whoever is given rule here,' Korkamani said firmly. 'The truth will seem to them that you are what you are – nothing more than a simple overseer of a farm.'

Siamun bowed his head in humiliation at that last insult.

'He is right, husband,' Naphren said sadly. 'We must take our chances and stand with those who have served us faithfully these many years.

'But what of the master's wife and son?' she turned to Korkamani. 'They will be in great danger here.'

'I will speak with them,' Korkamani said, and strode off to the house of Siamun with Talakh following at his side.

Within, they found the wife of Broken Nose sitting on a low wooden chair, her young son close by her, hugging her legs in the gloom. With her rich gown and long, braided wig framing her fine features, she looked the part of a lady. Talakh wondered how she had come to marry such a brute as Broken Nose.

'Who are you?' she demanded, her voice brittle as she drew the boy closer still.

'You do not need to fear us,' Korkamani held up his hand. 'We... we work the land for Siamun and his master, your husband,' he said calmly.

'What do you want?' the lady asked suspiciously, eyeing Korkamani up and down.

It was true that compared to Siamun and his household the two Napatans were roughly dressed, and Korkamani's grey-flecked beard was wild and bushy, giving him the look of a lawless man.

'My name is Korkamani. It seems to me that you are in need of help.'

'Why should I trust you?' the lady said, piteously close to tears as worry for her son ate away at her pride.

Korkamani thought for a moment, whilst he chose his words.

'Your husband is no friend of mine,' he said bluntly. 'But

still there is respect between us, and so you and your son are not my enemies. I think since danger threatens, your husband would trust me to know what to do.'

'Then tell me,' she cried, 'for I do not trust to the judgment of Siamun.'

Korkamani gave a wry smile at that. He had never trusted Siamun's judgement in anything either.

'My name is Sati,' she continued. 'I come here only because I have not heard from my husband and I do not know where else to go. There is no safety for me in my own house, now that my servants have fled and a mob roams the city.'

'Then what about Khaemwaset?' Korkamani said, doing his best to murder that name with his tongue. 'Is he not your husband's master? Does he not have a duty to shelter you?'

'I...' she started, hanging her head low. 'I do not...'

'You don't trust him either,' Korkamani nodded, finishing the words she could not. 'You are very wise in this lady, for he is evil itself.'

'Tell me, have you heard any word of my husband?' the lady Sati asked, her voice straining with the weight of her heavy heart.

'I have not seen him for many weeks now. Your husband will be off to the east doing Khaemwaset's bidding. As you well know, he has given that piece of dung his oath, so he has no freedom to be able to defend you.'

Sati bowed her head sorrowfully. 'It seems you know my husband well,' she sighed.

'Yes, we know him, though we have every reason to regret it.'

The wife of Broken Nose looked anxious again as she dwelt on Korkamani's last words.

'This is your son?' she said at last, trying to summon a smile for Talakh.

Korkamani looked at the boy and Talakh looked back up to him, to see his tall protector's dark eyes glinting in the dim light.

'Yes...' Korkamani said. 'His mother and father have passed to the other place. Now, I am glad to call him my son, for he is all that I have in the world.'

Now the tears started to burn in Talakh's own eyes, but he set his teeth and fought them back.

The lady Sati smiled back again, a sad smile, for she didn't know what to say.

'Where are you from?' Korkamani said finally, breaking the silence. 'That is, where does your family live?'

'I have two sisters, that is all,' she said distantly. 'They live a day's walk away to the south. They married two brothers, and together their families farm a strip of good land besides the Great River.'

'And you trust them? You trust their husbands?'

Sati thought about this, but only for a moment.

'Yes, they are honest men, both of them.'

'Then you must leave behind your fine robes, and hide your gold and jewels in a hole in the ground,' Korkamani said, guessing at what was in the small, ornamented chest that sat between the woman's feet.

'Hide them at the foot of a tree, well away from the river, that is the best place. If you have time, it is best to hide them in two or three different places, for then all will not be lost if one of your caches is discovered.'

'Thank you for your advice,' the woman replied. 'I will do as you say. But would you help me?'

'No, you must ask no-one for help in this task, except your own son there. Trust no-one else,' Korkamani said firmly. 'Do it tonight under cover of darkness. Take a dagger with you and make sure you are not followed. Then in the morning, you must take the road south to your sisters.'

'Would you come with me then?' she pleaded. 'For then we might pass for a family, and no-one would trouble us.'

'What makes you think I will be heading south?' Korkamani said bluntly, though Talakh could tell he did not mean to be so harsh.

'My husband is Siamun's master,' Sati said, her voice a little calmer now as she remembered who she was. 'I could ask this of you, as you are Siamun's man.'

'I may till his fields, but I am not his man,' Korkamani said through gritted teeth.

'Then perhaps you have your own reasons to leave this place?'

'Perhaps I do. I will think on what you have said,' Korkamani replied. 'But only if you give me your word that you will mention none of this to Siamun or anyone else.'

Sati thought for a moment weighing up in her mind where the greater danger lay for her and her son. She looked at Korkamani and then at Talakh with eyes that seemed to see deep into his heart.

'You have my word on this,' she said, standing up. 'I will take your advice and leave this place tonight, either in your company or alone.'

Korkamani bowed and they left.

'Will we go with them, Korkamani?' Talakh asked when they were outside again.

'I don't know. Perhaps,' said Korkamani quietly. 'For now we will go back to the fields and act as if nothing has changed. But tonight...' he whispered under his breath, 'tonight we will leave this place and return to our own lands, if Amun wills it.'

'What will we do when we get there?' Talakh's thoughts took voice.

Korkamani's face darkened and his eyes narrowed with vengeance and hate.

'When you are safe and returned to the care of the priests,' he said. 'And when I have told our young king of all that happens here, then... then I will return to this place and seek out that dog Khaemwaset. If he still lives I will make him pay a thousand times for what he has done.'

That evening, as the heat of the day diminished and the great orange sun disc hung low in the sky, Korkamani and Talakhonsu returned from the fields to their simple shelter at the farm of Siamun. They were not surprised that there was no bread for them, given the disarray in Siamun's household, and they had to content themselves with some stewed beans and barley from their own cache of food.

'No matter,' said Korkamani. 'We will make our escape from this place in the middle of the night when all but the dogs are asleep.'

'What of the lady Sati?' Talakh asked. 'Will we take her with us?'

'That, I have not yet decided,' Korkamani said, a thoughtful frown creasing his high forehead. 'Just as she is reluctant to trust us, so I hesitate to trust her. Travelling together, we would probably be safer, but also slower. And what if she betrays us?'

'Perhaps Amun will send you a dream, to tell you what to do?' Talakh said hopefully.

'Perhaps. But now, though it is still early we must try to sleep. The night will be long and we will need all of our strength for what is to follow.'

Talakh lay down on the woven reed mats that made for his bed and closed his eyes, listening to the evening songs of the birds and the croak of the frogs. Sleep did not come easy to him that night for his head was full of strange thoughts and dreams of freedom.

It seemed to Talakh that he had hardly been asleep at all, when he suddenly woke up with a start at the sound of Korkamani's voice, low and threatening.

'Harm the boy and I will kill you with my bare hands!' the voice of Korkamani spat.

Talakh opened his eyes, thinking that Korkamani was talking in his sleep, and tried to sit up, but a foot on his chest pinned him down.

'Don't move brat, or I'll skewer you,' a sly voice said.

Talakh felt the cold, sharp point of a spear pressing against his neck and he became very still, for he knew that the blade was poised, ready to end his life at the first excuse.

'Put your hands behind your back, Kush dog,' another voice ordered Korkamani.

'How do I know you won't kill us both?' Korkamani said bitterly.

'If we'd wanted to do that, we could have speared you in your sleep,' the man holding Talakh said.

'Ah, but if you want the boy to die that's all the same to

us,' sneered the other.

'Stop messing about and tie them up,' a third voice said impatiently.

Korkamani let out a great string of curses at the cruelness of their fate, to be bound and taken prisoner again at the last, just as they had planned their escape. But they were outnumbered and so there was nothing to be done but submit to their fate, at least for now. Talakh's wrists were bound tightly behind his back, and then the two prisoners were tied together with a length of cord about their necks and marched from the farm of Siamun, two men at their head and two more at their backs. In the darkness Talakh recognised one of the men as a soldier of Broken Nose who had been with the war chief in the Kemet raid on Napata, though his face was now scarred with a huge slash across one cheek and into his lip. It had not yet healed and where it had been crudely stitched together, the pink flesh below showed bright against the man's dusky skin, even in the dark of the night.

'Korkamani,' Talakh whispered.

'Be strong Talakh,' Korkamani urged the boy grimly as they stumbled on in the dark. 'We are not done yet.'

For two long, thirsty days the Napatans were marched north along the banks of the Great River. Always they were in sight of its cool waters but only twice were they allowed to drink. All the while, the hot sun blazed overhead, searing their heads, for their caps had been left behind. These things alone were not enough for their captors, who goaded and tormented them, taking great sport from demeaning Korkamani with their insults and spear trips.

Soon the Napatan's knees were red with blood from falling on the rough ground and Talakh's mind kept wandering back to their long, torturous journey into Kemet what seemed so long ago. What had become of their countrymen sold into slavery at Sesibi? And where was Broken Nose? The boy gritted his teeth against the stinging sweat that dripped into the weals around his wrists as he stumbled on.

When darkness fell at last and the searing heat of the sun

gave way to the chill winds of the night, Korkamani and Talakh lay on their sides in the dirt on the riverbank, their arms and legs still tied so that there could be no comfort for them in sleep, though both of them were too weary for words. While their captors laughed, ate and drank, the Napatans once again knew only thirst, hunger and despair, while the blazing stars burned ever bright in the desert sky.

The Kemet warrior Broken Nose, sworn by his oath to serve Khaemwaset, clenched his fists in anger and took a deep breath that swelled his great barrel chest. In his time as a warrior he had known many fights and many battles. Always, even under the rule of the Persians, Kemet's enemies had been a thorn in her side. There were the tribes who lay off in the desert lands to the west, to the east and to the south. All different, but all the same in their desire for the spoils of the land of the black earth.

Yes, Broken Nose had fought many times, felt the sticky blood of his enemies run warm down his sword arm as he ran them through, seen the look of agony and surprise on their faces as they fell into the dust. But never in all his time had he felt so ill at ease on the eve of battle.

He looked to his right. There somewhere off in the rabble of nervous, poorly armed men gathered into a makeshift army was Meketra and his war band. It was these men only that Broken Nose trusted, for they had fought together many times, sharing the hardships of battle.

Now he looked to his left across the flank of the other men in Khaemwaset's front line. A few he could pick out, but the rest he did not know. In this part of the line were many mercenaries from foreign lands, men who fought only for the promise of gold. They were driven by their heads, not their hearts. Men not unlike Broken Nose and his own warriors in many ways. But these mercenaries were not men to trust with your life, that much Broken Nose knew from his own past experience where he had seen them desert in droves when the cause was lost.

Yet still, amongst these landless and lawless men there

were some Greeks from the islands of the Middle Sea and beyond. Much as he disliked their arrogance, all the same they were proud warriors, with their polished bronze helmets, heavy shields and long spears. In the main these were men who valued their honour. They would rather die bravely than be branded a coward, though they were wont to bicker amongst themselves just the same.

Then there were the desert peoples from a number of scattered tribes, desperate men displaced from their homelands. These ones were the ancient enemies of his own people, Broken Nose cursed under his breath. They fought for gold and gold alone.

But where were the fighting men of Kemet? Where were the warrior kings, whose images were carved so deep into the temple walls? No, Broken Nose swore again, those days were long in the past. He looked across the rocky plain to where the dark, massed ranks of the Persians waited like a plague of beetles ready to devour the meagre armies of Kemet. There would be no victory here today, only a great slaughter and an even greater humiliation. Today was the day when the half remembered glories of old Kemet would finally be trampled into the dust.

'Lord?' Meketra's voice carried into the warrior's thoughts.

Broken Nose turned his head to find the tall, dark southerner now at his side. Meketra looked the same as he always did, at his ease, sure of himself in the full strength of his youth.

'Today,' Broken Nose said quietly, 'I am not your lord, Meketra. We will fight together as brothers you and I, but when the fight goes against us, and it will, you must look to yourself.'

Meketra's dark eyes narrowed and the slight smile that always waited in his face now left him.

'Commander then,' he said with a small bow of his head. 'You brought me to the great city and I have made my home there. I will fight for you, no matter what. I will fight for Waset and for the honour of Kemet too.'

'I do not doubt it,' Broken Nose said clapping his broad

hand on Meketra's sinewy shoulder. 'But remember what I say Meketra. You are young and there are many things ahead of you. Many times for you to prove yourself. Do not spill your life's blood for nothing today.'

'And you? What about your son? Your wife?'

'Do not ask me of these things,' Broken Nose said sadly, shaking his head. 'I can do nothing but trust to the gods for them. I can think only of the fight ahead.'

'You will fight well, as you always have,' Meketra said boldly. 'I will be at your side today and we will kill many of these Persians who think they can take back our lands so easily!'

With that he held his spear aloft, shaking it at their enemies.

'Well said!' a familiar voice boomed from behind them, though not many others joined it.

'Lord Khaemwaset,' Broken Nose turned to face his master with a respectful bow. For once the Kemet noble was plainly dressed in a simple white kilt, showing off his well muscled chest. A sword in the pattern of the Greeks hung at his waist, and a dagger beside it, but he had no shield.

'I will fight here, amongst my bravest and most loyal men,' the evil one said, looking at Meketra, then at Broken Nose in turn.

Though there was the familiar, handsome arrogance in Khaemwaset's chiselled features, there was also a strange glint of something hiding at the back of those dark eyes of his. Broken Nose had seen that look before. For though men said that his master was the only one of the Waset nobles brave enough to show himself against the might of the Persian army, Broken Nose knew the truth of the man. It was not vain pride alone which drove Khaemwaset to bring his men to this rocky, sun baked plain to do open battle with the Persians. In his delusions of madness Khaemwaset actually thought he could win.

'Tell me my general, when will you be ready to attack these Persian dregs?' Khaemwaset addressed him, as if to confirm his thoughts.

'Lord,' Broken Nose said in a low voice, so that the men would not hear. 'I am no general. There are none here that fit that title. But as I advised you before, we should remain where we are and let the Persians come to us. Our lines are thin, and not wide enough to draw around their flanks. If we charge them, the few men who are not cut down with arrows will be broken by their spearmen. Then their horses will encircle us to attack our rear...'

'You are an old man,' Khaemwaset interrupted him, sudden anger lighting up those distrustful eyes of his, 'Do you no longer have the stomach for a battle, is that it?'

Broken Nose felt his own temper rise and he almost shook with the rage that coursed through his veins.

'Lord,' he said hoarsely, 'no man has ever disputed my courage. We are too few to win, but do not doubt that I will die for your cause.'

'So you are to die? Then you will not die rooted here like an old woman, waiting for them to cut you down!' Khaemwaset said angrily. 'We will attack the Persians and scatter them to the four winds. We will break them and show them for the cowards that they are, that is my command! Would you question my will? Would you break your oath to me?'

Now Broken Nose knew that he was truly trapped.

'I am no oath breaker, Lord Khaemwaset,' he ground out his words as slowly as a stone grinds the corn. 'It will be as you say, though few of us will live to see the setting sun.'

'Yes, it will be as I say!' Khaemwaset spat, ignoring the warning of Broken Nose. 'For I, not you, am the one who will save this land. Through me our people will be free and the glories of Kemet will be restored!'

He shouted this last, so that all standing nearby could hear his rallying cry, and a small cheer went up again from the men.

'When the Kush slaves have been sacrificed to the greatness of Amun, then we will attack,' the evil one said quietly, turning his back on Broken Nose.

'The Napatans?' the war chief said slowly as he saw the

full spite of his master's madness. 'The boy?'

'Yes, the boy,' Khaemwaset turned around. 'Siamun has had enough use out of your little pets. When the sun disc of Ra is at his highest in the sky, then their throats will be cut and their blood will soak the sands in the name of Amun, Mut and Khonsu,' he sneered, the evil light burning fiercely in his dark eyes.

'The boy...' said Meketra quietly after Khaemwaset had turned his back and strode off back to his tent to escape the hot sun.

'Aye, and Korkamani too,' said Broken Nose bitterly. 'There is a brave man, an honourable man, Napatan or not. They do not deserve to die like the slaughtered calf.'

'Then what will you do?'

'I don't know Meketra,' Broken Nose swallowed hard, his voice hollow. 'May the gods keep us from this madness.'

For once, Meketra could see that his war chief doubted himself and now for the first time in his brief time as a warrior, fear crawled low across the back of the young man's mind as he looked out to where the Persian hordes waited. Gritting his teeth, Meketra left Broken Nose to his thoughts and went off to talk with his own men, for if they were to die then they should die with honour and pride in their cause he thought.

How things had changed for Meketra. It had not yet been quite a year since he had left his father's fields, yet now instead of herding goats, here he was gathering his men for a great battle. When he found them again he drew himself up to his full height and did his best to raise their spirits by talking of their bravery. Meketra looked on the sun glinting from their newly sharpened iron spear heads, noting the raised scars and lost fingers amongst his men. These ones knew how to fight when called to do battle and they would know how to die too if need be, with the blood of their enemies on their spears. They would not run. He looked around him, past his own men to those others who waited nervously nearby.

A group of Greek mercenaries stood apart from the fearful rabble, resting on their spears and their oddly shaped shields, most of them wearing their own armour of bronze plates strapped to their shins and forearms. Some wore the shining metal across their chests too. A few of them made offerings to their gods, burning fragrant tree resin while they talked in that slow, strange tongue of theirs. To Meketra's ears they sounded as if they were drunk, and in truth perhaps some of them were, for men will do many things to steady their nerves before battle.

Just then he spied another of his men who he had thought missing, perhaps deserted.

'Inherkau!' Meketra's voice rang out above the din. 'Where have you been? Why do you come so late to the battle?'

'Am I late?' Inherkau said casually, the lurid scar on his face rippling like a snake as he spoke. 'I don't see any Persians amongst you. Perhaps they have all gone home?'

Meketra had never taken to Inherkau, for though he was fearless he was also arrogant and foolhardy. Vicious too, often when there was no need for it. Since Broken Nose had given Meketra charge of these men, only this one had given him any trouble. His war chief had told him right from the start that a band of warriors are like a pack of dogs. If one of them cannot be brought into line, so the rest of them will run wild too. This was good advice that Meketra remembered well.

'There will be Persians enough for all of us when they come,' Meketra said bluntly, looking down on the stocky Inherkau to demean him. 'I ask you again. Where have you been hiding yourself without my leave?'

Now an angry glare came over Inherkau's face and the scar puckered on his face as if it had its own mind.

'I was sent on a mission by Lord Khaemwaset,' he said with hateful eyes.

'And you thought not to tell me?'

'Khaemwaset is our lord, above all others. If he asks me to do his bidding, that is what I will do. He is the one with the gold, after all,' Inherkau smiled sarcastically.

'And what was this mission that was important enough to draw you away from fighting alongside your brothers for your homeland?' Meketra spat out his words into the face of

Inherkau as his temper rose to a boil.

'I brought those two Napatan wretches here from the farm of Siamun,' Inherkau laughed harshly, resting his hand on the head of the war axe that hung from his belt. 'I hear the commander's wife Sati is there too. She's a pretty young thing. When things are finished here perhaps I will go back to Siamun's farm and get to know her better? After all, we all know the fat man won't leave this place alive,' he laughed again, looking around the other men for agreement. 'He will die like a fool for his pride and his oaths, while those of us who have better sense...'

He got no further with his slander as Meketra punched him full in the face with his bony fist.

'Perhaps that will shut your mouth, you worthless piece of dung!' Meketra cursed him.

Inherkau staggered back, but only for an instant. 'You will have to do better than that boy,' he said, drawing his war axe.

The two now circled each other warily as Meketra drew his own throwing sticks, backing off to give himself room. Now, Inherkau had seen Meketra use these weapons before and he knew the heavy, iron-bound weapons could be deadly in an expert hand such as Meketra's. Before Meketra had a chance to throw, Inherkau rushed at him swinging wildly with his axe, but Meketra had guessed Inherkau's move and deftly stepped around the rampaging warrior's swinging blow, bringing one of the heavy sticks down to land a glancing strike of his own on the other's spine. Inherkau grunted with pain, but he was not badly hurt and now he turned with a speed that belied his stocky frame, swinging his axe wildly from side to side. Meketra feinted one way then the other, dodging just outside of the fatal arc, then clipped Inherkau again on the back of his neck as he ran past his enemy to make some room for the throw.

Men were shouting, urging the warriors on, but to Meketra their voices blurred into the background. The mist of battle was on him now and it drew all of his thoughts towards killing his enemy as he brought his arm back, judging the distance without thinking. The chest, not the head. Yes, the safe throw was the one. The one that broke arms and crushed ribs. All of these things passed through Meketra's mind in the blink of an eye. But before his long sinuous arm could whip round and let fly the heavy stick, a voice rose up above all the others.

'Meketra! Stay your arm!'

It was Broken Nose their war chief, whose great bulk so belied his skill and speed in arms.

'You dare fight amongst yourselves on this day when I need every man I have?' he said striding between them.

Truly the big man looked a fearsome sight, for he had put on his crocodile hide armour and helmet. It was if the gods had transformed him into half man, half khamsa.

'You will not carry this bad blood into battle!' he said bluntly. 'Whatever your quarrel, bury it now or you will both have me to answer to.'

'I will not make my peace with this one,' Meketra spat. 'He has long been a thorn in my side, sowing discontent amongst the men where he can. And where has he been these last few days? Ask him that.'

'Well?' asked Broken Nose sternly.

'I was doing Lord Khaemwaset's bidding,' Inherkau replied sullenly.

'So, it was you who brought the Napatans here,' Broken Nose said, anger mounting in his voice. 'Remember that I pay your gold. You answer to Meketra first, and then to me, is that understood?'

'Khaemwaset also has gold,' Inherkau said rashly.

'So, you are Khaemwaset's man now?' Broken Nose poked him in the chest. 'He cares nothing for worthless dregs like you. Perhaps I should cut another scar in your ugly face to teach you a lesson?'

'No, this is my fight,' Meketra said steadily, as the big man squared up to Inherkau.

'Ah, but don't forget he insulted the commander's wife,' said another.

'Is this true?' Broken Nose roared, his face dark with fury.

'It is,' the man said. 'He swore that when the battle was

146

lost he would seek out your wife.'

'And what do you know of my wife, you little turd?' Broken Nose spat furiously in the face of Inherkau. 'For that I will take your life, do you hear me? I will piss in your skull!'

Faced with the rage of Broken Nose, fear now crept over the face of Inherkau, but there was nowhere for him to run. His tongue had got him into much trouble before, but this would surely be the last time. As Broken Nose threw off his armour, Inherkau made his move and attacked. Jumping high into the air, he brought a swinging blow down towards the back of Broken Nose, who deftly turned and parried it away with the hide breast plate. Now Inherkau was off balance and Broken Nose rammed his shoulder into the arm of the other and butted the side of his head so that Inherkau cried out in pain as his ear, already a swollen mass from an old injury, oozed blood from a ragged tear.

Broken Nose staggered back as if the butt had dazed him, but then as Inherkau swung round and readied his axe again with a roar of defiance and pain, so the commander raised his own axe overhead with both hands and threw it with all of his might. The weapon flew the short distance between the two and thudded bluntly into the chest of Inherkau with a sickening crunch. Now Broken Nose stepped forward and smashed his fist down on his foe's skull, knocking him to the ground.

As he looked on, Meketra knew that Inherkau was already as good as dead, a death he richly deserved, and yet his skin still crawled as he saw what the commander was about to do. As the dazed man lay on his back, his eyes rolling wildly, so Broken Nose stamped a sandaled foot on his forehead and took up his own axe again.

'So die my enemies!' he roared, swinging the axe down into Inherkau's neck as if he were chopping a log in two.

Inherkau let out a high scream that ended almost as soon as it had begun and a great spray of blood erupted from his neck. Death had already come for him and though Broken Nose chopped twice more with the axe, no more sound came from Inherkau's lips.

Broken Nose kicked the severed head into the watching crowd, his battle rage now spent, and threw the bloody axe to the ground. Meketra and the others grew silent now. Even for seasoned warriors, there was still something of horror for them in what they had just seen.

'Leave this goat shit where he lies!' the commander said coldly, as the flies started to swarm around the headless body. 'Let the crows have their fill on his stinking flesh.

'Meketra,' he glanced at his right hand man, a cold, dead look in his dark eyes. 'Gather the men together and bring them to me in the first line.'

And with that, the big man stomped off, rubbing the blood from his hands with sand as he went.

'Aye commander,' Meketra called after him. 'But your armour...'

Broken Nose turned to look at the crocodile hide breast plate and helmet lying discarded on the ground, for now he wore only the grieves of hide that protected his shins.

'Throw a dice amongst yourselves for them,' he said sullenly. 'I will not wear it today.'

Meketra looked on as his war chief stomped off through the loose lines of the Kemet army, men's eyes following him in fear and awe as he went, and a feeling of deep foreboding came over him. For the first time since he had known Broken Nose, he could see death stalking his master. Meketra turned his eyes back to the armour on the floor.

'Take it amongst you if you wish,' he said to his men. 'But do not think it will help you. That armour may ward of one spear blow, but the man wearing it will attract a dozen more. Better to leave it where it lies.'

Just behind the Kemet lines, the Napatans lay exhausted in the dirt, watched over by two young spearmen who were unknown to them. It had only been a short walk from the overnight camp of their captors, but after two days of being beaten and deprived of water, the captives were desperately weakened. Korkamani looked at Talakh's fearful face and tried to smile. The boy looked back up at him and bravely smiled back, both of them seeking to console each other against the awful fate they knew surely awaited them at the hands of the evil one.

'Do not be afraid, Talakh,' Korkamani said gently.

'Don't worry Korkamani,' the boy replied, his voice dry and cracked with thirst. 'I know this is the end, but I'm not scared.'

Korkamani smiled sadly, as the tears rolled from his eyes. 'You make me proud,' he said, his voice trembling. 'The garden of the afterlife where your mother waits for you will be a beautiful place you know. There will be palm trees and flowers, fish and fowl to be hunted in the marshes. All of the good things we love in this life, they also await us there.'

Talakh smiled at the thought of his mother.

'There will be cool water to bath in and a bed of softest feathers to sleep on,' Korkamani continued, 'and the gods will bless you and your mother. As you have honoured them in this life, so they will protect you in the next.'

'But what about you Korkamani?' Talakh asked. 'Will you not be there too?'

'I will have my own place in the afterlife Talakh, my own trees and my own gardens, but I will come to visit you and your mother often and we will all be happy there.'

'May great Amun make it so.'

'The gods will guide us there boy, have no doubt,' Korkamani said turning his eyes to the blue sky.

'Talakh,' he said after a pause. 'There is something I must tell you now. Something that I hoped to save for a better day, when you were older...'

The tall Napatan grew quiet now and he looked away as if he might find his thoughts amongst the distant hills.

'What is it Korkamani?'

'I hope you will not be angry boy.'

'Whatever it is, you should tell me. If it is the truth, I do not hide from it.'

Korkamani smiled.

'You should live,' he said proudly, 'for you would be a great man, of that I have no doubt.'

149

'No, I could never be as wise, nor as brave as you,' Talakh shook his head. 'Will you tell me now what it is that I must know?'

'You remember when we talked with Sati, I said that I was your father now?'

'Yes and I am glad of that'

'Well you should know that I have always been your father, Talakh. Your true father.'

'But my mother...'

'Yes, she and I were together once, many years ago,' Korkamani answered simply. 'You are my son Talakhonsu. My only son.'

Talakh looked at him, at his curly hair, his steady, deep-set eyes and the long, thin nose that was so different to his own. He could not see himself there at all, and yet he realised he had known this truth for a long time. Now it was clear why Korkamani had always been so kind to him. Why he had stayed with Talakh despite all of the hardships and dangers they had endured since their capture.

'Father,' was all that the boy could say as he tried to find words that would not come.

'I am sorry Talakh,' Korkamani said sadly. 'I should have told you before.'

The salt from his dried tears had left white crystals on his father's dark cheeks, but fresh tears came now to wash them away. Talakh could do no more than look up at the sky as if he might find an answer from the gods up there to the confusion in his mind.

It was then that the men of Khaemwaset came for them. The captives were hauled upright and the rabble that passed for the Kemet army jeered and hissed as they were led by their tethers along the lines. Korkamani could see that the end was near now and perhaps he almost welcomed it for himself. But to know his son was to die too? His face was filled with deep sorrow at that.

The jostling rabble finally parted to let them through and there Talakhonsu saw the man he had such cause to hate. Khaemwaset, bringer of great grief and sorrow to so many in the homeland of the Napatans. The evil one turned now to look upon his captives, a faint smile on his lips. Talakhonsu hated him all the more for that.

'Curse you,' the boy's dry voice croaked and he tried to spit in defiance, though his mouth was too parched for that.

'Hah!' Khaemwaset laughed sharply. 'See how the miserable Kush whelp suffers? It is a shame that he should die at all today when his pathetic suffering pleases me so much.'

Talakh had learnt the Kemet tongue well and he understood every one of those hateful words.

'And what of you, Kush dung?' Khaemwaset turned his amused sneer to Korkamani. 'Have you nothing to say before I take both of your miserable lives?'

Korkamani tried to stand up straight, but their captors had tied a tether between his bound wrists and ankles that kept him hunched over so that he could only raise his head with difficulty. With a great effort, he forced his dry tongue into speaking. 'My breath would be wasted on you, coward.'

The smile vanished from Khaemwaset's face.

'What did the Napatan girl say?' he asked those about him. 'He goads me, even as death awaits him!'

There was a crazed look in his burning eyes and Talakh now started to sob, for he knew what must quickly follow now.

'Your spear,' Khaemwaset cried at a guard, his voice high with the rage that now gripped him.

'Korkamani!' Talakh cried.

But already the evil one had taken the short spear, and pressed its point between the ribs of Korkamani, who sagged under the pain.

'What do you say now?' Khaemwaset hissed, his face contorted into that of a snarling demon.

Korkamani lifted his head and stared back into those evil eyes. 'The soul eater will take your spirit when you die,' his voice rasped. 'And all those who you have murdered will watch you piss yourself in fear...'

For a moment Khaemwaset was still. For a moment the hate left his face and he looked lost, his body trembling as if he might collapse. But this was only for a moment. With a strangled cry, the evil one heaved with all his might, thrusting the spear between Korkamani's ribs and out of his back with a sickening crunch.

Talakh felt himself grow cold and he started to shiver as Korkamani dropped to the ground with a gasp. There was not much blood, yet the boy knew that Korkamani's life was already near its end even though his father's eyes still saw and his mouth still sought for breath.

'Korkamani!' Talakh called out as he lay in the dirt. 'Father...'

Khaemwaset was smiling now, smiling as if the day was pleasant and a weight had just been lifted from his mind.

'Father, eh?' he said laughing mildly to himself. 'Father...' he laughed again. 'Do not worry boy, you will soon join him.'

And with that the evil one drew the long, bright dagger that hung at his waist.

Talakh tried to stare his look of hate into the eyes of Khaemwaset, but the sun glinted on the bronze blade as the evil one stepped closer, and he could not tear his gaze away from it. Khaemwaset's shadow of death stood over him, blocking out the hot sun and the air grew heavy with the pungent smell of the oils that anointed his skin. He grasped the boy's ragged bush of hair and Talakhonsu felt his head being pulled up, so that his neck was stretched out, ready to receive the blade.

'Men of Kemet!' Khaemwaset shouted to his rabble army. 'The gods, who favour me as your king above all others, have sent us this boy to offer in sacrifice for the great victory we will be granted this day. Hear me all of you! Not one of those Persian swine will escape today. Not one! We will spill their blood until the desert sands run red with it!'

Khaemwaset waited now for the cheer, for the roar of his men as they found their hearts and their courage, but what little shouts there were came only from his own guards who stood close by. This angered him all the more and Talakhonsu felt his head yanked back harder still until the sun blinded him. For an instant he watched Khaemwaset's arm rise high

152

above him, the gleaming dagger in his hand. Now the arm swooped down and the boy felt the edge of death, hard against his throat. He tried to cry out, but no noise would come from his dry mouth, and instead a strange calm came over him as his body went limp. His mother waited, Prainke waited. Soon poor Korkamani too would be waiting for him. Talakhonsu swallowed hard against the pressing blade as the keen edge rasped his skin.

'Khaemwaset!' a voice rang out loud and clear.

'Khaemwaset!' It was the voice of Broken Nose.

Talakh felt the pressure of the knife's edge ease on his throat, but still his hair was pulled hard back by the evil one's grip.

'What has happened to you?' he heard Khaemwaset laugh. 'You look as if you have started the battle without us!'

'I would speak with you in private, Lord,' Broken Nose said, bluntly.

'But I have unfinished business here,' Khaemwaset sneered arrogantly. 'These Napatans, they have lived on my grain long enough do you not think? See this one here? Stuck like a pig on my spear!' he laughed harshly at his own crude rhyme.

'It is a matter of great importance Lord,' Broken Nose said firmly. 'It cannot wait.'

With an annoyed sigh, the evil one pushed Talakh's head forward and he collapsed into the dirt. The boy looked up to watch the two men meet close by Korkamani's shivering form. The face of Broken Nose looked like thunder and his kilt was stained with blood, though it seemed it was not his own.

'Now,' Khaemwaset started to say, but his voice stopped short when Broken Nose drew his sword.

Talakh recognised it as the pattern of his own people. A short sword of finest beaten iron, stolen from Napata no doubt. The two faced each other, Khaemwaset still with his bronze dagger in hand.

'What are you doing?' the evil one asked, almost seeming to doubt his senses.

Broken Nose was silent for a moment, as if he fought a

battle of wills within himself, but when he finally spoke his voice was firm and unwavering.

'You will release the boy to me,' he said bluntly.

'What? You dare to tell me what I should do?' Khaemwaset spat, unable to believe his ears.

'I have dared many things for you,' Broken Nose answered, his voice as cold as stone. 'But today you butchered a brave man as if he were nothing more than animal. I will not let you do the same to the boy.'

'You will not let?' the evil one snarled. 'Who do you think you are, worthless low-born? Who are you to tell me anything?'

There was spit hanging from the lip of Khaemwaset and his shoulders hunched up grotesquely in his fury as he stabbed the air with his blade.

'I see no sons or fathers here, only my slaves!' he raged on. 'I see the enemies of Kemet! I see you. Are you finally my enemy too, oath breaker?'

Broken Nose stood unmoved by all of this, like a great boulder in the flood waters.

'I made my oath to a man I thought sane,' he said. 'For too long now I have done your bidding, you who murdered your own kin. You think to lead these poor men, these farmers against the Persians? Truly now I know you have lost your mind. I am done serving your cause Khaemwaset.'

'You are done with me? Oh, but I am not done with you,' Khaemwaset sneered. 'You!' he glared at his personal guards. 'Take him, take the oath breaker! Tie him and bury him up to his neck in the sand for the ants to eat. I want the fat pig to suffer a hundred deaths before he begs me for mercy!'

The guards shuffled from foot to foot, but they did not move, for much as they feared the wrath of their master, still they knew Broken Nose of old. They knew his reputation as a fighting man. They knew too that one of them at least would die before they would ever take him. The guards looked at each other, but none of them would move against the blood drenched warrior with the Napatan sword.

Talakhonsu tried to crawl away from the confrontation,

shuffling slowly on his side like a poor snake to try to reach the side of his dying father. A guard moved as if to stop him. He was younger than the rest, skinny and perhaps not yet in his twentieth year. The young can be rash.

'Leave the boy,' Broken Nose grunted a warning, but still the guard edged forward. 'Touch him and I will skewer your eyes and piss in your skull holes!'

The guard looked at the big man, unsure of what to do, but he reached down anyway and snatched up the tether that dragged behind Talakh. As the man took up the strain to pull him in like a fish on a hook, Talakhonsu felt his legs straighten out against his will but he was powerless to resist. There was a noise, like the wings of a swift bird close overhead, and a sharp crack. The tether went slack again as the young guard fell to the ground at his side. Talakh could see his temple was broken in and bloody, his dead eyes fluttering as they rolled back in their sockets. The throwing stick of Meketra had struck again.

'Who threw that?' Khaemwaset screamed. 'Who tries to kill me?'

'He is my man,' Broken Nose said grimly, 'and if he wanted to kill you, you would be dead already.'

Khaemwaset half turned to look over his shoulder, looking for the safety of his guards, but instead found his eye fixed on the boy who scrambled in the dirt, trying to crawl back to the side of Korkamani.

Broken Nose read the evil one's thoughts.

'Turn your back on me and my sword will split your spine, you snake!' he bellowed in a furious rage.

Khaemwaset turned back now to face his challenger.

'So! You think you can beat me?' he laughed. 'You think you can defeat a whole army by yourself? Hah! Suppose you take the boy? What then? When I have finished with the Persians, I will come for you and your wife and your own son. You will all die on spears, and the crows will have your eyes.'

'You won't leave this place, alive.' Broken Nose said, with death in his words. 'I will see to that.'

And so the two men faced each other again, each

unyielding, each ready to attack in the blink of an eye, while Talakh at last reached the side of his dying father.

'Lord Khaemwaset,' a foreign voice found its way to Talakh's ears as he lay by his father's side.

'You will have to fight this battle without my men,' the strange voice said. 'We return your gold.'

'So, the Greeks now lose their stomach for the battle,' Khaemwaset sneered. 'The Persians are your friends now that you face them, is that it? Is this the way that the Greeks fight? By running away?'

'Do not brand us cowards,' the Greek warrior said, leaning on his long, heavy spear. 'Since they took our lands, my men have fought the Persians many times, from your shores to our own. Sometimes we have fought for gold, but always we fight with our honour.'

'Then tell me, why do you not fight now that your enemies are before you and my gold is in your purse?'

Talakh looked up from the anguished face of Korkamani to see the one who spoke for the Greeks. He was a tall, lean man with bronze skin that matched the plates of armour on his forearms, chest and shins. His long black hair was tied back and a thin leather strip circled his forehead, but his hair still curled around it like Korkamani's. The man stared hard at Khaemwaset, his hand now resting with threat on the pommel of his sword. He let his silence speak for a long time before he opened his mouth again.

'Look around you lord of Waset,' he said, casting his outstretched hand around in an arc that took in the nervous, rabble army. 'Your men fight amongst themselves and even your trusted man here turns against you. You kill a defenceless slave and hold your dagger against a boy's throat, yet I am to fight for your glory? No, my men will not fight for one such as you, gold or no gold. There is only dishonour for us in that!'

Khaemwaset's face now seethed with anger untold, and he skewered the air with his sword in his impotent rage.

'I will gladly take your life if that is your wish,' the Greek warrior said with cool contempt. 'It would spare your own

156

people much if you were to die.'

'No!' Broken Nose interrupted. 'I own his death!'

'Ah, my old friend,' Khaemwaset mewed sarcastically. 'You will stand by me, only so that you can stick your own knife in my back?'

'Not in your back,' Broken Nose answered bluntly. 'Judge me not by your own standards.

'I will give you death for what you have said about my wife and my son, just as I gave it to Inherkau – in a fair fight. You will follow him into the dark places where the great serpent lives, and the sun will not reach you there.'

The tall Greek had listened to all of this, and nodded his approval at the curse of Broken Nose. Without another word, he dropped a heavy sack of gold at his feet and that was soon joined by another from one of his men, and then another.

Talakhonsu watched from the corner of his eye as the island Greeks followed their leader, forming up behind him in neat lines as they marched away. Smaller groups of Greek warriors joined them and those other mercenaries who fought for gold left too, though none of them returned their battle price.

'Men of Kemet!' Khaemwaset shouted his voice rising with desperation. 'Do not lose your courage. We don't need these cowards! Stay and fight!'

But his words were already too late. The rabble Kemet army was melting away into the desert, casting aside their spears so that they could run as fast as their legs would carry them back toward the far distant Great River. For it did not take a soldier's mind to know what would come next.

'Lord, do not waste your life here,' Meketra urged Broken Nose, glancing sideways at the seething Khaemwaset, who stood alone now that even his personal guard had deserted him.

'We can take him lord,' Meketra urged again. 'We can leave this place with him in bonds and then if you must you can give him a fair fight. Don't fight him here. Live to see your wife and son.'

Broken Nose stood silent and still, as if he had been turned to stone, and Meketra wondered if he had even heard his words.

'Lord!' he said again, his voice more urgent.

'I hear you. Leave this place Meketra,' Broken Nose said with the voice of the dead. 'Lead your men away. Take the boy and his father with you.'

'But lord, Korkamani...' Meketra hesitated.

'Spare him his suffering Meketra.'

Meketra knew what must be done then and he knelt down besides Korkamani. The Napatan's chest rose only slightly now, his life almost gone. Talakhonsu lay beside him, his eyes a well of tears as he looked on his dying father.

'Korkamani,' the boy said, quietly sobbing. 'Father...'

Meketra cut first Korkamani's bonds, and then Talakhonsu's. 'Come away now boy,' he said gently, laying a hand on the boy's shoulder.

'The brat is mine!' Khaemwaset spat, but though he made to lunge at Meketra, still fear of the sword of Broken Nose held him back.

'Come,' Meketra said again, taking the boy's hand.

'No! Father!' Talakhonsu cried pitifully.

'It is... alright...' the words came painfully from Korkamani. Half whispered, breathless words as dry as dead leaves.

Talakh touched his father's face, his hand dark next to Korkamani's pallid skin. Beneath the bushy beard flecked with grey, Korkamani's face felt cold to him.

'Remember...' Korkamani said. 'Always...' And with that his spirit slipped away from his body and he was gone from the world of men.

Pelia did not sob, though there were tears in her eyes just the same as she finished the sad tale of the death of Korkamani. He was after all the man from whose seed

Talakhonsu had sprung and therefore her own oldfather. Her tears were not the only ones.

'The world is such a terrible place when good men like Korkamani die in such a terrible way,' Cerian sobbed.

'Aye,' Pelia said drying her eyes, 'there is much evil in the world. But there is good too, we must not forget that. Otherwise the spirits of evil only grow stronger.

'Korkamani was a good man, loyal and true,' Cerian nodded, with a sad sigh. 'Do you think he did join with Talakhonsu's mother in her afterlife?'

'I would like to think so,' Pelia smiled. 'The people of those lands believe that when someone dies, their spirit becomes a little bird which flies off, carrying the essence of what they are to the afterlife. The spirit bird of Korkamani would have found itself a long way from his own lands, but his will was strong. I am sure he would have found his way back there so that he could love Talakhonsu's mother again, as he had loved her in life.'

Cerian thought on that for a while before she spoke again.

'Do you ever wonder what path your spirit might take?' she asked with the guilelessness of the young. 'I mean, when you...'

'When my time is at end?'

'Yes, though you are still young of course,' Cerian added quickly.

Pelia smiled at that. 'I always think it best to live for the time we are here and not dwell too much on what may happen after,' she said. 'But yes, I do wonder about these things sometimes. I hope I would see my mother once again.

'But if I could speak to Korkamani's spirit, that I would dearly love too. Perhaps it is possible to pass between both spirit worlds, ours and theirs. Or perhaps my spirit will wander the earth, not knowing where to go?'

'Let us hope not. But you must tell me, did Broken Nose kill Khaemwaset in the end?' Cerian asked, trying to take her friend's mind off of such things.

'Ah, that part I do not know for sure,' Pelia said, frowning. 'But I give too much away again. We will come to that part of

159

the story in good time.'

'I feel almost sorry for him now,' Cerian frowned

'Broken Nose?'

'Yes. He did many evil things in his life, but...'

'Ach, well there is good and bad in all of us,' Pelia frowned. 'He had more than his share of the bad, but even so in the end he came to no longer believe in his master. As the final battle loomed, he could see the death of so many men to be a hopeless cause.

'But I think it was only when he saw a helpless boy who had been through so many things about to be murdered... Only then could he fully see the evil of Khaemwaset.

'It is a strange thing but if it had not been for Broken Nose, Talakhonsu would have been killed and I would not have been born. Still I often wonder if he had been there when Korkamani was murdered, would he have stopped Khaemwaset then? But these things we can never know.'

'Aye,' Cerian agreed.

'Still, the longer I live, the more I see that all life is strange,' Pelia said thoughtfully. 'Ah well, I suppose we should fetch some fresh water from the spring before the last of the light goes. Then I will tell you more of what happened after the battle that never was.'

-ф-

When Meketra finally decided that all was lost for his war chief, he acted decisively as Broken Nose surely knew he would. He threw the grieving Talakhonsu over his shoulder and carried him away from the danger to a safer place amongst some rocks. There were no parting words between him and Broken Nose, for it is not often in the gift of warriors to find the right words at such times. Besides, the fixed eyes of Broken Nose invited no farewells as he faced Khaemwaset.

Meketra had two of his men retrieve the body of Korkamani after they had broken off the spear shaft that pierced his chest.

'What shall we do with him?' one of the men asked, nervously glancing over his shoulder.

Meketra looked on too. Across the far horizon, the army of the Persians squatted like a swarm of ants waiting to pick the bones of Kemet clean. With his keen eyes, Meketra could see small trails of dust, no doubt sent up by horse riders taking messages between the Persian lords. He tried to think as Broken Nose had taught him. For in war, bravery is seldom enough to live out the day.

In his mind Meketra imagined what the Persians would see from their ridge. Across the plain from them, the meagre Kemet army had simply melted away, leaving but a handful of stragglers and a few war chariots. The Persians would think their enemies were fleeing back to the relative safety of their city of Waset and its walled temples. But then again, they might fear a trap.

It seemed to Meketra, based on what Broken Nose had told him of his own skirmishes, that the Persians would be more likely to hesitate. The vast size of their army meant they would be slow to react whatever they thought was happening. Perhaps then there was still time for Meketra and his war band to cheat death.

'Bring that chariot over here,' he called an order.

'But it is the chariot of Khaemwaset!' one of his men said nervously.

'I said bring it here!' Meketra insisted. 'Cut a shroud from one of the tents, quickly now! Wrap Korkamani in it and tie him across one of the horses. I will drive him and the boy away from here. That is our commander's order.'

'And us Meketra,' another of his men said. 'What of us?'

'Do what I ask of you,' Meketra said firmly. 'Take a share of Khaemwaset's gold, but no more than you can easily carry at the run, otherwise you will be chased down in your greed.'

'Will we follow you then?' one of his men asked.

'No,' Meketra said grimly. 'The time for our war band is at an end. Run as fast as you can back to your villages and families. Throw away your weapons before you get there and hide your gold well, those are my orders. If we all live to see the day's end, we will soon see how the Persian king punishes those who are shown to have raised arms against him. Now go, and good luck go with you.'

When Khaemwaset saw Meketra's men rifle his gold and seize his chariot with its gilded wickerwork and fine, black horses, he erupted into a yet wilder fury, yet he was powerless to act. For Broken Nose, unyielding as stone, held him at bay, daring him to make the first move.

Meketra watched as his men made off back across the desert sands toward the river, splitting up as they went and he asked the gods that they would not let the Persians overtake them.

Across the plain, first one rider and then another rode out slowly from the far off Persian lines. No doubt they were scouts whose job was to ride forward of the main army to see if Kemet archers hid in ambush amongst the many depressions and rocks that strewed the shimmering desert. They would catch on soon enough that the entire Kemet army had fled, and then the game would be up.

Broken Nose saw the horsemen too, over the shoulder of his former lord and at last this spurred him into action. He struck fast, thrusting forward with his sword to force the grimacing Khaemwaset onto his back foot. The clash of their swords rang out clear and loud in the hot, desert air as Meketra pushed Talakhonsu onto the small platform of the chariot.

'Stay low boy,' he said urgently, but there was no reply from the young Napatan.

Meketra took the reins and whipped the horses into a fast trot across the rough ground, while behind him the furious clashing of swords told of a battle to the death between his war chief and the Lord Khaemwaset. Desperate though he was to see this battle, Meketra could do nothing else but steer the chariot over the rough, rocky ground that at any moment threatened to smash the fragile wheels and tip them over. To the river, to Waset and then to escape, that is all that the young warrior could think of as one of the horses reared its head, and the shrouded body of poor Korkamani was jostled harshly on its back.

The wind blew hard in Meketra's face as the chariot sped across the desert, but after a while it seemed to slacken off, though the horses galloped on just as fast. It was as if he now drove through a waking dream and so strange was the feeling that the tall Nubian wondered if a Persian horsemen had shot an arrow into his back and he was now no more than a spirit. Though he hardly dared to take his eyes off the ground ahead, something made Meketra steal a glance over his shoulder then. Rising into the sky behind him was a billowing cloud of sand, following hard on the breath of Amun. Back in his homeland further south, these storms of sand were dreaded by Meketra's people, for they choked the crops, scattered goat herds and forced the people to seek shelter, sometimes for days. Around Waset they were rarely seen, so it could only have been down to the will of Amun, the great god of the four winds, that the storm had chosen to rise up now to hide the flight of the chariot from any pursuing Persians.

The storm winds came up quickly, pushing the chariot on faster and faster until the sand cloud overtook them and the land grew suddenly cold as the sun god's rays were hidden. Meketra had no choice but to pull up the horses and slow the chariot to a walk, before finally stopping altogether to make what shelter he could from the windblown sand that choked the mouth and stung the eyes.

'Get under the chariot!' Meketra shouted to Talakh as he quickly hobbled the horses with their reins and tipped the chariot over to form a shelter of sorts from the driving sand. For himself, all the Nubian could do was sit with his back against the chariot, his hands covering his face as best he could while he waited for the storm to blow itself out.

It was many hours before the storm eased enough for Meketra to right the chariot and set off again. The sun was lowering in the west and so, though he was lost, he knew that he must head toward it if he was to come to the Great River.

Eventually as the sun started to cross over the horizon, the young warrior sighted the distant palm trees that marked the river's course through the heart of Kemet and he knew then that it would be safer to abandon the chariot here. The once great and powerful land of Kemet would soon be back under the heel of the Persians again, and anyone driving a war chariot such as this would be taken as an enemy to be killed on sight. Meketra pulled up the horses for the last time and stepped to the ground.

'I am sorry Talakh,' he said hoarsely, his throat dry from the windblown sand. 'We will take Korkamani to the Great River and bury him there amongst the palms, where his spirit may be at peace.'

Talakhonsu said nothing, for he was still too shocked to speak, having found and lost his true father on the same day.

Meketra cut one of the horses loose from its harness and slapped it hard across the flanks so that it galloped off across the desert, clouds of dust rising up from its hooves as it fled into the distance. Then he cut loose the horse bearing the body of Korkamani and led it away with Talakhonsu at his side toward the distant banks of the Great River.

So it was that the gilded war chariot of Lord Khaemwaset came to be abandoned in the desert, where it would lie until the sands claimed it for their own as they do all things in the end.

Chapter 9

Meketra's Gift

In the last of the evening light, Meketra used a flat stone to start digging the grave for Korkamani's body amongst some tall palms, well away from the nearest farm. It was only then that the boy finally spoke again.

'Can we not take him back to Siamun's farm?' Talakhonsu sobbed.

Meketra laid the flat stone down and turned to the boy, setting a hand on his shoulder.

'The Persians will already be in Waset,' he said, 'and if they find us with Korkamani's body, they will think we raised arms against them. Let him rest here Talakhonsu, far from the bonds that tied him to Siamun. Let him rest as a free man in this quiet place, where his spirit may be at peace.'

Talakhonsu, nodded silently, knowing that Meketra was right. Dropping to his knees, he too began scrapping away the dry earth with a small stone. For a moment Meketra thought of sending him away whilst he finished digging the grave himself, but then he saw that this was the best way.

'Your father would be proud, Talakh,' he said with a tremor of sadness in his voice. 'He was a good man, a brave one too. These things I know from what I saw of him. You must follow his way now.'

And so the young warrior and the Napatan boy dug the grave of Korkamani in the dry earth while cool night gathered in around them. As they worked Talakh spoke a little at last.

'Is Broken Nose dead too?' he asked, his voice small and dull with the pain of his father's loss.

Meketra frowned and then gave the faintest of smiles at the nickname given by Talakh to his master.

'I did not see the end, but he is a great warrior and he would be a match for Khaemwaset.'

Talakh spat at the mention of the evil one's name and then spat again. Once for himself and once for Korkamani. 'I hope he suffers a hundred deaths for all that he has done,' he said bitterly.

'Aye,' Meketra nodded, 'no good ever came from that one. It may be that they are both dead at the hands of the Persians. If that is so, then two good men have been taken from us so that one evil man might die. But still I will offer to the gods that the one you call Broken Nose is safe.'

Talakh thought on that for a while but he said nothing. In the years to come, whenever he thought of his father Korkamani, his mind would often turn to Broken Nose as well. Although the war chief had helped bring them both great sorrow, still in the end he had most probably given his life to defy the murdering Khaemwaset. And for that Talakh slowly came to realise that in a strange way he owed his own life to the big man.

When finally the grave was dug, Meketra carried the body of Korkamani over his shoulder from the shelter of a tree to that final resting place in the earth. The tall sinewy warrior had great strength in his limbs and he laid Korkamani down as gently as if he were a babe, while Talakhonsu stood silently by, not knowing what he should do. Then the two of them covered the shrouded body with heavy stones in case the jackals should try to dig down to reach it. Finally they spread the dug earth over the grave and scattered it with dead grass and litter until there was nothing to mark it out.

'We will watch over him until Ra returns to give his light to the land again,' Meketra said. 'You were to be a priest, Talakh. Will you say some words on Korkamani's behalf to the great god?'

Talakh thought on this for a moment, but then shook his head.

'I thought Amun would protect us,' he said angrily, 'but even though we made offerings to him when we had nothing, still he let Korkamani die. I think the god doesn't hear us any more, otherwise how could he let my father be killed?'

'I have no answer for you as to why these things have

happened,' Meketra said quietly. 'But I know that if Korkamani is to be received well in the afterlife, you should speak for him. They will judge him wisely then and grant him eternal life. Speak of Korkamani, Talakh, even though it saddens you. Speak of all that he did and all that he was, so that the gods of the dead will hear you and know him better.'

Talakhonsu heard the wisdom in the words of Meketra, and he thought of what Korkamani had told him of the beautiful land where he would now hunt and feast and live again in the afterlife. Summoning all of his courage, he spoke of Korkamani as Meketra had said, beseeching the gods to judge him well. He spoke of the kindness Korkamani had shown him and of how his father had nursed him back to health many times, giving up his own meagre food and water so that Talakhonsu might survive. Then he told the gods of the bravery Korkamani had shown on the boiling rapids of the Great River, and of when he had fought and killed the great lizard beast as he tried to save a man who was not even his kin or his friend.

All the while Meketra added his own words to confirm what the boy had said and add his own praises of Korkamani, until finally Talakhonsu could say no more and he collapsed in a sobbing heap next to the grave of Korkamani, wetting the earth with his tears.

Meketra gathered some fallen palm fronds then and draped these across the boy to keep a little of the cold of the night from him as he cried himself to sleep with exhaustion.

When Talakhonsu awoke much later there was a terrible thirst in his throat and an awful pain in his gut, worse than any hunger he had ever felt. The giants of the night still hung in the dark sky, their forms marked out by the brightest of the stars, and Talakh wondered if a part of Korkamani was up there now amongst the heroes. He shuddered in cold and fear, longing for the dawn in the hope that somehow the past day's events would be shown to be nothing but a nightmare.

Then Meketra's voice spoke out of the darkness and the boy knew that what had passed could not be undone and that Korkamani was gone forever.

'I am here Talakh,' Meketra's voice came, half whispered through the darkness. 'Come, now you are awake we will go to the river and drink. You need water.'

Talakhonsu slowly struggled to his feet, his limbs stiff and aching from his ordeal, but he did not speak for his heart was cloaked in a deep sadness.

They came to the river bank in a short while, drinking their fill from the muddy water. Some said that the spirits of the Great River could make you ill and most folk in these lands drank the cleaner water from their wells or settling pools, or else drank it boiled with the leaves and flowers of plants to flavour and cleanse it. But spirits or none, the muddy water was like wine to Talakh and Meketra and they stayed there a good while until their thirsts were slaked.

When they returned to the resting place of Korkamani, the dawn light was just starting to arch over the horizon and Meketra and Talakhonsu stood there in silence as the first rays of the sun god Ra returned to warm the land. Meketra started to sing a low, solemn song which Talakh could not make out the words to. Meketra's eyes closed and he held out his hands, palms uppermost in offering to the sun god whilst his voice grew stronger, bound in a rhythm that wound backward and forward in a chant.

Though Talakh could not make out many of the words, still he joined in as best he could, for the sound soothed him and he felt as though they must be singing the spirit of Korkamani up into the sky. Meketra's voice grew slowly quiet and Talakh's own voice followed it down into a low steady chant that dissolved into silence as the morning breeze carried away the last of their words out to the empty desert. For a moment there was a deep silence and then Talakh opened his own eyes, blinking against the bright yellow disc of the sun that now ascended into the sky.

'What was it that we sang?' Talakh asked, though he felt embarrassed at not knowing.

'It is an old, old song that an old, old man used to sing when one of our kin died,' Meketra said, a distant look in his eyes as he searched his memories.

'The words are the old tongue of my people. These things are now almost forgotten, but still we sang the song when my brother died. It tells us that Ra watches from his boat as he sails the sky. We ask the god if he will take up the spirits of the dead and carry them with him to the gates of the afterlife when he heads into the west.'

'Korkamani's spirit is a long way from our home. A long way from our priests and ancestors...'

'He will find his way,' Meketra said, his hand on the boy's shoulder. 'He was strong in life and his spirit will be strong too in the afterlife.'

Talakhonsu nodded with a faint smile. He thought of the spirit carrier, the Ba bird, of which Korkamani had sometimes spoken, and imagined it soaring high into the sky carrying his father's spirit. Perhaps the Ba bird would fly high enough to perch on Ra's boat as the disc of the sun god sailed up to the top of the heavens. From up there Korkamani's spirit would surely be able to see the Great River winding away to the south, back toward the sacred mountain of Napata and Amun's throne. If such things were possible, then truly Korkamani might still take his place in the gardens of the afterlife, the gods willing. The hope renewed in him that one day he would once again see his mother and Korkamani when his time came to cross over.

'Will you go to look for Broken Nose?' he asked, while the respite from his grief still lasted.

'First we will return to the farm of Siamun,' Meketra said. The smile that normally dwelt on his face was still absent and the young warrior's voice was tense now.

'We will see what news they have for us there Talakh, but we must be prepared for anything. The farm may be burned to the ground. Siamun may be dead and the Persian soldiers may be sacking Waset as we speak. But we must go there all the same,' he said. 'I need news and I must have it from those I know. Those I can trust.'

And so after Talakhonsu had said a final sad goodbye to the unmarked grave of his father, the two of them began to follow the river back toward Waset, begging a little food where they could as they went. Meketra was always vigilant for the Persian soldiers and their allies. He still bore his arms and they marked him out as a rebel against the Persian king, but in those uncertain times they could not tell what lay ahead of them. It was not until another day had passed and they were close to Waset itself that the warrior finally hid his long dagger and small war axe in a shallow scrape in the earth under some rocks.

Along the way they had heard plenty of news. Some men talked of the burning of the great temples of Waset, while others said that the Persians were spitting children on their spears and roasting them over fires for amusement. All spoke of the might of the vast army that had passed close by and their stories were filled with fear and suspicion.

At last they came to the farm of Siamun. The overseer sat outside his house, his chin on his hands.

'Ah,' he said as they approached, his voice heavy with sarcasm. 'A soldier returns from battle.'

'Do not bait me, Siamun,' Meketra answered angrily. 'No doubt you have heard that our army drifted away without a fight, but that is not the whole story. Don't speak of what you don't know.'

For a moment Siamun looked as if he might say something, but he wisely bit his tongue. Naphren appeared now and when she saw the cuts and weals on the body of Talakhonsu, her face turned from relief to anguish, then back again.

'Oh, Talakhonsu, you are alive!' she said, rushing over to gather him into her arms. 'The gods be praised for sparing you.

'But Korkamani...' she said, her voice trembling with what she surely knew had come to pass. 'Where is Korkamani?'

'He is gone,' Meketra said quietly. 'He died bravely.'

'No!' Naphren cried, disbelief filling her kind face. 'What evil is this? How could it be?'

'Khaemwaset would have killed them both,' Meketra said grimly. 'He wanted to sacrifice them to the gods for a victory. We managed to save the boy, but Korkamani was already dead. He was the boy's true father.'

'His father?' Naphren cried. 'I often wondered if it was so. Oh poor Talakhonsu!' she hugged the boy close to her as his own tears started to come again.

'Take him inside,' Siamun said bluntly.

'Yes, yes of course,' Naphren said. 'Come Talakh, let us clean your wounds and give you water.'

When they had gone into the house, Siamun spoke again. 'What of our master?' he croaked.

'I don't know,' Meketra shook his head. 'When I left him he was fighting Khaemwaset.'

'They fought? Why?' Siamun asked in disbelief. 'And how did you come to escape?'

'Be thankful you have a wife to grieve for you, Siamun,' Meketra spat angrily. 'Otherwise I would put you under the ground for what you imply.'

Siamun's face froze.

'I did not mean...' he started to say.

'I know what you meant,' Meketra snarled. 'He ordered me to take the boy away.'

'And he fought Khaemwaset? But why?' Siamun blurted again. 'He was honour bound to our Lord.'

'Still, he could not stand by and watch Khaemwaset slit an innocent boy's throat. If he is dead, then he died with a sword in his hand and honour in his heart. Let everyone you speak with know this.

'I will,' Siamun nodded.

'Be sure that you do. Now, what of his wife and son?'

'Sati has returned to her own people off to the south. They are simple farmers, but she will be safe with them. But you Meketra,' Siamun asked, 'what will you do now?'

'I will go back to the battlefield and look for...' Meketra stopped himself short.

'Naphren will care for the boy until you return,' Siamun said quietly. 'Then we will decide what is to become of him.'

'Treat him well,' Meketra said. 'His heart is sick and he needs Naphren's tenderness. I will leave in a while, but first tell me what has happened in Waset. What news is there of

171

the Persian army?'

And so, while Siamun's daughter brought Meketra food and drink, the overseer told of what he knew. There was much talk of the new king of the Persians, a one called Xerxes.

It was said that Xerxes himself had come to Waset and that his wrath had shaken the very walls of the great temples to the ground. He had already stripped the nobles of Kemet of all of their land and wealth, putting those Persians he favoured in their stead. But that was as nothing compared to the torture and bloodshed he had meted out to those he saw as leaders of the Kemet revolt. These ones were put to death with clubs, so that they suffered a long time before they died. Now their naked bodies hung from the pylon walls of the great temple of Amun, staining the whitewash red with their blood. The grand house of Khaemwaset had been taken by a Persian general who was close to Xerxes, so even if he lived, he too was now landless and stripped of his power.

These things Siamun told Meketra, though he had stayed on his farm and so had not seen them with his own eyes. Even so, Meketra did not doubt that the Persian king would exact a terrible revenge on his former subjects. Yes, the foot of Xerxes would rest heavily on the soil of Kemet and there would be no return to the benign rule of his father, Darius the great.

'And what of you, Siamun?' Meketra asked when the overseer had finished. 'The Persians have not come here yet?'

'Yes,' Siamun answered, some of the mistrust returning to his face again. 'Soldiers rode by looking for any our own fleeing army. Of course I told them nothing of our master and his role in things.'

'Good. If they return again, keep your mouth shut about me,' Meketra said with narrow threat in his eyes. 'As far as they are concerned, I am nothing but a worker of your fields.'

'As you say,' Siamun agreed. 'But what if they take my lands?'

'This is no land of yours,' Meketra said bluntly. 'You are just an overseer, remember that. If the Persians take the farm, you will have to prove your worth to them. Perhaps then they may let you stay.'

Anger showed in the face of Siamun again, but he knew better than to challenge Meketra and so he said nothing as the tall Nubian strode off.

'I will return in three days, if not before,' the tall warrior called over his shoulder. 'Look after the boy, and don't cross me Siamun, or you'll wish the Persians had taken your head too!'

After he had retrieved his arms from their hiding place, Meketra made the long walk back to that desolate plain where the ramshackle army of Kemet had melted away like mist on a spring day before the Persian hordes. Along the banks of the Great River he could blend in with the common folk who lived in the scattered settlements to the north, but this was not so when he struck out across the desert wastes, and he feared to come across Persian soldiers alone in a land such as this. For here, only solitary goat herders were to be found, scratching a living from the scrubby wastes.

So it was that the journey took Meketra many days as he sought out what cover there was behind rocks, searching the horizon with his keen eyes for the dust of horses. In this way he travelled little by day and much by night, snatching sleep where he could until finally his gut told him that he had come to the place. There was no trace of his war chief, Broken Nose, nor of Khaemwaset, nor indeed of Khaemwaset's camp. In fact, Meketra came to doubt for a while whether he had the right place at all, for the sandstorm had covered the many tracks that would usually have betrayed the passing of a great army.

At last though Meketra's luck changed when he stumbled upon a trampled shield of the type used by the desert peoples, and further on, the torn, blown down remains of one of the tents of Khaemwaset, half buried in the sands. Only then could he finally be sure he had found the field of the battle that never was. Close by only days before, Korkamani's blood had stained the sands red and Broken Nose had fought Khaemwaset as the Persian horsemen charged. But of bodies, of blood, there was none. Perhaps they were there, buried by the sands. Perhaps animals had fed on them. Perhaps their bones had been carried off and buried by the jackals.

Meketra tried to imagine what might perhaps have happened. Broken Nose was a great war chief it was true, experienced in battle, fearless, strong and faster than he looked. But Khaemwaset was younger and perhaps his sword arm was the faster of the two. Driven as he was by rage and madness, perhaps he might have bested Broken Nose. Perhaps too they might both have been ridden down by the charging Persians. These things he could not know, and so after another brief search, Meketra set off on his long, dispirited walk back to the farm of Siamun.

-φ-

The trials of the winter were hard that year for Pelia and Cerian. For days at a time, the storm winds lashed the settlement of Llan Huell with great sheets of rain that dripped through even the thickest thatch and left the land sodden.

When the storms were over, then harsh frosts came to freeze over the stream as the muddy spate waters abated. At such times, when Pelia and Cerian went to the spring to collect water they found the small pool there covered in a thick layer of ice that had to be broken with a heavy stone. Many across the land were carried off by the hand of winter, for it sought out all, young and old alike, and for Pelia and Cerian, as for all others in Llan Huell, times were hard and food scarce. Thank the goddess Brid then for her gift of fire that brought heat and light in those dark times, for without her there would have been no warm hearth for them to huddle round.

By the time the first signs of spring finally came to Llan Huell, all were sick of life within its timber walls. Finally they could tell themselves that though there were still frosts to come, perhaps even brief snow, still the days would quickly lengthen now and any such cold snap would not last long.

More than most, Pelia longed to roam far and wide beyond the sharpened stakes of the stockade wall, for the winter hardships meant that such things were beyond reason for all but the best hunters when there was little food and much danger amongst the hungry beasts of the forest. A few years ago she had heard of a man from a settlement in the next valley, who had chanced upon one of the great bears, woken early from its winter sleep under an old fallen tree deep in the silent forest. The bear had savaged him with its long claws, and though he escaped to tell the tale, he did not live long after the bear's angry spirit entered his wounds and gave him a high fever. Such are the dangers of the lonely woods in winter.

One evening as the twilight gathered in, Pelia and Cerian went to see Aneurin the hunter. Though most of the men were to be found in the hall of the chieftain keeping up their boasts and their gossiping, Aneurin was not amongst them. Mostly he preferred his own company. It was no surprise then for the pair to find him sitting outside his hut, as he liked to keep a fire going there in the spring evenings so that he could watch the moon and the stars until the chill sent him inside to his bed.

Sealgair the great hound lay by the hunter's side, but at the sight of his mistress, he lifted his long tail, which started to wag.

'Pelia, Cerian,' Aneurin inclined his head, as Sealgair wandered over to greet them with a friendly nuzzle of Pelia's side.

'You see?' the hunter said. 'I may feed him and leave him a space by my fireside, but his heart belongs to you Pelia.'

Pelia smiled back. 'Your words are kind Aneurin, but I think Sealgair looks to you as his master now. Once again I must thank you for his care.'

'You care for many others in these parts,' Aneurin answered graciously, 'so I will gladly look after Sealgair when food is scarce. He will return to you when the summer comes.'

Pelia once again felt the awkwardness of Aneurin's love

for her, though it was hidden well enough in his words. For a moment she could not think of a reply, until Cerian broke in.

'We are going to the woods tonight Aneurin,' she said brightly, 'and we wondered if you could unbar the gate for us when we return.'

'We will come around the stockade to your hut and call for you, so that you know when we are returned,' Pelia added. 'That is if it doesn't put you to any trouble.'

'It puts me to no trouble,' Aneurin said, though worry lines creased his forehead. 'Will you go far?'

'There is a grove in the woods that I know of,' Pelia said trying to reassure him. 'It is a way off.'

'I could come with you then,' Aneurin offered. 'It would be safer for you…'

'The moon goddess rises full,' Pelia shook her head, 'and there are things of magic that I need to gather. Things that the presence of a man might taint.'

'Oh,' Aneurin said a little embarrassed. 'I understand.'

'Besides, we both have our staves,' Cerian added, twirling hers around as she had seen the older boys do when they practiced their fighting.

There was the hint of a smile on Aneurin's thin lips, but though he no doubt laughed inside, he kept his amusement from Cerian, not wanting to offend her.

'If I cannot come with you,' he said, 'then take Sealgair. He would defend you with his life, just as surely as I would in his place.'

Pelia felt herself blush a little despite the gathering chill, and she lowered her head so that her eyes no longer met Aneurin's.

'You will not be long before you return?' the hunter asked.

'No, not long,' Pelia answered, turning to go.

'Then keep safe, both of you,' Aneurin said, his voice anxious as Pelia called Sealgair after her.

In the gathering gloom, the two young women left the high gate of Llan Huell behind them and headed for the edge of the woods, the great hound Sealgair loping off ahead of them as if he knew their way. Pelia felt a thrill of excitement in her spine. By day, she knew these woods as well as the back of her hand, but by night all was different. The light of the moon overhead strengthened against the gathering darkness, lighting their way with its silvery glow. Some said that at times like these the older tree spirits woke at night to whisper their secrets to each other, and that strange faces appeared in the knots of their trunks to scare any folk who dared to roam beneath them. Pelia shivered at the thought despite herself.

'You are cold?' Cerian asked.

'Ach no, I'm fine,' Pelia shrugged.

'Aneurin really likes you,' Cerian went on, trying to cover her own nervousness with talk as they passed a grinning oak tree.

'It is plain to see,' she continued when Pelia didn't answer.

'I know, I know…,' Pelia answered with a sigh.

'I think a woman could easily love him,' Cerian continued. 'He's very kind and quite handsome too I think. He will make someone a good husband.'

'He will...'

'I saw the way you pushed your hair behind your ear, when you spoke to him,' Cerian said again. 'It is what I find myself doing when I talk to someone I like.'

'Cerian,' Pelia shook her head. 'You are a terrible tease.'

Now the two resumed their silence, for this was a solemn time to be wandering in the deep, bare woods under the gaze of the moon goddess. With Sealgair once more at their side they came to a small clearing where many years ago two great oaks had fallen. Here the trees gave way to a grassy glade where primroses glowed, their yellowness banished to a pale blue by the silvery light. This was a place of magic it was plain to see, for here also were birch trees, tall and graceful, their white bark shining bright in the moonlight. Pelia approached one of them, and stooped near the foot of its trunk, where a clay pot was tied against it.

'Thank you for the gift of the sap,' she said, placing her hand on the smooth bark before she untied the pot and lifted it away carefully to the waiting hands of Cerian.

'It is nearly full!' Cerian whispered excitedly, lifting the woven reed lid.

Pelia remained silent as she withdrew the length of hollow reed from the round hole she had bored through the bark with a knife a few days before. Now she took from her purse a small piece of birch wood she had already made to use as a stopper and pushed it into the hole. It was too big, but after a little whittling it was soon a snug fit.

'Now we need a log,' she said to herself, as she cast about for such a thing on the forest floor.

In the moonlight she saw a heavy piece of oak and she hammered the stopper home with it, the dull thud echoing around the silent woods. After a few knocks, only a small part of its length stuck out and the hole was sealed.

'The sap is the lifeblood of the tree,' she explained to Cerian. 'If we don't stop up the hole, then the tree will bleed and may weaken, perhaps even die.'

Cerian nodded, her face pale and ghostlike in the moonlight against her dark plaits of hair.

'Now there is one more thing,' Pelia continued. 'We must bless the tree for its gift a final time. Make a ring with me around the tree.'

Cerian put the sap pot down and took up Pelia's hands on either side of the birch, so that they made a circle about its girth.

'Now that a ring is formed we must pass slowly, sun-wise around the tree. Close your eyes Cerian, while I ask for a blessing of the sap.'

And so they danced slowly round the tree three times, the magic number. Though Cerian could not see Pelia's face, she heard the wise woman singing softly as they stepped in time.

'Once for the maiden, once for the goddess, once for the old one,' Pelia sang quietly over and again.

Cerian joined in too, so that the goddess of the earth would bless the tree and the sap it had given them.

Sealgair watched on as they paced and sang, his head on his outstretched paws, though his ears twitched now and again at some other distant sound that passed by the ears of Pelia and Cerian.

When they had finished the dance, Cerian took up the pot and they moved on to another birch on the edge of the clearing, where another pot waited for them, and then to a third tree, performing the same ceremony at each.

'There are a few midges in this one, Cerian said, looking under the lid of the last pot they had collected.

'It often happens,' Pelia said, offering her a small twig. 'Here, fish them out with this. They will have done no harm.'

'I have heard the sap is sweet, but I can't remember ever tasting it,' Cerian said hopefully.

Pelia was surprised at this. 'Never in your life?'

Cerian shook her head.

'Well it is not so sweet as honey, but all the same. Go on, try some.'

Cerian hesitated. 'What will the magic do?'

'Don't worry,' Pelia smiled. 'The magic is not complete until the three pots are mixed, one with the other, and even then you would still need to lie with a man to fall pregnant. Some of the sap we can drink ourselves, or trade for grain perhaps. But that which is formed of the three I will keep aside, for it is a powerful charm for those women who do not easily fall pregnant.'

Cerian still hesitated.

'Go on, drink,' Pelia urged her. 'It will do you no harm.'

'There is one I like,' Cerian said. 'But I have not lain with him,' she added hurriedly.'

Pelia smiled. 'I know as much. But don't worry, even if you do have a tussle, the sap alone will not make you conceive. That will be for the goddess to decide.'

She took the pot from Cerian and drank from it herself, to show that it was good, then passed it back to her friend who also gently sipped.

'Mmm, it's good,' Cerian grinned, excited at overcoming her fears. 'I could drink this every day.'

'Ah, but then the trees would grow weak and die. This is why we must only take a little from each tree, and then only once, just before the leaves start to appear. Will you remember what we have done tonight?'

'I will.'

'Then the lesson is well learnt,' Pelia nodded. 'Perhaps one day you will pass it on to someone else, as my mother passed it on to me.'

'Perhaps,' Cerian said thoughtfully. 'Did they have this magic in the land of Kemet?' she asked as they covered up the pot again

'I don't think so. There are no forests there like ours, only the palm trees. My father's people had their own magic and their own gods. All very different to ours, as you have heard.'

'The earth goddess too?'

'They don't name her as such, but perhaps she appears to them in other ways. Still, the Greek tribes I told you of earlier, they are different again. They look for their gods in the sea and the sky as much as on the land.

'Anyway, we should walk back now. The forest can be a dangerous place, beautiful though the night is. We should not linger, even with Sealgair at our side.'

-ϕ-

Though his wounds slowly healed and Naphren watched over him with all the tenderness of a mother, the pain of losing his father stayed with Talakhonsu, and it would not ease. For he had also lost also his friend and constant companion, one who had been snatched away from him in the cruellest of ways. Yes, Naphren did what she could for the boy, but she could not cure his sadness.

After a few days a Persian man came with some soldiers, and another one who, though he looked like a native of Kemet, spoke both the Persian and the Kemet tongues. After a lot of talking, they went away leaving Siamun in a great rage and Naphren crying. The overseer had been told that the lands he watched over were now to be divided between two Persian lords and though he was to remain in his duties, they were only over one part of the farm now. Siamun's standing was much diminished as a result and from now on times would be leaner for his household, all the more so for Talakhonsu

Thoughts of Meketra would often come to the boy's mind in the evening when the day's work was done.

'Do you think he will return?' he would ask Naphren.

'Who can say Talakh, who can say?' Naphren would shake her head. 'Perhaps he has gone back to his own people?'

The weeks passed and then the months too with no sign or word from Meketra, and time dragged slowly on for Talakh as if he were in a strange dream. For now he was truly lost in the land of Kemet, not knowing what was to become of him. By day he worked listlessly in the fields with the sons of the other farm workers. In the evenings he sat staring at his feet, not wanting to talk or play with Siamun's daughter, though she tried many times to make him laugh. That part of him, that carefree boy who laughed and ran, had died with Korkamani. In these desolate times he had become a shadow of himself, living the days without a purpose.

The years passed, one, two, three, four of them, and Talakh grew from a boy into a tall, thin youth on the verge of manhood, his hair long ago abandoned to a wiry bush that others would make fun of. Sometimes, when the Persian yoke around their necks chided too much, the men of the fields would tell the old stories of their ancestors' victories over the hated Kush to the south. He knew they meant nothing by it. In their minds he was not of the Kushites, but then neither was he of Kemet. For as Talakh came to realise, even though he now spoke the Kemet tongue as well as any, still here in this place he would always be considered an outlander. Napata and his life in that far off place was nothing now to him but a sad, ever more distant dream.

There came the time when the river was in full flood, as it did every year through the will of the river goddess, so that the land would be rich again. The water crept ever wider over the fields, inundating the ditches and tracks that connected them, so that there was little work that could be done. When the floods had started to recede a little, kindly Naphren sent Talakhonsu on an errand to deliver some fowl eggs to their Persian overlord who lived in one of the grand houses near the edge of Waset itself. The youth did as he was bid, carrying them carefully in a wicker basket lined with old straw so that none would be cracked. He remembered the way well enough from a time when he and the older boys had been sent to whitewash the Persian lord's house.

After he had delivered the eggs safely into the hands of the keeper of this great house, Talakh wandered off with the empty basket toward the far distant walls of the great temple of Mut, goddess and wife of great Amun. It was then that the face of the hated one Khaemwaset suddenly flashed into his mind again. Anger rekindled anew in Talakh's heart as he remembered being offered to the temple priest of Khonsu and all that had come to pass after that. How he wished now that he had died then, for perhaps Korkamani would have escaped and would still be alive.

Talakh spat at the evil memories of this place and turned his back on Waset to make his return to the farm of Siamun. But he did not go straight there, for another face had come to him, that of Meketra. A curious thought crossed Talakh's mind and so he wandered around the network of paths leading away from the great city between the flooded fields, trying to remember a half forgotten place from long ago when he was still a boy.

Back and forth Talakhonsu wandered along the tracks for some while, until at last something sparked in his memory. Ahead of him lay Waset again, now hidden off behind a cloak of palm trees, while in the distance loomed the parched mountains of the dead on the western side of the Great River. The farm of Siamun was a way off to his right, but there, near a fork in the track. Yes, there it was, a leaning palm tree that looked as if a strong wind might blow it over. The sight of it took him back to when he had been led there by Meketra all those years ago. Beyond the leaning palm there were a few scattered boulders with dry grass growing around them, but one of them in particular caught his eye as he wandered off the path and deeper amongst the palms. It was a large rock that looked as if at some distant time it had been hewn into a rough block before being abandoned. Too heavy even for a dozen men to move, it lay out of the way by the foot of another palm. Yes, there was no reason for anyone to have noticed this rock amongst any of the others there really, Talakh said to himself with a wry smile. Yet only he and Meketra knew that it was the place where the tall warrior had hidden his cache of weapons all those years before. He could almost see Meketra kneeling down there to scrape out his hiding place with an old discarded rib bone from the side of the track. Meketra, once the right hand man of Broken Nose. What had befallen him?

Talakh crouched down as Meketra had once done and started to dig under the base of the rock with a stick. The dry, sandy earth gave way easily into a hole, but Talakh did not reach in straight away. No, he was careful now. For in such places as these, poisonous serpents dwelt that could kill a man with one bite. Instead he probed around in the hole with the stick, listening as he did so in case a snake might betray itself by hissing or rustling its coils.

When he was sure that nothing lived within, he scraped more of the earth away, looking warily behind him now and again in case anyone might be watching. Then he reached in with his arm and felt around. The hollow under the stone was deeper than Talakh had thought and he had to reach in almost up to his armpit to find its limits with his fingertips. There was nothing there, nothing at all. He cast his mind back to seeing Meketra wrap his long dagger and axe in a strip of cloth, together with some gold discs and one of his heavy throwing sticks. There was no sign of that parcel of things precious to Meketra.

Talakh sat down on the stone to think. Perhaps someone else had found the cache and stolen it? But then, no. If that had happened, he thought to himself, well then the earth would not have been packed back in so carefully to seal the hollow up again. No, it must have been Meketra who had returned to collect his weapons. But then that left another question, Talakh puzzled again. There would have been no reason for Meketra to seal it up again either, unless...

He got back down on his knees again and reached back into the hollow, this time letting his fingers trace around more carefully. Then with great excitement, he felt something smooth and round, something too thin to be a stone. He clutched it in his fingers and drew out his hand to reveal a small disc of metal, silver as the bright disc of the moon at night. Talakh rubbed it with his thumb and the metal shone even brighter underneath. Pressed into its face was the shape of a woman's head, whilst on the other side were rearing horses that pulled a war chariot. The bright metal had value and could be traded for many things, this much he knew. It was a beautiful thing and Talakh's heart soared as he realised Meketra must have left it for him.

He reached into the hollow again and felt something else that might have been the end of a twig. He could easily have ignored this, but something told him to see what it was and when he withdrew his arm this time he was holding a small bronze knife. The blade was fine, and though the bronze was dulled through being in the ground, still it had a sharp edge to it. Meketra had not forgotten him after all, Talakh was sure of that now. Why else would he have left these things, both precious and useful, yet small enough for Talakh to conceal from the prying eyes of Siamun?

Talakh stood up again, feeling the cool breeze on his face as it whispered through the palms, and he knew then in his heart that Amun had led him there. The great god had not forsaken him after all. He searched one last time to make sure that Meketra had left nothing else for him, then hid the coin and knife in a fold in his tunic, under the piece of cord that served him for a belt.

Talakhonsu's heart was much lighter walking back to the farm of Siamun, for now he did not feel so alone. The birdsong sounded sweeter, the bright sky seemed bluer, and the distant singing of men treading mud and straw to make bricks brought a rare smile to his face. For the first time since the murder of Korkamani, the friend and protector he had known only too briefly as his father, the young Napatan felt like there might yet come a time when his sadness would leave him. He told no-one of his discoveries when he came to the farmstead, though it was true to say that Naphren noticed a change for the better in the young man from that time on.

Whilst Talakhonsu hid away the silver coin where none would easily find it, he kept the knife about him constantly as a reminder of Meketra's friendship. When Siamun asked where it had come from, Talakh told him that he had found it on his errand to Waset, which was no lie. But though the overseer wanted the blade for himself, no doubt to sell or trade, kindly Naphren appealed to him that Talakh be allowed to keep it, as he had had little enough good fortune in his young life.

So it was that Talakhonsu, with memories of Meketra in his thoughts, began to carve himself a new throwing stick from a piece of heavy, dark wood he had found at the river's edge. It was a slow task, for the wood was hard, almost as hard as stone, but gradually it took a shape somewhere between a dog leg and the S of a crawling snake, just like the sticks of Meketra. When all was finished, Talakh sanded the wood smooth with a piece of rough stone, and then polished it with oil to stop the harsh sun from cracking it. This was the first thing he had made by himself with none to guide him and as he gave the stick a few throws his heart filled with pride. The stick flew straight and true, at least most of the time, spinning round on itself as it carried through the air.

And so in the evening when the work of the fields was done, Talakh would always have this new throwing stick with him. Sometimes he would practice with it in the fields against a target of old palm fronds, throwing and retrieving over and again to improve his aim. Other times he hunted amongst the reeds for waterfowl, listening for a rustle that might betray his prey, though around the farm of Siamun the birds were wary and hard to surprise. Rare were his kills and often were the times when he nearly lost his prized stick in the water of the canals, for the wood was so heavy that it barely floated.

Sometimes he would throw with his favoured left hand and sometimes with his right. He wanted to throw well with both, just like Meketra had, though for the time being he found that impossible.

It was not long after this that Talakhonsu put on a final spurt of growth as he neared manhood. He had his father's blood after all and Korkamani had been a tall, lean man. Within a short while he overtook by some way all of the other young men of the surrounding land, but with this change also came trouble. Once again it was easier for those around him to notice the differences between them and some of the others of his age were always at their happiest when they called him names.

There was an animal sometimes seen in those parts of Kemet, though it was very rare, called the giraffe. It was as tall as the trees, owing to its long legs and even longer neck, so that it could eat the leaves from the highest branches. Now, Talakhonsu was the giraffe, and the others took much fun from laughing behind his back and calling him this. Siamun too resented Talakh all the more, for in the young Napatan who towered over him he surely saw a stronger, more able man emerging. A cuckoo in his nest.

All of these things brought it home to Talakhonsu that he would never truly be accepted amongst these people. But if he saw that things could not remain as they were, still he could not see what path he should take in his life to change them. And so, although Meketra's gift of the coin of silver could have carried him away from the farm of Siamun and his tormentors, like Talakh's path through life, it remained hidden.

One day, Naphren surprised Talakhonsu by making him a gift of a kilt she had cut from some coarse linen. The cloth was not of a good quality, so it had come at a modest price, but even so when old Siamun saw Talakh wearing it out in the fields he was furious.

'Where did you come by this?' he raged, though he surely knew the answer already.

Talakh felt the anger burn in his throat, but he knew it would not be wise to answer back. The summer before, his voice had broken and, now that it was as deep as a man's, this seemed to anger Siamun all the more. Still, even though he held his tongue, this made the overseer angrier than ever. When he finally stomped off, cursing others as he went, Talakh knew that trouble awaited him when he returned to the farm. After the others went back to their homes that evening, the young man stayed in the fields taking out his anger with the throwing stick until his arms ached and the sun had set. Only then did he return to the farm of Siamun.

The smell of baked fish still hung in the air when he arrived there, but though the dogs barked to welcome him home, Siamun thankfully did not appear. Now that old age pursued him, the overseer often slept for a while after his supper. In the cool darkness of the old mud brick storeroom that was now his home, Talakh lay on his mattress of straw, alone with his thoughts until a while later he heard Naphren's voice whisper his name.

'Talakh,' she said. 'I have your supper for you.'

Talakh drew aside the woven palm leaf panel that served as a door and stepped outside into the starry night.

'Thank you,' he said taking the flat bread and bowl of stewed beans that she offered him.

'Go on, eat,' Naphren smiled, her teeth showing black by the light of her lamp.

She seemed to grow older every day Talakh thought, her eyes weakened by age. But then life was harder for her now that her daughter was married off and there was no servant to help with the jobs of the house. Now that Siamun's lands had diminished, the whole household was poorer. Talakh saw that he too made life harder for her, for he had come between Naphren and her husband, and Siamun could be a cruel man with his words to her.

'Thank you Naphren,' he touched her bony hand, a warmth in his voice that was kept only for the old woman. 'You have always been very kind to me.'

Naphren smiled sadly.

187

'I could not see you left alone and lost in the world when Korkamani died,' she said, her eyes glistening in the flickering light. 'He was such a good man. You must not forget him.'

'You know I never will,' Talakh said. 'I won't forget you either, kind Naphren.'

Naphren smiled her sad smile again as she guessed at what he meant.

'When will you go?' she said, lowering her head to hide her tears.

'I had not decided until now,' he said thoughtfully. 'But I think I must leave when the sun rises tomorrow. There are things that I must do.'

'I understand,' Naphren spoke quietly as the tears ran down her cheeks. 'You are almost a man now, but I will always remember you as the boy who came to us. I will miss you.'

'And I you,' Talakh said fondly.

He wished his own tears would come then, so that Naphren would see that he cared for her too, but they would not. He had been too badly hurt by the murder of his father and there were no tears left for anybody else. He hugged Naphren close to him all the same and kissed her wrinkled cheek.

'Will you ever come back?' she asked pitifully.

Talakh looked at the old woman, and saw the pleading in her eyes, but he could not give her false hope.

'Only the gods can know that,' was all that he could bring himself to say.

And with that he sent Naphren back to her husband, hoping that when he had gone the overseer would be kinder to his wife in the years that she had left to her.

Talakh slept but little after he had finished eating the bread and beans Naphren had brought him, so that when the first faint light of the day touched the night sky he was already wide awake. There was not much for him to take away, just his water skin to sling over his shoulder, and the new kilt that Naphren had made for him. He wore his old, patched tunic as the night was still cool and through his cord belt he looped the heavy throwing stick. His small knife, precious gift of Meketra, he hid in his old folded kilt and this he wrapped in his thin, cloth blanket, tied into a length so that he could carry it over his shoulder along with the water skin.

When Talakh stepped outside the store house for the last time, the dawn was gathering and the first of the morning birds sang cheerfully, but he had one last job to do before he left. A pile of wet mud lay under a tree, ready to be mixed with straw to repair the walls of the house of Siamun, and Talakh took some of this and carefully fashioned a tiny figure of a cow, using thin pieces of hollow reed for its legs and tail. He had not much time, and it was still quite dark, but still he surprised himself by how well it looked with its raised up ears and open mouth.

When it was finished, Talakh stole into the courtyard of the house, patting the two dogs that guarded there so that they would not raise an alarm with their barking. In the courtyard was a small covered shrine by the doorway to the house, dedicated to the god Bes, protector of households. Talakh left the cow figure on the small offering stone at the shrine's foot, whispering a plea to the god that he would watch over Naphren as she slept and keep her safe. He could hear the rattling snores of Siamun coming from within the house, but it would not be long before the overseer awoke, and so he left quickly.

In the cool morning air the young Napatan stole quietly along a track that led him to the place he had hidden the silver coin of Meketra and it was a great relief to him when he found it still in its hiding place, wrapped in its small piece of cloth. The silver shone just as brightly as always in the first light of the sun that now spilled over the horizon, but this time he did not wrap the coin back up and return it to the ground. No, instead Talakh dropped it into his water skin, a safe hiding place where none would think to look, he was sure of that.

Now, although he did not know much of the ways of trading for coin in the land of Kemet, still Talakh knew that the silver disc was too valuable to exchange just for food. The only way was for him to trade it for something else more useful and so he quickly made his way into the great city of Waset, thinking as he went of how he might try to find out the coin's true worth. First he went to a man he had heard of who traded in cloth and other rich things. Talakh knew he was wealthy despite the taxes of the Persians.

'My master is new to this place and sends me to ask how many pieces of copper you will give him for each silver coin he has,' he said to this one.

'He is from the south?' the man nodded, as if he knew everything there was to know about Talakh's imagined master. 'And what weight are these coins of silver of his?' he asked doubtfully.

'I do not know,' Talakh hesitated. 'But they are this big,' he added, drawing a small circle on his palm.

'If the coins are of that size and the correct weight, I suppose I could give one arm's length of my finest linen cloth for each silver coin I am prepared to trade,' he said, a greedy look in his eye.

'But my master wants copper, not linen!' Talakh protested.

'Then I would give him double the amount of copper pieces for the amount of silver ones he gives me,' the man said, his face beaming with a generous smile. 'But only, mark me, if the coins are true and haven't been clipped. Of course I would have to see them first.'

Talakh had at least heard of this practice of cutting off a part of a coin of silver to arrive at the right value in trade.

'The coins are not clipped,' he said firmly. 'My master is an honest man. I will tell him what you have said, but I don't think he will be interested.'

'You serve your master well,' the man said, smiling. 'As I am a generous man, I will offer my best price. Tell him he will have five and twenty pieces of copper for each ten of silver that he brings me. Provided as I say that the coins are true'

'I will tell him,' Talakh said and turned to leave.

'You will not get a better price in Waset!' the man shouted after him. 'Be sure to tell your master that!'

Now, Talakh did not trust the man at all, but still he knew a little more than he had before; a piece of silver was worth at least two of copper, though he suspected his coin was worth far more than that.

Next he went to a part of the city where a great many people traded their wares before the heat of the day grew too great for them. Of course there were many Kemet traders, but also some of the desert peoples. These ones came and went with the desert winds carrying their herbs, spices and scented oils from places unknown. There were Persians too, with their coiled beards and hair, their lighter skin and finely patterned clothes trimmed with many colours. Phoenicians also had their stalls here and there. They were traders of the sea who had long been allies of the great Persian kings. Looking around, Talakh saw many others besides, men and women whose homelands he could not even guess at, with their strange clothes and customs. Some were dark of skin like him, but most were much lighter, like the Persians.

It was then that Talakh saw a man and his family who were like no others there, for everything about them was different. The head of the family was a man past his best years, but still a formidable figure with his simple open tunic of plain white linen bound around his waist by a heavy leather belt so that he showed off a bare, broad chest. He wore wide leather bands about his wrists, as archers do, and another narrow strip circled his forehead to tie back his long hair which, though it was thinning a little, was the colour of sun ripened wheat.

His wife was there too, sitting in the shadow of a palm. Most of the time she looked down at the sewing in her lap, but now and again her dark eyes looked up. She was much younger than her husband, her skin the colour of pale honey and her hair was a mass of thick black curls raised up on top of her head. That is, all but a single strand which hung down the side of her face and onto her shoulder. She was a rare beauty and Talakh's spirits warmed at the sight of her. He was after all a young man, with a young man's yearnings of the heart. The woman had two sons, both younger than Talakh. One had long hair that shone like the sun and eyes the colour of the blue sky, just like his father. The other son took after his mother and was already marked out to be slighter of build and much darker than his brother.

'They must be Greek,' Talakh told himself, as he stared at their strangeness.

For their wares, these Greeks were traders in bronze it seemed and spread out on rush mats in front of them were all manner of things made of this metal, from bowls and spoons, to small mirrors for fine ladies to colour their eyes and lips by. They seemed wealthy enough, so Talakh approached them with the same questions as to the value of his silver coin.

'Do you speak the Kemet tongue?' he asked first, the nerves catching at his voice.

'Of course,' the man said, his accent thick and heavy.

My master is a wealthy man,' Talakh said boldly, though the Greek looked at him with some doubt in his eyes at this.

'Yes,' Talakh continued, 'a wealthy man he is. He has a number of silver coins which he wishes to exchange for copper, so that he can make gifts to the poor. What would you give him for each silver coin, he asks?'

The man looked even more doubtful now.

'And where is this master of yours boy?' he asked. 'Perhaps I have heard of him?'

The eyes of the man's sons and his pretty wife were on Talakh now and he felt like turning on his heels and running away from this challenge, but still he stood his ground.

'My master is at a house he has taken at the edge of the city,' he pointed. 'We are newly arrived from the south, so you will not know of him, but he is very wealthy.'

'And he sends you to trade his coins?' the Greek said, looking Talakh up and down. 'I will tell you what I think boy,' he said with a hint of anger in his voice. 'I think that your words do not ring true. Any silver you can lay your hand on has probably been stolen from your master.'

'I have not stolen anything!' Talakh protested, suddenly angered by the Greek's words. 'I came by the coin honestly enough.'

'Ah,' the man said with a glint in his eye. 'So now there is only one coin?'

'Yes...' Talakh hesitated. 'It was left to me by a friend. A man who saved my life a long time ago, when I was a boy.'

'Hah!' the Greek laughed. 'Some would say you still are a boy! Well, I should send you on your way, but I will hear your story if you have time to give it, for we men of Kypros love a good yarn. Spin yours for me, and if it is a good tale perhaps I will give you a piece of bread!'

The insult burned in Talakh's chest.

'I am no beggar!' he said fiercely. 'I have always earned my keep through honest work, as my hands show,' he said holding up his palms. 'I will tell you my story, but I will take no bread from you.'

At this the Greek man turned to his wife, who shrugged her shoulders and said something in their own tongue.

'My wife says you have an honest face, young man,' he said. 'And for myself, I say your pride does you credit. Now come, sit with my sons and tell us your story, for we would be pleased to hear it my young friend. I am called Miltiades, this is my wife Eulalio, my sons Paramonos,' he pointed to the dark-skinned one, 'and Zotikos,' he glanced at the other son with a face that beamed with pride. Zotikos was obviously the favoured son.

'Some bread and water for our guest, Eulalio,' Miltiades said to his wife, once Talakh had sat down amongst them. 'What is your name young man?' he asked, turning his sky-blue eyes on Talakh.

'Talakhonsu. But Talakh to my friends,' he answered proudly.

'That sounds like no name of Kemet that I ever heard,' Miltiades said, rubbing his chin with his broad, stubby fingers, one of which had long ago lost its end.

'I am not from Kemet,' Talakh replied. 'My homeland is far to the south in Napata, but I have no home there now. I will tell you my story,' he said, 'though it causes me pain. All of those who were dear to me are gone now.'

And so Talakh began his story, whilst Miltiades and his family listened. The sun grew hotter as he told of his childhood in Napata, of the priests who had taught him much, of his loving mother, and of how all of these things were swept away by the evil of Khaemwaset and his men.

Next he told of the journey over the cataracts of the Great River and of the hardships and horrors he had known. He spoke then of how brave Korkamani had protected him to his dying breath, and how only then had he learnt that Korkamani was his true father. As tears rolled down Eulalio's pretty cheeks, Talakh spoke of Meketra, and of how the young Kemet warrior had brought him to safety, before going back to search for Broken Nose.

'And so you see,' he finished, 'this was how I came by the coin of silver and the bronze knife that Meketra left for me.'

Miltiades nodded gravely. 'I see a terrible truth in your story, Talakhonsu,' he said. 'You have seen too many horrors for such a young man, things that I shudder to think of happening to my own boys.'

Eulalio nodded at that.

'You are very brave to have borne all of these things,' she said gently.

'Yes, very brave...,' Miltiades echoed her. 'But still you are here in spite of everything, with your pride intact, and a free man too. What will you do now? Where will you go?'

'I... I don't know,' Talakh answered honestly. 'Perhaps the gods will guide me.'

'Perhaps they will, perhaps they will not,' Miltiades shrugged his shoulders. 'But of one thing you can be sure lad, every man needs to think out a plan for themselves. Otherwise, how will you feed yourself? How will you find a woman and raise children?'

Talakh thought for a moment.

'I do have a plan,' he said finally, 'though it is nothing more than a place to start really. I must go to find the resting place of my father Korkamani, if I can. When Meketra and I buried him, I was still a boy. Perhaps his spirit will be able to see me from there. See me as I am now...'

'And this is why you want to change your silver coin into copper discs, so that you can trade them for food for your journey?' Miltiades guessed. 'Can I see this coin of yours?'

Talakh trusted Miltiades and his family now that they had treated him as a guest and shared their water with him, so he nodded his agreement, and reached for his own water skin. After taking a gulp from, he upended it so that the water glugged out onto the ground. There on the wet sand at his feet lay the shining silver coin.

'Hah!' Miltiades laughed and clapped his hand on his thigh. 'A clever place to hide your coin, young Talakhonsu. But did you know that we Greeks also do this to stop our water tainting on long sea voyages?'

Talakh shook his head as he offered the cool silver disc to Miltiades.

'Yes, silver has the quality of keeping the water sweet,' Miltiades continued, turning the coin over in his hand as he looked over it carefully.

'My people are scattered over many lands and islands, Talakhonsu, and there are many, many lords, many kings, and many tyrants who rule over them too. Most of the great cities and islands have their own silver coin, each with a different face to them, but otherwise more or less the same size and weight. Do you see the image on this side?' he pointed to the head of the woman with her slender nose. 'She is Arethusa, a beautiful water spirit, said to dwell in the streams of the great island this coin comes from.'

'Where is that?'

'It is a place called Sikelia, a greater island even than my own home of Kypros. It lies like a jewel far off to the west in the Middle Seas. There are rich cities there and a mountain that spews fire, where the gods of the underworld dwell!'

This fired Talakh's imagination all the more as he struggled to think of what a place such as this Sikelia might look like.

'See how these dolphins swim around the edge of the coin?' Miltiades continued. 'They are the messengers of Poseidon, great god of the sea, and also his eyes above the water when they leap. We Greeks never harm them, not just for this reason, but also because they have a great joy in life. Some say they have carried drowning men to the safety of the shore too, so you see they are a special animal to we Greeks and we love them as we love the sea itself.'

'I would like to see them with my own eyes,' Talakh, said as he tried to imagine the strange creatures that looked like a fish but were not.

'Well, perhaps you might at that,' Miltiades grinned back at him as he turned the coin over again.

'See?' he said, turning now to his sons. 'It is a coin from Sikelia. A tetradrachym. See the chariot? The Sikelians are proud of their games and through this coin they say to us, 'look at our wealth'. They are rich enough to have chariots for racing, not just for war.'

The younger son, dark haired Paramonos, asked his father a question in their own language, a puzzled look on his face.

'Ah, he asks what its value is,' he laughed, winking at his son as he turned back to Talakh. 'Well, it is worth what someone is prepared to trade for it, and that varies from city to city and from land to land.'

'I don't understand father,' Paramonos said now in the Kemet tongue.

'Well,' Miltiades said, rubbing his chin again with his stubby fingers. 'Let me put it to you like this, Paramonos. If I asked you to work all day for me for that cup of water at your feet, would you do this for me?'

'Yes father,' the boy smiled. 'But I would work for you for nothing too.'

'Ha, ha, ha!' Miltiades laughed heartily, tousling his son's hair. 'I know you would Paramonos, you are a good boy,' he smiled. 'But what about you, Zotikos? What do you say on this?'

The golden haired Zotikos turned his eyes to his father, and puffed out his chest as he crossed his arms, before answering his father in their Greek tongue.

'Speak the tongue of Kemet,' Miltiades chided his son. 'Go on boy, otherwise our guest will not hear your wisdom!'

'I said that soon I will be a man father,' Zotikos said boldly. 'And if I am to be a man like you, I would not work all day for a cup of water.'

'Aha! Miltiades clapped his thigh again, a stern look on his face. 'So Zotikos, you are a proud one to be turning down my offer. Your father's son, so your mother says and she is right by Zeus!' he laughed, gripping his son's shoulder with a broad smile.

'Now Zotikos, I will ask the question a different way. Imagine you walk for two days away from the Great River into the desert sands way out there beyond the city of the dead,' Miltiades said with a broad sweep of his arm.

'The sun is scorching, searing into your skin until it blisters like a burn from a fire, all across your back and shoulders. Your lips, they crack open and burn with the salt from your dripping sweat. You grow weak and though you cast around, there is no water anywhere to drink,' he said, his blue eyes wide and fierce. 'You look above you to see the vultures gathering in the sky overhead, waiting to pick your bones clean…'

'Miltiades, do not say such things,' Eulalio protested, her face a picture of worry.

'Now, Zotikos,' Miltiades continued, pretending he had not heard his wife, 'you see a man coming toward you out of the shimmering heat. A tall man with a broad chest and a noble brow. A handsome man, brave and strong, like a god striding the land! He is holding out a cup of water. You squint against the dazzling sun until finally you recognise his face. It is me!'

'Oh Miltiades! You are a terrible man!' Eulalio scolded him with a tap on his hairy arm.

'Yes,' Miltiades continued with a grin on his face, 'a handsome man. Brave, strong and now terrible too! Well, thirsty Zotikos, you look at the cup of cool clear water, and you want nothing more than this, for without it you will perish of thirst. I ask you now under the desert sun, will you work for me for two days for this cup of water?'

'But father!' Zotikos protested. 'You would only have me work for a day before. Now it is two!'

'And will you work for two days, or will you perish?'

Zotikos thought on this while his family and Talakh

looked on.

'I would like to say no,' he said finally, the frustration plain to see on his face. 'But if I did it would be a lie, for if things were as you have said, I would have no choice but to work. Either that or I would surely die.'

'A good lesson then for you my sons,' Miltiades beamed proudly. 'And for you too young Talakhonsu, I think. Where something is scarce it is always worth more. So it is with silver coin. It is worth what someone is prepared to trade for it, no more and no less.'

'And what would it be worth to you?' Talakhonsu asked coolly.

Miltiades turned the coin over in his hand again and said simply, 'I will trade you a knife and a loaf of bread for it.'

'But I already have a knife,' Talakh answered. 'I have no need of another.'

'Ah yes, the knife of Meketra you spoke of. Can I see it?'

Talakh drew the knife from its hiding place in the fold of his tunic and offered it to Miltiades, who now looked at it with some surprise.

'This is very old,' the Greek said, running his fingers along the length of the blade. 'See?' he showed the knife to his son Zotikos. 'Made of bronze, like the swords of the heroes of old. You have something rare here, Talakhonsu, for knives such as this have not been made for many ages.'

'It holds its edge well,' Talakh nodded.

'Not as well as hardened iron, I think, but it is a fine thing. As you can see, bronze is my trade, so I know good work when I see it.'

Miltiades sat for a moment more, looking over the knife as he turned it over and set his eye along the length of the blade to admire its shape. 'I will make you an offer young man,' he said finally. 'Leave the knife and the coin to my care and my son Zotikos will give you his iron knife in trade, and I will give you enough copper to feed yourself for a week. What do you say to that?'

'Father!' Zotikos protested. 'The knife is mine!'

'Do not worry my son,' Miltiades said, brushing aside the

objection. 'I will find another knife for you better than that one.'

'No, I will not trade the knife,' Talakh said plainly. 'Only the coin.'

'I offer you a good price,' Miltiades cautioned him. 'You will not get a better trade for an old knife and a silver coin.'

'I do not doubt you at that,' Talakh shrugged. 'You seem a fair man to me, but the knife was a gift from Meketra and the fact that it is old and rare means that he wanted me to keep it.'

'Well, perhaps you are right,' Miltiades said, rubbing his chin again.

'And besides I have found it very useful to me. For instance, I made my throwing stick with it,' Talakh said, drawing the heavy stick from the twist in his waist cord.

'Ah, the throwing stick!' Miltiades said with a grin. 'I have heard of these things, but I would sooner have a bow and a quiver of straight arrows than a piece of wood to throw at my enemy!' he laughed good naturedly. 'How is your aim with it?'

Talakh felt his skin prickle at Miltiades's words and so he could not resist a boast when he answered.

'I am better than anyone around here,' he said boldly.

'Ah, better than anyone?' Miltiades laughed again. 'I will set you a wager then if you are so sure.

'Zotikos,' he turned to his son, 'take that broken pot that lies in the dirt and put it in that bush over there so that Talakhonsu can aim for it with this stick of his.'

'What do you wager?' Talakh asked.

Miltiades rubbed his chin again. 'If you win, I will give you... say ten pieces of copper for your silver coin of Sikelia!' he said generously.

Talakh looked at the broken pot. It was small and the bush it now rested in was a long way off, but he knew that on a good day he would usually hit such a target. 'And if I miss?' he asked.

'If you miss, then you lose,' Miltiades said, the smile leaving his face. 'You only have one chance. If you miss the pot, then I keep your knife and the coin. But I am a generous man so I would still give you five pieces of copper.'

'The wager is too one sided,' Talakh said firmly. 'If I win, then you will give me twenty discs of copper for the Sikelia coin.'

'Ha, hah!' Miltiades laughed. 'You bargain well young man. I am in good spirits today and I like you, so I'll give you ten and five of copper, if you strike the pot cleanly.'

'Miltiades!' Eulalio scolded her husband. 'That is too much.'

'No Eulalio,' Miltiades said gently. 'We have much and the lad has little. The gods will decide who should win, but if he should loose, then he will be much worse off than we.'

With that Miltiades carefully placed the knife and coin on the ground in front of him. 'In your own time lad,' he said to Talakh. 'There is no need to hurry.'

And so Talakh stood up, trying to look confident though his heart was in his mouth.

'I will accept your wager,' he said boldly.

The two shook hands on it, but now Talakh was aware that others had overheard the bargain, for two men were placing a wager of their own on the outcome. He swallowed down his nerves as best as he could and hefted the throwing stick in his hand. His palm was sweaty, so he picked up a little dust from the ground to rub into his hands, trying to steady his nerves.

'Never try too hard,' the words of Meketra came back to him from all of those years distant when the young warrior had taught the boy how to throw. Talakh knew not to throw with all of his strength, otherwise his arm would be tense and he would miss. So he practiced, bringing his arm back over his shoulder, as smoothly as he could and then letting it fall forward, slowly uncurling until it had almost straightened in front of him and he could aim down its length toward the target.

In his mind's eye he saw the heavy stick leave his hand and spin slowly, end over end until it vanished into the bush, clearing the pot by an arm's length. He repeated this a second time, but this time his imaginary throw fell short and disappeared into the dust at the foot of the bush. Talakh aimed a third time and this time in his mind's eye the throw would surely have missed again. Fear began to creep into his mind, fear of losing, but then other words came to him, the words of Miltiades this time, 'the gods will decide'.

Something made Talakh turn his face to the north then, to feel for the breeze. It was gentle, but it was there all the same, the breath of Amun on his cheek. He invoked the great god's name to guide his hand, and bringing his arm back a final time he aimed at the bush and threw. The heavy stick left his hand cleanly and all eyes followed its gentle arc until it dipped down to hit the pot with a splintering crash.

'Yes!' Talakh cried, as he leapt into the air for joy.

A small boy who had been watching the wager ran to retrieve the stick for Talakh, and brought it back to him with a piece of the broken pot. When he handed them over, the boy looked up at the young Napatan as if he were a hero.

'Thank you,' Talakhonsu said, as the boy ran back to his mother's call. Now he turned to Miltiades.

'With that throw, you have cost me dear, young man,' the Greek said with a bullish look on his face, but then as Talakh began to doubt if he would honour the wager, Miltiades's face broke into a grin.

'Where did you learn to throw like that?'

'It was Meketra, who I spoke of,' Talakh smiled back. 'He is the one who taught me, but I will never be as good as him. He could throw just as well with either hand, and he never missed. I have seen him beat a spear man in a fight, armed with just his throwing sticks.'

'Was the other one asleep?' Zotikos laughed in disbelief.

'Quiet Zotikos,' Miltiades cautioned his son, who scowled at the ground. 'These are matters for men, not boys. Now,' he said, turning back to Talakhonsu, 'here is your knife back, and in exchange for the silver coin, there are fifteen copper pieces as we agreed. But do not put these in your goat skin, mark me, otherwise your water may taint!'

'I will head your advice,' Talakh said, taking back the knife and the small woven reed pocket that held the coppers safe. He thought about counting them out, but although he had been taught to count well by the priests, he did not for fear of offending Miltiades, who he had decided was an honest man anyway.

The small crowd of onlookers drifted away now, some winners who praised Talakh's aim, while those who had lost their wagers quietly cursed him.

'Tell me more of this Meketra,' Miltiades asked, inviting Talakhonsu to sit in the shade as his guest again.

'Well,' Talakh began as he sat down under the shade of the palm tree, 'when Broken Nose took him from his family he already had his throwing sticks, but he was just a farmer's son, not a fighter. Even so within a few days he had shown how good he was at hunting fowl with them in the marshes. And then he fought another warrior and broke his arm.'

'With the stick?'

'Yes. After that Meketra rose to be one of the most trusted warriors of the war band of Broken Nose,' Talakh continued while Miltiades and his family listened intently. 'But still, even though I was nothing more than a slave, he was always kind to me. It was a long time ago now.'

'Hmm,' Miltiades grunted, his blue eyes narrowed in thought. 'In my trade, I travel much between here and Kypros and I hear many strange tales and rumours. There is one that tells of a giant who throws sticks such as yours. They say he can take a man's ear off at one hundred paces! And he is dark, dark like you, but taller still. As tall as two men, so they say!'

'Meketra was very tall it is true,' Talakh frowned, 'though I was only a boy when I last saw him so he towered over me back then. But I don't think he was as tall as two men!'

'Ah, but we all love a good yarn,' Miltiades laughed. 'It's in the nature of men to exaggerate – ask any fisherman how big was his last catch!'

'But it could be Meketra,' Talakh said with hope in his voice that he might again see his long lost friend. 'Where might he be now?'

'That I cannot tell you,' Miltiades shook his head. Some say he sails the seas with a crew of cutthroats, raiding the trading ships of the Phoenicians. Others say that he lives in a deep cave far to the north along the Great River.'

'I would like to see him again one day.'

'Perhaps you will, but it makes no sense to look for him. Have you heard the saying, to look for a needle in the granary?'

Talakh nodded.

'Well, you will never find it, no matter how hard you look. But on the other hand, if you give up and sit down for a rest you might find it then – sticking in your arse, ha, ha ha!'

Talakh laughed too, as did Zotikos and Paramonos, though Eulalio covered her younger son's ears and scolded her husband for his coarse words.

'Such is the nature of fate,' Miltiades continued, unheeding. 'If the gods will it, you will find your friend.'

The Greek paused now and a more serious look came over his face.

'So we come to the same question again. What will you do after you pay your respects to your father's grave?

'It seems to me,' Miltiades continued, not waiting for an answer, 'that if you were to go back to your homeland, you will only find bitter memories there of the life you once had. You will know no-one and so you will be an outsider, just as you are here.

'Yet you have already made your mind up that you should leave Waset, and I think in this you are right. Your past will always dog you here and so you must go. My advice is to follow the Great River to the north and see where she takes you. Beyond where the river empties into the sea, there is a world that would be as full of wonder to you as Kemet is to me.'

'Your words are wise O Miltiades,' Talakh bowed his head in respect. 'I will take your advice and head north. But first I must say goodbye to my father a final time, for I will not pass this way again.'

'May the gods guide you to happiness and wealth young man,' Miltiades said gruffly, his blue eyes glistening with sadness. 'You have had your fair share of ill luck, that much I know.'

Chapter 10

The Ship and the Oxen

After he had taken his farewell of Miltiades and his family, Talakhonsu began the journey back to his father's burial place, an urgency gathering in him as he drew nearer. So anxious was he that he would not find the grave, that he could not rest in the heat of the day, nor in the cool of the night.

Finally he came to a small barren field surrounded by rock strewn ground that was dotted with a few palm trees. This was the place where he was sure he and Meketra had lain Korkamani's body in the ground many long years ago. With those bitter memories, so his boyhood thoughts came back now as if no time had passed at all between that day and this. The land here was higher than that lying about, out of reach of the floods of the Great River, but the clump of tall palms that he remembered as marking Korkamani's resting place under the dry earth was nowhere to be seen.

Talakhonsu walked further away from the river and then back again several times, each time his memory telling him that this must be the place and yet still he could not make out the exact place where his father lay. It was with much frustration and anger at himself that Talakhonsu finally had to admit defeat and he sat down with his head in his hands, his back to the rough bark of one of the solitary palm trees that dotted the land. So deep in his own thoughts was he that the world of the living dropped away from him and he was left alone in a darker place.

'Why do you cast about here on my land?' a voice suddenly spoke.

Talakh opened his eyes to see an old man there, leaning on a long stick. He wore a long linen tunic that hung to his ankles, as faded and worn as his dark, wrinkled face.

'I ask you again boy,' the frail old man said in his gravelly voice. 'Why do you come here? We have nothing for you.'

'Firstly, I am not a boy,' Talakh said, resentfully.

'Hah!' the old man cackled harshly. 'To my eyes you are.'

Talakh started to grow angry now, but then he thought of Korkamani and what his father would have advised him in such circumstances.

'I make my own way in the world now,' he said, calming himself as he spoke, 'and so I consider myself to be a man.'

'Hmm,' the old man pondered as he leant his chin on his stick. 'Have you taken a wife? Have you raised sons? Daughters? Do you have a family to watch over? No? Then some would say you are not a man until you have done these things.'

'I will not argue with you, old man,' Talakh sighed.

'Old? I am not old!'

'Then I am no boy either,' Talakh said firmly.

The old man laughed at that, so long and silently that Talakh thought he might laugh himself off to his grave.

'You have a quick wit, young man,' he finally allowed when he had recovered his breath. 'But still you do not tell me what you are doing here.'

'I am looking for the grave of my father, who I buried here when I was a boy. But,' he said sadly, 'the palms that marked the place are not here anymore.'

'Your father died here?' the old man looked puzzled.

'No, not here. But here is where we laid him to rest,' Talakh said. 'It is a long story that I do not wish to repeat.'

'Hmm,' the old man pondered again, his rheumy eyes screwing up so that they were no more than slits. 'Perhaps I can help you in your search. There were more trees here right enough, but I needed the roof of my house to be made up, and so the trees were cut down for timber.'

'Here you say?' Talakh said getting to his feet.

'Yes, I am sure of it. Right where you sit is the last of those trees. If you look under the sand you will still find the stumps of the old palms here and there.'

'But no... no bones were found?'

'No,' the old man said, leaning on his stick, 'nothing like

that as far as I recall. If this is where you laid him, then perhaps he is still here in the ground. But the animals, you know...'

'We covered him with heavy stones,' Talakh said, as he used his feet to scrape back the sandy soil. 'The jackal will not have had them.'

The old man hobbled over, his bones stiff with age. 'I will help you look,' he said, tapping the ground with his stick, as he searched around.

Sure enough, it was not long before Talakh found one tree stump, and then another. Then the old man's stick found a large flat stone under the sand that rang hollow when he tapped it.

Talakh dropped to his knees and scrapped back the earth until a layer of flat stones was revealed. He pushed the earth back to cover the stones again, knowing at last that this was the place and so he knelt in silence, his head bowed.

The old man's gnarled hand came to rest on Talakh's shoulder. 'You have found your father now I think, may his spirit always have peace,' he said. 'My name is Sekatu. Where are you from young man?'

Talakh wiped away his tears, so that he would not show them to the old man and got to his feet.

'My name is Talakhonsu. I am from Napata, far off to the south. The land of your enemies.'

'People are only my enemies if they steal my goats or do harm to my kin,' the old man said, leaning back with his head on one side, the better to study Talakh's face. 'Life has taught me that we have enemies enough in Kemet without looking for more of them beyond our lands,' he smiled faintly, offering his bony hand in friendship.

'Thank you for your help,' Talakh said gripping his hand. 'The years have not been wasted on you O Sekatu, you are a wise man.'

Sekatu inclined his head a little, to accept Talakh's compliment.

'Do you journey back to your own lands now?' he asked. 'If so, you have a long and hard walk ahead of you. Even the

Persian king doesn't care to take his army there.'

'No, I will follow the Great River north. That is where my path lies, so a Greek trader helped me to see.'

'The Greeks?' the old man laughed harshly. 'If ever there were a people to cause trouble, it is those ones! Ah but then, they are the enemies of Persia, most of them anyway,' his voice sank low, 'and Persia punishes us all with their grain taxes. Yes the Greeks are a thorn in the Persian king's side, so good for them I say!'

Talakh nodded, though really as he was not of Kemet blood these things mattered little to him.

'Have you any bread to trade?' he asked the old man.

'Hmm, bread,' Sekatu sighed, shaking his head. 'But then what have you to trade?'

'I have copper pieces.'

'Ho!' the old man cackled. 'Do you think I am the treasurer of the granaries? The copper has no value here! You must go to the temple if you wish to trade copper.'

'I have nothing else to barter with,' Talakh said, annoyed that his copper was useless here.

'Then you must go hungry,' the old man shrugged.

'I will go to the river and hunt,' Talakh said, though he was not sure that this would feed his aching stomach.

'Hmm,' the old man pondered again. 'I have an offer for you. If you will work three days in my fields, then I will give you bread. Not enough to make you fat and lazy mind, but enough to keep your belly from growling. On the morning of the fourth day when you leave I will give you half a loaf to be on your way with too, if I am satisfied with your work. That is my offer.'

'Have you no sons to work your land?' Talakh asked. 'No kin?'

'My three sons all walk together in the land of the dead,' the old man said, though there was no bitterness in his voice.

Talakh guessed their deaths had happened a long time ago now.

'I have just left a place where I was bound to the land,' he said with a sigh. 'But I am hungry and my stomach speaks louder than my pride. I accept your offer.'

'Then come young Talakhonsu, and I will show you to your work.'

Sekatu lived poorly with his wife in a simple house made of mud brick which looked to have seen better days. One end of it had fallen down beyond repair, and a rough wall had been drawn across what had been its middle to preserve the half that the old couple still lived in. The wizened wife of Sekatu looked on Talakhonsu with suspicion at first, scolding her husband for bringing another mouth to feed, though he took no notice.

But when Talakhonsu made good their roof with fresh palm branches, tilled their fields with a hand plough and then raised water from the river into other fields that he had freshly sown, so her scowl mellowed. The days passed and both Sekatu and Talakhonsu kept to their parts of their bargain. But though Talakh did not starve, still he lay awake on his bed of palm leaves under the stars long into the night, for his hunger was not fully sated, just as the old man had said.

On the fourth morning, when the sun began to warm the land again, Talakh returned to the grave of Korkamani and made a small offering of bread and water. This was in the hope that his father and mother would be together, happy in the garden of the afterlife.

So the time came for him to take his leave of Sekatu and his wife.

'I hope your harvest is a good one,' he offered, and the old man nodded, fixing Talakhonsu with his eyes, a faint smile on his lined face again.

'I hope you have learnt something here young man,' the old man Sekatu said. 'You have a good way with the land. A farmer's life is one you would suit well I think.'

'Yes, I have learnt something,' Talakh agreed. 'Many men make a life in the fields and are happy for it, but it is not for me. Not anymore.'

'But you are not afraid of hard work, I have seen that.'

'No, my labours have toughened my hands and

strengthened my back it is true. But other things call me now.'

The old man nodded, a twinkle in his eye.

'I knew this about you from the moment I saw you casting about for your father's grave, Talakhonsu. You would never be happy with the simple life we have here. Not until you find what it is that you seek.'

'I'm not sure I will know it even if I find it,' Talakh frowned.

'You will know,' Sekatu said quietly, his voice deep and gravelled. 'Yes, you will know.'

Talakhonsu left the house of Sekatu and his wife then, his goat skin full of clear water and half a heavy loaf of bread under his arm, wrapped in leaves to keep it from drying out in the sun. He did not look back. But he did wonder. Was the old man a seer of things to come? Did he know Talakh's path ahead? The young man, once of Napata but now of nowhere, shivered inside despite the growing heat of the day, as if a shadow were passing over him.

Talakh's path north back along the Great River was a curious mixture of things that came hard and things that came easily, things familiar and others strange, though he avoided Waset with all of the bad memories that place had for him. In the cool evenings he would hunt for fowl with his throwing stick if he came to a reed bed, which often as not he did. Still, the river level had now fallen to its lowest and only once did he manage to down a small duck, just as it took to the air.

When there were no reeds to hunt amongst, he would fish with a small wooden spear he had fashioned from a thin branch, sharpened to a point and hardened by the heat of fire. With this he did not have much luck, no matter how close the fish looked. For all his perseverance he only managed to catch a few small fish that were more stunned than speared. To have a net would have been a great boon to him.

There were times too when there were no settlements to seek a light from to start his own camp fire and without fire to ward of the beasts of the night, there was little sleep for him. Sometimes too he would come to great bends in the river leaving him with the choice of either following the longer route, or risk taking a shortcut into the desert. There were always paths leading away from the river, but only once did his curiosity get the better of him. Soon he had lost his way entirely in the endless sandy hills and had it not been for a goat herder who pointed him back to the river, his own bones might have joined those of the long dead beasts that shone white under the sun god's harsh stare.

Travel north though he might though, still there were none he could find who would trade his copper pieces for food, though some advised him that perhaps the temple priests might be prepared to trade in such a way. And so, Talakh sought out the great temples dedicated to the high gods of Kemet as he continued his journey, always in the hope that bread would soon fill his hungry belly. Sometimes the temples were on his side of the Great River, and sometimes on the far bank so that he was forced to beg a lift from a passing fisherman where he could. Where none would take him, Talakh had no choice but to empty his goat skin of water and fill it full of air to help him float across. Even though he was a good swimmer, the Great River was immensely wide and full of danger from the ferocious khamsa, the water cows and the dangerous currents.

In this way, Talakhonsu crossed the river many times, sometimes finding bread at the temples, sometimes not, according to the mood of the priests. Always his copper was worth less than Miltiades the Greek had said and now he really began to understand the lesson Miltiades had given his sons: that anything, no matter how precious it might be, is only worth what another is prepared to exchange for it. Sometimes that might be little, or even nothing at all.

So, Talakhonsu journeyed on farther and farther north, always following the river where now there were many fisherman casting nets from their small reed boats in the shallows. Farmers still lifted water from the falling river up onto their thirsty crops, but though many things were the same, many things were also different. There were far fewer people of his own skin, though there were more Persians with their colourful robes, strange pointed hats and curling hair and beards. These Persians, so men told him, were taxing the temples heavily, taking much wealth of grain and gold from them. Around many of the temples and the nearby riverbanks, scattered blocks of new stone lay in the dust, since many of the temple repairs begun by the great priests during the Kemet rebellion against the Persians were now abandoned. Yes, the Persians made the nobles and high priests of Kemet pay dearly for the trouble they had caused.

As he travelled, Talakh heard tell of a great city farther north still, close to where the Great River divided itself many times over amongst the vast marshes that bordered the sea. This place was called Menefer and the Persians had chosen to make it their chief seat of power, which in turn brought it up to be the wealthiest city in the whole of Kemet. It was to Menefer that Talakhonsu decided he must go, for perhaps there he might find what he looked for. It was on his long journey to this next great city that Talakh's luck changed at last.

Early one morning, while he was walking through a land of farms, rich fields and cattle, Talakhonsu came to a great ship, run aground in the shallows. He had seen nothing like it before, for it was far sturdier, broader, and longer than any of those he had ever seen. At the high prow of the ship, the captain bellowed orders at his men who were up to their waists in the water below him, pushing with all their might to try to refloat her. There were many of her crew, but none had the cast of the Kemet race, so it was obvious to Talakhonsu that this was a foreign ship.

The Udjat, symbolic eye of the Kemet hawk god Horus, was painted on her bow in blue, white and black. Talakh had heard that this one had been adopted by some of the Greek sailors to ward off evil, so he thought that the strange ship must surely be Greek. The eye looked down sternly at the men straining to free the ship, as if urging them to push harder, but there was no moving it. She was stuck fast and even though the current was slack, still the river's flow worked against their efforts.

It was plain as day for Talakh to see that even the gathered strength of her crew was not enough. He plucked up his courage and raising himself up to his full height he strode down to the river's edge to talk to them.

'Captain!' he shouted. 'Can I help your men?'

The dark haired captain stared down at Talakh, a curious look on his sun bronzed face.

'We need more brawn than your scrawny arms could give us,' he said in the thick accent of the Greeks. Some of his men laughed at that.

Talakh felt anger prickle under his skin and he thought of walking away then, but something made him swallow his pride. If he could somehow help them free the ship, then they might take him with them down the river to Menefer. And so for this reason Talakh resolved to try to help the captain and his crew, despite the Greek's rudeness.

'Perhaps my arm is stronger than you think,' he said. 'I will help you float your ship off the mud.'

The captain waved Talakhonsu away, saving his breath to give his men a further lashing with his tongue, as he cursed and swore at them to push harder.

The young Napatan turned around and retraced his path back the way he had come along the banks of the Great River, angry at the captain's rudeness, yet at the same time resolved to prove him wrong. He was thinking of what his father Korkamani might have done if he had still been alive, for Korkamani was a wise man who always knew what to do.

After a short while he came back to a ploughman he had passed earlier, cooling his pair of oxen in the water as they rested from the plough.

'You have the right idea,' Talakh grinned at the ploughman. 'The day is too hot for ploughing.'

The man said nothing, but nodded his agreement.

'You have a fine pair of oxen there,' Talakh ventured again. 'You know, I was talking to some Greeks who are run aground just down the river. I said to them that only a pair of Kemet oxen would be strong enough to pull them off the mud bank, but you know what Greeks are like. 'No,' they said, 'only a team of Greek bulls would be strong enough to pull us free.' You and I both know they are wrong in that.'

'The Greeks,' the ploughman nodded. 'They are always full of pride, when little enough is due to them.'

'Exactly,' Talakh replied. 'But still, they are better than the Persians.'

'Aye,' the man said grudgingly. 'But that does not say much either.'

'Perhaps we should have a wager with them,' Talakh said thoughtfully, as if the idea had just come to him. 'They are only around the bend there in the river. What if we were to go to them with your oxen and show them how strong these beasts are?'

The man turned to Talakh now and looked him up and down suspiciously.

'Boy,' he said dismissively, 'my master would be angry with me if I took his oxen on such a fool's errand as this one of yours. Why should I do such a thing when there is nothing in it for me but the pride of my oxen?'

Talakh's heart sunk as he realised his plan had not worked, but then the spark of another idea lit up his mind.

'You are a wise man,' he flattered the ploughman. 'If I were in your place I might think the same. But what if I were to offer you a wager of my own?' he asked.

The ploughman's eyes narrowed now as curiosity took over from the suspicion on his face.

'What kind of wager?' he asked.

'Well on your side, you would need to give only a few moments of your time. Just lead your oxen to this ship of the Greeks and show them a thing or two by freeing them. In return they may reward you, so you have little to lose.'

'And what about on your side? What will you wager?' the ploughman sneered, though Talakh had seen his eyes light up at the mention of a Greek reward.

'I will wager you these copper pieces, and this fine bronze knife,' Talakh said, showing the ploughman these things. 'The temple priests will trade these for bread if you have no need of them,' he added hurriedly.

'And what is the wager to be decided on?' the ploughman said eyeing the knife and coppers covetously.

Talakh had already thought on this and now he strode off some way before planting his fishing spear in the mud of the wide river bank. 'I will strike this spear from where you now stand, with my throwing stick,' he called back to the ploughman.

'With only one throw?' the ploughman called back to him.

'Yes,' Talakh agreed. 'One throw only.'

'The spear is too close,' the ploughman called again. 'Take it back another ten... No ten and another ten paces. Full paces mind!'

Talakh's heart sunk again, for that was far too far, but he was determined to push his luck.

'I will take it another five paces only,' he called back. 'Do you agree to that?'

The ploughman hesitated for a moment as he struggled to think in his dull mind how much closer this was, but his impatience got the better of him in the end.

'Oh alright, I agree to your wager,' he said. 'Now hurry up. I must get ploughing again soon or the overseer will be on my back.'

Talakh moved the spear the agreed distance and ran back to the ploughman, hefting the heavy throwing stick in his hand. Once again he was risking all on what Meketra had taught him and what he had learnt since.

'One throw only!' the ploughman reminded him again.

Talakh nodded. He had learnt now, not just from practising against targets, but also from using the stick for hunting that it was best to trust his arm and not to think too hard about the throw. Often all this did was cause him to hook his throw as he tried too hard, and the stick would then dig into the earth ridiculously short of the target. So instead of this, Talakh stepped from one foot to the other to make sure his footing was good in the rough earth, drew back his arm, and as he lunged forward, so his arm uncoiled like a striking snake, swift and sure. The throwing stick spun around on itself as it flew slightly off to his right, and for an instant Talakh felt his heart sink for it looked like he had missed. But then it curved quickly back to his left, as if the breath of Amun himself had blown it onto the target. To his relief the throwing stick clattered against the thin spear, knocking it clean over in a cloud of dust.

'Yes!' Talakh jumped in the air with a great shout, but no sooner had he begun to celebrate then the ploughman raised a protest.

'You took a step forward, he said sullenly. 'You cheated, so you forfeit the wager.'

For a moment, Talakhonsu was speechless, but then the anger swelled in him and his words were full of force.

'You dare accuse me of cheating, ploughman?' he demanded. 'I won the wager fairly, so do not try to break your oath to me on that!'

At Talakhonsu's angry words the man waved his hand dismissively. 'I will hear no more of this, boy. You must give me what I am due.'

Without a thought, Talakh took hold of the ploughman's outstretched arm and quickly twisted it behind his back before he could use his strength to resist.

'So, a cheat am I?' he bellowed hoarsely as the ploughman yelled in pain. 'A boy am I, you worthless piece of cow dung? You will honour your debt to me or I'll break your arm, and then we'll see how well you plough!'

So the words came from Talakh's mouth, though it seemed as if someone else was speaking them as a fierce rage coursed through him.

'I... I meant no disrespect,' the ploughman blurted.

Though Talakh was far taller than him, the ploughman was probably the stronger of the two from his years of steering the plough through the soil. And yet, as Talakh had already come to realise in his still young life, fear could weaken a man's strength and render him helpless, when he should be bold against his enemies. So it was with the ploughman, who now cowered before him.

'You will follow me with your oxen and help me free the

215

Greek ship,' Talakh said with words of iron. 'And don't think to trick me. I have bested far better men than you in my time!' he boasted, as he had seen the men of Broken Nose do amongst themselves many years ago.

The ploughman bowed his head, cowed in fear of this tall young warrior with the dark skin.

'I will do as you say,' he said quietly as Talakh released his arm and strode back to retrieve the throwing stick.

When he walked back toward the ploughman, the thin fishing spear in one hand and his heavy throwing stick in the other, it seemed to him that he walked taller even than usual, proud at what he had just achieved. For though the boy in him felt a little sorry for what he had done, the man that he was becoming knew that this was the way of the world.

Talakhonsu led the dejected ploughman and his oxen until they came to the stranded ship of the Greeks, where they found some children gathered on the bank, chattering amongst themselves and taunting the captain, who was now red with rage.

'So!' he bellowed in a fury as he noticed Talakhonsu. 'The boy returns. What do you want now?'

'As I said I would, I have come to free your ship from the mud with these oxen,' Talakh answered, pointing behind him. 'If you will pass a rope from the back of your ship, this man will tether his oxen to it. With the strength of the beasts and the will of Amun, you will be freed.'

'I don't know what to say,' the astonished captain beamed. 'Thank you young man, thank you and thank you again.'

'A moment please, great captain,' the ploughman spoke up. He stood the other side of his beasts from Talakh, and feeling surer of himself in the company of others, he once again tried to break his word.

'I am only here because this one tricked me,' he said. 'Great captain, I would ask for your judgement on him.'

'Is this true?' the captain demanded.

'I won a fair wager with him that he would bring his oxen here to free your ship if he lost,' Talakh answered firmly, glaring angrily at the ploughman. 'He stood to gain much from me and I would have honoured my debt if I had lost. But then he went back on his word, so I asserted my right over him.'

The captain looked between them for a moment before he spoke again.

'Hah!' he laughed. 'Young man, I think it is you who I believe. Though I don't pretend to understand why you risked what little you have for the sake of my ship.'

'Captain,' Talakh said. 'I hope only that you will see fit to reward me with passage on your ship down the Great River to the place called Menefer.'

'Hmm, Menefer eh?' the captain nodded agreeably. 'It will be as you say then. This man will honour his wager to you, but if after the ship is free... the gods willing,' he paused to look to the sky. 'If he still calls you a liar, then you should fight with your fists. The gods will show us who was in the right and who broke their oath.'

Of course, when he saw that he had no ally in the captain, the treacherous ploughman could only swallow his pride.

'I want no trouble,' he mumbled as he led his oxen into the shallows of the Great River.

It was not long before the captain's men had fastened the ship's mooring rope to the yoke of the oxen. As the beasts strained at the ploughman's goad, the captain joined Talakhonsu and his men in the water as all strove to push the ship free. Finally, with the rope as taut as a bowstring and the ship's timbers creaking like the bones of an old man, the hold of the sticky mud was at last broken.

But as the ship slid off into the water and the rope slackened, so many of the men, the captain and Talakhonsu included, fell flat on their faces in the muddy shallows with a great splash. Spluttering and spitting the water from their mouths, those who had fallen got back to their feet, soaked to the skin, while those who had not laughed their bellies sore at them. The captain was laughing too, almost to the point where Talakhonsu thought he might lose all the air in his lungs and never breathe again.

When finally he came to himself, he gripped Talakh in an

embrace of friendship, slapping his back.

'Your name my friend, what is your name?' he asked, with a white-toothed smile that stretched from ear to ear under his dark mass of wet hair.

'Talakhonsu is my name, but those who know me call me Talakh.'

Again a curious look came into the captain's dark eyes.

'Talakh it will be then,' he said, 'though it doesn't sound like a Kemet name to me!'

'I am from Napata, not Kemet,' Talakh said proudly.

'Ah, I have heard of this place. It is far to the south, yes? We call it in my tongue the land of the burnt faces. Men say that gold drips from the face of the sun there, and that the sun's rays are so hot they can burn an ordinary man's skin away as if he had leapt into a blazing fire! Only your people can survive there, that is what the stories say. Is it true?'

Talakh tried not to laugh at that. 'The sun is hotter than here, it is true, but not only my people live there.'

'Ah. And the gold?' the captain asked.

'I have never seen it drip from the sun's face,' Talakh said, 'but it is true that we have our share of gold, though not as much as there is here in Kemet.'

'Well Talakh, I am in great debt to you and we men of Kypros always honour our debts,' the captain said, giving the ploughman a sidelong glance as he unhitched his oxen. 'My name is Leontios and you are welcome on my ship.'

Now the captain barked orders to his men, who scrambled up the side of the ship to push her back into the mainstream with their oars, before he pulled Talakh aboard too. The ploughman stood watching from the bank with his oxen while the captain's men pulled the mooring rope aboard like a long snake. But if the ploughman waited for a reward, he was quickly disappointed.

'O oxen!' the captain shouted out as the ship began to drift downstream with the current. 'You have my thanks for your help. May Apis, god of bulls, look kindly on you.'

His men laughed at that, for the captain blessed the oxen with great solemnity.

'But you ploughman!' he called out again. 'If you had not lied, I would surely have rewarded you for your help. Go back to your fields with your shame, and remember this the next time you think to cross an honest man.'

So it was that Talakh found a place on the ship of Leontios and quickly became almost a part of the captain's crew. For though he could have rested easily as the captain's guest, still he had not been an idle boy and he was not to be an idle man either.

When the current was slack and the wind was against them, Talakh brought water to the men as they pulled on the oars, and when they went ashore at night to make camp, so he collected fuel for the fire and picked herbs and plants to add to the cook pot. How different this all was from his dark memories aboard the boat of Broken Nose.

Most of the crewmen were Greeks of one island or another and they spoke few Kemet words. One of their number though, a small, wiry man with equally wiry hair flecked with grey, was apart from the rest of them in that he spoke both the Kemet tongue and the Greek. During the day Talakh talked much to this man, whose name was Isek. He came from a village in the marshes near the mouth of the Great River far off to the north and had been with the captain many years.

'The captain seems very blunt with the men in the daytime,' Talakh said thoughtfully as he helped Isek carry their big cook pot back onto the ship one morning. 'Yet at night he sits and eats with us all and tells the men his stories,'

'Ah, that is always the way with the captain of any ship,' Isek said. 'On board ship, Leontios is captain and we all must follow his lead, for if a storm comes when we are out at sea he will know what to do and he will give us our orders. He knows the seas as well as you and I know the back of our hands. But most of all he is a lucky captain, and when a prize comes his way he shares it fairly amongst all.'

'A prize?' Talakh asked.

'Yes, a prize,' Isek said in his dry, reedy voice. 'You see that we are traders, yes? We bring wine and oil from Kypros and trade it here for spices, incense, linen and whatever other good things we can strike a bargain on. Now, when we are at sea if we come across a friend we will help them if they need it. But,' Isek said, his narrowed eyes almost disappearing amongst the wrinkles of his face, 'if we come across an enemy, and my Greek comrades have many of those, well then we will take their ship before they can take ours!'

'You fight?'

Isek thought for a moment.

'Not often,' he shrugged his shoulders. 'But the Greeks are a fierce and proud people. Faced with the captain's battle rage, many a strong man has cowered on his knees and begged for his life. The captain is a good judge of such things and if he thinks the odds are against us, or that there will be a hard fight, then we will pull on the oars until we are safely away from danger. That is why Leontios is the captain, and why we stay with his ship.'

All of this shocked Talakh greatly, for he had thought that the captain seemed a good man, a likeable man. And yet he was a fighter; if the chance came, some might call him a thief too. Still, Talakh found that despite himself it was impossible to dislike Leontios.

As the days passed slowly in the slack current, Talakh would often stand by Isek, listening as the older man told him of the many settlements and temples they passed by. He learnt also of the great city of Menefer, where the Persian invaders held their court, and of all the riches that lay there. He also used the time to learn some words of the Greek tongue, though they were harder to speak than he had first thought. One day he knew, this might be useful to him.

Isek told him something too of the Greek beliefs and legends of which they were so proud, and when the crewmen told their stories in the evenings, Isek would help him to understand their meaning. The tales spoke of the many gods in the Greek lands who might take the form of man or creature to come amongst the world of men in order to do good or ill. Stories too they would tell of the great heroes of old, and of their quests and adventures in far off lands, where huge monsters dwelt. Isek would murmur these same words in the Kemet tongue so that Talakh might understand what was spoken of, and in this way Talakh picked up more words himself, speaking them back to Isek and the other crewmen.

'You learn the words of the Greeks well,' Isek said to him. 'You have a rare gift Talakh, to do this so quickly.'

'But you understand them well enough yourself,' Talakh answered, not wanting to accept this praise lightly.

'Ah yes, but I grew up in a place that was visited by traders from many lands, chiefly the Greek peoples. So, I have been learning the words of that tongue from when I was a boy, and that is a long time ago now!' he laughed. 'Ah, but still I do not know them all. No, you have your Napatan, your Kemet, and now you have some words of Greek to add to them.'

'Isek,' Talakh said thoughtfully. 'You don't bear me ill feeling because I am Napatan?'

'Why should I do that?' Isek laughed dryly, showing the ruined teeth that made eating a slow task for him. 'If it had not been for you and your cunning Talakh, we would still have been stuck on that mud bank even now! No, I bear no ill will to you or your people.

'Besides the quarrel you speak of is one between Napata and the lands of Upper Kemet. I am from the land of Lower Kemet, where we go now. This is where the first and greatest kings of Kemet came from,' he said proudly. 'You will see soon enough wonders that put even the temples of Waset into the shade!

'But anyway, I lose my track. Whether the Southerners see it or not, it is the Persian king who is their biggest enemy now and has been for some time. It is to him that they should direct all of their anger, not your people. Perhaps one day Kemet will be great again and the Persians will be overthrown once and for all? Or perhaps it will be Napata that will rise once more, who can say? Such things will not happen in my lifetime, or yours, nor even your sons. I am sure of that at least.'

Isek grew quiet now with his thoughts and Talakh thought

it best to leave him to them, but as he turned away the wiry man spoke again.

'Anyway, judge others by their own deeds, not those of their fathers. That is what I say,' Isek grinned.

Talakh had plenty of time to consider what Isek had said as the ship floated slowly on.

'What do you think on, young Napatan?' the captain's voice came to him as he sat deep in thought that afternoon, his legs dangling over the side of the ship's prow above the shimmering water.

'I wonder what the fates have in store for me, captain,' Talakh answered him honestly.

'Ah, it is a good thing to be young and have your whole life ahead of you!' Leontios laughed. 'We Greeks believe that the gods are always watching us Talakhonsu, since we are their chief sport. They will have plans for you, I am sure of that, for they love to see boldness in a man. Only if you settle to your lot will the gods lose interest in you and perhaps not even then.

'But come young man, you should take a turn at steering my ship. Follow me,' he gestured as he walked over the benches and the cargo stores to the rear of the vessel.

Talakh followed, and stepped up alongside the captain and the steersman on the raised platform at the ship's stern. The captain spoke with this one, Akakios and he stepped aside, beckoning Talakh to take his place at one of the two steering oars.

Talakhonsu took hold of the oar, nestling it under his armpit as seemed the right thing to do.

'See how she handles,' Leontios continued proudly. 'Better by far than any Kemet ship, eh? Ah, we Greeks are the greatest sailors in the world you know, whatever those dogs the Phoenicians might say!'

Talakh thought then of how he had found the Greek ship run aground on the mud. But though he smiled, he said nothing, not wanting to offend the captain.

'Now,' Leontios said, perhaps guessing the Napatan's

thoughts, 'when the ship runs as slowly as it does in this current, you need to work both the steering oars in turn to keep her straight. Your eyes must be far ahead looking for any sharp bend or shoals that might wait to snare us. Pull the left oar round into the current and we will swing to the left. The right oar and we swing to the right. Go on, try it.'

So Talakh pulled against the left oar, but still the ship ran straight on, carried by the gentle current into the oncoming breeze. 'I feel the oar strain, but nothing happens captain,' he frowned.

'Wait a moment,' the captain said. 'There you see! Slowly she comes round to the left. Now the other oar, quickly lad!'

Talakh did as he was bid, pulling against the right oar. Again the ship hesitated to change her course and for a moment Talakh's heart was in his mouth for they were now on course to run into the bank. Finally after what seemed an age, the ship started to swing back into line.

'There, she is back on course,' Leontios said with satisfaction in his voice. 'You see Talakh, to steer a great ship is no light task. You cannot take your eye off the river. You have to think!' he said tapping his temple hard with a stubby finger. 'For if you don't then the wrath of Leontios is great against the man who runs my Kallisto onto the mud shoals!' the captain laughed, though there was a hardness in his eyes just the same.

'Kallisto,' Talakh said the word slowly. 'I wondered if that was her name. Do all Greek captains name their ships?'

'Why of course they do!' Leontios said cheerfully. 'My people always name our ships, whether they be a great ship like Kallisto, or the lowliest of fishing boats.'

'I like the way that the name sounds,' Talakh said. 'What does it mean?'

'Ah, Kallisto was the beautiful nymph who was desired by great Zeus, chief amongst our gods. It was after Kallisto that my wife was named by her father, and so my ship is named for them both, nymph and earthly woman.'

'You have sons?' Talakh asked. 'Daughters?'

For a moment a dark look furrowed the brow of Leontios,

but then deep sadness came to his eyes.

'No, lad,' he said finally, with a heavy sigh. 'My wife died trying to give me a son. I have not taken another woman since, for there are none to compare with her beauty and her.... what is the word in Kemet? Her kindness,' he said quietly.

'I am sorry,' Talakh said simply. He had already lost much himself and he knew that words alone were no help when the heart had old wounds as deep as the captain's.

'I think my line will end with me, but this is the way things are,' the captain set his teeth. 'Yet still I will show great Zeus!' he clapped his outstretched hands together loudly. 'Through my deeds, if not through my sons, I hope the name of Leontios will not be forgotten.'

Leontios was silent then for a while, staring along the river as Talakh steered the ship, slowly getting used to the sluggishness of her steering oars. Soon he realised his nerves had left him and thought then of what it would be like to be master of a ship.

'You handle her well Talakh,' Leontios said, shaking himself from his thoughts at last. 'As though you were born to it.'

Talakh's heart swelled with pride as the captain clapped his shoulder before making his way off down the deck to talk to the tall one Akakios. While the hot sun beat down and Talakh steered the ship on, the captain talked, sometimes quietly, sometimes heatedly with Akakios. As for the rest of the crew, they dozed or rested until the day grew cool enough for them to row again.

The disc of the sun god Ra was far into his slow descent back down to the horizon when Isek came up to stand alongside Talakh.

'The captain likes you I think,' he said with satisfaction in his voice. 'He is a good judge of character.'

'I hope so,' Talakh answered. 'But still, is he not afraid that I will ground the ship?'

'No, no,' Isek grinned. 'Leontios is always the steady hand in the stormy sea. He sees you have a steady hand too and that your mind does not wander from the task, and so he trusts you. This is your river after all, not his, and even here so far away from Waset you will still know its ways well.'

Talakh thought of all that he had seen pass on the Great River in his time, both in Kemet and in his Napatan homeland, and he saw that Isek was right.

'That makes sense,' he nodded thoughtfully.

'It should,' Isek grinned. 'I've been with Leontios long enough to know him better than I know myself. You watch him tonight though. He always grows restless when we are becalmed like this. Yes, tomorrow will be a hard day for those at the oar, you can be certain of it.'

Sure enough, after the men had rowed the ship to tie up safely near the shore that evening, Leontios was sullen and sat apart from his crewmen, sharpening his knife on a stone. For the first time then, Talakh saw him as a menacing figure, his long dark hair hiding his stubbled face in shadow as the light failed.

When the men had roasted some fish they had bartered from some fishermen, and baked some flatbreads, they all sat down to eat. Only then did Leontios join them, though he was still silent, only speaking when one of the men handed round a flask of wine.

'Water the wine well tonight,' he said stonily. 'I want no fuzzy heads tomorrow. We will reach Menefer by the close of the day, even if we have to row from dawn till dusk.'

As Isek whispered the captain's words in the Kemet tongue for him, Talakh wondered how the men would take this. Until now they had been merry every night, but none spoke a word against their captain.

'I am sick of this river,' Leontios muttered, taking up a flat bread. 'It is time we had some salt air in our nostrils again!'

'Pay him no heed,' Isek said to Talakh as the captain strode off back to where the ship lay, silhouetted against the moonlit water. 'A ship such as the Kallisto is made for sailing across the wide seas, not for drifting down a river. Leontios knows that the men will lose the fire in their hearts if they are idle too long.'

'Perhaps he needs to keep moving so that his memories do not trouble him,' Talakh said thoughtfully.

'He told you of his wife then,' Isek nodded. 'It is true enough that those things drive him onwards, as they would any of us. There is no family waiting for him to return home to, only his own sadness. This is why he is only truly happy with the wind at his back and the open sea before him.'

'The captain,' Talakh said to Isek as he finished his share of the sweet tasting fish. 'I know he must be the leader on the ship, but he shouts a lot at the men.'

'Mmm,' Isek mumbled. With his missing teeth he could not eat as quickly as Talakh. 'You will have heard the older men answer him back just as hotly though.'

'I had noticed that,' Talakh nodded. 'Is all well between him and Akakios?'

'Hah!' Isek laughed his dry laugh, his face so screwed up into a mass of wrinkles that his eyes almost disappeared again.

'Don't trouble yourself on that, Talakh,' he grinned. 'You see it is just the way of the Greeks. They shout and they point and they jab a finger in the other's chest. They wave their hands in the air like madmen and then turn away as if in disgust. Just as quickly they will turn back around to argue again, and then after all that they will embrace! It is their way, nothing more. When they shout like they do at each other, they don't curse, and so no harm is meant by it.

'But when it comes down to it the men of the Greek tribes live by their pride, so they will not lose face lightly. That is why there is all the shouting,' Isek grinned again.

'With my people,' Talakh said, 'if a man shouts at another like that, it is because he wants to fight.'

'Ah, not so these men of the islands,' Isek shook his head. 'See them speak with an enemy and they are as cold as stone. They save their hot words only for their friends!'

Talakh left Isek to his thoughts then and made himself a place to sleep for the night on some fresh palm leaves he had climbed a tree to cut down.

The next morning, Isek roused the crew of the Kallisto just as the first of the birds had begun to call to the coming day.

'Eat some bread Talakh,' he said. 'You will earn it at the oar today. Drink plenty of water too or the sun will bake you alive.'

Talakhonsu rubbed the cold of the night from his bare arms and looked around him in the dim dawn light. Every day that he had travelled north, the sun god rose above a different view, changed from the day before, yet unchanging. For there was always the river, always the palm trees, always the blue sky and always the sun. There were times like today when the young Napatan wondered if the river went on like this forever and that he might spend his whole life following it, never to find its end.

'Here,' said Isek interrupting his thoughts. 'A draught of honeyed water to warm your bones.'

Talakh took the small, steaming clay bowl from Isek's hand.

'The others do not drink?' he asked, looking around at the rest of the crew.

'No, they will not drink this,' Isek grinned his wrinkled grin. 'They think it unmanly, but we will not listen to them, eh?'

The young man of Napata and the old man of Kemet took turns sipping from the bowl of sweet water, taking care not to swallow the bright red petals that gave it a scent above even that of the honey. As Isek had said, it did go some way to warming Talakh's bones in the chill of the dawn.

'Teaching our friend your odd ways Isek?' Leontios said cheerfully, seeming more his usual self.

'There are none odder than the Greeks and their ways, captain,' Isek screwed up his face in a wrinkled smile. 'Especially those from Kypros.'

Leontios laughed at that, clapping Isek on the shoulder.

'Perhaps you are right old friend,' he nodded. 'We all have our customs. Take Talakh here. He hunts with that stick of his, when any Greek would use a net or bow to catch a fowl.'

'It is a custom here, as you say,' Isek shrugged his

shoulders. 'Perhaps we like to give our quarry a fighting chance?'

The captain laughed again, but then turned to Talakh with a more serious look on his face.

'So,' he said, 'do you think you would be a match for a spearman with your throwing stick?'

'I am no warrior,' Talakh shook his head. 'I was to be a priest when I was a boy back in Napata, before I was taken away.'

'You must tell me more of those days once we reach Menefer,' the captain nodded thoughtfully. 'If you have not gathered as much by now, we Greeks like a good tale, and it seems to me yours would be worth the telling.'

'I will,' Talakh said. 'But to answer your question about the throwing stick, I once knew a great warrior, a man from the south. He fought with throwing sticks in battle and hunted with them too. He taught me, though I am nowhere near as good as he was. When he threw the sticks it was like the strike of a snake, his arm moved so fast.'

'What was the name of this warrior?' Leontios frowned.

'Meketra,' Talakh answered, 'he was my enemy once, but he proved to be a good friend to me in the end. If the gods will it perhaps I will meet him again one day to repay his kindness.'

'Meketra,' Leontios played with the name on his tongue, speaking it over again. 'I have heard this name before. His skin is dark like yours?'

'Ach, such dark warriors are not uncommon Leontios, as you know,' Isek said grumpily. 'These stories are just the imaginings of drunkards who do not water their wine.'

The captain grunted indignantly, then turned to Talakh again.

'Pay no heed to Isek, Talakh,' he said. 'This one I speak of and your Meketra are likely enough one and the same, for they say he too is deadly with the throwing stick. He sails the western seas, raiding the Sikelian traders there, so I've heard.'

'Sikelia?'

'You have heard of that island?' the captain asked, a little surprised.

'Yes. Meketra left me a silver coin that was made there.'

'You have it now?' Leontios held out his hand.

'No, I traded it with a Greek when I was still in Waset, a man from Kypros named Miltiades.'

'Hah! Miltiades? That old rogue?' the captain clapped his hands together. 'He had blond hair, yes? Well, probably silver by now if there is any of it left! Yes, Miltiades... At least that's what he calls himself these days.'

'You know him then?'

'Know him? Yes I know him well. He's a gambler and a cunning one at that, a thief and a cheat too when he puts his mind to it. All in all, a rogue through and through. He is like a brother to me!' Leontios laughed heartily.

Talakh laughed too at that, the first time that he had laughed in a long time, and it felt good.

'So what did my friend Miltiades trade you in return for Sikelian silver? Just those coppers of yours? No don't tell me, he told you the story of the man dying of thirst in the desert didn't he? And how things are only worth what someone is prepared to trade for them?'

Talakh bowed his head, shamed at being deceived by Miltiades when he had striven so hard to make the best bargain he could with him.

'Ah, don't be offended by what I say Talakh,' Leontios said, realising he had hurt the young man's pride. 'Of course Miltiades is right with his story in any case, but if you meet him again you will be ready for such a ruse next time. Now come! We must ready the ship and get her under way before the morning wind comes up!'

When all were aboard, the men of the Kallisto poled her slowly away from the shallows where she had tied up overnight and into the midstream of the Great River. Soon enough the small current and lack of a headwind had her making a fine speed as her oars dipped in and out of the calm waters.

'Keep your oar blades shallow! Save your strength!' Isek called out to the men. 'You'll need it when the wind comes against us!'

This was a day that would stay fresh in the mind of Talakhonsu all of his life, for it was the day when he became as a brother to the crewmen of the Kallisto. A day when he proved his strength, and a day when, as Isek had foretold him, he would see the great works of kings of old. It was well into the midmorning when the river wind sprang up from the north, as it often seemed to.

'The breath of Amun,' Talakh thought to himself, though Isek had told him they were now in a land where other gods were just as strong.

Still, as the morning wore on so the breeze stiffened and the men at the oars ran with sweat as they suffered in the heat of the noon sun. Talakh took them water, holding the deep wooden spoon just in front of their mouths, so that when they were ready they could reach their necks forward to drink without missing their stroke. He took the captain water too as he stood on the high steering deck at the stern of the ship with tall Akakios.

'See the wealth of the land, Talakh,' Leontios said. 'We draw closer to Menefer now lad. We will see its white walls before the sun has set, I'm sure of it. Look at my men! None can row as they can!'

Leontios was right enough. The crew chanted as they rowed and were an impressive sight, as they timed every stroke so that the oars all hit the water at the same time with hardly a splash.

'I would like to row too captain,' Talakh found himself saying as he watched them.

'I have seen you sit at the oar with my men before Talakh,' Leontios said. 'But today is very different. Today we row with purpose.'

'If he wants to row captain, let him take the last oar,' Isek grinned. 'He is young, but he is keen and youth has its own strength.'

Leontios growled, unhappy at having his word challenged.

'He should take the last oar,' Isek said again. 'Pamphilos is just about all in anyway, so why not let Talakh take his place?

Let the boy prove himself a man, just as you once had to.'

Despite himself, Leontios could not help but relent at this, and he nodded his agreement.

'Though I hate to say it old man, you are right. He deserves his chance. Go to it Talakh!'

So the young Napatan went forward to the last oar bench and swapped places with Pamphilos. He was eager to prove himself without a doubt, but this was not to be as easy as he had first thought. He tried to put in a good stroke, but could not match the speed of the Greeks, and his oar dragged in the water as he pushed it forward, clipping the one in front as it came back too quickly for him to get out of the way. An angry shout went up from the man in front of him, and he saw that Leontios glared at him from his vantage point up on the steering platform. Talakh sweated now, not from the heat of the sun but with embarrassment.

'Take your time boy,' Isek said quietly as he walked through the ranks of oarsmen and past him to the prow.

Talakh heeded his advice and held his oar back out of harm's way while he watched the stroke of the man in front. The oarsman pulled the blade powerfully through the water. At the end of the stroke, it rose dripping from the river, then glided smoothly back toward him, before dipping sharply into the water again as smoothly as a kingfisher dives for fish.

Talakh watched again and again as the cycle repeated until he was sure of his timing, then finally he pulled his own blade through the water in a short clean stroke, lifted the oar, brought it back behind him, dipped cleanly and pulled the stroke through again as he braced his feet. This time he made no mistake as he found his own rhythm, for though his stroke was not as powerful as the man in front, it was at least clean. A smile crossed the face of the young Napatan and he felt the pride in his heart that comes when a task is done well. The men's chants grew and Talakh joined in, though he did not understand the words of the Greek song.

'Now you have it!' Isek grinned as he edged past again with the water bucket. 'But watch your grip on the oar, or your hands will blister until they bleed.'

Talakh looked up as Isek passed back through the ship and saw the captain on the steering deck, arms folded. His frown had disappeared now.

The men of the Kallisto rowed her onward at a good speed along the vast river, despite the troublesome headwind, and as they went so their chants were louder with every Kemet boat they overtook. Talakh took many draughts from the water spoon as the stinging sweat dripped into his eyes and his arms ached.

In the early afternoon when the men were too spent to row any longer, Leontios ordered them to rest and eat, though they did not put in to the bank, for every yard that the current carried them was a yard less to be rowed. All too soon though, they were under way again. Yet though Talakh's muscles were on fire and his back ached, still he would not stop rowing until the captain commanded him.

It was late in the afternoon before Leontios finally relented and gave the crew the order first for them to slow their stroke by half for a while, then finally to rest at the oars altogether as the breeze fell away. It was a beautiful evening, the sun casting a rose coloured glow over the fields, the palms and the far distant desert, as Ra's red disc sank toward the horizon.

Isek brought the men some dry bread moistened with beer, and when he came to Talakh he crouched next to him to talk.

'How do you feel, Napatan?' he asked, a wry smile creasing his face.

'Worn out and hungry,' Talakh grinned, stuffing a piece of bread into his mouth. 'These Greeks are men of iron.'

'They are,' Isek nodded. 'Stubborn too. Whether they come from the island tribes or from their mainland far to the north across the great Middle Sea, the Greeks are many nations united by three things only. Their gods, their tongue, and most of all their pride.'

'How many islands are there besides Kypros and Kriti?'

'Hundreds lad, hundreds, if not thousands. Many are small, but some are vast. Most of the crew come from Kypros, Hippolytos comes from Kriti, and young Pamphilos comes from the small island of Skyros far, far off to the north in the sea of the Aegeans.

'There are many, many more such islands of the Greek peoples, scattered far and wide across the seas. Perhaps one day you if you are lucky you will see some of them, though you can be sure you will never see them all.'

'I would like that,' Talakh said, a far look in his eyes as he chewed on the bread and looked into his mind to try to imagine the green islands rising from the deep blue of the sea, as this was what had stuck with him most from the stories of Leontios and his crew.

'Ah, but, there is no ship to carry me across the seas to those places,' he said after he had swallowed the last of his bread.

'No? Do not lose your hope Talakh. Menefer is a big place and many ships come and go, some of them bound for the sea like the Kallisto. Perhaps you will find a place on one of those ships if you can show your value to its captain?'

'Perhaps, if Amun wills it,' Talakh nodded.

In his days on the ship of Leontios, he had forgotten both the past and the uncertain future, happy in the friendship of the captain and his crew, but now these thoughts came back to him again.

'Do not concern yourself,' Isek said placing a hand on his shoulder. 'We will all celebrate tonight when we come to Menefer. The captain will speak with you then I think and we will see what we will see.

'But there!' he pointed to a gap in the palms on the western bank. 'The halls of the dead. What do you see, Talakh?'

Talakhonsu looked on in wonder at a distant hill that rose smoothly into the sky from its broad base until it narrowed to a sharp point. Its sides were straight and it glowed a dusky pink in the last rays of the sunset. Clearly it had been made by gods or men, since it was not a thing of the natural world.

'It is the tomb of a king!' Talakh said. 'We have them in my own land to hold the bones of our nobles until they journey to the afterlife.'

'But not like this,' Isek shook his head.

'Yes, of course like this,' Talakh answered. 'The priests

who taught me as a boy, they told me of such things.'

'I think your priests were mistaken,' Isek frowned. 'We call these tombs 'mer', though to my Greek brothers they are known as 'pyramid'. There are many, many mer in lower Kemet and they were all built from huge blocks of stone each bigger than a storehouse. These mer are big enough, but there are three others off to the north that rise up to a point so high that they touch the roof of the sky itself! I do not wish to offend, but your own people could never raise such immortal things as these.'

'If your people can build them, then why not mine?' Talakh said defiantly. 'It is said that our kings once conquered and ruled all of Kemet, so perhaps we learnt how to build these mer from your people. But then, who is to say it is not the other way around?'

'Oh, that is good!' Isek laughed his reedy, high pitched laugh. 'You have a sharp mind Napatan. If your ancestors had your brains then perhaps they did build their own mer, though I know in my heart that my people built them first.'

'It is a mighty thing in any case,' Talakh nodded, not wishing to offend the older man as the pointed mer disappeared behind the trees again.

'It is,' Isek smiled his wrinkled smile. 'The Persians are jealous of our achievements and the Greeks have no equal to them either, despite what they might tell you! Tomorrow morning you should go to the ridge above the city and then you will see a sight, I can tell you lad. That is if you aren't still drunk.'

'I have never been drunk,' Talakh thought aloud.

'Ah! Never drunk?' Isek grinned. 'There is a first time for all things Talakh.' With that he wandered off chuckling to himself as he took more water to the tired rowers.

When at last the Kallisto came to Menefer, the city of the white walls as Isek called it glowed in the gathering dusk. Here the river bank had been built up in smooth stone slabs to form a level platform along which many other boats and ships were moored. Leontios steered his ship toward the stone quay, but while the men shipped their oars, Talakh saw that they were cutting off the line of a smaller Kemet vessel that was also making for the same mooring place. The two rival captains shouted many a curse at each other, but the Kemet boat was forced to give way to Leontios all the same.

'Pay them no heed Talakh,' Isek grinned. 'Their mouths will be closed when we see them ashore. That is,' he laughed, 'if they have any sense at all!'

As the Kallisto ran up alongside the quay, Kleon and Pelagios, who were as close as brothers even though they often squabbled, leaped onto the stone steps that helped men ashore when the river was at its lowest, as it was now. Soon they had tethered the ship prow and stern, so that the Kallisto was securely moored.

'Get the cargo unloaded,' Leontios ordered. 'Isek! You go and find your man.'

'You must come too captain,' Isek called back to him. 'And Talakhonsu. He should attend us.'

Leontios nodded his agreement and then barked an order at tall Akakios to watch over the ship and the men while he was gone, before climbing ashore to join Isek and Talakhonsu. Talakh carried a basket of goods as the three of them strode off along the bank, passing many roads that led away from the Great River into the heart of the mighty city of Menefer. All of these were thronged with people of many trades, all going about their business, and the smell of baking bread and roast meats hung heavy in the cool evening air.

'Where do we go?' Talakh asked after Leontios had finished talking with Isek.

'To trade some of our cargo,' Isek answered. 'In the basket is some of the incense and fragrant wood from the far south. These things are worth far more here than where we traded them below Waset.'

'Who will we trade them to?' Talakh asked curiously.

'Who would you think?' Isek asked the question back, with his wrinkled grin.

'Hmm,' Talakh thought for a moment. 'The temples? The priests?'

'Good,' Isek nodded. 'But not right. No, there are men here

who will buy from us and other passing traders. In turn they will then sell at a higher price to the temples.'

'But why should we not take the higher price and trade with the priests ourselves?' Talakh asked, a little confused by the ways of this business.

'Ah, I often ask myself this question Talakh but...'

'The man in the middle gives us a quick trade,' Leontios put in. 'It is like this Talakh. He will know all of the priests and perhaps more important, he will know their officials. He will know when they last bought, and when they are likely to buy again. So it is with him that we will reach a deal quickly and then we can be on our way to our next port and our next trade. If we chose to go our own way, we might be here weeks before we find a good price and a willing buyer.'

'So the middle man is worth his price in the end,' Isek nodded. 'Come, this is the house of the man I know of. His name is Kagemni.'

The house of Kagemni was painted white like many of its neighbours and was narrow and very tall. Talakh guessed that like other houses he had seen in Waset there was an upper floor, perhaps even two, reached by a ladder or stone steps. A chink of light shone through a narrow slit window let high up in its mud brick walls.

Isek stepped forward and rapped on the low door loudly enough to wake the dead.

'What do you want?' came a low, tarry voice from inside.

'My name is Isek. I am known to you Kagemni through my friend Meru, son of Metu of Per-Bast. We come to trade.'

'Trade what?' the bad tempered voice of Kagemni answered.

'We have the finest incense of all kinds and fragrant woods from the south. You will find none better than our cargo.'

'Ach,' Kagemni muttered moodily. 'The market is no good for such things.'

'But neither is the market bad,' Isek replied slyly.

'Humph. Well, I suppose there is no harm in hearing you out, though I promise you nothing,' Kagemni said. 'Step away from my door and I will come out to speak with you.'

There was silence for a few moments and then they heard the sound of a heavy bar being lifted from the door, before it creaked open on heavy iron hinges. Kagemni now joined them outside, while behind him the door was drawn closed and barred by someone unseen.

Though it was dark, Talakh could see that this one Kagemni was a tall, thin man of the same lighter skin as Isek, with a short, grey beard and a white cap on his shaven head. His black, restless eyes roved around suspiciously, giving Talakh a sidelong glare. He did not look a man to be trusted, Talakh thought.

Still all the same, Isek brought out some fine woven reed pouches from the basket Talakh carried and gave Kagemni some samples of the incense resins and gums, together with some small pieces of fragrant woods. Kagemni pored over them, sniffing some samples and nibbling others with his yellow teeth in such a way that he reminded Talakh of an old goat. Finally he straightened up and handed the samples back.

'Well?' Isek asked.

'I will not lie to you,' Kagemni said, feigning sincerity with his hand over his heart. 'These things are well enough, but the only price I could offer with things as they are…,' he paused, sucking the air between his long teeth as he shook his head. 'No, no, I could not offend such a great sea captain as your master with such a low offer.'

Isek nodded his head slowly, his eyes no more than slits again as his face wrinkled into a fixed, unchanging grin.

'I am sure you are right, O Kagemni,' Isek said at last after what seemed like an age. 'Truly you are a wise man, a wise man indeed. But still we are very weary, for the day has been long and hard for us. It would be a sad thing if two great men such as yourself and my captain Leontios here were to meet and yet not be better known to each other?'

'But Yes,' Kagemni nodded, a sly smile on his face. 'Perhaps I might offer you some refreshment?' he said, snapping his fingers so that the door was unbarred and opened again from within.

They followed Kagemni into his house, and Talakh began to see that Isek and the devious trader were playing a kind of game, sounding each other out to see who was in the strongest position to bargain. They found themselves in a kind of storeroom with boxes, baskets and sacks neatly arranged against the walls. The air was filled with many pleasant smells, a blend of both the familiar and the strange, mixed in with an oily smoke that came from the small lamp that was set into the wall above a tiny shrine. Steps led to an upper floor, where no doubt Kagemni lived with his wife, if he had one, which Talakh somehow doubted. He could not see how any woman could bear such a loathsome man. Two stools had been placed in the centre of the room and a small boy with a scared look on his face brought down a third from the upper floor, so that all had a seat except Talakhonsu, who stood by the door feeling awkward.

The boy brought cooled wine for them, but of course none was offered to Talakh as he appeared to Kagemni to be nothing more than a roughly dressed servant.

At first they talked of news, Isek and Kagemni. News from the south and news from the north. Kagemni told of the harsh rule of the Persians in Menefer, for they now taxed the temples so heavily, he said, that the priests were too poor to burn incense except during the festivals of only the highest of the gods.

Isek nodded, but maintained that, though the Persians were a plague of locusts on the land, still the priests were so wealthy and powerful that it was in fact only the poor who really suffered. So it was that they slowly worked around to talk of gold and silver, and then on to the kind of price that a man like Kagemni might be prepared to pay for such a cargo as the one on offer from Leontios.

All of this while Talakhonsu looked on and Leontios drank more wine, saying nothing though he glowered at Isek and Kagemni with a dark mood brewing in his eyes. Then suddenly, without warning the captain rose up from his stool, knocking it to the floor.

'You Kemet dogs are all the same! As thick as thieves!' he

bellowed,' glaring at Kagemni and Isek in turn. 'Well, you won't make a fool of me! Tomorrow, I take my cargo elsewhere and do my own bargaining!'

With that he made for the door.

'Captain, captain,' Kagemni said, getting to his feet. 'Please, please, stay a while longer,' he snapped his fingers again. 'Some more wine for our honoured guest!'

'Stay? Why should I stay?' Leontios jabbed his finger at Kagemni, his other hand resting on the handle of the long knife that hung from his belt. There was the threat of a drunken man about him as he swayed and glared.

Isek too got to his feet. 'Master!' he pleaded, holding out his upturned palms for pity.

'Good captain,' Kagemni said in his oily voice, 'if I have offended you, then truly I am sorry. Times are hard and it is not easy to make a living, but for you I am prepared to offer my best price! Please take some more wine with me, O Leontios.'

Leontios wavered now, and after more plaintive gestures from Kagemni, he was persuaded to sit again, though he turned to Isek who had a piteous look on his face and poked his finger in the older man's chest.

'Do not fail me, cur,' he said through gritted teeth, 'or you'll be looking for a new ship.'

With the threats of Leontios hanging over them, Isek and Kagemni went back to their bargaining, swapping offers back and forth like the blows of the sword smith's hammer. Even so, every time they agreed on a price over a certain weight of incense or scented wood, Leontios would grunt and growl until the price would nudge a little higher. When he was finally prepared to shake Kagemni's hand, Isek had wrung every last grain of silver he could from the trader's bony grasp.

'Isek will bring some men with the cargo in a short while,' Leontios said then. 'And do not seek to cross me Kagemni. If you go back on your word, I will come back to your house an angry man.'

With that they left the house of Kagemni and walked off in

silence back down the river bank to the Kallisto. Talakh carried the basket behind Isek and Leontios in the gathering darkness, fearful for his friend after Leontios had abused him so harshly. Tired as he was from the day's rowing, it seemed to the young Napatan that the world had become a sad place when a great man like Leontios treated one so loyal as Isek in such an ill way.

They had not gone far though when Isek made a fist of his bony hand and tapped the captain's brawny arm with it.

'So!' he said. 'Going to throw me off your ship are you, you old tyrant?'

Leontios laughed quietly. 'I am sorry my friend,' he said with a smile, putting his arm around Isek's shoulder. 'I take every one of those words back, you know I do. We showed that snake Kagemni a trick or two though, eh?'

It was only then that Talakhonsu realised Leontios had feigned his anger in order to get a better deal from Kagemni.

'You will have learned something today Talakh I think,' Isek said, turning to him with his wrinkled, smiling face. 'When you want to trade with a man like that it is often better to look like you don't want to trade at all.'

That evening Isek and three of the ship's biggest and fiercest men took the sacks of cargo to the house of Kagemni to be weighed in order that they could claim the price of silver for Leontios. When they returned, they brought a little of the cargo back with them, for Kagemni had sworn on his soul that he had not enough silver to buy it all. Still though, Leontios was pleased with them. The bargain was a good one and there was great celebration amongst the crew as the captain divided the coin up amongst each of them. Every man had his share according to both his worth and his time served with Leontios, who as captain of course took by far the largest portion. Without his ship and without his silver to buy and carry a cargo, there would have been nothing for any of them.

'Now men,' Leontios said to them all. 'You rowed your hearts out today to bring us to Menefer, and you have your silver for it. Go ashore and enjoy yourselves. Eat! Drink! Find a dancing girl, if you have the strength left to entertain her,' he laughed. 'But stick together, for this is a strange city and there will be some who would cut your throats for your coin. Stay out of trouble with the Persian soldiers too and be sure to be back here when the first cock crows. We sail for the sea tomorrow!'

The men cheered at this, and heaved their captain up onto their shoulders as men would a victor in battle, for they were proud to serve Leontios.

'Will you not go ashore with the men Talakh?' Isek asked as the others began to leave.

'No,' Talakh answered, 'I am too sore and tired from the day's rowing. Besides,' he shrugged, 'tomorrow is another day and there may be many of those for me here in Menefer after the Kallisto sails on.'

'Hmm,' Isek nodded.

It was dark now, but Talakh could still see the familiar wrinkled smile that the old man always wore when he was scheming something.

'I have little enough copper left anyway,' Talakh continued, 'and I have no idea what its' worth will be here.'

'Then what will you do?' Isek asked.

Talakh laughed now, though he was not sure why. In spite of all, his heart felt light.

'As the captain told me,' he said finally, 'it is good to be a young man, free of ties. I have enjoyed my time on the Kallisto, so I think I will try to find a place on another ship.'

'Ah,' Isek said, lifting his head up. 'Another ship, yes. It is a pity that there is no spare place on the Kallisto, for although the captain was happy to carry you this far to honour his debt to you, still there is no place for a passenger when we put out to the sea.'

'Yes, I know that,' Talakh nodded thoughtfully 'But I have learnt much from my time with you, so perhaps that will help me. I will not give up, Isek. If not a Greek ship, then perhaps one of the Kemet river boats will need an extra hand?'

'Perhaps,' Isek said with the familiar sly smile that hid his eyes in their slits. 'We should talk with the captain now,' he said as Leontios returned aboard the ship with a cooked fowl and some wine. Isek took these things from the captain and brought out some bread and some cooked beans and fresh leaves that one of the men had bought for them earlier.

'Come Talakh, join us,' Leontios offered when all was prepared.

'Thank you captain,' Talakh answered, 'I will have a little bread, with you, but much more than that I have not earned.'

'Hah!' Leontios boomed. 'You rowed with the best of my men today, so you have earned your fair share. Besides,' he continued, pouring some sweet, red wine into small clay vessels for the three of them, 'without your help I might still be swearing at my men to get me off that mud bank.'

The three of them laughed at that. So they ate and talked and drank the blessings of the gods on each other, Greek, Kemet and Napatan, until finally the fowl was eaten and the un-watered wine had warmed them through.

'Now Talakh,' Isek said. 'I have some news for you, something that will gladden your heart I think, just as it saddens my friend the captain here.'

Leontios did indeed look sad.

'You see Talakh,' Isek continued, 'although I know I don't look my years, still they are at last catching up with me,' he grinned. 'So when we sail past my home on the way to the sea, this last time I will leave the Kallisto to settle for good with my family.'

'I wish it were not so, my old friend,' Leontios said. 'But though I am sad for myself, I am happy for you. Few enough of us who sail the seas live to grow too old for them.'

'Too old? I am not too old!' Isek said testily. 'There is plenty of life in me yet, you young pup!'

'Yes, yes, I know,' Leontios laughed. 'I joke with you while I still can, Isek. The time will come too soon when you are gone from my side, back to your wife and your sons and daughters, and their children too. We will all be sadder for it,' he frowned, casting his dark eyes down at the ship's wooden decking.

'You will always have a welcome in my house, Leontios,' Isek grinned now, trying to lift his mood. 'We will feast together, you and I in the years to come when you visit, and we'll tell the stories of our past adventures, though few will believe them. My family and my kinsmen know only the Great River, the fields and the marshes. They have not seen what we have seen.'

'This is true,' Leontios said, managing a grin. 'Still I will miss your wisdom.'

'You have enough of that yourself between those ears of yours,' Isek grinned, knocking his knuckles on the head of Leontios. 'Besides,' he said, 'the lad...'

'Yes,' Leontios said, turning to Talakh and staring him hard in the eye. 'Isek here is a good judge of a man, do you not think so Talakhonsu?'

'I do,' Talakh agreed, though he was not sure why the captain had asked him this.

'He says that as I will be a man short, you should join my crew,' Leontios frowned. 'But I am not so sure. You have the makings of a man about you, but you are still young. It takes guts to conquer your fear when the great god Poseidon raises a storm, for then the sea builds itself into angry great mountains that loom high over the ship from all sides and threaten to drown all aboard! The wind howls like a thousand wolves and the waves push us toward the reefs where great rocks rise from the depths, jagged as teeth, waiting to tear the belly from any ship that strays too close!'

The dark had returned to the captain's eyes now and his face was as cold as stone in the small light of the waning moon, for it was plain that he had seen the terror of such things with his own eyes.

'Can you swim well, Talakhonsu?' Leontios asked bluntly.

'I can, captain,' Talakh replied. 'I have swum in the Great River for as long as I can remember and there are few better than me,' he said boldly.

'A good swimmer then?' Leontios nodded. 'But that alone won't save you when the sea drags you down into the depths, and squeezes the breath from your lungs,' he said, smacking his fist loudly into the palm of his hand to make the point.

'You say I am young,' Talakh answered, his temper rising

now as he looked back on the horrors of his own life. 'Well that is true enough, but I have seen death close by many times and I do not fear it now, for I know that if I die well I will go to the afterlife where those who I loved wait for me.'

'Hmm,' Leontios grunted, surprise on his face. 'What else do you have to say?'

'I will never turn away from the things I must face,' Talakh said, the words coming to him without thinking.

'Well said young man!' Isek clapped his hands together in delight.

Yet in spite of Isek's praise, Talakh was still a little angry, and his next words came just as boldly as those that had gone before.

'Give me a place on your ship captain,' he said, 'and I will show myself to be a man!'

'Calm yourself Talakhonsu,' Leontios said quietly. 'I have seen with my own eyes that you would fight rather than bear an insult. But the sea is a place by turns both beautiful and dangerous. There is a place for you on my ship, and I know you would join my crew gladly, yet it is only right that you should know of the dangers you will face with us.

'If not Poseidon, then the Phoenicians, the Persians... even some of my own people are our enemies. These are the things that will await you. So I ask again, do you still want to sail with us, Napatan?'

Talakh thought for a moment, as the eyes of Isek and Leontios watched him. It was true that he desperately wanted to join the ship, but even if he had not, he knew he had little choice. Tilling the soil and tending to crops was all he knew and he could not go back to that in the land of Kemet. For this was the land of the killers of his mother and father. It was not his land, this much he had not forgotten.

'I will gladly serve under you, captain,' Talakh said, placing his hand on his chest. 'You will have my loyalty always.'

'Then you will have reward enough in time, Talakhonsu,' Leontios said, 'though it will not come easy.'

'Few things in life ever do,' Isek observed with his narrow-eyed smile. 'But you have an old head on your shoulders, Napatan. You know these things already I think, as well as any of us.'

Chapter 11

From the Mer to the Secret Marshes

Great clouds of fading white blossom still hung about the blackthorn trees in the deep of the woods as Pelia and Cerian walked the paths left by animal and man from clearing to clearing, accompanied by the pungent smell of crushed herbs beneath their feet. It was once again time for folk to be busy as the bees are, and so the two young women looked for the first shoots of spring, both those for eating and those for healing. It was a time for learning too, for now Pelia could show Cerian the plants she must know if she were to become wise. In this way her own knowledge of these things would pass to another and so would not be forgotten.

'These will help the sick in small ways,' she said to Cerian as she gathered some violet flowers and the first few tender leaves of sorrel. 'Still, when the summer comes again it will do more good than I ever can for them.'

'The two things go hand in hand,' Cerian said, showing the brightness of mind that Pelia had seen in her from the first. 'The sun warms our bones, but still the sick need your cures and your magic.'

'Thank you,' Pelia smiled, 'but it is not my magic really. When we make a healing draught from flower, herb, tree bark or toadstool, we only take into our hands the charms that are already there, hidden in the forest. These things are gifts from the earth mother, there to help us pass through our lives more easily. So you see it is the knowledge of these things that is mine, not the magic in them?'

'You are clever all the same, to remember them all,' Cerian smiled.

So they continued at their work, safe in the knowledge that the men of the village were felling trees nearby to join two clearings into a larger one along the edge of the forest. The sound of the iron axes echoing through the woods was comforting to the two women, as a sign to any strangers that their kinsfolk were at work there. A sign also to wolf and bear that this was a place of man and therefore a place to be avoided. But still the sound of the axe was a melancholy one too.

'We bless the trees when we collect their sap and their bark,' Cerian said, 'and yet now the men chop others down. It makes me sad when I think about that.'

'It is the way things are,' Pelia said gently. She knew that it was Cerian's time of bleeding and that this made her sensitive to such things. 'Though you won't hear them admit it, the men will thank the spirit of the tree for its sacrifice before they fell it. The tree spirit will be warned and will go down into the earth, or on to a new home.'

Just then a sudden crash made Cerian start.

'It is nothing,' Pelia said, 'just a falling tree.'

Cerian looked embarrassed. 'I thought perhaps a boar was running out of the woods at us,' she said with a sigh of relief.

'Well, you are right to fear them in the spring,' Pelia said. 'Now they have young, the sows will charge anything that passes too close by.'

'Like any good mother,' Cerian laughed.

'Yes, I suppose,' Pelia laughed too.

'The palm trees in your father's story then,' Cerian said, her mood lightened a little. 'They have their own spirits too?'

'Hmm,' Pelia thought aloud. 'Those lands are so far away. Even though I have often tried to put myself there in my mind's eye since I was a child, and even though I often think about how things must be there, still they are strange lands to think of.

'But there is always the earth and always the sky, always the sun and always the moon watching over all. The Great River's spirit is felt in my father's lands and I am sure that where the palm trees grow old and tall, then they will have their spirits too. Let's start back and on the way I will tell you more of what my father saw in the great city of Menefer.'

After receiving the news that he was to join the crew of the Kallisto, Talakh spent that night under the stars, hardly sleeping for excitement at the good fortune that great Amun had sent his way.

When the first rays of the sun broke over the rooftops of the great city, he rose early from his sleeping place on the quayside. The other men lay snoring around and about, like a band of sleeping boars. Even Isek who had drunk his share of the wine twice over was still asleep. Of the whole crew only Leontios was awake, looking around his ship to make sure that all was as it should be for the journey that lay ahead of them along what remained of the Great River and out to the sea.

'You wake early Talakh,' the captain called across to him. 'I wish the same were true for the rest of them, but they were all drunk last night, so I will let them have their rest a little while yet. They miss a beautiful morning, do they not?'

'Yes captain,' Talakh answered thoughtfully as the two of them looked over the still surface of the Great River to the peaceful crop fields and palms beyond. 'Who knows, this may be the last time I am ever here, unless we come back on the ship. Can I walk around the city a little, to see for myself what it is like, captain?'

Leontios nodded with satisfaction.

'Aye, why not lad. Some men pass through this life thinking only of women and drink, and the food in their bellies, but whilst we all need our share of these things, they alone are not enough for a man with any brains between his ears. Go on then and have a look around. There are few cities greater than Menefer.

'But be sure that you are back well before the noontime,' Leontios called after Talakh as he wandered off. 'We sail then, if you are here or not!'

So, with that fear in his mind, Talakh wandered away from the ships and smaller vessels that lined the stone quay, up onto a wide road where the traders of fish had their stalls. There were a great many people, despite the early hour of the day, all looking over the traders' wares. Baskets of tiny fish glinted silver in the sun, like the ones he had netted as a child in the shallows of the Great River in far off Napata. Those days seemed almost a dream to him now in the strange city.

There were huge fish too, some almost as big as a man, laid out on smooth stone slabs under canopies of palm leaves, to keep them cool. These ones were the beasts that lurked in the deeper channels of the Great River, coming out into the shallows only rarely to terrorise women as they washed their linen, though in truth the fish could do them no harm. Their great gilt eyes stared unblinking at the blue sky as Talakh passed by and he wondered what they had seen in their lives, down in the deep places of the river.

Next he came to a place where the road of the fish traders joined a wider road still and the pungent smell of fish gave way to far sweeter scents that filled his nose and made him smile. Here were great sacks of spices in all hues from yellow, to earthy brown, to clay red, some of which were familiar to Talakh from his far away homeland. There were finely woven baskets full of seeds and grains too, and the bright green of fresh herbs mingled with the duller green of others from far away which had been dried.

The spice traders seemed mostly to be wealthy men, for they wore jewellery about their arms and necks, and wigs of finely coiled black hair that set off the white and gold of their clothes. Most were of Kemet, but some were clearly Persian judging by their beards, and pointed hats. Talakh passed through the throng of people milling around, eager to see more of the sights of great Menefer, though the road of the spices seemed to carry on and on without an end.

After a while, he came to another wide road headed away from the river, where those who traded fine linen cloth had their stalls. Wealthy women walked up and down here, shielded from the sun by servants who held canopies above their heads, so that they always had shade wherever they went. Some were old and wizened it was true, but others were very beautiful to the eyes of a young man like Talakhonsu. Their servants eyed him suspiciously as he walked past, no doubt making him out for a thief, yet still it was more than he could do to resist looking at their mistresses with their dark rimmed, catlike eyes and painted lips. Before he had finished walking the length of this road it was true to say that the young Napatan had lost his heart many times over.

In this way Talakh walked the great city, wonder filling him as he passed a huge stone temple dedicated to Ptah, chief god of Menefer, and then another where the bull god Apis had his halls, both decorated with a great many carved and brightly painted symbols. On a ridge up ahead now stood a beautiful, low built palace which stretched wider it seemed than the width of the Great River itself. It was painted a pure white so that its walls shone gold in the light of the early morning sun. Surely it must be the home of a king, Talakh thought to himself.

'What is that place?' he asked a man who had a friendly enough face.

'Ah young man, I see that you are a stranger here. From the south, yes?'

'From Waset,' Talakh answered, thinking it best to keep his Napatan root to himself.

The man nodded. 'A great city so they say, though it is not the equal of Menefer, would you not agree?'

'They are both great cities,' Talakh replied wisely.

'Greater still before the Persians came,' the man's smile waned. 'But in answer to your question, the palace up there was once the home of a great Pharaoh. Now only our friends the Persians hold court there,' he shook his head.

'Ah.'

'Yes, none may enter it now but the Persians and those nobles of Kemet who do them homage. But I am forgetting myself!' the man said, his smile returning. 'There is a greater sight than this or even the temple of Apis, which you no doubt already passed. Walk with me toward that rise over near the palace and you'll see a sight all visitors to Menefer should see, to remind us of the glory of our former times! My name is Kesi, by the way,' he added. 'And yours?'

'Talakhonsu.'

'Then come, Talakhonsu. Let me show you something that will fill your heart with pride.'

Being a Napatan, there was nothing for Talakh to take pride in, but he followed the man Kesi nonetheless until they came to a road which led them upwards toward the palace.

'Now look over there on the plain,' the man Kesi said proudly as they turned to face to the west. 'See there, the tombs of the great pharaohs.'

Beyond the green farmland and palms on the distant far bank of the Great River the desert sands stretched endlessly, but they were far from empty, for Talakh could count many mer, the great pointed tombs of the pharaohs rising into the sky. Some seemed quite small, others much larger, but all had a similar character, their four sides sloping upward from a square base to join together in a point. One of the larger mer had huge steps cut all the way along its sides but the others were smoothly built from stone the colour of honey.

'It is a wondrous view,' Talakh could not help but reply.

'Wondrous, yes,' Kesi nodded. 'But look there!' he pointed further down the green swath of the Great River as it stretched far off to the north.

Talakh followed Kesi's gaze to where three more distant mer lay in a neat line, two of them far bigger than the third, though size apart, each of them seemed to follow the same shape as its neighbours exactly. 'They are more beautiful still,' Talakh said in awe.

'Beautiful, yes,' Kesi agreed. 'But tell me young man, how long would it take you to walk to them do you think so that you could rest a hand on their stones?'

Talakh narrowed his eyes and he stared hard at the mer as they shimmered in the growing heat of the desert sun. 'They must be half a day's walk from here,' he said, surprising himself with his answer.

'Easily that, unless you can run like a hare!' the man Kesi

251

laughed.

'But they must be huge,' Talakh scratched his head. 'The work of the gods!'

'As big as mountains!' Kesi said proudly. 'Some say the ancient pharaohs buried in those places were greater even than Rameses the Great himself.'

'The river passes close by them,' Talakh said thoughtfully. 'I will see them close up with my own eyes soon enough.'

'You journey there?'

'Yes, I am a crewman on a Greek ship,' Talakh said proudly.

'A Greek ship, eh? These are strange times, when a young man has to look to a Greek captain for a living,' Kesi shook his head. 'But then you are lucky all the same. There are many I know in Menefer who have never been over there to see the Great Mer, even though they live close enough by. I wish you well on your journey Talakhonsu. May the gods watch over you.'

'And over you,' Talakh returned the blessing. 'But now I must go, for my captain sails at noon.'

The two of them clasped hands in farewell and Talakh walked off back down the road toward the great city. He looked round, not wanting to ignore any wave of farewell from Kesi, but the older man still gazed at the far off mer.

When Talakh came back down to Menefer, he passed a small temple dedicated to great Amun and wandered through the outer walls into an inner court paved with stone. The smell of fragrant incense drifted faintly on the breeze from within the god's dark sanctuary and he knew from his boyhood that Amun dwelt there, his spirit filling the small statue that would serve as his earthly body in that place. Only the priests could enter there, so he approached the low stone table where the common people were allowed to leave offering. Under the suspicious eye of a temple official, he left the few copper pieces he still had next to the flowers and fruit that lay on the flat offering stone and asked the great god to watch over the ship of Leontios in the coming journey across the sea.

It was still well before noon when Talakh returned to the quay beside the Great River, for the sun was not yet at its full height in the sky, but of the Kallisto there was no sign. Talakh's heart sank into his stomach as he looked for the ship left and right. He kicked the dirt in his anger, stubbing his toe so that his rage only increased, but just then he heard a familiar voice behind him.

'What troubles you Napatan?'

'Isek?' Talakhonsu turned to see the old man's familiar, wrinkled face. 'But where is the ship? Where is the captain?'

'Not far,' Isek said, taking his arm and walking with him along the bank. 'We are moored downstream, outside the city.'

'But why?'

'Ah, the Persians,' Isek grinned his narrow eyed grin. 'They have a mooring tax here and when the tax collector came to take silver from him, the captain did not like the price. So, we moved outside of the city.'

'You didn't know about the charge?'

'Of course I knew,' Isek scowled. 'But in Menefer there is now one price for a Persian ship, another for one of Kemet, and yet a third for a Greek ship.'

'Ah.'

'Yes. You see now why we moved? The Persians resent the Greeks more with each passing day, so they charge more than for anyone else, far more. But also I think that conniving old jackal Kagemni had something to do with this. He probably told the Persians of our hoard of silver in the hope they would reward him.'

'Hmm,' Talakh nodded, 'I thought he looked like a snake. Did soldiers come?'

'Soldiers? Not yet, but they will without a doubt. When they find us gone, they will come after us for dodging their tax, that much we can be sure of. They do not take kindly to their authority being challenged. Still, the Persians are always slow in every action they take, so they will be lucky to catch us.

'But now, tell me of what you saw in the city while our

captain was annoying the Persians.'

So, while they hurried downstream along the river bank, Talakh told Isek of the huge temple of the bull god and the Great Mer he had spied off in the distance, though he did not speak of the beautiful women. In his youth, he was still too shy of such things.

It was some while after they had left behind the last of Menefer before they finally saw the Kallisto up ahead. She was slowly drifting with the current out in midstream, but one of the men had climbed the mast to keep a look out and this one waved to them now. As Talakh upped his pace and Isek struggled to keep up, the Kallisto steered toward the near bank, the men putting out their oars so that they could back them against the steady flow to hold her station. When finally they had caught her up, the ship was still some way off the bank, for the wide river margins were too shallow to moor.

'Any sign of the Persians?' Leontios called across.

'They are still combing their beards!' Isek called back in the Greek tongue, and the whole crew laughed heartily at that.

'Nonetheless old friend, the river is too low for us to put in,' Leontios called back. 'Talakhonsu, you swim across and pull the rope back for Isek,' he said throwing it across the water as far as he could. 'The old man swims like a rock!'

'Hah! I'll have none of that!' Isek said, wading into the river shallows in a fit of pride.

Talakh took off his tunic and wrapped it around his waist, then followed Isek into the cooling water, fearful that his friend might drown. Soon the rope was in Isek's hand and with Talakh's help to keep him afloat, he was pulled quickly to the side of the ship.

'Good to have you back aboard safe,' Leontios grinned, lending them both a hand as they pulled themselves up the knotted rope that hung over the side.

It was only then that Talakh realised that Isek had risked his own place aboard the Kallisto by waiting for him to return from his wanderings around the city.

'I owe you a debt, Isek,' he said. 'Thank you for staying behind for me.'

'Ah, debts,' Isek shrugged his shoulders. 'We all owe something to someone along the line. As crewmates this is what binds us together. You will return the favour if ever I have need Talakh, I know that. Now come, there is work for you at the oar!'

Isek was right, for once they were out in the mid river again, Leontios gave the order for the men to row at a fierce pace. The captain knew well that though it might take the Persians a while to organise a chase, still they had swift horsemen and they would not allow such a slighting of their authority to pass. So, they rowed through the heat of the day and though Leontios did not drive them quite as harshly as he had in the run to Menefer, still he drove them hard enough.

With his back to the north as he rowed, Talakh did not see the three great mer that he had spied from a distance in Menefer until the Kallisto had already begun to pass them by. These giant mountains of stone or pyramids as the Greeks called them, were so high that they seemed to hold up the sky itself just as Isek had said. Still, though they were an awe inspiring sight, Talakh dared only to steal a glance at them as they rose up beyond the treetops, for fear of missing his stroke. Slowly, ever slowly, the mysterious pyramids passed behind them as the Kallisto pressed onwards, her crew sweating in the boiling heat of the day.

That evening they moored close by an island in midstream which hid them from the eastern bank, as that was the side along which any pursuit would likely come. Leontios posted a lookout on the island amongst the palm trees, while the rest of the crew ate their supper of bread, dried fish and sweet honey cakes bought from Menefer. But though the men made light of their danger, and though it was not certain that the Persian soldiers would launch a pursuit, still it played on their minds all the same.

When Talakh had finished his supper, Leontios sent him to lookout in the place of Hippolytos. The stocky Kretan was nowhere to be seen and it was only after Talakh had crept a short way, whispering his name, that Hippolytos showed himself.

'It is my turn to watch,' Talakh spoke the Greek words that Isek had taught him to say.

'Your Greek is terrible,' Hippolytos said, a scowl on his swarthy face.

Talakh understood these simple words well enough, but he needn't have worried, for Hippolytos broke into a smile then.

'Better than my Kemet though, eh?' he said, clapping Talakh on the shoulder with his hairy fist.

'I will learn,' Talakh grinned.

'Hmm,' Hippolytos nodded. 'Now...' he started to say, though Talakh lost the meaning of the words that followed, so that the Kretan had to use signs instead, pointing at his eyes to show that Talakh was to keep a keen lookout.

'Crocodile,' he said next, pointing to the river. 'Khamsa!'

Talakh understood these names well enough. He knew that smaller islands where man seldom trod were often the sleeping places of the feared lizard beasts. Twice in his life he had seen grown men taken to the underworld by their jaws and he had no wish to join them. So, when Hippolytos had returned to the Kallisto, instead of crouching down behind a tree as the Kretan had done, he shinned up the smooth trunk of a tall palm and clambered into its topmost branches. It was a perch more for a bird than for a man and his blistered hands were sore in the climbing, but Talakhonsu made himself as comfortable as he could up there.

From his lofty seat, if he craned his neck round, he could see the top of the Kallisto's tall mast and behind it the orange ball of fire low in the horizon where the power of the sun god now waned. To the south stood the three great pyramids, coloured rose pink by the setting sun on their flanks. In their shadows lay something he had not seen when they had passed by on the river, a great beast of stone with the head of a man. This was the guardian of the Great Mer which Isek had told him of. It was a beautiful sight, one that was to remain in his mind's eye always.

Talakh settled to his task as the quiet of evening came upon the Great River, for all of the boats had put in for the night and the workers of the land too were done with their labours. The black earth was rich here, Talakh thought, extending much farther on each side of the river than it had in Waset. Beyond it there were no mountains, just a few low hills with the desert plains beyond, those empty places where wise men feared to tread.

He craned his head around to the north, where the darkened river lands fanned out either side in a great expanse that stretched ever wider. The Kallisto had come at last to what Isek referred to as the land of the many nomes, those provinces where the river split itself into countless branches, wandering far and wide across the fertile fields and marshes of lower Kemet.

The sound of distant singing came to Talakh then on the faint breeze. Perhaps the celebration of a man and woman wed, or the welcoming of a newborn child. He could not make out the words, but many people sang as one voice, bound together in their happiness. The Napatan listened for a long while before the breeze dropped and the voices were lost to him again. He would never know their joy, he was certain of that, but still he had the ship and her crew. They were to be his family now. He smiled at the thought of the adventures that lay ahead of him. There would be dangers yes, but he was amongst friends now and they would all look out for one another.

So, as the darkness gathered in around him and the reflections on the Great River melted away into the night, Talakhonsu steeled himself to keep his eyes and ears open to any movement or sound that might signal the approach of an enemy.

Time passed slowly on and there was little to see in the darkness that cloaked the land, though there were still the calls of the night birds and the rustling of a beast in the bushes far below to keep him alert. He grew weary all the same, his unblinking eyes tired with watching, but then just when he had grown so tired that he thought he might easily fall asleep, a glint of light caught Talakh's eye off to the south along the far bank of the river. No sooner did he see it, than it was gone, yet as he began to doubt his senses there it was again, closer now, then closer still until Talakh heard the distant fall of horses' hooves in the dirt. Riders were coming! One, two, three, four of them passed by, holding their horses at a quick trot despite the darkness. Torchlight glinted from metal helmets and lit up their bearded faces. Persian soldiers! Talakh's heart was in his throat, for he could just make out that they were armed with bows across their shoulders, but he told himself to be calm and so he watched them until they passed on out of sight and all was quiet again.

His mind leapt back to the battlefield of long ago when the evil one Khaemwaset had murdered his father. The Persian horsemen had charged then in a huge cloud of dust, bristling with spears as Broken Nose had confronted Khaemwaset. Talakh had seen their great army with his own eyes, escaping only by the good will of Meketra, and he knew well enough that they should be feared. He watched on for any sign of their return until some while later he heard a familiar voice from below.

'Talakhonsu,' Isek's dry voice called softly as he sought out Talakh's hiding place.

'I am up here,' Talakh whispered back as loud as he dared. 'Up the tree.'

'Ah, the tree,' Isek said in his familiar way, and Talakh could imagine the wrinkled grin that would surely be on his face.

'Kleon is here to take your place on watch,' Isek whispered up to him.

'Good,' said Talakh, 'I have news for the captain.'

'Ah, news,' Isek answered without any surprise in his voice. 'What did you see, lad?'

'Wait for me to climb down,' Talakh said, 'but watch for the khamsa. I think I heard one pass this way a while ago.'

'Now I see why you are in the palm tops,' Isek chuckled to himself.

To climb back down was not a task to be rushed in the dark and Talakh took his time, but when he had finally planted his feet on solid ground again he told Isek of what he had seen.

'And you didn't think to bring this news to the captain?' the man Kleon asked through Isek.

'Yes, I thought of that,' Talakh answered, 'but then I thought it better to keep a watch until someone came to replace me. If I had left my tree, then who is to say that more Persians might have passed by without us knowing?'

'You made the right choice,' Isek nodded. 'Come. While Kleon keeps watch, you must tell Leontios what you have seen.'

So, leaving Kleon behind, the two of them carefully felt their way back though the darkness until they came to the Kallisto, where Talakh told Leontios of the bearded horsemen. The captain frowned and his eyes pierced Talakh through in spite of the dark.

'There will be trouble awaiting us,' he said grittily. 'Pelagios,' go and join Kleon. If you see anything more, one of you must bring me news while the other stays behind.'

'You will find him up a palm,' Isek called after him. 'That is if the crocodiles haven't eaten him already,' he winked at Talakh.

'This is no time for joking Isek,' Leontios said grimly. 'Those few horsemen couldn't trouble us on their own, but that is not their purpose I think.'

'Yes,' Isek nodded. 'The Persians have no need to send an army after us. Their soldiers are everywhere in the land.'

'Then they are messengers?' Talakh asked.

'Messengers, yes,' Isek grinned his wrinkled grin. 'The Persians will have searched close by Menefer at first but now they see that we have made our escape.'

'They will be waiting for us at the next settlement along the river,' Leontios said darkly.

'That will be Avasais,' said Isek. 'We must be past that place before the sun rises, so that we can lose ourselves amongst the smaller branches of the river. There they will not find us, for no Persian knows the river here as I do.'

'But if they catch us in the open...' tall Akakios joined in. 'If we do not give ourselves up to them, they will rain arrows

259

down on us from both sides of the river until we are all dead.'

'Give ourselves up to Persians?' Leontios growled. 'That we will never do!'

'That was not what I said!' Akakios said, offended by Leontios' slight.

'You Greeks,' Isek shook his head. 'It will be well for me when I am away from your arguments and back in my village.'

'Where your wife has a lifetime of nagging waiting for you!' Hippolytos laughed, doing his best to lift the mood.

'Ah, my wife, yes,' Isek's face screwed up again.

'Well,' Leontios said, 'we are a match for any bunch of Persians stupid enough to challenge us... and you Akakios, it goes without saying that I do not doubt your courage. Kretans, Kypriots, men of all the thousand islands,' the captain addressed his crew.

'We are all bound together by the gods, as Greeks with a common tongue and proud hearts. The gods look to us for their amusement, so let us give mighty Zeus something to cheer! We will be as wise as the owl, and fly by night toward our enemies, but they will not see our coming or our going. It will be as if the Kallisto has taken to the air and vanished over their heads,' Leontios said boldly and the men cheered at that.

'Ready the ship!' Leontios gave his orders. 'We'll take our chances tonight.'

So when all were back aboard, the Kallisto slipped her mooring and drifted off slowly downstream on the slack current, the men gently dipping their oars in silent time to keep her speed up. Leontios ordered Isek and Talakh to the ship's prow where they stood watch, looking for the deeper channels of the river and those tell tale ripples on its surface that marked the mud shoals and shallows.

'There to the left,' Talakh spoke in a low voice, pointing to a mud bank that lay close to their course.

'Ah, the river,' Isek nodded, signalling the steersmen with his arm to edge to the right. 'It changes all the time. But your eyes are keener than mine in the dark, Talakh. Keep a close watch, and if the gods are with us then we will not go aground again.'

'Let's hope the Persians don't see us,' Talakh said worriedly.

'They will be in their beds by now!' Isek chuckled. 'In their minds only a madman would sail a ship like the Kallisto on a moonless night. No, the Persians are not given to the boldness of the Greeks. They plan and plan again until they are sure of success. So you see, until day breaks, we have only the fates to fear. The Persians will not trouble us until the sun is up.'

And so it proved. The night was as quiet as the dead, with not a soul to be seen or heard, and only once did the Kallisto sigh as her keel slid along a submerged mud bank, though that was enough to bring the sweat to Talakh's brow. The night was long for them all the same, though all aboard the Kallisto wished it longer still, for the darkness cloaked them well.

Then at last came the dawn, a lightening of the horizon so slight that at first Talakh couldn't be sure that his tired eyes didn't deceive him.

'The light will come quickly now,' Isek answered his thoughts, 'and then we will see what we will see.'

As the dawn came, so Leontios had the men row faster, then faster still until the Kallisto surged forward with every stroke. They passed a waking village, and then a little farther on in the early morning haze Talakh started to make out the outlines of a larger settlement.

'There!' he pointed for Isek. 'Another city?'

'A city, no,' Isek shook his head. 'This is Avasais, usually a quiet place, but for us a dangerous one today...' he tailed off thoughtfully and stared ahead for a while.

Talakh felt the heaviness of fear in his belly, fear of the unknown that lay ahead. In times like these he had learnt that men will often laugh and joke to make light of danger, but this was not his way.

'Ah,' Isek said to himself, his face breaking into a wrinkled smile.

'What is it Isek?'

'Keep a steady watch Talakhonsu,' Isek grinned as he

started to make his way back along the ship through the ranks of the oarsmen. 'I have an idea.'

Talakhonsu watched as Isek spoke quickly to the captain. Leontios thought for a moment and then ordered the crew to ship their oars and lay them down flat in the bottom of the ship. Then the whole crew including Leontios himself crouched low against the ship's side, out of sight from the shore. Only Isek was left now at the steering oars, and only Talakh at the prow, to guide the Kallisto as she coasted along on the current as close as they dared to the far bank.

Talakh saw that Avasais was a smaller place by far than Menefer, hiding its simple houses behind large earth banks that were no doubt there to keep the annual flood of the Great River at bay. Yet Avasais was not quiet, despite the early hour. As they drew close, a man lifting water from the river for his cattle waved and called out to them. Talakh waved back, but said nothing, leaving Isek to return the man's greeting of the morning.

Down in the hull of the ship, Leontios and his men gripped the handles of their long knives and swords, while tall Akakios and a few of the others had laid arrows to their bows. Talakh too felt for his throwing stick, though he knew that if they were caught in midstream it would be of little use against a rain of Persian arrows. Still the Kallisto drifted on unchallenged as they slowly passed by Avasais, until at last they were clear of it.

Up ahead lay a large island dividing the river in two. Isek steered them down the left branch of the river, and when they were out of sight of Avasais he at last gave Leontios the all clear.

'Were we noticed?' Leontios asked.

'No, but there were horses,' Isek answered. 'The Persians will be there, but we should not trouble ourselves all the same. They'll be in their beds a while yet.'

'Then your plan worked well,' old friend, the captain smiled, shaking Isek by the shoulder as the cheer returned to his face. 'With the gods' will, the Persians will forget about us now.'

'Ah, the gods,' Isek said nodding his head. 'We will do well enough without their help. It is the river we must fear now, or the lack of it.'

Some of the men muttered amongst themselves at what Isek had said, but it was Hippolytos who spoke up.

'It is not wise to disrespect the gods,' he muttered.

'I do not disrespect them, Hippolytos,' Isek answered, and for the first time Talakh saw the smallest trace of anger on his face, though it was the kind of anger that a father reserves for a wilful child.

'These lands are my lands,' he said firmly, 'and the gods of these lands are my gods, not yours. It is not their help that we need, but the good will of the Great River only.'

Hippolytos turned his head away then and kept his silence, for though he did not think that Isek was right to ignore the gods, still he did not want to argue with one who was his elder and commanded great respect on the Kallisto. Besides Isek was his friend, and friends should not seek out arguments with each other, even if they do disagree.

The channel the Kallisto had taken was not nearly as wide as the one she had left, for now the Great River had split its course for good, so Isek said. As the heat of the day grew great with the noon and then slowly eased away again so they passed more channels branching off on either side.

The land slowly changed out of any recognition, with great stretches of wild marsh replacing the tilled fields and palm groves. It seemed that in this new land, water had taken a hold over the desert, banishing the sands far away beyond the horizon. Tall stands of reed sighed in the slackening evening breeze and the beautiful blue lotus flowers, beloved of the priests of Kemet, sprang from the water everywhere along the shallows.

A gentle peace reigned amongst these marshes, broken only by the dipping of the Kallisto's oars and the alarms of heron and stork taking wing as the ship bore down on them. This then was the land of Lower Kemet, Isek's land that he had often spoken of. But of the people who lived there, few were to be seen apart from solitary fishermen casting their

nets from small reed boats. Isek bade the men to back their
oars so that he could speak to one such man who had his
young son for company, a sure sign that a village must be
close by.

'May Bast watch over your house, fisherman,' he called in
friendly greeting as the Kallisto coasted slowly toward the
reed boat.

'And over yours,' the man answered. Like Isek, his skin
was a little lighter than Talakh was used to in Waset. He wore
a piece of white cloth tied around his head that draped on his
shoulders to keep the sun from burning him while he was at
his work. His son was darker and wore his hair in the side
lock as Talakh had done as a boy, with the rest of his scalp
shaved.

'Where are you bound?' the man called out.

'Ah, to the sea,' Isek returned, 'but on our way we will
pass my home in a day or so.'

The fisherman nodded, seeming not surprised, though his
son stole glances at the strangers, most of all at Talakh.
Perhaps he had never seen someone with skin so dark before.

'Your village is close by?' Isek asked.

Now the fisherman looked wary.

'Your ship will not reach it,' he said quickly. 'The channel
to my home is only for small boats such as this.'

His boat was small indeed, no more than a narrow floating
platform of tightly bound reeds on which he and his son
balanced.

'Ah, it sounds like my home,' Isek said, his face wrinkled
up with his familiar grin. 'Do not fear us, for we are all honest
men like you,' he added. 'If you would trade us some fresh
fish and bread, we have good wine from Waset.'

The man looked along the line of the ship's crew, with
distrust still in his eyes, despite what Isek had said. 'I will ask
the headman,' he said anxiously.

'Ah, the headman,' Isek smiled. 'Yes, of course. We will
wait here awhile, and if he comes to trade we will receive him
well. Here,' he held up a small clay jug, 'take this gift of fine
Greek oil to your headman so that he will see we come only as

friends.'

Still the fisherman was cautious and he first paddled his small boat over to a small island that the low river had revealed, leaving the boy there with a few whispered words.

'I know what you are thinking,' Isek turned to Leontios as the fisherman paddled his reed boat back toward the Kallisto's side to collect the gift of oil. 'Why do we bother with this man and his village?'

'I know you well enough, old friend,' Leontios sighed, 'You have your reasons. We are lost aren't we?'

'Ah, lost,' Isek grinned, with a shrug of his shoulders. 'A man is never lost when he is in his own land, captain. But there are things we will learn from him concerning the river ahead, and of course our friends the Persians.'

But Talakh had seen something that made Isek's words grow distant from him, for as the fisherman's boat drew alongside the Kallisto, his eyes caught a rippling on the water. As he watched, the ripples closed in on the small island where the boy waited alone.

'Khamsa!' he shouted, leaping over men and oars as he ran to the Kallisto's stern. 'Crocodile!'

The little island was nothing more than a low strip of mud which at most times would have been submerged, so there was nowhere for the boy to shelter and no tree for him to climb. The crew watched in horror as the long snout of the crocodile, the feared lizard beast, broke the surface of the water and quickly started to crawl ashore on its stubby legs.

Now the fisherman shouted in terror to his son as the boy started to cry, cowering back along the length of the island as the crocodile crawled quickly toward him, its long tail carving a trail in the mud.

'Back oars! Back oars!' Leontios shouted to his men, and the crew swore and cursed at each other as they pushed their clashing oars away with all their might.

As the Kallisto slowly began to struggle back against the gentle current toward the island, the captain took up a bow and strung an arrow from its quiver in the blink of an eye. Drawing it without a pause, he loosed the arrow, but although his aim was true, the hide of the khamsa was too tough at that range and the arrow glanced off its back without harming the beast.

'Son of a dog,' Leontios cursed. 'More speed men! Bend those oars!'

Talakh had taken a steering oar but as the Kallisto sought to overcome her bulk and make way upstream, he could see the crocodile hurry forward, its jaws open and ready to strike. Though it was not full grown, still it was big enough to seize the boy in its jagged teeth and drag him into the river. There it would drown him and take him down to the underworld. Talakh could feel his father's spirit watching him and he knew he too must act. 'Here!' he shouted to Isek. 'Take the oar!'

Another arrow bounced off the scaly back of the lizard beast, as it closed on the fisherman's son, too close now for Leontios to shoot at its eye for fear of hitting the boy. But Talakhonsu, summoning all of his courage, jumped onto the wooden rail that edged the steering platform. Shouting his battle cry at the lizard beast, he drew the carved throwing stick from his belt and brought it back over his head. His long arm snapped forward like a whip as he threw the heavy weapon with all his might. Talakh almost fell off the side of the Kallisto, such was his effort, so he did not see the throwing stick flash just past the fisherman's shoulder, but he heard its heavy weight strike the crocodile with a hollow thud, just above the eye so Isek told him later. As he recovered his balance, Talakh saw that the beast hesitated, perhaps stunned by the blow.

Now the fisherman paddled furiously toward the island, shouting all the curses of the world at the crocodile. More arrows flew over his head and this was enough to drive off the beast, for it now turned aside and clawed its way back into the river, its scaly tail thrashing the water. While the father rescued his sobbing son, the Kallisto finally started to make headway toward them and was soon alongside the island where it held station, Leontios and tall Akakios holding their long spears at the ready in case the crocodile should return.

'A thousand blessings on you and your men captain,' the fisherman thanked Leontios, tears in his own eyes now, as he paddled back to the Kallisto with his son.

'It is to this young man that you owe your thanks,' Leontios smiled. 'Talakhonsu was the one who stunned the beast with his throwing stick.'

'I have it here,' the fisherman said, handing the weapon up to Talakh. Thank you.'

'I have seen the khamsa kill before when I was a boy,' Talakh answered. 'I only did what I could to help you, praise be to great Amun for guiding my aim.'

'You speak the tongue of Kemet well stranger,' the fisherman said. 'My name is Ayut. Where are you from?'

'I am Talakhonsu and I grew up near the city of Waset, far to the south, but the kingdom of Kush is where I was born, in a place called Napata.'

'You are the first of your people that I have met,' the man Ayut bowed his head. 'You are welcome here in these lands Talakhonsu. You use the throwing stick better than any I have seen.'

'I was taught it as a boy,' Talakh said, remembering the face of Meketra.

The fisherman's son had stopped crying now and he stared up at Talakh curiously. 'Why is your skin burnt?' he asked with the honesty of a child.

'Khai!' the fisherman scolded his son.

'Do not trouble yourself,' Talakh laughed as he leant over the side of the ship to speak to the child. 'You are a brave one, young Khai,' he smiled. 'But to answer your question, my skin is just the same as yours, only darker. In my land the sun is hotter than it is here.'

'Why is that?' the boy asked, his young face a puzzle.

'Well the sun is closer to us there. My people say that our gods took pity on us for this and so they let our shadows fall on us all of the time, instead of just following us around. In this way our skin wards off the worst of the sun's great heat, and this is why it is darker than yours. But underneath we are the same as you.'

'Does your blood run black?' the boy asked again, looking down at a red graze on his knee from where he had stumbled on the island in his terror of the crocodile.

'No, that is the same as yours too,' Talakh smiled as the boy stared back up into his face curiously. 'Here,' he said taking out his small bronze knife and pricking his thumb with the point of the blade.

'See?' he said, squeezing a few drops of blood from his thumb. 'The same as yours.'

The boy stared up in wonder, but his father had heard enough from him.

'Be quiet now, whilst I speak,' he said, making his son sit down cross legged on the reed boat.

'Captain, what I said before is true enough. The channel to my home is too narrow for your oars you see, but I will gladly bring our headman to you. He is my father and he will want to thank you for saving the life of his grandson. My kinsmen will come too and we will hunt down the khamsa, but then we will feast with you in your honour.'

'You will be our welcome guests,' Leontios smiled.

Ayut went ahead of them and guided the Kallisto to a place where the river channel ran deep enough that the ship could be safely moored, before paddling his strange craft off back to his village, his small son holding onto his leg as they stood together.

The village of Ayut could not have been far, as it was not long before the fisherman returned with his father and a number of their kin. But though they sought out the crocodile for some while, it was not seen again. Talakh knew well enough that this was the way of the lizard beast, for it could lie asleep at the bottom of the river for many days, if it so chose.

While Ayut and his brothers hunted in vain, the headman came aboard the Kallisto with two boys, who carried with them baskets of fresh bread and fragrant fish cooked in plant leaves with sweet herbs. There was a small basket full of the sticky, sweet fruits of the date palm, and a larger one with many pieces of roasted fowl inside it. Last of all they brought clay vessels of fresh, clear water aboard.

'You honour us with such a feast, O chieftain,' Leontios greeted the headman warmly as his crew fed themselves on these good things.

'I am no chieftain, O captain,' the headman answered humbly. 'My name is Ayit and I am headman of this place only. I owe you my eternal thanks for saving my grandson.'

'Any man would have done the same,' Leontios nodded.

'Perhaps,' Ayit nodded. 'But perhaps not.'

He was about the same age as Isek, but though he was more upright and had less wrinkles on his face, he still looked the older of the two, Talakh thought. He hobbled with a limp, one of his legs being shorter than the other. Long ago it had been broken, judging by the bony lump half way down Ayit's shin. Truly he was lucky to still walk, but there was an air of sadness behind the headman's smile all the same. He had lived long enough to have grandchildren, so no doubt he had seen his share of death too. Perhaps he had lost a favoured son, or perhaps a wife. Perhaps both.

Still for all that, Ayit did his best to find good terms with Leontios, and for his part Leontios did the same. Isek brought wine for them to drink and Ayit begged his new friends to eat their fill of the food his people had brought.

'Please,' Leontios gestured as his men brought forward two vessels of fine wine, 'accept this gift in thanks for your hospitality.'

'I thank you, but no,' Ayit answered him. 'You have already given me a greater gift than this by saving young Khai. And,' he added as Leontios began to protest, 'I already have the gift of oil you sent back to me with my son, so nothing else is required. Let me instead enjoy your company and hear your news from the south.'

'If you will tell us your news in return,' Leontios nodded with a friendly smile.

And so they began to talk, with Isek listening intently as Ayit told of the grip of the Persians and how it had not yet fallen on his own people's lands, as they were so remote.

'Ah, nor on mine,' Isek said. 'The Persians will never

control our people here unless they stop up the Great River.'

'Hah!' Ayit clapped his hands. 'They might as well try to change the course of the sun god as he sails across the heavens!'

Leontios laughed at that. 'You are right my friend. The Persians think their power knows no bounds, but it will not last forever.'

'There are few things that do,' Isek agreed. 'But tell us O Ayit, will this branch of the river still have water enough to carry us all the way to the sea?'

'Old friend, I thought you knew our course from here?' Leontios frowned.

'Ah, the course, yes,' Isek grinned. 'I know where we are captain, and I know where we must go, but the Great River has its own mind on these things and she changes much from year to year. What was once passable may now be choked with mud.'

'That is the truth of it,' Ayit said, as his son Ayut and the small band of hunters tied their reed boats alongside the Kallisto. 'The Great River is fickle as you say, O Isek. When I was a boy a great flood caused it to change its course and claim my father's village,' the headman said sadly as he took a draught from his cup of watered wine.

'We all had to move our homes then and I dare say that one day we will have to move them again. But to answer your question, you must leave this part of the river, for you will not reach the sea by it to my knowledge.

'No, instead you must follow another channel on your right, a few hours downstream. You will not want to take it, for it is narrower at first and your men may have to use their oars as poles to make any way. But little by little the channel will widen as other waters join it, and before the day's end you will rejoin a wider branch of the river.'

'Ah, as I thought,' Isek said, looking into the evening sky as he searched the memories of his mind. 'Then it is not far until my own village.'

'May Bast watch over your house,' Ayit raised his cup.

'And over yours,' Isek grinned back.

The crew of the Kallisto and their new found friends feasted a while longer, the Greeks raising their cups over the ship's side to Ayut the fisherman and his hunters as they stood on their reed boats. They had not much common tongue between them for the most part, but these things do not matter where there is goodwill between men.

At last in the gathering dusk Ayit returned to his son's boat and many farewells were said before they paddled off into the marshes. Talakh watched them out of sight as the last of the evening light slowly faded from the sky and darkness gathered in around the ship. The marshes had seemed tranquil by day, but the attack of the crocodile on Ayut's son was a reminder that this was a wild place, a place at the limit of the settlements of man. The crew of the Kallisto were alone now in the darkness with its strange calls and noises, and only the mosquitoes for company. Even had he a comfortable bed to lie upon, Talakh would not have slept soundly in such a place.

When at last the sun returned its light to the land the next morning, the men scratched their mosquito bites and ate some bread and water, before Leontios had them row gently along to ease their stiff sinews back into life once more. The words of Ayit the headman were soon proven right when the Kallisto came to another branching of the river as he had predicted, yet it was no easy decision for Leontios and Isek to follow his advice, and tall Akakios counselled firmly against it.

'This is madness,' he shook his head. 'The ship will surely ground if we take this ditch. There's not enough water in it to float a twig let alone a ship!'

Akakios might often be proved right, Talakhonsu thought, but still he would never be a leader of men. He was always too cautious for men to follow.

'I am not saying you are wrong, Akakios,' Leontios said, 'but we must trust to Isek and the man Ayit on this matter. What other choice do we have? They say there is no way to the sea unless we take this path, and so I must heed them in this. It is their land after all and in any case, we cannot go back with the Persians watching for us. We have no choice but to go on.'

It was as Ayit had warned and soon after they had turned into the channel it narrowed to a point where the men could row no more and instead had to pole with the oars between the thick rushes. It was slow progress, and several times the Kallisto ground her belly against submerged mud banks, so that the men had to back her around the obstacle. Akakios was far from pleased and muttered many a curse under his breath all the while, but little by little, other waters joined their course until at last it had widened enough for them to dip the oars again.

By the day's end they had rejoined a much broader stretch, yet still Isek said this was not the branch of the river they had left at Avasais. For in what the Greeks called the delta, the Great River spread itself far and wide to cover the land of Lower Kemet in a mass of waterways, like the web of a great spider so Isek explained.

In the evening they came to a place near a small settlement, where the banks of the Great River were solid enough for the Kallisto to moor. That night the men slept ashore, around a welcome fire that kept both the damp air and the troublesome mosquitoes at bay.

Leontios awoke in one of his dark moods the next morning in spite of the bright sun that rose into the clear blue sky.

'Well Isek old friend,' he said ruefully. 'I think at last we come to the parting of our ways.'

'Ah, captain...' Isek tried to smile his wrinkled smile. 'We have lived through many good times, you and I. Many dangers too, though always we have come through them by the will of the gods. But yes, my home is close now. If the men row, we will get there by the afternoon.'

'I would rather they row backwards,' Leontios said with a wry grin. 'Then I would not lose you so soon. But I know you look for our adventures to be at an end,' he sighed.

'I cannot lie,' Isek shrugged. 'My wife and my children,

and their children in turn... They have all earned their time with me.'

'And you with them,' Leontios conceded. 'And you with them.'

Isek bowed his head. 'Tonight we will drink and feast, as if tomorrow may never come,' he grinned. 'And when it does, your head will be so sore, you will wish it hadn't. Then you will be glad to be rid of me and leave these lands with a happy heart.'

Leontios said nothing, but just looked Isek in the eye and shook the small man's bony shoulders with his big hands.

'Talakhonsu,' he said turning to the Napatan as they boarded the ship, 'you have proved yourself many times over in the short time I've known you. Yet still you have a long way to go before you become half the man that Isek is.'

'Ach, he will surpass me before he grows his first beard,' Isek grinned, and Leontios laughed at that.

With the men at their oars and Leontios and Isek on the lookout for any trouble from the Persians, the Kallisto made good progress along the river that day, passing many small craft and some even of their own size. One such ship proved to be another Greek vessel, the Phaeton, and the two ships slowed, then backed oars as they hailed each other. There in the midstream, the two captains and crews exchanged greetings and news, much of which was lost on Talakh, for he was still learning their tongue.

'Diokles, their captain, is an old friend of Leontios, bound for Menefer,' Isek explained after the ships had separated and gone their separate ways once again.

'Did they have news of the Persians?' Talakh asked.

'Not of those who pursued us, no,' Isek screwed up his eyes. 'But then we have come to this place by a route those Persians could never guess. They will have tracked up and down the main course of the river many times on their horses between Avasais and Menefer, but all for nothing!'

'You think they have given up by now?'

Isek shrugged his short neck down into his shoulders.

'I think so. Yet who can say? When you sail away without

me I will pray to the gods that you will all have good fortune and that the Persians leave you alone.'

It was early in the evening before the Kallisto finally coasted in toward the bank, at last bringing Leontios and his trusted man Isek to the parting of their ways. The village of Isek was set back a little from the river, on a slight rise of palm fringed land that in those flat regions was as close to a hill as most of the people were ever likely to see. An earthen bank encircled most of the simple mud brick houses, though the enemy it was built to keep at bay was water, not other tribes. Outside of the bank's protection a few newer houses had been built.

'Ah, the young,' Isek said. 'They do not remember as I do the time when the river flooded right up to here. Let us hope they build their own earth bank before the next great flood comes.'

A group of men appeared on the top of the bank. Standing tall with their fishing spears, they watched the strangers approaching on foot with suspicion, for though Leontios had left most of his men to guard the Kallisto, still the arrival of a strange ship brought with it a threat that had not gone unnoticed.

'What do you want?' one of the men called out defiantly.

'I want a bed for the night!' Isek called back, 'And food and drink! I want my wife and my daughters and sons and my kinsmen around me.'

One of the men lifted his spear, readying himself to throw it if need be, but the man who had called out stayed his hand.

'Isek?' he called again. 'Can it be you?'

'No other,' Isek called again, and Talakh saw that tears fell from his narrow eyes, tears of joy at his homecoming.

More faces appeared now at the top of the bank until the whole village was gathered to greet them, shouting and cheering. Isek wiped away his tears and stiffened his back as his wife and children streamed out to greet him, almost knocking him to the floor as they showered him with their kisses and hugs.

So, Talakh saw what it was for a man to be loved and to come home at last to his family.

'You should have sent word ahead that you were coming!' the wife of Isek scolded her husband even as she kissed him. 'I could have prepared a feast.'

'We will feast tomorrow if not tonight,' Isek grinned as his wife first slapped his arm and then kissed him again.

'I have missed you,' she said looking deep into his eyes.

'And I you, my love,' Isek said with a tenderness Talakh had not dreamt was in him. 'Now where are my sons? And where are my princesses?'

And so Isek called each of his two sons and his three daughters by their names and received them in turn, kissing their foreheads and holding them tight to him, as Leontios, Talakh and the others looked on with a deep happiness for their friend.

'Thank you captain Leontios, for bringing my Isek safely home again,' the wife of Isek touched Leontios on the hand.

'Home for the last time, Unnefer,' Leontios nodded with a smile as he held her hands. 'From now on he will take his ease here with his lovely wife and the comfort of his children.'

'He has earned that right,' Unnefer nodded, a tearful smile on her face.

She was plump and it was plain she had never been a beauty, but still as Leontios had said, she was a lovely woman.

'But enough of my tears,' she said, drying her eyes with the hem of her long white dress. 'Welcome Leontios, welcome to you and your men.'

'You honour us greatly,' Leontios said warmly as he kissed each of her hands. 'These young men are Pamphilos and Talakhonsu, and you may remember Hippolytos from our last visit here?'

'Lady Unnefer,' each of them said, bowing in turn to her.

'Unnefer is enough,' the wife of Isek gave a modest smile.

'But you are the wife of my oldest friend,' Leontios bowed, 'You are Isek's greatest treasure and so you are a treasure to all of us.'

Such was the way of Leontios with women, Talakh came to know. He could charm them all, though the sad memory of his lost wife would never allow him to take another.

That evening Leontios stayed with Isek and his family, though Talakh and the others were not sent back to the boat empty handed, for they were provided with fresh bread, roasted fowl and fish enough for a feast. It was always the harvest season in the land of the black earth and food was plentiful in the village of Isek's people.

The next morning, Leontios returned to his ship, but he did not come alone. For knowing that the proud ship of the Greeks and its treasures could not be left unguarded, Isek had arranged for a great feast to be held down on the river banks in honour of his crewmates. The sons and daughters of Isek carried with them cook pots and firewood, woven mats to spread on the ground and a great many other things to make the men of Leontios comfortable. There they set these things up in the shade of the tall palm trees.

While the cooking began, games were played and the Greeks demonstrated their skill with the bow and their strength with the spear throw. For Talakh these things did not come easily and his efforts fell well short of the others, all except for Pamphilos, who was slightly built and like Talakh still to reach his full strength. While the others boasted of their efforts, he and Pamphilos stood to one side muttering, their heads down.

'Ah, spear and bow,' Isek grinned at them. 'These things are not easy to learn, but you will get better. Still Talakh, you have another skill. Let us see the throwing stick fly from your hand, as it did when you gave that khamsa a headache!'

'Aye, go on Napatan,' Leontios urged him. 'Show us your best throw!'

Yet Talakh was not so sure of himself. 'I have not practised much for a long while now,' he said. 'I was lucky to hit the khamsa, and luckier still that the blow was enough to scare it off.'

'My husband has told me of what you did,' Unnefer added

her words, 'and it seems to me that if the gods in your southern lands gave you such skill you should not lose it. It does not matter if you miss this time, but you should honour the gifts you are given.

'Go on Talakhonsu,' said the sweet voice of Ketet, one of Unnefer's daughters. She was perhaps a year younger than Talakh, but had a rare beauty that he could not help but think wasn't to be found in either of her parents. Unlike her younger sisters, she no longer wore her hair in the side plait of childhood, a sign she would soon be thinking of marriage.

'I have seen boys use these things to scare fowl out of the reeds and into their father's nets. But I have never seen a man throw well enough to defeat the khamsa.'

Being called a man flattered Talakh greatly and pride welled up inside him.

'I will be honoured to show you what skill I have,' he said, bowing his head as he had seen Leontios do, which made Ketet smile.

A tall bundle of straw that had served as a target for the spears was moved away by one of Isek's sons until it was almost as far as the bowmen's targets, and Talakh could at least be content that no-one would think the task had been made too easy for him. He looked from the corner of his eye to make sure Ketet was watching and then threw hard. Even before the heavy throwing stick had left his hand he knew that he had missed, for his arm had not snapped out to its full length and sure enough the stick fell well short, kicking up a cloud of dust as it bit spitefully into the earth.

'Damn it!' he cursed in his own Napatan tongue. He had forgotten the first thing Meketra had told him about trying too hard.

'Not so good,' stout Hippolytos shook his head. 'Let me try,' he said, holding out his hand to receive the throwing stick from Isek's young son who had run to fetch it. Hippolytos tossed the heavy stick in the air like a toy, watching its angled shape spin end over end as it fell back towards his hairy hand. The Kretan was a strong man, making up in muscle what he lacked in height. He raised his foot off the ground as he hung the stick over his shoulder and then with a loud grunt he threw his weight forward, stamping his foot into the dust as he threw with all his might. Talakh watched as the weapon flew at great speed toward the target, though it curved away and fell harmlessly well off to one side.

'Not so easy,' Hippolytos conceded, a puzzled look on his broad face as he scratched his head.

Once again the boy brought back the weapon, a wide smile on his young face, and this time Talakhonsu held out his hand to receive it. Before he had time to dwell on the thought of missing again, he brought his long arm back and snapped it forward like a striking snake as Meketra had shown him. Everyone was watching as the throwing stick soared through the air in a low arc, spinning around on itself until it swished through the straw target as a scythe cuts through the corn. Talakh breathed a sigh of relief and a broad smile spread across his face as Hippolytos clapped him on the back.

'Well done,' Unnefer smiled. 'Now, come and sit with my daughter. Ketet is curious about your people and their ways.'

So Talakh sat down on the woven mat next to Ketet and the two talked, awkwardly at first, whilst his crewmates joked with each other at his expense.

'I cut father's hair for him before he went back to the sea last time,' Ketet said after they had talked of Napata for a while. 'Perhaps you will let me cut yours before you leave us?'

'I would like that,' Talakh agreed. His hair had grown bushy and every time he saw his shadow, he worried that it made his head look too big for his tall, skinny body.

'Come with me back to my home and I will use my mother's shears.'

Talakh looked at Unnefer for her approval, which knowing her daughter well, she gave with a smile.

'Go on then, but do not miss the feast,' she said.

Ketet stood and took Talakh's hand. 'You are very tall,' she said leading him off back toward the village. 'Are all the men of your people as tall as you?'

'No, not many as I remember. But it is hard to say. I was

only a boy then, so everyone looked big. But my father, he was tall.'

'Tell me of your father, Talakhonsu. Was he dark like you? He must have been very handsome?'

Ketet's words brought out the shyness of youth in Talakh, but also bitter memories of the death of Korkamani.

'You look sad,' she said as they stopped in the shade of a palm. 'Have I offended you?'

'No,' Talakh shook his head, 'not you Ketet. My father was strong, tall like me though not as dark, and his hair was more like yours,' he said, looking at the curling waves of dark, shining hair that framed Ketet's heart shaped face. 'He taught me many things, for he was as wise as any priest.'

'It sounds like he was a great man,' Ketet gave a comforting smile, and touched his arm gently, seeing in Talakh's words that his father had long gone to the afterlife.

'He was,' Talakh hung his head, swallowing hard. Although he often thought of Korkamani, he had forgotten just how heavy the weight of grief still was upon him.

'I will remember him too when I think of you, Talakhonsu,' Ketet looked up into his face. Her hand looked tiny in his.

'You will think of me, Ketet?'

'I will Talakhonsu, when you are gone far to the north, to the places my father has told me of. I will make offering to the gods that they may watch over you and the Kallisto, as I always did for my father when he sailed away.'

'You are kind,' Talakhonsu smiled. 'And pretty.'

Ketet said nothing, but instead led Talakh over to the stump of a felled palm tree and stood on it, so that they were the same height. And then to Talakh's surprise, she leant forward on her toes and kissed him gently on the lips. This was the first time he had kissed a girl and Ketet's lips felt soft and warm against his as she drew back for a moment and then gently kissed him again.

'Think of me when you are far away,' she smiled

Talakh felt a great surge of happiness in his heart then, even though his path was soon to take him away from the village of Isek, Unnefer and their lovely daughter. They had only just met, yet somehow he already knew that he and Ketet were meant to be together.

There are none more happy than the young in love and by the same turn, none more unhappy when the fates part them. But for those moments Talakh and Ketet felt only joy in each other's company as they slowly walked on to the home of Isek laughing and smiling, their fingers entwined.

'Your hair is a little like my father's,' Ketet said when she began to cut it.

'A little less grey though, I hope!' Talakh joked.

'In time I would like to see it turn to grey,' she said, looking away from him as he glanced up at her. 'When Leontios lays up his ship for the season of the storms in the north, will you return to us here as my father always did?'

'The season of storms?'

'Yes, what the Greeks also call the winter, when the rains fall in their lands and the storms raise white spray from the seas. At least that is what my father tells us. He says that their days grow short in the far north and that sometimes it is so cold that water turns to stone on the mountain tops. This they call ice and sometimes it even falls from the sky in white flakes like salt, though again it is only water. Will you come back to us when the winter is in the north?'

'If your father accepts me here, then I would gladly return,' Talakh promised.

'My father likes you, and my mother too,' Ketet said resting her hand on his bare shoulder after she had brushed away some of his cut hair. 'Will you talk with them before you leave?'

'What will I say?'

'Say only what is in your heart,' Ketet said quietly. 'That is, if you like me as I like you.'

That evening after the two young lovers had returned to the feast, Talakh steeled himself to speak with Isek. And yet as the time drew on he found that he could not. Had he dreamed of this love that had suddenly blossomed like a spring flower?

Had he dreamt Ketet's kisses? The wine in his cup was watered too much to give him much courage, yet not enough to save muddling his thoughts, so that he could not find his voice.

So the evening wore on and while a goat was roasted by Isek's sons over the low embers of a broad fire, the crew of the Kallisto wrestled each other, as is the sport of the Greeks. Ketet sat next to Unnefer, stealing glances at Talakh while she talked softly with her mother.

Eventually, after Hippolytos the stocky Kretan had beaten Leontios by throwing him onto his back, the wrestlers went to bathe in the river to wash off the dust of their battles, and it was then that Talakh finally found his courage.

'Isek,' he said nervously. 'Can I speak with you?'

Isek looked on Talakh, his narrow eyes twinkling in the firelight. 'Of course,' he said, with his familiar, wrinkled grin that was so hard to read. 'Ah, the fire is roasting me as much as it is that goat! Let us walk along the riverbank a while so I can cool down a little.'

Isek stood up stiffly and led Talakh away, his arm through the Napatan's own, as Talakh stole a glance at Ketet.

'Now, I am guessing you want to speak to me about my daughter?' Isek asked very plainly when they had gained the peace of the riverside, away from the bathing Greeks.

'How did you know?' Talakh asked, trying not to sound surprised.

'I was young once like you Talakhonsu,' Isek smiled, his eyes distant in the darkness as he looked back on his memories. 'Ah, the pretty girls!' he laughed. 'There were many that caught my eye, but I was never a handsome lad like you, even in the best of my years.

'Now I am getting old and the years fly away from me quicker all the time. Ah, but still I know what it is to fall for a girl. You like Ketet?'

'I do,' Talakh said honestly.

'Ah, and she likes you too. She has told her mother this at least.'

'Oh,' Talakh said, surprised at that.

'She has always been a headstrong one, my Ketet, despite her sweet face,' Isek laughed. 'But until now she has shown little interest in marriage.'

'She wants me to return here when Leontios lays up the Kallisto for the winter.'

'And you? Do you want this too? After all, you have only just met each other.'

Talakh looked for hostility in the face of Isek, but found none there. He steeled himself to speak plainly.

'It is true that I hardly know her. And yet it seems when I speak with her that I know her well.'

'It was the same with Unnefer and I,' Isek nodded. 'But the young heart is easily swayed. She is pretty, my daughter, and you are tall and strong. Your ways are strange to each other and so you are both curious to learn more of these things.'

Isek turned to face Talakh then, fixing him with his dark eyes.

'You see, Ketet does not want a farmer or a fisherman for her husband, as much as anything because these things are too dull for her. She has eyes for you because you are different Talakh, this much is plain to me. Ah, but the yearnings of the young are not enough on their own to make for a happy marriage, do you not think?'

'You are a wise man Isek,' Talakh answered. 'After my own father, the wisest man I have known.'

Isek nodded at this, but just grinned as was his way and said nothing.

'I like Ketet, and I felt my heart lift from the first time I saw her,' Talakh continued. 'I would like nothing more than to return here when the winter cold is in the northern places, but she is your daughter and this is your home. I will heed your words whatever they may be,' he bowed his head.

'Hmm,' Isek nodded. He was silent for a while as they walked on, his head nodding still before he spoke again.

'You will be welcome back here Talakhonsu, but not this winter,' Isek said at last. 'Stay with Leontios when he lays up the Kallisto. Stay on Kriti and learn the tongue of the Greeks well. Learn their ways and the ways of the sea. When your second season on the Kallisto is at an end and the season of storms comes again, then you can come back here to us, if that is what you still want.'

Talakh nodded. 'I will do as you wish,' he said, his heart heavy.

'Do not trouble yourself,' Isek put his hand on Talakh's shoulder. 'Leontios may return here from time to time as his voyages allow, and perhaps you will see my daughter then. The time will pass quickly for you, every day a new adventure.'

'But Ketet...'

'Ah, for Ketet, the time will pass very slowly, but if your love for each other is strong it will keep you in each other's thoughts until the fates bring you together again. By then you will know your mind as well as your heart, and so will she.'

'I will do as you say,' Talakh agreed. 'And when I return I will have made something of myself, this I swear.'

'Then I will give you my hand on it and we will return to the feast,'

As Talakh took Isek's hand he felt two heavy discs fall into his palm. 'What is this?' he said looking at the silver coins that Isek had passed to him.

'There will be things that you need,' Isek grinned. 'A new tunic and a cloak for a start. Sandals too. You will need many things for your new life on the Kallisto, Talakhonsu.'

'But I cannot take your silver!' Talakh protested. 'You have worked long and hard for it.'

'Think of it as a loan to you that you can pay back in good time when you have earned silver of your own, as you surely will,' Isek said, closing Talakh's fingers around the coins.

'I will return,' Talakh said solemnly, 'and I will repay you O Isek. I swear it before Amun.'

And so, after the two of them had walked back to the feast, Talakh told Ketet of the will of her father. She was bound to accept it, in spite of the heartache it brought them both. While Leontios and his men feasted and drank the health of Isek, the two young lovers sat apart from the others saying little with their mouths but much with their eyes. They were filled with the happiness of love and yet also sadness. The dawn would soon part them for who could say how long.

Chapter 12

Poseidon's Realm

Long after Unnefer had taken her daughters back to their house, long after her sons had joined them, and long after the Kallisto's crew had drunk themselves into a stupor, only Isek, Talakhonsu and Leontios remained awake by the dying embers of the great feast fire.

'I will miss these times,' Leontios said, as he chewed meat from a thigh bone of the roasted goat.

Isek nodded, his tired eyes now no more than mere slits.

'I will miss them too, but...' he looked across at Hippolytos, who was snoring loudly, 'some things I will miss less than others though, eh?'

'The old boar!' Leontios laughed.

'The old boar,' Isek nodded. 'You must be careful of these Greeks, Talakhonsu,' he said, winking at Leontios. 'They are a strange people, with their god of the sea and their superstitions. They think it brings evil if blood is spilt on their ship, even if by accident.'

'So watch out for splinters!' Leontios grinned, slapping Talakhonsu on the back.

'Ah, as you have seen, they also have a strange sense of humour,' Isek grinned. 'But they are shaped by the things they see in their own lands, which are scattered far and wide across the seas in the thousand islands and the mainland far beyond that.

'When the Kallisto comes to the mouth of the Great River, Talakh, be sure you make an offering to their god Poseidon as you cross into his realm of the sea. The men will know then that you respect their ways.'

Leontios raised up the meat bone to salute his friend's wisdom at that, and Talakh saw it was time to leave the two old friends to the last of their stories, so he took himself off to sleep on the straw that Unnefer had laid out for the men.

There were many sad farewells the next morning between Isek and his crew mates, but Leontios was anxious to be away.

'Talakhonsu!' he called as the Napatan stood on the river bank with Ketet.

'I must go now,' Talakh said sadly, as he faced the girl who had stolen his heart.

Ketet hung her head, the tears coming to her eyes. 'Will I see you again?' she asked quietly.

'I promise that you will,' Talakh said, lifting her chin with his finger so that he could look on her pretty face a last time. 'Will you wait for me Ketet?'

'My heart tells me that I must,' she answered. 'I will think of you every morning when I wake and every night when I go to sleep.'

'And all the hours in between I will think of you,' Talakh kissed her hands each in turn. 'When I return I will have made myself a man. I will be worthy of your love then.'

'Talakh!' Leontios called again, impatience in his voice, and this time Talakhonsu knew he must obey.

'May Amun protect you,' Ketet called to him as his hand slipped from hers and he walked up the boarding plank onto the Kallisto.

'Bast protect you and your family,' Talakh called back to her as he took his place at the oars.

After the Kallisto had been poled out into the river, the crew began to row, striking up a song of their hero Heracles and his seven labours as they slowly gathered speed downstream. Talakh looked up to see the last of Ketet, Isek and all their kin, but Leontios did not look back. Instead he stood on the steering deck proud and upright, his right arm fast around the steering oar. Tall Akakios stood beside him, leaning against the other steer oar as Isek had often done.

Talakh felt sad for the captain then, now that he had left his closest friend behind. Yet Leontios was not in the mood to dwell on such things that day, happy as he was for Isek.

'Sing out men!' he bellowed. 'Let me hear your voices!'

Talakh joined in and Leontios filled his lungs too as the crew of the Kallisto raised their voices around the rhythmic chant of Heracles.

This then was their final farewell to Isek, but also the farewell of Talakh to Ketet. The land of Kemet that he had so much reason to hate, he now came to see had become part of him, for just as some had shown him only spite, still others had treated him kindly. And now there was Ketet too. The daughter of Isek had awoken something in Talakhonsu that he had never felt before. The love of two young hearts brought together, even if now they were too quickly parted.

Leontios had the men row steadily all that day to strengthen their sinews for the rougher waters of the sea that lay ahead. They grumbled at times under the hot sun, but Talakh did not. At least for him, the effort took his mind away from his sadness.

The Kallisto moored far from any settlement in the late of the afternoon as the sun dipped low, and Talakh helped Pamphilos in his duties of making the cooking fire, while some of the men hunted for fish and fowl amongst the reeds. The young Skyrian was a bright lad, very different from the other hardened sailors and the two young men enjoyed each other's company.

Soon there was cooking to be done when Kleon and Pelagios speared two great fish between them, one as long as a man's leg and another of a different kind, almost as big. They were still trying to outdo one another as they returned to the Kallisto, much as they always did.

'Your fish is a sprat compared to mine,' Pelagios laughed, his own fish slung over one shoulder. 'I can hardly carry this one it is so big!'

'Huh. Yours is all head and tail,' Kleon sneered. He carried his own stouter prize across his shoulders, the better to bear its huge weight. 'Look at mine!' he said proudly. 'Its belly is as big as Hippolytos'.'

'I heard that you young whelp!' the Kretan bellowed,

hurling a small fowl that he had caught. It hit the back of Kleon's head in a cloud of feathers, and the whole crew laughed at that, even tall Akakios who was the most sombre of men.

'Well, I have never seen such fish caught from a river,' Leontios praised them both. 'We will eat well enough again tonight my friends.'

Talakh prepared one of the fish with his small bronze knife and then swam in the river to cleanse himself of the silver scales that shone against his black skin. Perhaps he would have stayed brooding by the riverside as his skin dried in the warm evening air, but the gathering mosquitoes were hungry for blood and would give him no peace. The smoke from the fire called him back to where the insects would not follow so readily. Hippolytos came and sat next to him then and started to speak in a mixture of Greek, Kemet and signs so that Talakh could understand him.

'Tomorrow boy,' the hairy Kretan said to him. 'We come to the mouth of the river and the sea! What do you think of that?'

'I never thought I would come to the sea,' Talakh said plainly.

'It is home to all Greeks,' Hippolytos said proudly. 'We sail where the Persian dogs will not. Now drink!' he said, turning his dark bearded face to Talakh. 'You will forget the girl, when we come to the sea.'

Talakh put the cup of watered wine to his lips. To forget Ketet would spare him much pain, he knew. And yet he did not want to forget her. In his mind's eye he remembered her full lips and the warmth in her dark eyes. Her curling hair that fell to her shoulders and her bright smile that was like sunlight playing on the water's edge. He sighed, but brought a smile to his face anyway as he passed the cup back to Hippolytos.

'May the gods bring us good fortune, Hippolytos,' he managed to say in the Greek tongue.

'Uh,' Hippolytos shook his head. 'Your Greek is still terrible!'

'So is your Kemet!' Talakh grinned, and they both laughed at that.

That night the men ate until they might burst, filling their stomachs with the great roasted fish, together with the fowl and some sweet fruits that Pamphilos had collected from a palm tree. When the ship put to sea, so Pamphilos told Talakh, there were often days when there was only dry bread and water for them, sometimes not even that, so when there was plenty, so the men ate plenty. Yet Talakh had known great hunger in his life and so the thought of dry bread and water did not seem so bad to him.

The next morning, many of the men awoke with the itching bites left behind by the fearsome mosquitoes that had plagued their sleep through the night with their bloodsucking ways. All were now keen to be away from the Great River and out to the freedom of the open seas, so that such pests would be left behind in the fresh sea breezes.

After they had poled out into the mid channel, Leontios once again had the men row with purpose down the ever widening river until by the mid morning they had come to a place where the banks finally disappeared from view.

'The sea!' Leontios called to the men, and so it was. 'Talakh! Pamphilos! Ship your oars,' he ordered the two young men. 'Now you, Talakh. Stand on the prow and tell us what you see!'

Talakh did as he was bade and saw that before them the waters of the Great River had spread themselves far and wide across the whole of the world, stretching in an unbroken expanse from horizon to horizon.

'The land is drowned!' was all that the Napatan could think to say, and the crew laughed at that.

'The realm of the god Poseidon!' Leontios called to him proudly. 'This is where my Kallisto belongs. Here we can sail as we will, without a river telling us where we can or can't go!'

'But there is so much water!' Talakh called back to Leontios. 'Does it all come from the Great River?'

'Some of it,' Leontios nodded. 'The rest comes from the

rivers of the lands to the north.'

'But I can see no land to the north,' Talakh called back. 'There is nothing there!'

'Ha!' Leontios laughed heartily, and explained Talakh's words to the others who laughed in turn. 'There is much for you to learn if we are to make you a man of the sea!' he shouted back.

'I will learn,' Talakh thought to himself as the ship rowed on. The priests had told him something of the seas when he was a boy, but he had never dreamt he would see such a thing with his own eyes. The wide waters were calm, a beautiful mix of blues and greens that sparkled in the sunlight. Talakh stared in wonder for a long time, thinking of how the sea came to be, and he asked many questions when the captain came to join him in the prow.

'How deep is it?' he asked, and, 'Where is it that great Poseidon lives?' and, 'Are there temples to the god on the land, or does he have his halls under the sea?' until finally the captain grew exasperated.

'You wish to know more of the sea, Talakhonsu?' Leontios asked him. 'You wish to see great Poseidon? Then ready yourself!'

Then the captain called the men to ship their oars, and he strode forward through their ranks to where Talakh stood on the ship's prow.

'We Greeks are born always to the sea, and it is in our blood, whether we are fair or dark. But for you it is different. To know what we know, you must greet the sea yourself!'

And with that, he pushed Talakh over the side of the high prow.

With a splash and a cry of surprise Talakh hit the water, but he was a good swimmer. Almost as soon as he had gone under, so his head appeared back at the surface with a cough and a splutter as he spat the salty water from his mouth.

'Now,' Leontios called to him with a broad smile as the others laughed. This time he spoke slowly in the Kemet tongue, making signs so that the others could understand too. 'You must swim around the ship and come back to where you began. This will bring us good luck!'

'Aye,' Hippolytos called, his bearded face leaning over the side. 'Bring us luck boy!'

And so with a grin on his face, Talakh swam under the high graceful curve of the Kallisto's prow and down one side in the cool sea, for in truth he was keen to show the men his skill at swimming.

'He swims like a fish!' Pelagios laughed.

'He does,' Leontios agreed. 'Men let us leave him in the care of Poseidon. Back to your oars!'

Talakh swam faster as the oars suddenly bristled out again from the Kallisto's side over the top of his head, until he was clear of them at the ship's stern. At first he thought the captain meant to make him swim around the oars when he reached the far side of the ship, to make his task harder. But then Leontios gave the command and the oars dipped into the water, then dipped again as the men found their stroke. Talakh looked up to see tall Akakios grimly staring down at him as the Kallisto found her legs and began to pull away from him out to sea.

For a moment Talakh trod water, unable to believe what his eyes told him, but then he heard Leontios call another order and the front ranks of oars were shipped again. As Talakh watched, the Kallisto's sail beam was winched up and the heavy sail unfurled in the freshening breeze, cracking and flapping as it billowed out.

'Captain!' Talakh shouted out. 'Hippolytos!' he called again, but it was to no avail.

With the power of the wind and the men rowing strongly, the Kallisto gathered pace and Talakh knew then that as good a swimmer as he was, he would never catch her. He had been betrayed by those he thought would be his friends for life. But why? How had he offended the captain so badly that Leontios would abandon him in such a way? Talakhonsu racked his brain time and again, but he could not think of a reason.

As he watched the Kallisto sail slowly out of sight, fear rose in the Napatan's throat and for a moment panic began to overwhelm him. He was far out to sea and the land was a distant thin line beyond the chops and the waves. He would never reach the shore, never. His heart beat fast in his chest and his mind reeled when he looked once more out to the empty sea, then up at the hot sun soaring high in the blue sky above him. Had he endured so much only now to die in this chill realm of Poseidon? Talakhonsu closed his eyes and took in a deep breath, then struck out for the shore, trying not to think of the grim fate that surely awaited him.

The Chronicles of Talakhonsu conclude in Book II

Beyond the Pyrene

Published in November 2016

From around 2,500 BC, the history of the ancient kingdom of Kush is intertwined with a series of raids and invasions by her more powerful northern neighbour, Kemet ('the land of the black earth' - modern day Egypt). For many years Kush fell under the rule of the great pharaohs of the New Kingdom of Kemet, who established their own temple to their greatest god Amun at the foot of the mountain of Jebel Barkal in the Kush city of Napata.

Gradually the Kushites themselves adopted the Kemet gods and customs as their own. However, when the Kemet New Kingdom slipped into decline and fall, Kush rose again and very quickly the Kushite armies turned the tables on their former rulers, invading as far north as Thebes. For a brief period in the 8th century BC, the Kushite kings ruled as pharaohs in their own right, reinforcing the cultural influence of ancient Kemet on the Kushite people and customs, until they too were driven back to their own borders by an Assyrian invasion.

As is often the case with competing nations, the peoples of Kush and Kemet had much in common in their beliefs and customs, despite the contempt in which the Kemet rulers often held their southern neighbours. The enmity between the two kingdoms would continue for many centuries to come, as their fortunes ebbed and flowed, until the power of Kemet finally faded into history.

This book is set at a time of huge upheaval in the ancient world, in the early 5th century BC. The vast and ever expanding Persian Empire holds sway across Asia Minor, the Middle East and the kingdom of Kemet, its only challenge coming from the powerful Greek city states of Athens and Sparta. In 490 BC the Greek allies under Athenian leadership had repulsed an invasion by the Persians, defeating the armies of Darius the Great at the battle of Marathon.

After the death of Darius, his son Xerxes thirsted for revenge against the Athenians, but even as he planned another invasion of the Greek mainland, the Kemet nobles revolted against their Persian overlords, the Satraps, in around 486 BC. Very little is known about the events of this rebellion, nor exactly when it was finally suppressed by the Persian armies of Xerxes. It is into these events that Talakhonsu, a young Kush boy destined for the priesthood of Amun, is cast.

Glossary of place names

Buhen	A great Kemet border fortress (now submerged beneath the waters of the manmade Lake Nasser)
The Great Middle Sea	The Mediterranean Sea
The Great River	The Nile
Kemet	'The land of the black earth' – the land later called Egypt by the Ancient Greeks
Kriti	Crete
Kush	An ancient kingdom in what is now northern Sudan
Kypros	Cyprus
Menefer	Capital of Lower Kemet (Menefer was a former name for Memphis and was located south of modern day Cairo)
Meroe	A southern settlement of the Kush Kings (still called Meroe, located in Sudan)
Naukratis	A Greek colony in the Nile delta, later lost to history.
Napata	The northern capital of the Kush Kings (near the modern day town of Karima in Sudan)

The Narrow Sea	The Red Sea
Nubia	The desert lands between Kemet and Kush
The Syene	The lake formed by the great Nile cataract in what is now known as Aswan
Thebes	The Ancient Greek name for Waset
Waset	Capital of Upper Kemet; home of the greatest temple of Amun (Waset was known to the ancient Greeks as Thebes and is located within the modern day city of Luxor in Egypt)

Acknowledgements

The author would like to thank fellow author Peter Knyte for his immeasurable advice and support in the publishing of 'Beyond the Black Earth'.

Thanks are also due to Peter Harding, Zigi du Toit, Michael Blake and Peter Boardman for their advice and insights on archaeological, anthropological and historical matters in connection with this book. Also, to my wife, friends and family for their support and encouragement.

Finally, thanks to Dorian Fabre, for his invaluable proof-reading input.

www.ingramcontent.com/pod-product-compliance
Lightning Source LLC
Chambersburg PA
CBHW032208190626
46810CB00019B/2191